Robert Hillstrom, a n...
distinguished career in li... ...ic writer,
he divides his time betw... ...ontana and Florida.

Intent

Robert Hillstrom

First published in hardback in 1998 by
HEADLINE BOOK PUBLISHING

First published in paperback in 1998 by
HEADLINE BOOK PUBLISHING

A HEADLINE FEATURE paperback

10 9 8 7 6 5 4 3 2 1

ISBN 0 7472 4135 X

Typeset by
Letterpart Limited, Reigate, Surrey

Printed and bound in Great Britain by
Mackays of Chatham PLC, Chatham, Kent

HEADLINE BOOK PUBLISHING
A division of Hodder Headline PLC
338 Euston Road
London NW1 3BH

ACKNOWLEDGMENTS

The celebrated criminal defense lawyer Earl Gray was indispensable to me in writing this novel, as well as in law school thirty years ago. Novelist Toni Volk, my dear friend, provided me with more encouragement and professional guidance than anyone has a right to hope for. I am indebted to Diane Elliot, Edward Robb Ellis, my agent Rita Rosencranz, and Anne Williams for advice and support, and to Susan Ransom, Victoria Routledge and Richenda Todd, all of whom helped with the manuscript. Had it not been for Carol Smith, my agent in the UK, this book would not exist.

Nothing is easier than to denounce the evil-doer; nothing is more difficult than to understand him.

Dostoevski

For Patricia

and
in memory of Lorene Hillstrom
1955 – 1996

Too soon her voice was gone;
Too soon her race was run.
For one more chance I'd give
The earth, the moon, the sun.

1

The long walks with her mother had been the best times of Rebecca's growing up. She had been in high school then and they had hiked along Lake Michigan. They acted like boys and ran and jumped and skipped flat stones across the water. Her mother's name was Julia and her skin was shadowy bronze. She had fine high cheek bones and a slim nose with nostrils that flared wide when she was out of breath. She did exotic things with her coarse black hair, before everybody was doing the elaborate braids they do now. Some high school kids Rebecca knew were embarrassed by their parents, but she was proud of her mama. She liked to drag Mama Julia along wherever she went. Mama Julia was a tall beauty with big oval eyes that never stopped smiling; she saw some humor in everything, until she first noticed the lump in her breast. A week after Rebecca got the letter from New York University telling her that she had been admitted to the law school, Mama Julia died. But she smiled those last days of her life because she was certain, she said, that her daughter was going to become a judge.

'Your honor, what we're talking about here is fairness. There is nothing more basic to our legal system than simple fairness.'

Harry Scott's navy pinstripe draped softly from what were once the shoulders of an all Big Ten linebacker. In the windowless wood-paneled courtroom, he stood behind the counsel table, never glancing at the yellow legal pad in his left hand. The long fingers of his right hand rhythmically

1

caressed the air like a pianist tapping out a riff. One by one, he catalogued the grounds that demanded Judge Rebecca Goldman step aside and let his client be tried by an unbiased court.

Rebecca felt the sharp points of each carefully selected dart. Harry Scott knew all the tricks. She had seen him ply his trade six years ago in the trial of William Schmid. She shuddered at the recollection.

Scott's voice rose a notch or two. Up came the left hand, the legal pad a warning yellow flag. 'You know, Judge, your activities with the battered women's shelters could tend to give you a biased view toward a man accused of a violent act.'

Calmly meeting Harry Scott's deep-set blue eyes, she relaxed the muscles of her face and spread her lips to a friendly smile. This smart-ass lawyer would not see her rising anger. A whole litany of her associations with feminist causes disqualified her from presiding over *State of Minnesota v. Thomas Phelps*, Harry Scott argued.

According to the state's complaint, Tom Phelps, after a primary election party last September, had tied Dinah White to a bed in the Marriott Hotel. Against her will, it further alleged, he had had sexual intercourse with her. All lies, Harry Scott had told the press; Ms White and her accomplices are conspiring to ruin Tom Phelps's political career.

An editorial in the *Tribune* that morning posed the question: is it because she is black or is it because she is a woman that Tom Phelps does not want to be tried in Judge Rebecca Goldman's court? She had been surprised that they hadn't also mentioned her Jewish upbringing.

'. . . And, your honor, with respect, from your past, perhaps even present membership of such feminist groups as the National Organization for Women, the National Women's Political Caucus and the Women's Legal Defense fund one could infer a built-in bias against a man standing accused of rape.'

Rebecca wet her lips. Time for a few darts of her own. 'Excuse me, Mr Scott, does it necessarily follow that if a person is repulsed by a certain kind of crime she must then have a bias against a defendant accused of it?'

The interruption in his argument returned the closed-mouth tight little smile to his face. 'Of course not, your honor. In the case at bar, I'm just trying to show the likely effects of an accumulation of factors.' He flipped a document to the Assistant DA, then walked round the counsel table and approached the bench.

To get rid of Judge Goldman, Scott must prove actual bias. It was for her alone to decide whether he had or not. She was skeptical. Scott had pointed to nothing specific. If mere allegations were enough, defendants could effectively pick their own judges. Scott held the document out to her.

'I'm sorry for not filing this earlier, Judge,' he said, 'but my clerk just got it to me minutes ago. As you can see, it's the Governor's affidavit.'

Rebecca scanned the page. It was brief and to the point. Self-serving bullshit. Like most successful politicians, the Governor was a control freak. But she shouldn't be too hard on him. After all, seven years ago *he* had appointed *her*. She accommodated his liberal agenda perfectly, representing three classes routinely discriminated against: women, Jews and African-Americans. A woman columnist had called Rebecca Goldman's five-year career as a public defender distinguished. The bar at large howled. She was only five years out of law school; the Governor was passing over many more highly qualified candidates, including women.

Even before Rebecca finished reading the document, Harry Scott pressed on. 'As you can see, your honor, the Governor clearly recalls you arguing with the defendant, my client, Tom Phelps, at a fundraiser the year before you became a judge. You accused him of a chauvinist attitude toward women. You even suggested that there was sex discrimination in his department in the capitol.'

Rebecca looked up from the document. Phelps slouched in a chair at the counsel table, a superior look on his plump face, sloping shoulders wrapped in brown tweed. He wrote the Governor's most important speeches and stood ready to engage any problem the Governor might find too complicated or unpleasant for his other lackeys in the capitol. When Phelps was indicted, the papers called him the Governor's right-hand man. Regardless of Phelps's lofty post, Harry Scott would be sure to wipe that smirk off Phelps's face before any juror ever had a look at it.

'Counsel, I don't recall the alleged incident, but I do remember that two different women won sex discrimination suits against the Department of Human Relations. Wasn't Mr Phelps running that office at that time?' Rebecca said evenly. 'If I had heard about those lawsuits, I don't doubt that I mentioned them to Mr Phelps. But chauvinistic – that simply isn't a word I would have used. But I forgive the Governor his cloudy memory. One can hardly expect any-one to accurately recall such an insignificant event, espe-cially eight years after. Have you anything more, Mr Scott?'

'Your honor, I think, upon reflection, you will agree that I need nothing more.'

'Perhaps, Mr Scott.' But don't hold your breath, she thought. 'If I understand your argument, you contend to have a right to somebody who isn't opposed to rape. Such a judge might be hard to find were I to grant your motion for my recusal.' The tone of her voice said, and you know I'm fair, you've been here before. Since the Schmid trial, his dark brown hairline had receded some, maybe giving him a more distinguished look, but no gray yet, maybe a few more fine lines around the eyes. When relaxed, most faces sag into a frown. Not Harry Scott's; his built-in smile disarmed witnesses and juries alike.

'That certainly is not my point, your honor.' A trifle close together, Harry Scott's gleaming eyes accused: you're a woman; you can't give my client a fair trial and, worse, like you, the alleged victim Dinah White is black. You mean to railroad my client. The thought hung between them as clearly as if he had written it on a chalk board.

'I'll take it under advisement, counsel.' There *was* one relevant event that the judge might have revealed in a perfect world, but the imperfection of this one was beyond dispute.

The Assistant DA, face almost hidden in a puff of blonde

4

curls, made a routine argument in opposition to Scott's motion and the morning's business ended.

That morning Rebecca had listened to six motions, all on criminal matters. As a freshman in law school, she had seen herself in flowing robe, making swift rulings in electrifying trials, the courtroom throbbing with tension, Judge Rebecca Goldman in complete control. Fifteen years later, the reality was that much of her work was tedious. Courtrooms were often places of punishing boredom. There was more financially rewarding work: criminal defense, corporate litigation. Sometimes she even considered politics. Then a case like *State of Minnesota v. Thomas Phelps* came along and she would eagerly head for the courthouse in the morning, ready for anything.

Coming to Minneapolis a dozen years ago she hadn't imagined how quickly she would become a judge. Sometimes she relished the role: the ceremony, living at the center of the system, and the symbolism of her courtroom. Everything in its proper place. From the five rows of seats behind a low rail, like pews in a church, split by an aisle down the middle, anyone could watch justice dispensed. Fourteen swivel chairs in two rows filled the jury box along the wall to her left. To her right, Bailiff Henry Pettiford in his tan sheriff's department uniform sat behind a desk pushed up against the wall under the clock. The two counsel tables were directly before her, side by side. The witness box was to her left, at the end of her bench. To each side, in her peripheral vision, the silky colors of the state and federal governments hung from wooden masts. Except when she presided over the criminal arraignment calendar and the place was filled with whores and miscellaneous miscreants, her courtroom remained neat and uncluttered like her personal life. From day to day, she saw to it that not a speck marred the rich texture of the maroon carpet. This was where it happened, where she belonged.

The morning's work had gone well. Harry Scott was back in her court again. Trying cases with able lawyers was a treat. This would be different from William Schmid's murder case. That trial had its own special place in her history.

Schmid was one of a kind. This time it was a rape, but not just any rape. *State v. Phelps* was the highest profile criminal trial in recent memory. All should have been well in Rebecca Goldman's world.

Tom Phelps had said he would stop by Harry Scott's office after his lunch appointment. Harry skipped lunch and hurried back to his lair in the Roanoke Building. His office was nothing to write home about, but it did the job without the frills clients expected at the big firms. Criminal lawyers tried to keep the expenses down. They didn't enjoy the steady cash flow produced by padded bills rendered to corporations. The dark tones of a reproduction of a Rembrandt self-portrait contrasted with the light-colored walls. Behind his desk, framed licenses and degrees hung in neat rows.

Today the heat was turned up too high. Sweat dampened Harry's tight shirt collar. He had eaten his weight up ten pounds thinking about his damn divorce. He returned several calls. The last pink slip reminded him to call Chet Ronning. If only the whole divorce mess would go away so he could practice law unfettered, the way it used to be.

'Mr Phelps is here.' Vivian's soft telephone voice stirred Harry Scott. Even though almost ten years had passed and she had found a loving husband, Harry still thought of her as a lover. That would never change. Friends can become lovers, but lovers can never be just friends. Yet it was still a relationship, though not the promise clad in silk it once was. Without sex, but not without love, it was a reliable, committed link, the only one he had left.

'Let Phelps cool his heels a while, dear,' he said into the phone. 'I've got some calls to make.'

He always called Vivian dear, but Joyce, the other secretary in the two-man office, would not hear of it. 'If my name was John, and I had a two-inch beard, would you call me dear?' she had asked Harry the week she started. 'Whatever you say, Miss Kromarty,' he had said. Joyce would be just fine, she assured him. No need for the *Miss* business. The Joyces came and went, but Vivian must always be there.

Without her he couldn't function. She balanced his check book, remembered his wife's and daughter's birthdays and listened to the miseries and secrets of his heart. Her disciplined presence reminded him that there was a right way and a wrong way to live your life.

Chet Ronning was handling Harry's divorce. 'Hiya, Chet . . . Yeah, I got the figures . . . Surprising, eh? Those pension plans build up over twenty years . . . She won't be satisfied unless we divide it in half? Christ, Chet, what about the three hundred grand cash? . . . Yes, I read the Flynn case but Flynn was a top guy in a big-shot firm with hundreds of regular clients. His partnership was worth plenty. But me, what would this practice be without me? There's nothing ongoing here . . . Draw it up. I'll take a look at it. But we'll still fight over the alimony . . . Shit no, I'll go to trial if I have to . . . Maybe I'll get Flynn to represent me.' Harry was laughing when he hung up. What's so goddamn funny? he thought.

Vivian held the office door open for Tom Phelps.

'That a new dress?' Ignoring Phelps, Harry smiled at Vivian. 'Looks great on you.'

The color deepened in the cherubic face, which resembled that of the actress Sally Field. Vivian let her eyes fall self-consciously toward the gray wool skirt. She was only a couple of inches over five feet, still a perfect size six. 'Thank you, Mr Scott,' she said.

'Better hold the calls,' said Harry, 'but this won't take long.' This was a warning to Phelps that he didn't have all day to talk about what Rebecca Goldman might or might not do.

Tom Phelps had his usual glad-hander grin in place. Harry didn't like the sonofabitch. Never would, either. He had represented murderers he had grown to like, at least a little. Even that spooky William Schmid had had his moments. But Phelps was another matter.

Without getting up, he waved Phelps to one of the two low-backed chairs on the other side of the desk. Harry skipped the formalities. 'The chances of Judge Goldman removing herself are slim to none, my friend.' He used 'my friend' only on those who weren't. He swiveled his chair toward the window. The only view from the fourth floor was the massive front of the Marquette Inn across the street. The stubby gray image of the Roanoke Building reflected in the colorless glass wall of the hotel. Like the birds, color left Minnesota by late November.

'That bitch'll hang me.' Phelps's voice was always louder than necessary.

Bitch put Harry off. Who was this ward heeler to call Rebecca Goldman a bitch? For emphasis, Harry twisted back to look into Phelps's little brown eyes. 'She can't hang you. Only a jury can hang you. If you're convicted, she's gotta sentence you according to the guidelines.' The grinning lips shrunk to a worm-like frown, the beginning of a scowl that spread like a stain over his florid face. But she could make it tough, Harry thought. Her rulings on the evidence might be the difference in this one.

A layer of fat had kept any lines from forming in Phelps's middle-aged face. 'Anyhow, everything you said this morning is true. She's been a scissor-bill for every goddamned woman's cause that comes along. You didn't even name them all.'

'It's all smoke, my friend. Every judge in the courthouse has been political in one way or another, or they wouldn't be there. What I cited ain't enough to show the kinda bias we need – but you never know.'

'What's that supposed to mean?'

'I'm sure we got her thinkin'. If there's some real bias in there somewhere – you know, that we don't know about – it might make her consider takin' herself off. But don't bank on it. Not even a little bit.'

'When will she rule?' Phelps asked.

'Soon. This judge doesn't fool around. And she'll put it on for trial in a few months.'

Phelps leaned forward. His fingers spread out on the edge of the cherrywood desk, ten stubby little sausages. 'It's still my word against Dinah's. Remember, Counselor, I got important people who'll come in and testify what a great guy I am.'

'I've told you before that could open a can of worms. You put on a character witness, they will too. Maybe somebody that doesn't like you so much. Otherwise they can't.'

'I got nothing to hide.'

'Most of us have something to hide,' Harry Scott said. 'And everybody thinks they can hide it. Then it pops out in the open when we least expect it. The DA's liable to come up with some surprises – maybe some broad from way back.'

Phelps shook his head. 'There's nothing, Counselor, nothing at all. Now, that might not be true of that cute little coon who says I fucked her against her will. There'll be a lóta guys willing to talk about her.' The smirk was back.

'Rape shield law's supposed to protect her from that kind of testimony. You get me their names anyway. Might be able to get some mileage out of 'em.'

'It's her word against mine and she didn't go to the cops until the next day.'

'Yeah, Tom, I know. It's those damn rope burns on her wrist that are gonna be hard to explain away.'

Phelps's voice quieted. 'I've told you about that. You believe me, dontcha?' Absently, he pushed his graying forelock back into his halo of bushy auburn hair.

'It ain't what I believe, my friend,' said Harry Scott. 'It's the jury, what they believe. That's what counts. It's the whole fucking ball game.'

A fire truck roaring down Marquette drowned out the goodbyes and Harry Scott's thoughts returned to Judge Goldman: large soft brown eyes that searched yours out and told you she meant exactly what she said with those sensuous full lips. He meant to get to know her better, much better. Whatever it took. Should he let a little technicality like *State v. Phelps* stand in his way? Life goes by too damn fast. With motions and appeals, Tom Phelps's case could tie him up for years. That would be too long a wait to approach Rebecca Goldman. It might even be worth some risks. Maybe even dump the case, but with his divorce settlement looming, he needed the money. Still, coming home every night alone to an empty bed in the frigid Minnesota winter was no bargain.

2

After a salad with her clerk Tess in the Government Center basement cafeteria, Rebecca returned to the twentieth floor. In the powder-room mirror she studied the tiny folds that threatened to merge into little bags under her wide-set brown eyes. She closed the door on one of the stalls and slid the latch. Sitting with her pantyhose stretched round her thighs – thunder thighs some asshole on the beach once called them – she thought ahead to her birthday three months away. Forty had been a shock, but she had got over it quickly. Forty-one should be easy.

Back in front of the mirror, she leaned forward to touch up the faint blue eye shadow. A couple of muted acne scars barely showed through the make-up. Her caramel skin was a diluted legacy of Mama's beautiful dark bronze dusted with shadow. Rebecca sometimes wished she had inherited Mama's face rather than Papa's. Not that his wasn't a good face, but Mama's was gorgeous, with high cheek bones and eyes as dark and bright as black onyx. Papa Nathan, raised an observant Jew, had mortified his parents when he brought dusky Mama Julia home from a trip to Santo Domingo right after the war. She appeased them by embracing the Jewish faith, but Rebecca knew Mama never took temple very seriously.

Papa had operated a restaurant in Milwaukee. When he opened it in 1946, ever conscious of local attitudes, he changed their name from Goldman to Coleman. Coleman's served the finest prime rib in town, and Papa spent almost every waking hour at the club, as he called the restaurant. Leave 'em alone and they'll steal you blind, he said. At the

University of Wisconsin in the late sixties, Rebecca defiantly changed her name back to Goldman. No one was prouder than Grandma Esther who had never got over the shame of Papa's denial of the family's good name.

But Rebecca did have Mama's lush lips without the enslaving cigarette that had always been part of Mama's face. Lips wonderful for kissing, said more than one suitor. As soft as fairies' pillows, said Reggie before he married her. Papa's chromosomes had passed along his formidable nose and Grandma Esther's commodious breasts. In high school Rebecca had hunched her shoulders in a vain attempt to hide them. Vestiges of her self-conscious gait still plagued her posture and she walked with a noticeable forward lean, especially in heels.

Appropriate to the judiciary, her thick chestnut hair was conservatively waved. She took a step back from the mirror to survey the whole picture. Not bad. She liked the professional look: dark blue suit, white blouse, narrow red tie. She could stand to shed ten pounds. At five foot five, 120 pounds would be just perfect. What the hell. Who was she to complain? Sitting as a district judge, in the best of health, esteemed by most of her peers, or at least she thought so. To top it all off, every trip home from work was filled with excited anticipation. Her fourteen-year-old daughter Julie, the best kid anyone ever hoped for, joined her for dinner every night of the year.

She crossed the hall to her chambers. Through the wall of windows the entire south side of the city to the suburbs on the heights of land beyond the Minnesota River stretched out before her. Compulsively, she kept her desk polished to a high sheen. The glare from the windows bounced off the varnished walnut, the broad top clear except for a silver-framed picture of Julie on a black and white pony. Reggie had snapped it up in the Catskills when she was nine.

Tess had left the mail in the center of the leather writing pad. On top of the inch-thick stack of correspondence an envelope lay, unopened. 'PERSONAL' was typed in the lower left corner. Rebecca knew what to expect inside. He deliberately misspelled her name. G-o-l-d-m-e-n. It was

11

postmarked Wolf River, MN. This was the fifth letter over the six years since the trial. A stream of ice water trickled down her back. The pace of her thumping heart quickened as though she had just run up ten flights of stairs. The spacious room felt more empty than ever. Her first impulse was to sweep the letter away like an ugly bug, throw it in the waste basket or send it over to homicide without reading it. She sank into her brown suede sofa and sliced open the envelope with a brass letter knife. Careful to preserve any latent prints, she held it by the edges. She had to read the letters. Maybe she hoped that he had had a change of heart and would reassure her that he had never meant any harm. It was neatly typed. Only the first had been handwritten.

Dear Judge Goldmen,
    Greetings from Wolf River. I trust you have not forgotten me. I have not forgotten you. Just a reminder. As repayment for your arranging my stay here, you will get the same as Alice got. You can bank on it. The only question is when?
                    With utmost sincerity,
                    William Bruno Schmid

Her hands trembled as she scrutinized the words. Slightly changed since last time, the essence was the same. She sometimes managed whole days without thinking of him, but never two in succession. There were too many reminders. Whenever Harry Scott's name was mentioned or she even heard about a murder case, the montage of images from William Schmid's trial played in full color on the screen in her head: lush red hair stained by bloody fingers; the scalpel, perverted from its life-extending purpose, lying steely in its clear plastic envelope on the wooden table; Alice Wahl's abdomen preserved in its ghastly moment on a glossy eight by ten; and the petri dish, the dreadful petri dish.

    It had been the first murder trial in her court. Harry Scott had tried to take over the courtroom, but she was satisfied with the way she had handled that trial. Schmid had stood beside his lawyer at the arraignment, one of many scenes hanging like bats in the caverns of her mind. The prisoner had been brought before her in chain manacles. Perfectly erect, his body tapered to a smallish head with thinning, dark blond hair. He seemed taller than the six feet listed on his sheet. There was little substance to him, shoulders hardly evident. He had worn a white shirt with nondescript slacks, gathered to his narrow waist by a belt with a gaudy silver buckle. One didn't forget the eyes, or any part of his lean face. Like a bird of prey, the intense blue eyes were shining and alert. Blanched skin stretched taut over sharp cheek bones with a slight sag at the jowl. The thin nose pointed directly at her. But it was the eyes that startled the novice judge. As a public defender, her clients had varied from shoplifting housewives to foppish pimps. One had murdered three people. In five years, there had been hundreds, but in this face there was something different. From time to time he had smiled at her – small even teeth, and thin yet vivid lips, the color of fresh meat. He seemed not to notice his chains: the two connecting wrist and ankles were met in the center by a third.

The charge was first degree murder. Extensive publicity would make it hard to pick a jury, and Rebecca had been surprised when Harry Scott failed to request a change of venue. That day Schmid had pleaded not guilty. Later, Harry Scott had filed notice with the court adding the plea of not guilty by reason of insanity. Schmid was held without bail for a trial that played out four months later.

Her mind came back to the moment. Her breathing was irregular. She took one very deep breath and blew it out slowly. A couple of tears coursed down her face. She had done her best. She had only wanted to do what was right, morally and legally, especially legally. She was there to decide the law of the case. What she said was the law *was* the law on any given day in her courtroom. For doing her duty precisely as she understood it, the mind of the defendant William Schmid held her responsible for his present predicament. At times like this her old job seemed preferable to sitting in judgment on her fellow human beings. As public defender you were always on their side. As judge you were supposed to be neutral, totally unbiased. But try to tell that to any criminal serving a long term. Try to tell that to William Bruno Schmid languishing in the state hospital for the criminally insane at Wolf River. Other judges told her the letters went with the territory. Of course, they were right. But when she opened each one she felt so vulnerable, so completely alone. The promise was crystal clear. William Schmid would see to it that Julie became an orphan.

3

On the sixth and top floor of Wolf River State Hospital dwelt those criminally insane classified as violent. Two rows of ten cells lined the two long outside walls. Their single steel doors with a tiny square window opened on two hallways. In the center, with doors on each of the corridors, six windowless rooms were used for group activities or by the administrative staff. A nurses' and orderlies' station occupied the northernmost of these rooms. A guard was posted in the southernmost with wall-width windows on each corridor. Hospital policy required his presence twenty-four hours a day. The elevator shaft adjoined the guard's room on the south, and beyond, a stairwell abutted the outside wall. The elevator, stairwell, and all the rooms on the floor could be accessed only by keys chained to the belt of the guards and several senior employees.

A flock of crows wheeled on the air currents above the gray second-growth forest across the river. The steel mesh and the grime on the outside of the glass clouded William Schmid's view. The sight and sound of the foamy bottle-green water rushing among the huge boulders below soothed his active mind. Through six winters he had watched the quieter waters freeze and thaw.

He left the window and lay down on his narrow bed. He spent hours lying on top of the green blanket staring at the dirty ceiling, always thinking methodically. His was a methodical mind. Since his trial, William had existed in this ten-foot cube labeled cell 615, halfway down the hall from the nurses' station.

The water closet stuck out brazenly in the corner. Beside

it a chipped white sink jutted from the wall. Above it a small stainless-steel mirror reflected only circular blurred images, reminding William of the ghoulish paintings of Edvard Munch. Toothpaste, brush, safety razor and mouthwash were arranged neatly on the top of a three-drawer chest below the window to the right of the sink. A faint stink of Lysol constantly tickled his nostrils. He had one chair and a small table for his portable Olivetti. It clacked along for several hours on most days. Recreational breaks in the yard provided his only enjoyment, apart from reading and writing and his sister Wilma's visits. He somnambulated through the weekly therapy sessions on the fifth floor and he met with a psychiatrist irregularly. One hour of calisthenics in his cube daily toned his muscles.

On occasion, standing before the dirty window, usually when bright sunlight illuminated the citrine surface of the river, William created a dialogue between professor and student on some issue of quantum physics, taking both parts in different voices, often letting the student win the point. Sometimes the student was Alice Wahl. He often thought of Alice. She was smart. Pretty. A whiz with numbers. A redhead, like his stepmother. Some of the head shrinkers thought that sharing his stepmother's hair color had cost her her life, an absurd theory in William's mind. He wished he hadn't killed her. It was the goddamn headache. Except for the headaches, he had enjoyed his life at the university. The headaches ruined everything. They had begun in high school. Not so bad. He almost always remembered what happened, but in college they had become worse. As the choices became more difficult, the headaches weren't far behind, indescribable pulsating pain you couldn't touch with aspirin or any analgesic. Then the memory lapses began.

He rolled over on the bed, facing the bookcase, stuffed to capacity beside the door. Books kept him sane, he thought ironically; yet the endlessness of his predicament had driven him to consider desperate solutions. If that jury had found him guilty of second degree murder he would have been out soon, ready to go back to work. But that do-gooder judge had known better. She had buried him alive in here. She would pay. He remembered how his father used to say that he would do something or other if it was the last thing he ever did. With mean Konrad Schmid, it had been just a manner of speaking. For William, it was ultimate reality. Settling accounts with Rebecca Goldman *would* be the last thing he ever did. She had made turning the ceiling light on and off the only control he had over his environment.

When he had first walked into his cell he was as sane as any of them: Harry Scott, Goldman, Bannon the cop – any of them. If it was convenient, the goddamn lawyer would pay too. But the judge was the one he wanted, the smart-ass presumptuous bitch, no different than his step-mother. Of course, when the headaches overwhelmed him, he slipped out of reality. In two or three minutes of blankness he had condemned himself to a lifetime of cheap gray denim with STATE HOSPITAL stenciled across the back. The first psychiatrist had said that the blackouts were a conditioned escape, not insanity. The others had alleged other symptoms, adding up to psychosis, but it was all guesswork. The jury didn't believe them. They didn't think he was crazy. Any true scientist knew that psychology wasn't a science. One of the lawyers had posed a question at the trial. 'Isn't it a statistical fact, Doctor, that any man on the street has as good a chance of predicting future violent behavior as a licensed psychiatrist?' The psychiatrist had agreed. But, in spite of the lack of any real proof, that woman judge decided he was insane – as a matter of law, she had said. The very nature of the crime was persuasive, she said. 'The very nature of the crime,' he said out loud in a sickeningly feminine whine. So here he lay, or sat, or paced, always waiting. Waiting for what? He had no options, except one. He was sane when he got here, but now he was not so sure.

A key turned in the lock. He had an appointment with Dr Perlman. The one positive in this whole mad dream was Perlman's prescription. One capsule delivered by an orderly daily in a tiny paper cup had subdued the headache dragon.

'Good afternoon, Herr Schmid.' Slim Olson, in green

17

scrubs, filled the door with his huge frame, his neck and jaw encased in a scarf of fat.

'You never tire of vacuous humor,' said William, sitting on the edge of the bed.

'What'sa matta, William? Not happy today?' Smile crinkles pinched Slim's pale blue eyes almost shut.

William never missed the hint of pity in Slim's deep voice and familiar grin. 'Is anybody happy in here?'

'Henry Ford, down the hall, is coming out with a new model next month,' said Slim. 'Air bags even in the back seat. He showed me the drawings. He's very happy.'

'I thought he was Sikorski working on a new helicopter,' said William.

'That was last week. You ready to go see Dr Perlman?'

'I am tired of him. He says the same thing every time. Same questions. Same answers.'

'Now, now, William. That's what you said last time.'

'And probably the time before,' said William. 'Perlman must be incompetent or he would not be working in this godforsaken place.'

'He would not like to hear you say that, William. He thinks you're so smart.'

'You are not going to tell him?'

'Not to worry. I don't like the little schmuck either. He's always talking to me like I'm one of the craz— patients.'

'You can say crazies,' said William. 'They all are. Except Thurgood – and me, of course.'

'C'mon, I'll walk you down the hall.'

'I can go alone. All the doors are locked. Who would I harm?'

'Rules, y'know. You don't want me to lose my job, do ya?'

'No, I do not want you to lose your job, Slim,' said William. He liked the big Swede.

In tandem, Slim in front, they plodded down the hall to the first door before the nurses' station. This session would be no different. Some new trick questions, mixed in with the same old ones about Alice and his childhood and Wilma, his twin sister.

The conference room's bright lights hit William's eyes.

18

Behind the desk stood a stubby, bristly-browed man. 'Dr Perlman' was embroidered in red on the breast pocket of his white jacket. A man in a tan sport coat leaned back on the sofa with his legs crossed, giving William the once over. An easy smile spread across his squarish face, lightly speckled with fading freckles.

'Not again,' said William. 'She get another letter?' His tone was friendly, at least for him.

'You know she did, Schmid. You didn't think I came way up here to invite you to Thanksgiving dinner.' Kevin Bannon's thin lips made a tight line, but there were laugh lines around his eyes. Seven years before, Bannon had arrested William for the murder of Alice Wahl.

Dr Perlman asked William to sit. 'Detective Bannon has some questions,' he said.

'I tell you every time you come. I have nothing to do with any letters. It is some crank. You have checked my typewriter before – and how would I get them out of here?' William didn't sit down. His voice whined with the sound of honest frustration.

'How did you know it was typewritten?'

'Oh, Jesus Christ, Bannon. You have asked me that before. Why would you have checked my typewriter if they were not typed? Except the first one, of course.'

Dr Perlman sat down behind the desk. 'Sit down, William. Please sit down. You know these letters aren't helping your record.'

'I have nothing to do with them. I tell you every time. Besides, what is the difference? You are never going to let me out of here anyway.' He sat down in the chair in front of the desk and looked at Dr Perlman for a reaction.

'Your problem can be treated,' said Perlman, 'if you cooperate.'

In a black and white photo above Perlman's head, Freud lectured to an unseen audience. 'I've been doing my best,' William said. 'You do not think I would ruin it by getting involved in a scheme writing more letters to a judge?'

From under a floppy cinnamon forelock, Bannon's eyes, no longer young, stared with green contempt into William's.

19

'You're having your sister Wilma do it.'

'Ask her.' William knew Bannon had – a dozen times.

'It's a dumb game, Schmid,' said Bannon. 'You're way too smart for this kind of shit. Why scare that nice young woman?'

'The know-it-all judge?' William blurted.

'She's a damn nice dame,' said Bannon.

'She stuck me in here.'

'Better than the pen,' said Bannon.

'You get *out* of the pen,' said William. 'Even lifers get paroled.'

'Some,' said Bannon. 'You can get out of here too if you get well, right, Doc?'

'Of course, that's what we're here for,' said Perlman.

'Mr Bannon,' said William, 'why waste a trip up here? It is over a hundred miles. I have always told you, except for the first one, I have nothing to do with the letters, and apparently so has Wilma told you.'

'You forget our little meeting after the first one, six years ago. You weren't into righteous denial then.'

William felt the skin of his face tighten. 'You have said that every time also.'

'Of course I have, Schmid. Because I'll never forget what you said.'

William fell silent. He remembered, just as he had remembered on Bannon's other visits. He had spoken too quickly. It was before he had analyzed his situation comprehensively, before he realized any sign of ferocity on his part would be counterproductive. The trial and incarceration had traumatized him. It was the first time he had been totally without any control since his father had died.

'You quoted your letter verbatim with your best smirk. You said she would be getting it, like Alice got it.'

'That was just an offhand remark. You told me you never repeated it to her.'

'Big deal. Those letters repeat it, almost word for word.' Bannon's face flushed.

'I cannot help what they say. I did not write them. That is the truth. But I must say I am not unhappy that she gets a

20

little reminder of what she has done to me.'

'I've never told you that word was in any of those letters,' said Bannon. He turned toward Dr Perlman.

'Neither have I,' said Perlman.

'What word?' said William.

'Reminder. How would you know anything about a reminder?' Bannon shook his finger at William.

'What is that supposed to mean?'

Bannon leaned forward and slid to the edge of the sofa. 'The word "reminder" is used in the last three letters,' he said.

'So what?' said William.

'How would you have known?' said Bannon.

'Please,' said William, 'Mr Bannon, you are grasping at straws.'

'I'm not so sure,' said Bannon. 'I'm going to say one more thing, Schmid. Dr Perlman tells me you have made progress here. Eventually, I'll prove you're connected with those letters. Then how do you think Judge Goldman will feel about approving your release? Never. You'll never be released if she believes you continue to write these letters. So, for Christ's sake, knock it off.'

'Of course, I have thought of that. If she is the fair person you claim her to be she would not hold something against me that I did not do.' William had no illusions that Judge Goldman would ever allow him to go free.

Bannon's eyes locked on William's. 'I'm good at my job, Schmid. There's others working on this too. The Feds, for instance. You are using the US mail in violation of—'

'What else can I say, Mr Bannon? I simply did not write them – or have any of them written, for that matter.'

Bannon's expression indicated a new idea. 'Would you take a polygraph on that?'

'Of course, if Mr Scott approves.'

'I thought you hated him too.'

'He was my attorney at the trial. I will take his advice.'

'You know Hard Head Harry won't approve.'

'Then why do you keep asking that question?'

Bannon just laughed. After a bit of almost friendly banter

21

he took his leave. William wondered what he had hoped to accomplish.

'Care to talk a little today, William?' said Dr Perlman.

'Isn't my time up?'

'Oh, we have a little time.'

'I am ready for some group activities,' said William as he drew his chair up closer to the desk. A familiar sweet smell faintly tantalized his nostrils. He thought it was Old Spice. Wilma used to buy it for him for Christmas, but he never wore it.

'I don't know, William. There are some areas we haven't made much progress in.'

'But Thurgood is participating in the groups.'

'Who told you that? I know you haven't had a chance to talk to Thurgood since he joined the games group.'

'Word gets around,' said William.

'I must learn who told you.'

William didn't want to upset Perlman. Slim Olson had told him about Thurgood. 'Roger Davis told me on Monday.'

'It's not like Roger to break the rules,' said Perlman.

Roger would lose his job if Perlman believed it. 'I was surprised too,' said William. 'What about groups? Thurgood killed *two* women.' The papers had been full of Thurgood Jefferson's murder rapes five years ago.

'Each case is different, William. Shall we talk about Alice?'

'I'd rather not. That was the old me.'

'Do you remember why you killed her?'

'No,' said William.

'If you remembered, maybe we could help. What *do* you remember, William?'

Sometimes he was tempted to lie, to tell Perlman just why and how he killed Alice. That might make his stay in this nuthouse more pleasant. But that was a lie he could not tell. 'Nothing. As I have told you many times, Doctor, I have never remembered anything about Alice's death. Only what the doctors and police told me later on.'

Perlman scribbled with his pencil. 'What did they tell you?'

William knew he must be consistent. But it wasn't difficult. He only remembered one set of facts. 'As I have told you over and over again, I have pieced it together from everything they have told me. I killed Alice with a scalpel. My fingerprints were on it and I had Alice's blood on my hands.'

'What else?' said Dr Perlman.

'Nothing else. I remember nothing else.'

'What about those letters you have written to Judge Goldman, William?'

'I have told you,' William said, looking directly into Dr Perlman's yellowish-brown eyes, 'Except for the first one, I haven't written any letters to Judge Goldman.'

'I find it very hard to believe that you are not involved.' Perlman added a benign little smile to the soft expression of his doughy face.

'Wilma might have written them, but I have asked her, and she says that she has not,' said William.

Perlman scribbled, then mentioned William's stepmother.

With minor variations the stepmother questions had been posed several times during the first three years William was at Wolf River. But Perlman hadn't brought her up for a long time. Perhaps he had just forgotten about her. Who knew his methods? Perlman must have a hundred patients. William had only talked about his stepmother once – when the psychiatrists who testified at the trial interviewed him. It could not do any good to talk about these things now. Anyway, Perlman must have read the transcripts. He must know the worst of it.

'I just do not remember anymore,' said William. 'I have put her from my mind. I hate her. She is dead.'

'But she isn't dead, William. You know Wilma has heard from her.'

'She is dead,' said William, 'and I can remember nothing of her.' The hatred and the image of the gingery pelt of dank pubic hair had faded with time. He had more important things to think about.

4

Tess, Rebecca's law clerk, had walked the letter over to police headquarters in the basement of the old limestone courthouse across Fifth Street. Later that afternoon Rebecca had called Kevin Bannon. He had promised to check into it and get back to her. She was surprised to get his call in chambers on a frosty Friday morning before she went on the bench, less than forty-eight hours after she had opened the letter. In the past it had sometimes taken up to a month.

'Judge Goldman, Kevin Bannon here.' His voice was upbeat, like a life insurance salesman hoping for an appointment.

'So soon,' said Rebecca.

'I interviewed Schmid yesterday.'

'In person?'

'Yeah.'

He had driven all the way to Wolf River on a routine matter that had occurred several times before. Incredible. Maybe this time their dusting had produced a print. 'I'm impressed. Have you found anything?'

The line was silent for a moment. 'Could we talk about it over lunch today?'

'That important, Sergeant?'

'Kevin,' he said.

'OK,' she said, 'Kevin. You know how the court likes to avoid fraternization with the police.'

'Sure, your honor, but do you really believe anybody would think you would ever favor the cops?'

Her curiosity tempered the sting of the reference to her

24

reputation for soft treatment of criminals. 'I suppose once wouldn't hurt.'

'The Willows?'

'Dutch?'

'If you insist,' he said.

'I insist.' That boyish freckle face must bring out the mother in every woman. She remembered that he was single. Supposedly a childless marriage had broken up years ago.

'Noon, OK?'

'See you there, Sergeant.'

'Kevin,' he said.

'Kevin,' she said.

Kevin Bannon's innuendo rankled. You apply the law. Rulings in favor of criminals on evidentiary questions were the cops' problem if they ignored the law. She had no choice. Still, the editorials and letters in the newspapers were irritating. She didn't want to be a minority judge. She wanted to be a fair judge. Come one, come all.

Worse was the conversation she had overheard. Just hearing Bannon's name brought the heat of embarrassment to her cheeks. Sometimes it replayed verbatim, like an audio tape on her Walkman. The visual images were only imaginary. She had heard, not seen.

It had been less than a year ago. She had been looking for a missing transcript in her court reporter's office. The door was open a crack. A few feet away, the door to her chambers was wide open. Anyone looking in would assume she was gone.

The first voice she heard was Henry Pettiford's, her bailiff, employed by the county sheriff. 'How's it goin', Knuckles?'

She had heard Bannon's nickname before.

'OK, Henry. I got a warrant. Is the judge around?'

'Ain't seen her,' said Henry.

'Too bad. I'll go to McGregor. By the way, Henry, what's it like working for that broad?'

Behind the door Rebecca winced.

'Ain't too bad, Knuckles. Mighty fine, I should say.'

25

'She looks pretty good with that robe off.'

'You got that, man, them's pretty fine.'

Rebecca's face burned. Bannon must have made some gesture with his hands.

'Must be thirty-six, D cup,' he said.

'Wouldn't know for sure,' said Henry.

'You know, Henry, I size women up in four categories: face, tits, ass and hair, and sometimes a little extra for legs and general proportions – whatever you wanta call it.'

'Yeah,' said Henry.

'Now on a scale of one to ten, I maybe give her face a five. A little too much nose, y'know, but those big brown eyes, uses 'em like bullets. She drills ya, right?'

'Right,' said Henry.

'And those lips are somethin' else. Complexion's a little rough, but that light tan is real nice.'

'Yeah,' said Henry, whose face was the cordovan brown of high-priced shoes, 'mighty nice color.'

Rebecca's pulse raced. She held herself as still as a rabbit in the weeds, too anxious about what he might say next to recognize her anger.

'Best I can do on the ass is a four. A little wide.'

No sound from Henry.

'I might give her a seven on the hair. It'd feel great between your fingers. But not as nice as those Hispanic babes down in traffic, nice and dark and long.'

'Yeah,' said Henry.

'But she fixes it nice. Yeah, at least a seven on the hair. Course, if you're into tits you gotta give her a ten, but I say about the same as the hair, maybe a seven. Now that all only adds up to about a six. Hardly ever see her legs and then only from the knees down, dammit.'

Rebecca thought of her thick thighs and was tempted to open the door. A whirling tornado of emotions held her back.

'But she's got great ankles and nice calves.'

'Yeah,' said Henry.

'So maybe I give her a seven overall.'

'A seven?' said Henry.

'Yeah, just a seven. But I'll tell you what, Henry. There

must be a lot of nines around the courthouse and tens over at the mall in the summer, right, Henry?'

'Right, Knuckles.'

'But my system's full of shit, Henry.'

'What the hell you talkin', Knuckles?'

'Because none of 'em look as good as Rebecca Goldman with that robe off, and that's a goddamn fact, Henry.'

'You got it, Knuckles.'

'And Henry?'

'Yeah.'

'Knock that Knuckles shit off, will ya?'

Rebecca had waited several minutes before emerging from concealment. She never did sort out her feelings. Overhearing an attractive man say she was the best looking woman in the neighborhood wasn't that hard to take, but the way he said it – the heat came back to her cheeks. Even a little guilt about eavesdropping lurked in the wings. She wasn't that surprised by the copper's plain talk. Reggie's friends used to be much worse. Kevin Bannon covered a lot of territory. *None of 'em look as good as Rebecca Goldman.*

Now, what could Bannon have to tell her about William Schmid that was so hot? Seven years back, Schmid had stood beside Harry Scott as the clerk read the verdict: guilty of first degree murder. A carefully pressed dark blue suit had replaced the casual dress of the arraignment. The real trial was to follow, a tournament of forensic psychiatrists, the champion's lance only as powerful as his acuity in revealing the innermost secrets of the defendant's mind at the time of the crime. After witnessing all this jousting, the law presumed the jury – or perhaps the judge – would become imbued with the knowledge to determine whether the defendant Schmid was disabled mentally to the extent that he should not be held criminally responsible. The questions: Did he do it on purpose? Or was it an accident somehow associated with his nature? Could William Schmid really tell right from wrong?

But there was no more time for speculation about what Kevin Bannon might tell her at lunch today. In a few minutes Rebecca would charge a jury that had been listening to an automobile accident case off and on for two weeks. The jury charge was as important a function as the trial judge performed. Sergeant Kevin Bannon and William Schmid would have to wait.

Some considered the Willows in the Hyatt Regency to be the finest restaurant in downtown Minneapolis. It was too far from the Government Center to walk. Her cab motored down the Nicollet Mall, off limits to private cars. Getting ready for the holiday season, workers strung lights in the scrawny trees lining the wide sidewalks in front of the fine shops. Rebecca rarely lunched or dined at the Willows, too pricey, and her occasional dates since she had ascended to the bench had chosen more modest venues. At ten after twelve she wove her way through the crowded lobby. Kevin Bannon, in a smart blue blazer with a red pocket square, waited just outside the entrance to the cafe.

'Hello, Judge.' He smiled broadly and held out his hand.

She took it. 'Sorry I'm late, Sergeant. Nice to see you.'

'No problem, and the name's Kevin.' He finally relaxed his firm grip on her fingers.

'Of course. Kevin. You are persistent. It's only fair then that you call me Rebecca.' She wasn't ready for Becka, the name her closest friends and family used.

The hostess led them to a table in the center of the dining room. The leafy decor went with the name. Kevin gave the waiter the order, then stared at Rebecca with a maddening little grin twitching slightly at the corners. The overheard conversation came back and she resisted the impulse to fold her arms across her chest.

'Charge a jury this morning?'

'How'd you know?'

'I walked by about an hour ago and saw the door was locked.'

'Thirteen days, counting today,' she said, 'and I bet it'll settle over lunch. The defense didn't like my instructions. Liability's clear – egregious, in fact. Just a question of money. Guy's a quad. They're talking in the millions.'

'Whose case?'

28

'Holloway. He'll make at least a mil for two weeks' work.' She knew there was preparation, but still the contingency fees were outrageous.

'What are we doin' workin' for the people?' Kevin said.

'You tell me, Serg— Kevin.'

'You're learnin', Rebecca.'

'What about Schmid? What chased you up there so fast?'

'Aim to please, and a good excuse to get you out to lunch.' His laughing green eyes looking straight into hers said he wasn't kidding.

'I appreciate your interest.' That didn't sound right. Interest in her or Schmid, or her and Schmid.

The ends of his grin started twitching again. He was there to see *her*. Socially. She mistrusted the little high gained from the knowledge. 'Please tell me what you've found.'

'Not much.'

She wouldn't ask him why the lunch. She waited for him to go on, and her effort not to smile turned into a giggle.

'Ah, she can laugh,' said Kevin. 'I talked to him yesterday. With his psychiatrist. Of course he still denies having knowledge of the letters. And he's changed.'

'For the better, one would hope,' said Rebecca.

'That's just it. Too much for the better. He almost seems like a nice guy. Not so stiff. And this sonofabitch ain't no nice guy.'

'Meaning?'

'I don't know. He brought up the bit again about being in the booby hatch rather than Stillwater. Said he might have got paroled.'

'Sure, when he was an old man.'

'Last time I talked to him he said he thought he could've got murder two if Harry Scott had asked for a lesser included charge. With second degree he might have been out already.'

'He had his hearing on that and an appeal,' said Rebecca.

'Anyway, Rebecca, something's different about the guy. I just wanted to tell you face to face. Here's a tape of the conversation. I had a recorder in my pocket.'

'You tell him?'

'Now, Judge, why would I tell him? We've already got this guy locked up.'

'What about the shrink?'

'You'll see. He said nothin'.'

'I appreciate your interest.' She felt awkward again.

'How's the teri-yaki?' he asked.

After some small talk about the criminal calendar, Rebecca changed the subject. 'Kevin, why do so many people call you Knuckles?'

'I'm afraid, er, that's a long story.' His ruddy complexion darkened. 'Ask me something easier.'

'OK. Where are you from originally?'

'Grand Rapids, up on the range. Judy Garland's hometown.'

'The iron range?'

'Yeah, that's right. You're not from around here, I guess. The natives all know range means iron range.'

'Is it a nice place?'

'Great place to grow up, especially if you like hockey, and I did. Played for the high school. And there's great fishing and hunting and hundreds of miles of trails in the woods.'

'Why'd you leave?'

'Didn't really plan to. Got drafted and sent to 'Nam. Came back and went to the University for a couple of years, pre-law. Decided I'd rather be a cop. Here I am.'

In New York Rebecca had carried signs against the war. She didn't want to talk about it with Kevin. 'Word is you're very good at what you do,' she said.

'It's a life. There hasn't been much else for quite a while.'

'Do you still have friends or relatives on the range?'

'Sure. My mom's still living in Grand Rapids and a few old friends. Dad's been dead for twelve years. He worked in the Greenway Mine for thirty years. I drive up there three or four times a year.'

'Sounds fun up in the north woods,' said Rebecca.

His wide smile showed a row of even teeth. 'You'll have to check it out one of these days.'

'I think I should wait until summer. My mother was a big fan of Judy Garland.'

'Summer'll be fine,' said Kevin.

Rebecca felt her face flush. She looked around for the waiter.

Alone in the cab on the way back to the Government Center, she remembered the concern in Kevin's eyes when he said that William Schmid had changed.

As she expected, the accident case settled before the jury had finished their lunch – $4,500,000. It worked out three million less expenses to the quad who was learning to steer his wheelchair by blowing across a tube placed in front of his mouth. His attorney Larry Holloway got $1,500,000. What it meant for Rebecca was home early on a Friday afternoon.

From the garage under the courthouse she pulled her Buick out on to Third Avenue. Heated parking was one of her favorite perks. A steel-gray canopy of low-hanging clouds covered the entire city and people could already see their breath as they hurried along the sidewalks. She headed south on Third Avenue and stopped for the light on Eighth Street. As she reached up to move the mirror for a quick look at her face, she glanced at the person driving the car behind her. Rebecca froze. Could it be Wilma Schmid? The same narrow face, the rimless glasses, the parting through the center of her dark blonde hair. A car two or three back beeped its horn. The light had changed. As Rebecca proceeded through the intersection, the woman made a left on Eighth. It was a black car. Rebecca didn't know makes.

She watched the mirror all the way to her building on Lake Calhoun. It could have been a coincidence. Anyway, she wasn't sure it was Wilma. And what if it had been? Wilma had a clean record. She had never hurt anyone, but she might be the one writing those awful letters. She couldn't be normal. Who could be with that childhood? Rebecca remembered the testimony that Harry Scott had drawn out of that young woman.

Wilma testified in both cases. She was called by the prosecutor in the phase determining guilt. Harry Scott called her in the mental illness phase. It was the latter Rebecca remembered clearly.

Every seat in the spectator's area was taken. Wilma Schmid sat in the witness box in a gray suit, her hair drawn back tightly in a chignon. She was pretty in a skinny sort of way and seemed incapable of smiling.

Scott prepared judge and jury for what was to come. 'Miss Schmid, I know the questions I am about to ask will be a source of shame and humiliation to you. Try to remember we are here only to enable this court and this jury to fully understand the state of your brother's mind at the time of Alice Wahl's death. Do you understand that, Miss Schmid?'

Like a wilting lily, Wilma Schmid nodded and dropped her gaze to the floor.

'Miss Schmid, it is necessary that you respond audibly so that the court reporter can make an accurate record of these proceedings. I take it your nod meant yes?'

'Yes,' she said.

'Do you love your brother, William?'

'Yes,' she said.

Harry Scott spent the following hour asking gentle questions about her childhood with William, her fear of her father, the failure of her stepmother to develop a nurturing relationship with the two children, and Wilma's growing dependency on her twin brother.

Scott asked Rebecca for permission to approach the witness. Quietly, 'Miss Schmid, when you were twelve years old, did you begin a sexual relationship with your twin brother?'

Even more quietly, she answered yes.

'How did this come about?'

'It just happened.'

Scott began to guide her through the details. The prosecutor didn't object to the leading questions.

Finally, 'When did it stop?'

'About two years later.'

'Why?'

'My father caught us.' For the first time she looked

32

directly at the jury. 'He decided he wanted me for himself.'

Deep in her reverie, Rebecca almost missed the turn into her garage. It was her imagination, she decided. A lot of women look like Wilma Schmid, especially when seen from a rearview mirror fifty feet away.

5

Whitlow Strom was serving his third four-year term as District Attorney. His twenty-foot square office was set in the corner of the nineteenth floor of the Government Center. Prints of ducks and geese hung wherever there was space. A sofa along the wall and four chairs in a semicircle before the wide mahogany desk were covered with tan leather. A hand-painted duck decoy with a green head sat serenely on the front of the desk. Several rust-coloured expanding files covered the top of the coffee table in front of the sofa. Because both he and Tom Phelps were Democrats, some suggested that Strom would not prosecute vigorously. They didn't know Whitlow Strom. He wanted Phelps convicted and he wanted to do it personally. It was the first case he would try himself in almost five years.

Phelps's alleged victim Dinah White was seated on the sofa. Strom wished she wouldn't smoke, but there were more important considerations, not the least of which was the pain in his lower back that had been nagging him since noon. He walked round his desk and maneuvered one of the chairs to face the sofa. After settling gingerly on to the chair he tried his best to turn on a radiant smile for Dinah White. She had the narrow brown aspect of a starving child, entirely redeemed by large brown eyes in a face relaxed by a sullen mood. Beside her, Barbara Bird, an Assistant DA specializing in rape cases, jotted notes on a yellow pad lying across her knees. Her black face with its broad nose and full lips was more classically African than Dinah's. Straightened hair glistened like fresh tar.

'I told Harry Scott we'd dismiss if Phelps's story held up

34

on a polygraph,' Barbara said, her voice deep for a woman.

'I can tell you just what he said,' said Strom, tilting the chair back slightly. He rubbed his right hand over the bare dome of his large head which was turned toward the long window framing the tops of skyscrapers. Strom always spoke slowly and precisely as though each word was being carefully considered. ' "I'm insulted," Scott said to you. "I have been trying cases for" . . .whatever his current number of years are . . . "without subjecting my clients to lie detector tests. I'm not going to start now. Besides, I need the money." Then he laughed.' Strom leaned forward and extended his hand holding a pair of black-rimmed glasses toward Barbara Bird. 'How close am I?'

'Pretty close, Whit.' The ebony contours of her face shifted into a soft smile, showing straight bright teeth. 'Twenty-four years, he said. And he said he needed the bread, not the money. How were you so sure?'

'Years back I tried three cases against Scott – everybody still called him Hard Head then – a murder, a kidnapping – and aggravated arson, I think.'

'And,' said Barbara. She winked at Dinah.

'And I lost 'em all,' said Strom. 'I remember offering the firebug a lie detector. Probably would have forgotten all about it if I hadn't lost a case I thought I had wired. Jury was out more than a week. After they acquitted the guy, I asked Hard Head, if this guy was so innocent, why didn't he let him take the polygraph when I offered it? That's when he added the part about needing the money. Ya gotta hand it to him. Not only is he a great lawyer, he's probably the best center linebacker the Gophers ever had. But that's a long time ago. Now at two hundred and ten pounds or so, he'd be too small.'

'I shouldn't have asked,' said Barbara.

'I take it you two have gone over all the facts again?'

'We've been at it all afternoon,' said Barbara. 'Right, Dinah?'

Dinah nodded. She put her cigarette out and folded her hands in the lap of a short white dress, brown legs crossed. Her toe tapped cadence in the air to some silent drum.

Strom thought her face might be showing fatigue more than anger. Dinah quickly disabused him. Both hands came up chopping the air, gold rings on most of the fingers. 'I want that bastard convicted. I wish you could get him the death penalty – or at least castration.' The big dark eyes narrowed.

At their first meeting Strom had explained the problems of prosecuting rape. Their conviction rate was low. Juries were reluctant to take the alleged victim's word against the defendant's, especially when they were friends or associates of one kind or another, especially when the woman was black, especially when there was drinking involved. Dinah had been worried about lies and innuendos. Would she become the victim all over again? Would the defense bring in a bunch of men to claim that she was a loose woman whom they knew from personal experience? After all, Phelps had friends, had done political favors for people. Both Barbara Bird and Strom had rushed to reassure her. At the trial she would be protected by the rape shield law. Minnesota was out in front on that issue. No evidence of her past sex life or any of her sexual proclivities would be admitted. Dinah had been single-minded. I want to go all the way with this, she said. Win or lose. Let them bring in whomever they might. The jurors would know liars when they saw them.

Barbara Bird, skin even darker than Dinah's, tall and straight in a blue suit, got up and walked over to the window. She looked out over the city. 'Do you think there's any chance Goldman will remove herself?'

'Almost none. At least based on Harry Scott's brief,' said Strom. 'I've got mixed feelings on Goldman. She's given our prosecutors fits in the past.'

'Tell me about it.' Barbara turned to her boss, her black hair glinting under the ceiling light. 'I tried the Clayton case in front of her. You remember the bigtime dealer with the fancy apartment at the Towers. She ruled the search warrant was no good and Clayton walked. You weren't too happy.'

'I remember,' said Strom. 'But we've got a couple of

verdicts on rapes. Year before last Pennington tried one in her court. Of course the big one was Schmid, that weird physics professor six or seven years ago. I tried that one.'

'Before my time,' said Barbara.

'It wasn't long after Goldman was appointed. Jury found him guilty of first degree murder. By the way, that was another one of my cases where Harry Scott defended. Goldman got on her high horse and took it away.'

'What do you mean?' said Barbara.

'Just that. Hard Head made a motion and she ruled that Schmid was insane as a matter of law. I really didn't give a damn because she committed him to Wolf River. He's still there and I wouldn't be surprised if he stays until he croaks. Actually better for everybody. He might have got out of Stillwater.'

'He would have done at least twenty,' said Barbara.

'Sure, but Schmid didn't think so. He was pissed. But Harry Scott was happy. He considered it a big win. After all, he had entered the insanity plea.'

'Are you saying,' asked Barbara, 'that you'd just as soon have Goldman take herself off Phelps?'

'No. I've got a feeling on this one. I think Goldman and Dinah here have got more in common than their race.' Strom turned to Dinah White on the sofa. 'I remember when Becka Goldman was active in the party. She must know what a prick Phelps is. That can't hurt us.' Strom caught Dinah's eye. 'How about it, Ms White?'

'It wouldn't surprise me,' she said. 'He's always sniffin' around young women. The more power he got, the more aggressive he got. A regular Mike Tyson, all hands. But most of his power has come since Rebecca Goldman was active in the party. Still, to use your word, you can be sure that Phelps has always been a prick.'

'Obviously there must be some who don't agree with you,' said Strom.

'Obviously,' said Dinah White, 'but there's got to be some other women he's hurt – if they'll come forward.' A cord stood out in her neck.

'We've got the word out,' said Barbara Bird.

Strom knew Phelps did well with some women. As a party regular he had heard the quips. Phelps had a tongue like an anteater. If Phelps had one wish, it would be for nostrils in the top of his head. It was pretty funny actually, but Dinah White might not think it was so humorous right now. Her foot still bounced to the same nervous beat.

'I appreciate how hard you two are working on this,' Strom said. 'I'm sure we'll be ready when the time comes.'

'We're gonna get this guy,' said Barbara Bird.

Strom liked her enthusiasm, but he wasn't so sure. They needed more than they had, and Dinah White wasn't known around the party as the Virgin Mary, either. The nagging pain in his back was getting worse. It had been a cold windy day up on Bowstring Lake nine autumns ago. He had steadied his duckboat in the waves with two long pipes driven into the lake bottom. If only he hadn't tried to pull those pipes out of the mud so fast, just so he could chase that crippled mallard all over the lake. If he had just let that duck swim away, the God awful ache in his back wouldn't be there now. But he had been obsessed to get that duck. It was the only one he had knocked down that day. He wanted this guy Phelps just as bad.

6

Though only the most persistent leaves clung to the trees, Indian summer had returned to Minnesota for a day. Through the ten-foot high chain-link fence, roofs of houses in Wolf River, a half-mile to the south, lined up against the sky like teeth on the edge of a saw. The scent of wood smoke rode the warm breeze wafting in from the village. From where he stood in the exercise yard, William Schmid couldn't see the old bridge that passed over the river just east of town, but Wilma's picture postcard had fixed the structural details firmly in his mind: only about twelve feet wide, wood pilings sunk into the riverbed, frail metal railings. Just one car could cross the river at a time. In winter the water gushed past about ten feet below.

Twice a day the sixth-floor patients were allotted a half-hour of exercise in the yard. One guard supervised their activities. The so-called violent patients were never allowed out in groups of more than four. From the fence William walked back to the bench where he had left his book. He was re-reading everything he could get by Stephen Hawking. When William taught physics at the university, to stimulate their interest he assigned Hawking to his students for outside reading. William's course in quantum mechanics was popular among the undergraduates. He was promoted to associate professor just six months before his arrest. Alice Wahl had been his teaching assistant.

Slim Olson lowered his wide bottom to the bench beside William. 'Readin' that complicated shit again.'

'I have a paper due to a publisher in January.' Part of his

plan, he had been working diligently in his cell for the past two months.

'Wanna shoot some hoops?' said Slim.

'Sure. Why not?' William wanted Slim to like him.

Over the years Slim had regaled William with tales of exploits on the basketball court in his youth. He had led Wolf River High School to the Class B state championship. After he had used up his scholarship at a junior college in Duluth, he met a dead end. Slim opted for the job at Wolf River. Now married, he was in the process of raising three children.

A hundred pounds less, Slim might have been as good as he said he was. His blubbery six-foot-five frame had become more handicap than help. William's only sport in high school had been basketball. He was taller than most of the kids and he had learned to shoot and dribble well enough to make the intramural all-star team. At the university he kept a ball in his small apartment. When he got the time he shot some buckets in the park across the street. In the Wolf River exercise yard he had learned to make a little fake, then dribble round the out of shape Slim for easy lay-ups. Even so, Slim enjoyed the games immensely. Since William had begun to formulate his plan, he had let Slim win their one-on-one games most of the time. In the laboratory, scientists learn there is no substitute for patience.

Time to go in. Slim stood panting under the basket.

William walked up close. Holding the ball on his hip, he looked up into Slim's face. 'That last hook was like Kareem.' William remembered Slim's favorite player.

'Hey, buddy, we don't want to be late. You know how mean that bitch can get,' Slim said.

'Just one second, Slim,' said William. 'You said you were working on Thanksgiving, correct?'

'Yeah, it's my turn for the holiday, plus double time, y'know?'

'I have been thinking,' said William. 'Nothing ever changes in the holidays. We will have turkey instead of chicken – that's about it. And this year Wilma cannot make it up here. I just thought it might be nice if you and I, and say Thurgood, had our exercise time alone. You get a thermos of coffee and some nice Danish. I will pay for it. And we could have a little party here on the bench. Maybe shoot some hoops. It would seem like old times on the outside, sort of.'

'I'd have to ask the bitch.'

'I see no reason.'

'You know her goddamn rules.'

'There's no rule against you just having two for exercise, is there?'

'Guess not, but what about coffee and rolls?'

'She won't be here on the holiday. She never is. And even if she found out, it is Thanksgiving.'

'I just heard they let that night orderly Davis go. Big hush-up thing. He broke some fuckin' rule about tellin' stuff to the crazies.'

'He was not a good man like you, Slim. I am sure they were just looking for an excuse.'

'I dunno, buddy.'

'That is the point. We are basketball buddies, Slim.'

Slim's gray eyes wandered up over the top of the fence toward the flimsy high-flying clouds. Maybe he could hear the band playing 'Win Wolf River'.

'And I have something for that daughter who is doing so well in high school.' William handed Slim a book – Hawking's *A Brief History of Time*, still in the blue dust jacket.

'I can't accept anything from the patients or their relatives.'

'You not accepting anything. It is a gift to Sarah Jane.'

The simple logic appealed to Slim. He held the book in his teeth as he struggled into his jacket, then shoved it in one of the big pockets.

'You will get the thermos and the rolls?' William looked into his eyes expectantly, forcing his best smile.

'Why not?' said Slim. 'Fuck the bitch.'

The following afternoon Wilma visited. They were allowed to meet in the conference room next to the nurse's station. A guard was always present. They sat beside each other on the sofa where Kevin Bannon had been sitting a few days before. The guard always insisted they stay at arm's length. Wilma's visits were the high points of William's life. From a knife-like parting her dark blonde hair was drawn tightly back and down to a low chignon. Sometimes the guard let them sit on the bench in the exercise yard, but the weather had turned cold. The air in the windowless room was barely breathable. In spite of the rule, someone had been smoking recently.

'So, William, my sweet, how is the article coming?' Her voice was light and happy.

William glanced at the guard. He was reading a newspaper. 'I have planned for it to the hour. It will be finished at three in the afternoon on Thanksgiving Day.'

'Wonderful,' she said. 'I can't wait to read it.'

'Is everything going all right at the railroad?'

'Of course, they think I'm indispensable.'

'I know how they feel,' he said. 'And your spare time? Are you having any fun?'

'What's fun, my brother? Since you have been here nothing is fun. I read a little.'

'What are you reading?'

'A woman at the office told me about a book called *Silence of the Lambs*. She said there was a man in it who was locked up in a place like this. So I read it.'

'Did you like it? Shall I read it?'

'I don't think so. I found it rather depressing.'

'Was the man like me?'

'No, not at all. He was truly mad.' She edged a couple of inches closer to him.

'Did he kill anyone?'

'Yes,' she said. 'But it was very bizarre.'

'Certainly, what happened to Alice could be called bizarre. You agree with that?'

'This book is fiction, William. Don't bother with it.'

'I have too much to do anyway.'

The guard was completely hidden behind the newspaper. The twins' blue eyes met. William lunged toward Wilma and wrapped his arms round her neck. Their lips met in an open-mouthed kiss.

'Hey, you two, cut that out. That's against the rules,' the guard brayed.

They held the open-mouthed kiss. Wilma's tongue pushed a large bean-like object between William's teeth. A metallic taste spread through his mouth.

The guard continued to yell. 'That's it. That's the end of this little session. You're lucky if Mrs Hess doesn't cut off your visiting privileges.'

He tugged at William's shoulder, but he held on and nuzzled his face into the softness of Wilma's neck. Images of the crows and the river and the bridge he had never seen flickered in his brain like scratchy scenes on movie film.

7

Cleck-cluck-cleck-cluck-cleck-cluck . . . chang. Harry Scott, moisture dribbling down his high forehead, thrust himself deep inside her. He had the penis of a stallion, and he whinnied when he came. The grandfather clock in the hall awakened her. Goddamn clock. Her body covered with sweat, Rebecca writhed among the twisted sheets. She gently massaged her wet clitoris in a steady rhythm. Release swept over her, harder and stronger than it ever had, even with Reggie.

She lay still, staring into the dark. Her friend Susan had urged her to get a vibrator, but Susan was truly liberated, and what if Julie found it? Why was it always Harry Scott she dreamed about? Their only contact had been professional. A drink or two sipped together at the annual judges' social, nothing else. She had never touched him, never even shaken his hand, that she could recall. He was an outstanding lawyer. But in the light of day, that was it, and he was married. Anyway, she had never felt a strong physical attraction to him. But in her dreams he was wonderful. That damn clock.

Chastity sucks. Worse, being alone sucks. Touching. She needed touching, sharing. Julie was wonderful. But it wasn't the same. The warmth of intimacy had eluded her for far too long. On a winter day when Julie was about a year old, chills surged through Rebecca's body as she sat in Con law. They were stating cases on the Commerce Clause. She guessed the flu. Better go home; cut Evidence. She walked along Washington Square heading for their little apartment in an old townhouse on Thirteenth Street. Her stomach

44

roiled. She visualized the amalgam of digesting food, enzymes and random fluids at the source of the disturbance. She climbed to the third landing. Little Julie's faint cries came through the door. Reggie took care of her when Rebecca was at school. He played tenor saxophone in various Village clubs at night. He never locked the door. It swung open easily. The overheated air was heavy with cigarette smoke. They had an old wine-colored sofa that made into a bed in the living room. It was presently so deployed. The bedroom door muffled the baby's sobs. Reggie was propped against the sofa back, his long legs spread and stretched out deep brown against the white sheet. Between them a broad pimply pink back tapered to a white ass propped up on kneeling legs, equally pale and covered with fine blond fuzz. Long brown hair veiled the head. The face was buried in Reggie's crotch.

'Becka, Jesus Christ, what are you doing home?' Glinting dark irises swam in wide white eyes.

'I got sick.'

The long-haired head withdrew from Reggie's crotch leaving his penis pointing skyward, like an artillery piece aimed over the horizon. Standing on its knees and turning toward her, the body revealed a stiff penis of its own. The surprised face looked familiar. Rebecca's stomach chose that instant to expel her lunch in a bilious pile on the frayed gray carpet.

'Jesus Christ,' said Reggie.

'Not cool,' said the pink man. 'Later for this.'

In a stoop-shouldered hunch, drool running down her chin, Rebecca looked from one face to the other and back to the mess on the floor, then charged into the bedroom to join her wailing daughter. After she closed the door, she remembered the name. The pink man was Voytek Milanowski, an artist near the top of New York City's pop art genre, whose paintings sold for a hundred thousand and more. They hung in museums all over the world.

Rebecca changed Julie's diaper in the crib, wrapped herself in a blanket, and sat down on the single chair in the tiny shadowy bedroom, holding Julie in her bunting. Wee

little gurgling coos replaced the sobbing. The winter afternoon light barely penetrated the worn ecru shade. The
nausea was gone, the chills subsiding. An all alone shakiness
spread out from her navel. She was lost in this vast city.
Reggie had been fucking her almost every day. She had had
no idea he might be interested in anyone else, let alone a
man. Eventually, the door squeaked open and he eased up
behind her and gently touched her cheek.

'I love you,' he said.

The two and a half years had been glorious. They had
met the second day Rebecca was in New York looking for an
apartment in the Village. He was playing in a club and
bought her and her friend a drink. When she found herself
pregnant, he wanted to get married. She considered an
abortion. It was three years after *Roe v. Wade* and abortion
had been readily available in New York City even before
that. Reggie wouldn't hear of it. He wanted to be a father. It
was time. After all, he was almost thirty-six years old, he
said through his luscious smile.

A couple of years later in that dim, closet-sized bedroom
she rocked her sleeping baby, side to side.

Reggie's fingers played with her hair. 'I love you,' he said
again. 'I really do, you know. I've given you every nickel I've
made. Just kept enough for cigarettes.'

She kept her eyes on the little brown face in her arms. She
remembered a rocking chair she had seen in a used furniture store on Fourteenth Street and wished she had bought
it.

Reggie knelt down beside her. 'I meant to stay straight . . .
for you,' he said, 'but it just isn't normal for me. You know the
ability to love both sexes, to share sexual pleasure without
regard to gender – that's a true indication that one loves a
person, not just a gender.' His voice was as mellow as his
tenor sax. 'That's the way Voytek thinks too. He has a girl
friend.' Reggie stopped for a few seconds as if he was hoping
she might respond and then he went on, 'It was just a lark.
This thing with Voytek. There are no other women.'

No other women. How well she remembered that ambiguity. As though that made a difference, and for a moment

it did. But in the next moment she realized the absurdity in her wishful thinking. The marriage was over. There was no resentment. None. Reggie was what he was, and it was futile for him to try to be something different. She knew he loved her, and she loved him, but marriage to a bisexual wasn't for her.

For ten years he stayed in close touch. He visited Julie and she went to visit him. No one was prouder than Reggie Smith when Rebecca was made a judge. He always paid his fair share of Julie's support, until he died of AIDS four years ago. Rebecca still worried about the virus and had her blood tested every year, always negative. She had had Julie tested until she was ten even though doctors had told her it was unnecessary. Nothing must ever harm Julie.

For all that time there had been few other men and sex only rarely; a short fling with a guy she met in the bar review course, then an Assistant DA took her out for a few months. They ended up in Hawaii for a week. It just didn't work out. Rebecca sensed it was racial. His father was anti-Semitic, for sure; probably a racist too. On the Northwest flight through the night from Honolulu to Minneapolis they decided to end it. Rebecca was disappointed. Not that it had ended, but that it ended when it did. She thought the sex was getting better and he kept her laughing. They had a room in the Royal Hawaiian on Waikiki and Donald insisted he had lost his contact lens in her pubic hair. The last night he had spanked her until the tears squirted out of her eyes. It was wonderful.

A year later she became a judge. People began to keep their distance, except for the ass-kissers who were looking for some kind of an advantage. Many lawyers were simply in awe of the bench. It was silly, but the simple truth. Young men and women, sometimes leaders through high school, college, and law school trembled when they entered a courtroom. Some never got over it, choosing to draw up wills or incorporate businesses. Ironically, the judge, like as not, had a lower IQ, GPA, and LSAT score than the timid lawyer standing terrified before the bench, his or her only inferiority being political. The judge had probably stuffed envelopes or knocked on a thousand doors in political campaigns, or he was the relative of someone who had. And then there were the glib little demagogues who sought to intimidate, assuaging the personal fear inspired by the knowledge of their own mediocrity. These types roamed the courthouses in every venue, working like hell to get re-elected. And intimidate they could. How could a trial lawyer buck a judge? Worse yet, in the knowledge of the power of incumbency and in hopes of winning favor, lawyers perpetuated this intellectual dilution of the judiciary by filling the incumbent judges' campaign chests with gold.

Of course, there were a few exceptions. Rebecca thought she was one. Cornelius Dahl, Corny to his colleagues, stood at the top of the list. He treated everyone who came before him with utmost respect, never gave way to his moods, never found the need to assert himself. He knew his function and delivered on it precisely. Lawyers treated him as a judge wanted to be treated and thought of him as a judge wanted to be thought of. There was never any question of bias. You knew he would be fair. Whether you supped with him or shared his duck blind – he was an avid outdoorsman – your cause would be considered in the same light of impartiality as your opponent's.

Very few lawyers would chance asking a judge for a date. Most of them were married anyway. In her seven years on the bench, Rebecca had dated a judge, a state senator, two doctors, a CPA and the owner of a chain of supermarkets. Nothing came of any of those. For the last two years she had tired of it all, avoiding the singles milieu entirely. Now, after fighting incipient recognition for several days, she finally owned the truth of her feeling. Though for some arcane Jungian reason buried in her unconscious she dreamed of Harry Scott, it was freckle-faced Sergeant Kevin Bannon, male chauvinist, cynic and pragmatist, who had touched her heart like no one since Reggie. When he had called her yesterday morning she had agreed to one drink at the Marriott and stayed for two. The grin, twitching at the corners, filled the small gaps in their conversation. His green eyes never left hers. Impulsively, she had invited him to share Thanksgiving dinner with her, Julie, and Papa Nathan who was flying in from Milwaukee tomorrow night.

Rebecca wasn't attuned to early mornings, yet she made sure breakfast was good mother-daughter time. A little lecture to herself in the bathroom mirror got the day rolling despite an inclination to speak only when forced. She was already eating her cereal when Julie breezed into the kitchen.

'Good morning, your honor.' A big yawn squeezed her bright dark eyes shut, leaving silky dark lashes and flawless brown skin.

'You're running a little late, darling,' said Rebecca.

'I don't need to catch the bus this morning, Mom. I have a ride.' Julie looked out the window over the lake. Already taller than her mother, she had Reggie's long legs. Her high school basketball coach eagerly awaited her going out for varsity next year. Pink lipstick and blush on her high cheek bones gave her dark skin an exotic look. In the multicolored print dress she bloomed like a tropical flower. 'Mom, somebody still hasn't gotten their sailboat out of the water . . . You know the smell of toast is the best thing about mornings?'

'That skirt's a bit short, don't you think?'

Julie sat down and started on her cereal. The toaster on the counter popped. 'You should see the other girls' skirts,' she said.

'I'd rather not. Besides, you'll freeze your you-know-what off out there this morning. Who's picking you up?'

'That kid I told you about. Teddy McHendry. The one in that picture with me and Monica.'

'The tall white boy?'

'Ya, and I'm the tall *black* girl.'

'You made your point. I'm sorry,' said Rebecca. She wasn't entirely comfortable with Julie running around in cars with boys, but to school in the morning shouldn't hurt.

'You're coming home on the bus though, right?'

'Sure, Teddy's got basketball anyway.'

'How old is he?'

'I think he's seventeen.'

'You know he's seventeen.'

'So what?'

'You know the talks we've had, Julie. Seventeen-year-old boys are driven by their hormones.'

'I can handle myself.'

Rebecca remembered similar conversations with her own mother, Julie's namesake, Mama Julia. Would it be easier raising a boy than a girl? Probably not for a single mother with no mate who truly understood those hormones.

'By the way, honey, clean up your room after school and pick up the apartment a little. Mrs Higgins will be by after lunch to vacuum and do the kitchen and bathrooms. I'm having my hair done after work. We have another guest for dinner tomorrow.'

'Oh, wow. I should get mine done too.' Julie's hair was done in elaborate corn braids.

'Your braids look great, silly.'

'I'm getting tired of them,' she whined, 'but who's coming to dinner?'

'Kevin Bannon.'

'Who's he?'

'A detective I know.'

'Do you like him?'

'Would I invite him if I didn't like him?'

'You know what I mean. Do you *really* like him?'

Rebecca still hadn't cracked the code. 'Put it this way, honey, he seems like a very nice man . . . maybe a little rough around the edges.'

'White?'

'Look who's talkin'.'

'Is he?'

'Yes, with freckles, and kind of reddish-brown hair. Though it's almost as dark as mine.'

'How long have you known him?' Julie was hoping her mother would mate again.

'Maybe ten years. I don't remember for sure, but way before I went on the bench.'

'You been going out with him long?' Julie's voice dropped a level.

'No. I've never really gone out with him.'

'Then why dinner?'

'Should I tell him not to come? Oh, I'm sorry, honey. I shouldn't have said that. You've got a right to know. I've been talking to him lately and I kinda like him, so . . .'

'Bannon. Oh, I remember. Wow, he's Knuckles, that cop they call Knuckles. I've seen him on TV. Oh, Mama, he worked on the Schmid case, didn't he?'

Rebecca had never told Julie about the letters.

'Has this got anything to do with that case?' Her voice rose again. 'Oh my God, Mom. Look at the time. Do I look OK? Teddy'll be waiting and we'll be late.' The lobby signal buzzed. 'My math book, where's my math book?'

'Isn't that it on the big chair in the living room?' Rebecca pointed through the arch.

Julie grabbed it on her way out the front door. "Bye, Mom.' She rubbed her forefinger under her perfect little nose and with full lips puckered into a pretty pink rose she blew Rebecca a kiss. Half the Cheerios still floated in the milk.

'Don't forget we're picking Grandpa up at the airport tonight,' Rebecca yelled at the closing door. In four years Julie would head out that door for college. The insurance policy on Reggie's life would pay the whole freight anywhere. With Julie at Smith or Radcliffe, or maybe even Stanford or Harvard, Rebecca would be alone. Too alone.

8

The icy air of Thanksgiving Day morning rolled across the warmer waters of the Wolf River. Swirling clouds of vapor rose among the naked branches along the banks. William Schmid had hoped for a more temperate day. Lying on his back on the narrow bed, a tide of anxiety engulfed his body. Ripples of nervous energy radiated concentrically from deep in his center. A fountain of fear had bubbled up in his heart that morning. Now it receded beneath the quiet surface of his desperate need for deliberate precision.

Just after lunch Slim Olson stopped by his cell. A frost of incipient whiskers overlay his weather-reddened face. 'Too cold for hoops today.'

William sat up on the edge of the bed. The big bulbous Swede's words hit like nails through William's ears. 'You promised,' he said.

'Well, I didn't think I'd hafta freeze my nuts off. Bet Thurgood won't want to go out there, either.'

'If you tell him he must, he will.'

'That don't sound right to me,' said Slim.

William tried another tack. 'Did Sarah Jane like the book?'

'I almost forgot, she says thanks very much.'

'My pleasure,' said William. He felt himself slowly rocking forward.

'Yeah, her teacher wants to borrow it already. You know how them smart kids like to butter up them teachers.'

William let his head hang. The silence mingled with the redolence of disinfectant.

'What'sa matta?' asked Slim.

'I counted on your promise. There is not much to hope for in here.' He stared at the colorless carpet.

'Oh, don't worry about it. We can shoot some hoops when it warms up a little. Maybe tomorrow.'

William didn't reply. He reached up and rubbed his eyes.

'Oh geez, Schmid. We'll go out. And I'll make Thurgood go along. I guess you're the best friend I got around this place. I don't wanta fuck it up. OK?'

'OK,' said William. 'Thank you very much. I appreciate it very much.' He wondered if Slim noticed the long draught of air that he let blow out of his lungs. 'Three o'clock like we planned?'

With William's eyes following him through the door, Slim stopped and turned round. 'Yeah, I'll come getcha at three. Don't go nowhere now, will ya?' He laughed uproariously like a honking goose.

Wilma gazed down at him from a gold-framed picture on the wall. Shivers spreading through his upper arms like electric shocks turned into goose flesh. There was no other way, Wilma had said. It is you or them. The headache would be the only thing to stop him now. Stress could bring it on in spite of the pills. As though warning it away, in a circular motion William gently rubbed the thin layer of hair lying limply across his scalp. Two years of furtive whispers, quickly exchanged sentence fragments, during Wilma's visits had brought him to this moment. He thought there might be a better way, but she had insisted. There would be only the one chance. Clearly defined problems required clearly defined solutions. All possible variables had to be eliminated. So he had agreed.

The three of them huddled together by the bench, the moisture of their breath condensing around their heads in miniature white clouds. Like a gallows before the descending sun, the basketball backboard atop its steel pole cast a long stark shadow across the yard. Slim set the thermos, three styrofoam cups and the bag of rolls on the bench. A crow perched on top of the chain-link fence surrounding the compound contributed a ready falsetto caw.

'You and Thurgood play to five points; I'll play the winner,' William said to Slim.

'Hey, man, it'll be purty chilly without these big coats.' Thurgood, a black man almost as big as Slim, was already pulling off his jacket. 'You think a skinny guy like you can beat big guys like us?' he said to William.

'He ain't bad,' said Slim. 'You'd be surprised.'

William had only talked to Thurgood a few times in five years, but he liked his good-natured manner. It was Thurgood who had told him how much better it was serving time in the state prison at Stillwater than here at Wolf River with the crazies.

'When I beat dat skinny white boy I'm goan take him down and fuck his white ass.' Thurgood giggled like a girl.

William shuddered.

'Watch your mouth, Thurgood, or I'll hafta take ya back in.'

'Sure boss, just jivin'.'

'Here we go,' said Slim. He dribbled around Thurgood toward the basket and reached up to lay the ball in off the board. Right behind him, Thurgood whipped his long arm across the top of Slim's head and upraised arms, propelling him into the steel post. The ball banked through the hoop.

'Hee, hee,' wheezed Thurgood.

'Jesus Christ,' said Slim. 'Tryin' to kill me?'

'Just trine to block the motherfucker,' said Thurgood. 'You done made it anyways.'

'Take it a little easy,' said Slim.

'One to nothing in favor of Slim,' said William from the bench.

'My turn,' said Thurgood. He dribbled with a little hop step, feet jumping off the ground in unison with the ball.

William began to screw the cover off the thermos.

Thurgood was dribbling and backing into Slim, trying to move him toward the basket. Attempting to break up the dribble, Slim flailed with both hands, but couldn't reach round the black man's huge bulk.

William pulled the rubber stopper out of the thermos.

Thurgood wheeled and shot the ball over Slim's outstretched arms. The ball missed the rim and Slim grabbed the rebound. He dribbled it out to take another try at scoring. Probably remembering his responsibilities, he looked over at William without breaking the dribble. 'Hey, don't drink the coffee without us.'

William took a little sip directly from the thermos. Just then Thurgood lunged for the bouncing ball, grabbed it, and headed for the basket, Slim at his heels. William quickly extracted the capsule from his shirt pocket and dropped it in the thermos. The bitter smell of almonds mixed with the rich aroma of the fresh coffee.

'Hee, hee,' giggled Thurgood. 'One to one.'

'I wasn't lookin',' said Slim. 'Watch this.' He arched a long one-hander right through the net with a swish.

'Two to one,' said William. The cold penetrated his coat and his ears were getting numb. Time was passing too quickly and Thurgood was dribbling backward again as if he thought he was Magic Johnson.

After Thurgood missed one and Slim hit another swisher, William yelled, 'Slim wins.'

'Whadaya mean, honky motherfucker, he's s'posed ta get five.'

'My friend,' said William, 'we will not have time for the coffee.'

'Who gives a fuck about da coffee?' said Thurgood.

'C'mon, Thurgood, let's have some coffee,' said Slim. 'Y'know wid a little practice you'd be damn good.'

The two mammoth men sat down on either side of William. He handed them each a cup and poured.

Slim took his hand and held it up towards the two of them. 'To my pals.' He took a gulp and another. Seconds later he pitched forward on to the ground.

'Hee, hee,' giggled Thurgood. His eyes rolled back in his head just before he fell off the end of the bench. William set the thermos on the ground. He walked evenly across the exercise yard to the ten-foot chain-link fence. He dropped his gloves on the ground and took off his shoes and socks. With a claw-like hold in the ice-cold wire, he grabbed the fence just above his head. He pulled himself up and clutched his first step with his toes. With the surge of excitement, he barely noticed the pain in his feet. In a few seconds he swung over the top rail and eased his way down until he stood barefoot on the frozen ground.

He walked slowly along the fence to the gravel cart path that led to the county blacktopped road one hundred yards away. There was no sound, except the idling engine of Wilma's black Chevy. He jumped in on the passenger side.

'Is he dead?' Wilma asked.

'They both are, Wilma. At least they looked dead.'

'The black was there too?'

'Yes, Thurgood was invited to the party.'

She pulled the car out on to the blacktop road. 'Were there any problems?'

'No. I do not think anyone saw me. Everyone stayed in because of the cold.'

Some place inside of him there was a feeling he didn't try to identify. No one would miss the killer Thurgood, but he wondered what would happen to Sarah Jane, and Slim had treated him very well for years. He wished he might have used a strong sedative in the coffee. It wouldn't be foolproof, Wilma had maintained. Cyanide would leave less to chance. As Wilma drove slowly toward Wolf River, William wriggled into the top section of the black rubber suit that had been waiting on the front seat. They passed one car heading in the opposite direction before Wilma stopped behind a green station wagon parked on the shoulder. When he finished stretching the headpiece into position round his face, William stepped out. He pulled the bottoms to the wet suit on. From the back seat he retrieved a scuba device attached to an olive oxygen bottle.

'Goodbye, Wilma,' he said. 'You will hear from me as we planned.'

'Goodbye, my love,' she said.

The back of the driver's seat in the station wagon had been forced all the way down to accommodate the tank on William's back. The engine started with the first turn of the key. Wilma waved as she passed, headed for Minneapolis.

The sun had sunk below the tree line and dusk hurried in. A half-mile ahead the straight road narrowed into the outskirts of Wolf River. William's mind focused on the configuration of the bridge on the other side of town. The bridge was the biggest gamble in his plan. It was ancient, built before the turn of the century and continually modified for the use of automobiles and small trucks. The gross weight limit for vehicles was four tons. Anything larger had to come into town from the other direction.

9

On Wednesday night when they returned from the airport with Papa Nathan, Rebecca pinned a white towel apron on her skirt, then pressed Julie into service preparing tomorrow's dinner. The brightly lit kitchen counters were covered with bowls, bottles and shopping bags.

'Have you gone berserk, Mom? Since when have you been so into cooking?'

'Since I'm having company for dinner. They deserve better than McDonalds.'

'Grandpa or Knuckles?'

'Both, and he doesn't like the name Knuckles.'

Rebecca thought of the headlights, too consistently in the mirror, as they had headed down I-35W to the airport. 'Here, start putting this together.' She handed Julie the file card with Great-grandma Esther Goldman's recipe for turkey stuffing.

'We won't have all of this stuff,' said Julie.

'It's in the biggest bag, there on the counter. I stopped at Lunds on the way home from work.'

'Wow!' said Julie.

Rebecca would never have noticed the headlights if William Schmid's letter hadn't arrived last week, if she hadn't thought she saw Wilma last Friday, if Kevin's eyes hadn't looked the way they did. Kevin's eyes gave him away. Only the shell was tough. He had eyes like Mama Julia and like Tootsi, her childhood cocker spaniel back in Milwaukee, eyes that said I have secrets I need to tell you, eyes that said please don't hurt me; people have, you know.

By midnight they had everything in covered dishes and a

58

pumpkin pie ready to go in the oven. The big bird was thawing. A spicy aroma lingered in the air.

At 1:30 a.m. Rebecca was still staring into the dark. A siren screamed down Lake Street. Her thoughts danced from Julie to William Schmid and the goddamn letter, to Kevin Bannon's face. Would she ever know him well enough to tell him she was listening behind that door while he discussed her body with her bailiff? She imagined the pink flesh filling in among the freckles. A brittle male ego might shatter from such shock. For now, she would keep her peace.

If Kevin's purpose was to get close to her, it was working. Was inviting him here a compromise? How much was her fear of Schmid involved, or even Wilma? In spite of the letter, fear had been only a subterranean trickle of anxiety. Now it had leaked out from under the bed to seek more visible venues. If she continued to preside over criminal cases, she must not let the cases preside over her. But the Schmid case had. There had been other letters from disgruntled defendants. None with any persistence. *State v. Schmid* was unique. Rebecca and the jury had listened to days of testimony on one issue: was Schmid psychotic – the defense's contention was chronic paranoid schizophrenia and that Schmid lacked the capacity to appreciate the criminality of his conduct – or was he a so-called sociopath, a condition that the law failed to recognize as negating criminality? Up-to-date psychiatrists called it antisocial personality disorder.

Dr Aaron Phillips had been first. He took the oath with an easy smile shrouded in the black bristles of a neatly trimmed beard. Yes, he had examined William Schmid. In response to Harry Scott's questions, Dr Phillips told the jury he had spent twelve hours with Schmid over a period of six weeks. It was during Phillips's testimony that William Schmid chose to focus on Rebecca. When she glanced at him, the animated blue eyes would be examining her. Trying to see inside, she felt, to read her mind. She decided not to look again. Still, peripherally, she felt monitored by those eyes like a television camera in a bank vault. She

59

imagined his thoughts. How can you judge me if you don't even look at me? Of course, he knew. She was afraid. William Schmid's person was not fearsome. The exhibits were the fertilized seeds from which her fear had grown. They had been brought to court early in the proceedings: the scalpel, the glossy photographs, the hair samples, the petri dish. Just as he had a right to confront the witnesses against him, didn't a defendant have the right to have the judge look at him? Maybe so, but not this judge, Rebecca had thought at the time. Would she ever know how much her fear had to do with what was to follow?

'Dr Phillips, please share with the jury your observations of William Schmid,' Harry Scott said.

'Object, form of the question.' Prosecutor Whitlow Strom had wanted a more precise examination, enabling him to interpose objections before the jury might be exposed to prejudicial statements by the witness.

'Overruled,' said Rebecca.

With a steady eye behind thick lenses, Dr Phillips went on, 'At our first meeting the subject was alert, co-operative, anxious. I would say over-controlled.' His gaze dropped to his notes. 'I found him to be quite rational in our discussions of his teaching, his relationships to his students, even his relationship with his twin sister. We took the time we had for background. My outside investigation revealed that much of what the subject told me was delusional.'

Delusional was the last word in Rebecca's conscious mind before the alarm clock went off at seven, reminding her to put the turkey in the oven.

Papa Nathan was already up, reading the morning paper. 'Dropped below zero overnight, *mein kint*. Were you warm enough?'

'Papa, my bedroom is heated, just like yours.'

'So I won't ask. When does the goy arrive?'

'Look who's talking. Mama was a goy.'

'She was different.'

'So maybe is Kevin. And enough of this. I can't believe my ears.'

★ ★ ★

60

At two, Kevin arrived in what had to be a brand new double-breasted blue blazer with tan pants and a blue paisley tie. The matching pocket square said, you don't always have to think of me as a gumshoe.

'You look marvelous.' Rebecca felt suddenly embarrassed by her enthusiasm.

'Not so bad yourself,' he said.

Rebecca had paid a fortune for her simple white dress. She introduced him to her father who offered a hand too limp for shaking, and then to Julie in a red blouse, smiling broadly.

'I've seen you on television. The man called you Knuckles.'

Rebecca felt like smacking her.

'Yeah, some people call me that just before I give them a knuckle sandwich,' said Kevin.

'What on earth's a knuckle sandwich?' said Julie.

Kevin shook his fist in her face.

'Geez,' said Julie.

'And you wouldn't like the taste,' said Rebecca.

'Oh, Mom!'

With a gentle nudge on his elbow, Rebecca steered Kevin to the living room. Papa Nathan, looking fearful of winter in a baggy sweater, had already sat down in the big chair. Kevin dropped on to the sofa. Vivid greens and yellows and blues flickered on the tube. The Lions were playing the Packers.

'You like football?' said Papa Nathan.

'I've been going to the Viking games since they started,' said Kevin.

Rebecca listened from the kitchen in between picking at Julie for bringing up Kevin's nickname.

'I'm a Packer man,' said Papa Nathan.

'They're doing all right with that new quarterback,' said Kevin.

'Po-lock,' said Papa Nathan. 'He can throw it.'

A white-suited Lion got behind his man in the end zone and caught a pass for a touchdown. The play-by-play announcer went wild.

'The goniff pushed off. I saw 'em,' said Papa Nathan.

'They'll do anything to win,' said Kevin. 'Lotta money involved.'

At half-time Rebecca asked Kevin to carry the turkey to the table. Papa Nathan grumbled that he wished she would wait until the game was over. The turkey would dry out and he could sit where he could see the game, she said. Julie said a prayer in Hebrew and Kevin carved the turkey. It should have been a wonderful afternoon.

10

Straight ahead through lightly falling snow the county road intersected with Wolf River's broad Main Street at a four-way stop. One minute after he had started the engine of the green station wagon, William approached the turn on to Main Street. As he sized up the intersection, his body tightly confined in the wet suit and scuba gear, he was almost unaware of the two-story frame houses set in the trees on either side of the road. No cars approached from any direction. He pushed the accelerator to the floor and wheeled the station wagon sharply to the left, tires whinnying round the corner. He didn't see the bespectacled old man stepping off the far curb until his front right fender just missed him. Gaining speed, he headed the station wagon through the business district. Main Street was only three blocks long. Beyond was the bridge. The sidewalks were empty. Several cars were parked diagonally, headed into the curb in front of a building on the right in the next block, probably a restaurant serving Thanksgiving dinner.

William sped by the darkened store fronts, awnings drawn up. In the late-afternoon November light the street lamps burned, dimly glowing globes atop colorless painted steel posts, lining the street on both sides every hundred feet or so. Still speeding. Past the diners' cars, past a lone small boy on a corner holding a large black dog by the collar.

One block to go; no sign of any pursuers. No sign of anyone but the old man he had nearly hit and the boy with the dog. Just before the bridge, a black on white sign: 'LOAD LIMIT FOUR TONS GROSS WEIGHT'.

The bridge had no superstructure, just a two-lane plank

floor with light steel railings. The wooden planks rumbled under the station wagon. William pulled the diver's mask up over his face. Then he pressed the brake pedal nearly to the floor and turned the wheel sharply to the right. The station wagon skidded a few feet, the railing disappeared below the hood with a scraping noise. It felt as if he had stopped, but then the front end teetered down. Foam streaked the flow of fast black water. The impact made the same sound as when he had cannon-balled from the high board as a boy, only magnified. His head snapped forward, but his arms and the seat belt prevented him from crashing into the windshield.

The car floated, listing to the front end. It slowly spun round in the current, revealing a panorama: first the rocky rip-rap on the town side, then the black creosote-treated wood shoring, then the bridge, only ten or twelve feet above the water, supported by thick, round, wood pilings, then the blackened wood shoring on the far side, then more rip-rap. His door banged hard against a giant boulder. Water flooded the floors; the front end nosed down below the surface. He lowered the window and the river rushed in. After clamping the scuba mouthpiece between his teeth, he released the seat belt. A frightening surge of dark water filled the car as it settled to the bottom, lying on the passenger side. With the oxygen bottle on his back he couldn't get through the window. For a few seconds a sense of panic gripped his insides. Against the current, the door resisted his effort to push it open.

The station wagon slid along the bottom, scraping across the rocks, pivoting in the stream. He had planned too carefully, living this moment over and over again in his laboratory-trained methodical mind, to give way to panic. He pushed on the door with his shoulder again. It opened. William shoved himself away from the sunken vehicle. He floated free in the river, shadowy light penetrating from the vague surface. The flow at the very bottom was much slower. He got his bearings and with his hands he attempted to maintain a course along the river's bed, moving downstream with the current like a feeding catfish.

He glided over rocks of all sizes, past a tire silted over

with sand. A grayish-green northern pike nearly three feet long leered at him with one unblinking eye. Further downstream, a startled beaver swimming above responded with a sharp crack of his tail on the surface. William remembered happy times in other rivers. Soon darkness obscured his vision and he navigated by feel alone, drifting downstream in the slow current.

By the luminous diver's watch Wilma had brought him, he had been down eleven minutes. When he bobbed to the surface, the bridge and town were nowhere in sight. Fading light reflected from a sheet of ice covering a quiet backwater to his right. Against the steely sky, leafless trees starkly lined boulder-strewn banks. Only now did he feel the cold creeping into the wet suit. But it was better than he had expected. He would be in the river an hour, and the water was much warmer than the air. Comfort wasn't the problem. The problem was finding Wilma's marker.

11

The four of them sat around the glass-topped table working on the pumpkin pie with whipped cream, Rebecca and Kevin Bannon at the ends, Julie and Papa Nathan at the sides. Papa Nathan's brown eyes squinted through gold-rimmed trifocals at the big TV screen twenty feet away. Julie fired question after question at Kevin. Have you ever shot anybody? was the last.

'Yes,' Kevin said.

'Who?' said Julie, aghast.

'Nobody you know,' said Kevin.

'You mean knew,' said Julie.

'OK. Let's change the subject,' said Rebecca.

Papa Nathan finished his pie. 'S'cuse,' he said, heading for the football game; some coffee splashed over the side of his cup on to the pale gray carpet. Rebecca ran after him with a roll of paper towels.

'Who'd you shoot?' Julie resumed her interrogation.

'You got nose trouble,' said Kevin.

'The public has a right to know!'

'Change the subject.' Rebecca was back and irritated. 'Forgive my child. She seems to have a hearing defect.'

'Oh, Mom.'

Kevin agreed to more coffee. Seconds later a series of beeps emitted from somewhere in his suit. He excused himself to use the phone.

'I bet somebody held up a bank,' said Julie.

'They're all closed today.' Kevin disappeared through the open kitchen door.

Both Julie and Rebecca listened to his voice, Rebecca

with a tinge of embarrassment. She remembered eavesdropping on Kevin before.

'Please turn down the TV, Grandpa,' said Julie.

Papa Nathan ignored her.

'Say that again,' said Kevin's voice in the kitchen.

For several seconds the only sound was a fifteen-yard penalty against the Packers. Papa Nathan yelled, 'Meshugas!'

'OK,' said Kevin. 'I want two uniforms assigned to Lake Vista, Apartment 1201. I'm there now.' He gave them the telephone number. 'Call me as soon as you know anything. *Anything.* Got that?'

Rebecca felt the hair rise on her arms.

Kevin stood in the kitchen doorway. 'William Schmid escaped forty-five minutes ago.'

'Oh! Oh my God!' Rebecca saw the hawk-like blue eyes gleaming at her, the meat-red lips and the small, even teeth.

'Mom, what's wrong?' Julie turned back to Kevin. 'And why did you have them send policemen over here?'

Rebecca wanted to conceal her fear from Julie. Maybe it was a false alarm. 'We'll just have to wait and see.'

'What in the world does that mean, Mom?'

The phone rang. Kevin answered it.

Again mother and daughter listened to Kevin's voice, Rebecca holding her breath.

'OK. I'm heading up there right now.'

Kevin came back through the kitchen door, his mouth crimped, eyes gloomy. 'I have to go to Wolf River. Two witnesses say a car crashed into the river just after Schmid escaped. One identified him from a picture. They've got divers going down.'

'In the dark?' said Rebecca.

'Yeah, they've got powerful lights, but I remember the current's awfully swift. Whatever. I gotta get goin'.'

'What about us?' Rebecca remembered Schmid's last letter, word for word.

'There are two police officers on their way over here right now. They'll be here in a few minutes. Wolf River is almost two hours away.'

'Are we safer with you, or two cops who know nothing about Schmid or me or any of us?' Rebecca's constricted throat raised the pitch of her voice.

'OK,' said Kevin, 'get your coats. It's cold out.'

'Wow! Cool,' said Julie.

'C'mon, Papa, we've got to go for a ride.' Rebecca used her sweetest tone.

'The Pack's on the fifteen and driving,' said Papa Nathan. 'I won't be going nowhere.'

Rebecca looked at Kevin. 'We can't leave him here.'

'There's two cops on the way.'

'No. I don't want to leave him here.' Her father one-on-one with Schmid was unthinkable. But she didn't want to excite him. He carried nitroglycerin for his heart. 'Julie, go get our coats, please.'

Rebecca grabbed Kevin's sleeve and led him over to Papa Nathan. 'Papa, it's important to me that you go along.'

'It's important to me that I stay here.' The furrows in a face formed over seven decades frowned in declaration more distinct than his words.

'Papa, I really mean it. I don't want to talk about it in front of Julie.'

'So don't talk about it.'

'I brought your black one, good for a somber occasion.' Julie had donned a puffy jacket in a chic brocade.

'No, honey. Get the down-filled one. C'mon, Papa.'

'The Pack's on the three. Now he should roll out.'

'We gotta get goin',' said Kevin.

'I can't leave him.' Julie's presence kept her from screaming at her father: A man has threatened to kill me, he's on the loose!

The intercom buzzed. Kevin grabbed it a wink before Julie. 'OK,' he said and hung up. 'An officer's on his way up and there's one staying in the lobby.'

Five years a lawyer, seven a judge, Rebecca understood when alternatives at last narrowed to one. 'OK, Papa. We're going.'

'Mazel,' he said.

'We could use a little,' said Kevin.

'What's going on? C'mon, you guys, clue me in!' Julie's dark brown eyes brimmed with the moisture of excitement.

The bell rang. A uniformed cop and Kevin whispered together in the foyer. Turning back toward Rebecca and Julie, Kevin, grim-faced, said, 'Time to go, you two.'

'Good, the game,' said the cop.

'It's fourth and goal on the one,' said Papa Nathan.

'They gotta go for it,' said the cop.

Julie led the way to the elevator as Kevin pulled the door shut behind them.

Heading north into a lace curtain of falling snow, Kevin had to use his low beams. The car's occupants were silent. The lights from the dash illuminated the little red plastic purse clutched in Julie's hands. Sitting between Kevin and Rebecca, she was in a pout because her mother had cut off her last question.

Rebecca confronted the part of her mind that hoped William Schmid was dead. He was truly a sick man, incapable of controlling his behavior. She saw Dr Phillips on the stand testifying to Schmid's chronic paranoid schizophrenia. Bearded, bespectacled, he exuded wisdom, like Freud himself.

'Eventually, Mr Schmid was willing to talk about his childhood. His earliest memories are of severe punishment administered by his father, repeated whippings with a belt or razor strap on the back and buttocks, and with a ruler across the hands. His father, Konrad Schmid, was a tall man, strong and sinewy. His pictures remind you of Lincoln without the beard.'

'What was his occupation?' Harry Scott interjected.

'He was a preacher – some extreme fundamentalist sect. I think it was called the True Church of Christ and His Disciples. One of a kind. He had left the Four Square Church.'

'Did he say how old he was when the beatings started?'

'He recalls back into his third year. Wilma told me her stepmother said the physical abuse began before he was a year old.'

'Did he treat Wilma as severely?'

'No, on the contrary. He babied Wilma.'

'What happened to William Schmid's real mother?'

'She died giving birth to the twins. Wilma said her stepmother told her that Konrad said it was just as well she died, that Satan was in her. Apparently she never bought into Konrad Schmid's brand of religion.'

'And Konrad Schmid's second wife, William Schmid's stepmother, how did he treat her?'

'Wilma says he beat her on occasion. I have never interviewed her. William was vague about the way his father treated his stepmother. I suspect he has blocked out certain extremely unpleasant memories; I think an incestuous relationship between William and his stepmother likely occurred. Of course, technically it couldn't be incestuous. She was not related to him by blood. But a similar psychological impact would probably be obtained. William remained mute on any questions leading into that area. But I'm convinced the incidents of the father's brutality are authentic.'

'Were you able to learn of any specific incidents?'

'Yes, one in particular. Both William and Wilma spoke of it in some detail.'

'I renew my hearsay objection,' said the prosecutor.

Rebecca overruled the objection. Experts had a right to state the basis for their conclusions, hearsay or not. Harry Scott asked his witness to continue.

'William was sixteen. The family had attended the state fair in St Paul. William had spent much of the time in the scientific exhibits, mostly astronomy and geology, as I recall. He brought his camera along and took some pictures of the exhibits and he collected a number of brochures, including one that discussed the process of evolution and various fossil evidence. After they got home, Konrad Schmid examined what William had collected. When he found the brochure on evolution, he smashed William across the face. He ordered the boy to drop his pants and bend over. Then, with his belt, and in front of Wilma and the stepmother, he whipped William repeatedly across the bare buttocks.

70

Wilma remembers vomiting at the sight of it. The father screamed the word 'Out!' with each lash – he contended that he was driving the demons out, Wilma said. After the whipping, he gave William a pair of scissors and ordered him to cut all of the material he had acquired at the fair into small pieces. He also opened William's camera and exposed the film. He directed William not to use the camera for any purpose for a period of one year. Photography was one of his hobbies.'

'How long did William Schmid suffer at the hands of his father?'

'He still does, but I suspect your question refers to a more direct influence.'

'Yes, Doctor.'

'Konrad Schmid's corporal punishment of William continued until he was a freshman in college.'

'Why did he stop?'

'Konrad died.'

The car droned on northward through the falling snow. Sarah Vaughn was singing scat on NPR.

'It's getting slippery,' said Kevin.

Rebecca didn't comment. The vivid lips in William Schmid's animated face repeated each word of the letter. Julie's head rested gently on her shoulder. Was it too much to hope that William Schmid *had* drowned? Or should she be hoping that he was alive? He was a human being after all. A very sick human being.

12

As the dusk congealed into night, William drifted downstream in the belly of the river. A small quantity of water had accumulated inside his mask, but it was the darkness that obscured his vision. From here on, the shroud of night should ensure unobserved passage on the surface. Working towards the west bank, he thrust his head above water. In seconds, big snowflakes plastered the lens of the mask. Elated, he pushed it up on his forehead. Biting cold stung his damp face, but nothing could suppress the victorious feeling fostered by the heavy snowfall. If his pursuers found evidence downstream that he had survived, they would hound him until he was recaptured. A thick blanket of snow would cover any trace of his leaving the river. They wouldn't know he hadn't drowned. Only rarely did these northern rivers regurgitate bodies devoured in winter until after all the ice had melted in the spring. The police could only speculate, any ardor for the chase inhibited by doubt.

A flock of ducks evading the strange shape come into their midst startled William as they leaped into the blackness above. He coughed and sputtered. His quick intake of breath mingled with river water. Above him, veiled in gloom, wings thumped the air searching for another roosting place.

Using a steady breast stroke he maneuvered close to the bank, bouncing along with the current, touching his foot on the bottom from time to time. Still, for long stretches, even at the very edge, his extended toe reached nothing beneath.

The accelerating rush of water swept him wide into a bend. At the last second he hooked his elbow on the edge of an ice shelf near the bank, his legs flailing below. Slipping beneath the ice would mean a cold, wet death. Brittle pieces along the edge kept breaking under the pressure of his arms. A reaching toe tickled a gravel bar, then made solid contact. He inched along the sharp edge. Suddenly he broke free into fast current. He pulled himself toward the middle of the river, oblivious of the raucous thrashing his crawling stroke created on the smooth surface. The plan had almost self-terminated right there. Judge Rebecca Goldman's life would have continued despite her grievous wrong. Though he might perish under the ice in the dark, there was no question of fear. Determination to achieve his single purpose ruled all other emotions.

Another flock of ducks erupted. Sometime later a hoarse buzz, pulsing from low to high frequency, penetrated the dark from the direction of the highway to the west. Maybe a motorcycle engine revving. Not likely in this weather. Maybe some logger's chainsaw. William repeatedly consulted his watch. He had ridden the river for eighty minutes. Distances had been carefully calculated months before. The marker should have appeared. No sign of the red light. Just after a bend, Wilma had promised. Could the battery have failed in the heavy snow? Could someone have taken it? Surely not the police. They would allow it to flash, hoping to capture him when he emerged from the river. If he missed the marker, he would fall victim to the unmerciful icy weather or be recaptured by the police. He much preferred the former. Perhaps he had overestimated the velocity of the winter water flow. This was his best hope.

In yet another bend, the fast current forced him tightly to the west bank. A glimmer of red. It immediately disappeared. A large object loomed ahead. Helpless, William plowed headlong against it. A tree trunk extended out into the river from the bank, recently fallen, branches and all. The river sucked him under. He stuck there among the branches, the scuba mouthpiece dangled uselessly below his chin. The current pressed his body into the snarl. Gurgling water roared in his ears. Futilely, he tried to push back into the torrent. He would drown. He needed to breathe. Shoving his face up into the tangle, he caught a breath.

Water mixed with the air choked him. He found a branch below his knee and pulled with every ounce of remaining energy. His head went down, feet up. The current whisked him free. He shot straight downstream on the surface, directly toward a red light blinking on the bank. The wet suit's rubber feet skidded in gravel. He stood up in three feet of water, the third phase of his plan complete.

He shut off the flasher. Wilma's soft hands had held this same cold metal just hours before. William saw her face and dreamed of her warmth. She had saved him again.

In the black of night, lit by starlight barely perceptible behind the thick layer of clouds, William scrambled up the low bank, feet slipping on icy rocks. Ahead in the trees, the car squatted, black as a bush. He opened the door, grabbed the keys from the ignition and opened the trunk. An owl's hollow call rolled down out of the branches above. The glare of the trunk light made the rest of the world disappear.

From the footlocker in the trunk he took a set of thermal underwear, a woolen shirt and pants and a pair of scuffed Oxfords with companion overshoes. Warmer air had accompanied the clouds that brought the snow, yet his teeth set to chattering during the change. The car's heater would feel good. He proceeded quickly, methodically: wet suit in the footlocker with the flasher, scuba gear loose on top. Giant spinning flakes filled his footprints.

He turned the ignition key. The engine's throaty growl settled to an even purr. He dropped the lever into drive. The wheels spun. The car didn't move. The friendly snow had turned its coat. William opened the door, then closed it. Time to think, not time to move. Perhaps some branches would provide traction, but the slope ahead was long. If the branches got him rolling, the speed might keep him going.

He browsed among the trees. There were fallen branches everywhere. He gathered an armful, carefully arranging them in front of the rear wheels across the depressed tracks of the woodland trail.

Behind the steering wheel again, he pressed down on the accelerator. The tires spun, a throbbing whirr as though the car was suspended in air. On his knees in the snow, he shoved some smaller branches more snugly under the rubber. This time they caught. The car lurched forward over the six-foot band of limbs. The rear fishtailed to the left, jumped out of the track, stopped, wheels spinning freely as before. Ahead, still more than a hundred feet of slope disappeared into the darkness. He let the car idle. He pondered. They had discussed the possibility of snow, indeed fervently wished for it. But he had overlooked the negative. Too long away from the lab. Had Wilma overlooked it? He grabbed the keys from the ignition, leaped from the car, opened the trunk. A dirty cloth bag was wedged in beside the footlocker. He probed its surface. Hard and lumpy. Tire chains.

He had to lie on his back in the snow to get them on. Precious time elapsed, at least a quarter of an hour. Two whole hours had passed since he had crashed through the bridge railing. Possibly they were already searching downstream. But they couldn't know how he was equipped. In two hours they would know very little. He couldn't even be sure they would assume he had been in the car that plunged into the river. They would eventually. He had left his hospital cap stuck between the seats.

The chains bit into the snow and ice. The car sped to the crest of the slope. The headlight beams followed the trail snaking through the trees up another slight grade. Everywhere snow transmogrified the flora into shimmering forms, a midnight museum of abstract statuary. At the top, the twin tracks, mere depressions under the white blanket, made a straight line to the state highway running south from Wolf River. William turned the lights off and drove slowly with his head out of the side window. Snow crystals prickled his face. In the distance, where the trail emerged from the forest, red and white flashes from the head and tail lights of occasional cars blinked past.

Still hidden in the trees, he stopped. No cars in sight. William's station wagon rolled out on to the highway and headed south, the chains ringing on the harder surface like bells on a sleigh. His pulse slowed. The warmth of the heater soothed his body. Ten miles south he would head straight west.

75

13

Kevin Bannon held the car at an even fifty as they pushed on north through the Thanksgiving Day snowstorm. Periodically, they passed cars in the ditch, some already enveloped in wooly wrappings of snow. Eventually, the traffic thinned out and the forest closed in on the highway.

'How much further to Wolf River?' Julie had awakened from her nap on Rebecca's shoulder.

'Between fifteen and twenty miles, I think,' said Kevin.

Headlights approached. The two cars met and passed. 'What was that noise?' Rebecca asked.

'Tire chains,' said Kevin. 'Not much in use around here anymore.'

They discussed how slippery it was and how they hoped they would make it without mishap and they speculated about what might have been accomplished by the time they arrived in Wolf River, small talk to avoid satisfying Julie's curiosity over the import of it all. Julie had slept most of the way.

When Rebecca was little, she would sit in the rear seat of her father's car, her eyes on the back of his head, and sometimes she stood on her knees and watched the dark go by and wondered who lived where the windows were lit. Mama Julia would sleep in the front seat. When she awoke she would smoke a cigarette and the smell made Rebecca sick. Traveling through the night down strange roads still meant adventure.

She tried to gather strength for what they might encounter, to behave like a judge of the district court, and she was determined to protect Julie. She had thought of dropping her off with Susan, but it didn't seem foolproof. She wanted a strong man involved. Who better than Kevin? He knew Schmid and he knew how to shoot people. Although the letters had refreshed ugly memories, after each one, Rebecca's confidence had returned. The key to the only door out of Wolf River's maximum security was in her hand. The news media and the victim's family had openly criticized her. She had fallen for Schmid's act, they said when she granted Harry Scott's motion for a judgment of insanity, notwithstanding the jury's verdict to the contrary. Whitlow Strom, the prosecutor, did not appeal. He was satisfied that Schmid would never be released from Wolf River. Rebecca made sure. Her commitment order contained a provision requiring the trial judge's approval of any proposed release of Schmid, no matter how far into the future. Schmid's appeals were long since exhausted. Six years later, heading north into the Minnesota winter, she wondered if she could have given such approval – under any circumstances, ever.

The sign said: 'WOLF RIVER Pop. 1837.' The next one said: 'State Hospital Half a Mile'. At the four-way stop, Kevin turned right. Several blocks ahead, red and blue lights rotated on the top of police cars and maintenance vehicles. One approached on the left, its huge blade pushing the snow from Main Street up on the curb.

'Wow,' said Julie.

Kevin pulled in behind the last police car parked on the right, about one hundred feet short of the bridge. He jumped out of the car and walked through the snow toward the bridge in his dress shoes and top coat. Rebecca looked at her pumps, hesitated, then opened the door to follow.

'You stay here, honey,' she said to Julie.

'No, I'm going with you.'

'No, you're not. I'll come back for you if it's OK.'

'Why can you go?' Julie pouted.

'I'm an officer of the court; it's my duty,' Rebecca lied.

'Oh, you're just a grown-up and grown-ups are never fair to kids.'

'Oh, please.' Rebecca stood in the snow talking through the open door. 'I'm going to close this door. You lock it from the inside.'

'Geez,' said Julie. Rebecca waited until she saw Julie depress the button.

Kevin was already out of sight in the crowd of cops and onlookers up ahead. Vainly trying to keep her feet dry, Rebecca jumped along in Kevin's tracks.

A big white wrecker extended at an angle across the road closing off the bridge. The river downstream from the bridge was lit up like a night ball game. From the winch on the back of the wrecker, a cable, taut as a harp string, extended at least two hundred feet downriver where it disappeared below the surface.

A huge man with a cigar burning inches from Kevin's nose spoke through clenched teeth. 'We got a kid down at the station saw the whole damn thing. Green station wagon skidded right through the rail. He was too far back to see what happened after.'

'He see the driver?'

'No, the car was goin' like hell. He was hangin' on to his dog, keep it from gettin' hit. But we got a guy did see the driver's face. It was daylight when he turned down Main Street off the highway. Odmar Wojihowsky. He says the guy damn near hit him. We showed him a picture of Schmid. No doubt, he said. It was Schmid, sure as hell.'

'Corky,' Kevin said, 'meet Judge Rebecca Goldman. She's on the district bench, Hennepin County. Sheriff Corky Montgomery.'

Cigar still in place, Corky pulled his glove off and stuck out his hand. 'Pleased ta meetcha, your honor.'

Cold and damp, his hand wrapped round hers like a two-pound rib eye. 'Hello, Sheriff.'

'I'm speshly inter-ested,' he said it like two words, 'in gettin' this guy. Slim Olson was well-liked around here.'

Rebecca questioned Kevin with a look.

'Schmid poisoned two people,' Kevin said. 'I didn't want to say it in front of Julie.'

'Oh my God!'

'Might as well tell her now,' said Kevin. 'It'll be front page tomorrow.'

'Any sign of Wil—' Rebecca stopped. 'Kevin, did anybody think to check on Wilma?'

'Jesus. No. Lemme get to a phone. Better, Corky, can I use your radio car?'

'Hop to it, right next to the wrecker.'

Kevin left. Rebecca finished her question. 'Any sign of William Schmid, Sheriff?'

'Car was empty. Door flopped open. No sign of the body.' Corky took his big fur hat off, a complete animal of some type, Rebecca suspected. He smoothed his thick black hair down with one hand and replaced the creature on his head. 'The water's fast down 'ere, and purty deep. Guy's drowned or froze ta death.' The puff of frosty breath added emphasis to the latter.

Rebecca started stamping her feet. Her toes were getting numb. The tip of her nose stung and the air bit her nostrils. How could they permit Schmid enough leeway to escape? A small measure of relief after the sheriff's pronouncement of Schmid's death was overcome by guilt. William Schmid was ill. Others should have been protected, and he should have been protected from himself. A judge should be confident that anybody she commits to an institution will be adequately restrained.

'You better get in a car 'fore you freeze to death too,' said Corky Montgomery.

'I will, Sheriff. Thank you.'

Julie made her knock on the window to get the door unlocked.

'Why didn't you tell me this William Schmid man killed two people today? I heard it on the radio,' Julie said.

'Kevin didn't tell me.'

'Why not?'

'Crack the window a little, honey. We may be sitting here for a while yet.' Then she went on and told Julie the whole story, letters and all.

When she had finished, Julie asked, 'So now he's dead? For sure he's dead?'

'The sheriff says he must be.'

'But they haven't found him, right?'

Kevin slipped in behind the wheel. His nose, a drop of moisture on the end, showed apple red in the light before he closed the door. 'They got the car out. Hospital cap in it. We ran the plate through the computer. It's William Schmid's own car. A nine-year-old Chevy wagon. Somebody's been keeping the license up in his name. Can you beat that? Must be Wilma.'

'Have they found him?' This time Julie directed her question to Kevin.

'Not yet,' he said.

'When they do, I'll believe he's dead.'

14

His body still tingling from the effects of the river, William had driven for three hours on headings generally west. Humming melodies under his breath, mostly Chopin, in an attempt to assuage the melancholy of being completely alone, he sped away from the only person he cared about. After one hour he had removed the chains. In two he was traveling under clear starry skies, the only sound the steady whine of the tires and the even hum of the engine. He pulled into a small roadside park. The air was warmer but, in spite of his weariness, it was too cold to sleep in the car. The thermos of coffee Wilma had provided had kept him awake. He wondered if even the great mind of Hawking could have conceived a plan as practical and workable as his had thus far been. Theoretical minds often only opened doors a crack. It was practical brilliance that walked on through.

On the back seat in a small box Wilma had left him the materials for a disguise: a brunette wig with mustache to match, and spectacles of plain glass. There was also a box of sandwiches and cookies and some apples and oranges. Underneath the sandwiches was a fully loaded Smith and Wesson .38 Special and the remainder of the box of cartridges.

He put the revolver under the front seat and stuck the wig on his head. In the glow from the dome light he adjusted his new hair, looking in the mirror as he pulled it down snugly all round. Suddenly, headlights showed through the rear window and a car pulled up beside William's Ford. He looked away and slipped on the glasses. A state trooper

81

walked through the beams of his own headlights and up to William's window. He rolled it down.

'There's no all-night parking in here,' said the trooper.

'I know. I am driving right through to Montana,' said William. 'Just stopped to have a wake-up coffee.'

'Where you from?'

'Sheboygan, going to visit my brother,' said William. This was part of the plan; a Sheboygan address and Wisconsin plates.

'I better take a look at your license.' From the patrol car came the faint sound of a radio transmission. 'Just a minute. I gotta take that call.'

William reached into the glove compartment for the wallet Wilma had prepared. Then he pulled the revolver from under the seat and stuck it under his thigh. The license with his picture on it might not pass muster.

The trooper's feet crunched on the gravel. 'There's a wreck on the interstate. I gotta run. Have a good trip.'

The patrol car, tires screeching, headed back on to the highway. We are both very lucky, William thought. Lucky, indeed.

Less than an hour later he continued west across the Minnesota border into South Dakota. Formulating his plan, he had considered Montana and Wyoming as places to bide his time while pursuers got used to the idea that he had drowned. He had finally decided against them. While even more thinly populated than the Dakotas, Wyoming and Montana consisted mainly of threads of civilization running along the highways. But in South Dakota, especially east of the Missouri River, people were scattered across the plains like seeds broadcast randomly in the wind. William had decided to become one of those seeds and alight somewhere close to the rich Dakota earth. Tonight he planned to find a motel in Sisseton. Perhaps stay two days, get the rest his trembling body demanded.

He found a small motel where he could park directly in front of the door to his room. With part of one of the thirty-five one-hundred-dollar bills Wilma had left in the wallet, he paid for two nights in advance. Had to catch up on his sleep, he told the clerk.

At two the following afternoon William looked at the diver's watch still on his wrist. He didn't remember why it was there. The door was stained, made of wood. Wilma's picture was gone, a calendar in its place. His head ached and the space heater had dried his lips and mouth. The sound of an occasional passing car accelerating blended with the hum of the heater fan. His cell had no heater. You couldn't hear cars in his cell.

William sat on the edge of the bed. He gently massaged his tender temple. Fine print covered a card in the center of the door, headed 'SOUTH DAKOTA MOTELS'. What was he doing in South Dakota? He stood up. Pain shot through his right metatarsus. He shifted his weight to his left foot. Stiff muscles further inhibited his hobble to the window. Outside, the sun glinted off the hood of the blue Ford. Wisconsin plates. The parking lot was otherwise empty. Whose car was it? He had to pee. Went to the corner. No toilet. Round the bed to another door. A whole bathroom with shower. He peed, then stood before the mirror. A dark mustache hung loose from one side of his lip. The narrow face was weathered raw. He wore only a pair of white shorts and a gray T-shirt.

Back to the bed. A dark pile of hair lay on the night table. He eased his head back on the pillow and let his lids fall closed. It wasn't a dream. He had seen none of this before. Had he been drugged and brought here? Were they conducting some sort of test? Was he somebody else? Would Slim Olson be in on it? Could they still play a little basketball? Had they told Wilma where they had taken him? Why South Dakota? Did he need the medication again? The heater droned on. He let himself drift into sleep.

Just before 10 p.m. he awoke again, mouth dry as road dust. The metatarsus hurt as he hobbled through the open bathroom door. Coming out, he noticed the TV and switched it on. The face was talking about some Russian politician. 'A big dump of snow on Minneapolis and St Paul had luckily missed them,' the inexpert young anchor woman said. Jesus. There was his own face. What an odd smile. He hadn't seen that picture before.

'The body of William Schmid has not yet been recovered from the Wolf River,' the woman said. She had the face of a sheep, broad space between the eyes, and pointy chin. 'Schmid is believed to have drowned on Thanksgiving Day when the car he was driving crashed through a bridge railing and plunged into the Wolf River near the town of Wolf River. Schmid had escaped from the state hospital nearby after allegedly fatally poisoning a hospital employee, Sven Olson, and a patient, Thurgood Marshall Jefferson. According to Sheriff J.T. Corky Montgomery, the car has been recovered but there was no sign of a body. However, Sheriff Montgomery said that it would have been impossible for anyone to have survived the plunge in the zero weather. William Schmid had been incarcerated at Wolf River State Hospital since his trial for the murder of Alice Wahl several years ago. We will keep you posted on further developments in this rather bizarre episode. Now, have you thought of changing to a more effective herbicide for next spring's planting? Lyle Schafer who—'

William switched the TV off, stretched out on his back and stared at the cheap light fixture on the ceiling. Again he let his eyes close. He spoke aloud to hear his own voice. 'What is happening?' The tone was tinny, didn't sound like himself. He was wide awake. His foot? His face? The diver's watch? He had been in the Wolf River? He rolled over and grabbed the pile of hair off the night table. Jesus, there was a pistol under it. A wig. He sat up again and picked up the revolver. There was a cartridge in every chamber. He would call Wilma. She would know about everything.

There was no phone in the room. It was getting late. In a small town everything he did would be conspicuous. Police would be driving around. How could he have poisoned Thurgood? Who was Sven Olson? My God, could that have been Slim? He turned the light off. Blood roared through his head. He asked himself a thousand more questions before he succumbed to sleep for the third time since checking in.

★ ★ ★

84

He awoke, clear-headed, muscles stiff and sore. The diver's watch said 9:00 a.m. He flipped on the TV. There were cartoons on every channel. Cartoons were on Saturday morning. This had to be Friday. Thanksgiving is always on Thursday. He had checked in early Friday morning. He switched channels. Got CNN. In a few minutes Reed Collins said it was 10:07 a.m. Eastern Standard Time, Saturday morning. He had slept for more than twenty-four hours. Not possible. But it happened. The wig was on the floor, the .38 Special on the night table. He remembered covering it with the wig just after he checked in. He must have knocked it off when he got up to pee. He wondered if the TV had carried any news of his escape. It was time for him to shower and shave and move on west. His head felt cool and refreshed. He sensed a clarity of thought he hadn't experienced in years. It was the pills, or rather the lack of them. There would be no pill this morning. Nor was there yesterday. Nor would there be tomorrow or any day after that. He had considered burglarizing a drugstore. Just stay calm. Enjoy the open space. His first in seven years. Perhaps he would not need pills. He hoped there would be a backboard and hoop wherever he ended up. To execute the remainder of his plan he needed to stay in good physical condition.

15

Rebecca watched the interrogation of Wilma Schmid through one-way mirror glass. The room was bright and bare, except for a table and four steel chairs.

'My brother is dead. You ask me all these questions. I have no answers. I told the other man, I haven't seen him since last Sunday.' Wilma, in a black cardigan with a blue scarf, her face tired and white in the bright light, threw her arms wide, palms up. A blue vein throbbed in her temple. Her dark blonde hair was pulled back to a tight knot on the back of a smallish head. She was well-proportioned and she sat erect with her chin up. She seemed completely confident. Although she had been almost seven years younger at the time of her brother's trial, now, even in the wee hours, she seemed to have become a more handsome and stylish woman.

The perfect press of Kevin Bannon's elegant blue blazer had disappeared with the day. He sat across the table from Wilma beside another detective whose five o'clock shadow was worse than Nixon's. It was well after midnight. An hour ago they had dropped Julie off at home with Papa Nathan and the cop. Rebecca wondered if they had Mirandized Wilma. If she had aided William's escape, she would be charged with felony murder.

In spite of the hour, Kevin displayed his best little-boy face. 'Now, Miss Schmid, we've known each other a long time – all right if I call you Wilma?'

She shrugged. Then made Kevin wait, maybe half a minute. Finally she said, 'Much longer than I have cared to, Mr Bannon.' Like William, she had the straight pointed nose, the large nostrils that tonight flared wide with each statement.

Rebecca wondered if Kevin would have pulled the first-name business on a man.

'Call me Kevin,' he said. 'Wilma, I've always been fair to you – and William for that matter.'

They were twins, but there were differences. Wilma's face was fuller, more balanced. Her washed-out blue eyes looked into space between the two men. There were no tears.

'Haven't I always been fair to you?' Kevin let his lips form a soft smile, and waited for Wilma to look at him.

'Mr Bannon, I suppose you have been fair to me. I can't remember your being unfair.'

'I deserve fairness back, right?'

'Your crude logic is better spent on juveniles.'

Behind the glass Rebecca silently agreed. Kevin looked disappointed.

'OK, Wilma, just tell us where you were between noon and nine earlier today.'

'Again. I was home.'

'Alone?'

'As usual.'

'Haven't you gone to visit your brother every Thanksgiving Day since he has been at Wolf River?'

'Again. I might have.'

'We know somebody had to have helped William escape from the hospital. His car was there waiting for him. You'll agree someone must have helped him.'

'Agree, disagree. What difference does it make? It was not me. And he is dead. All of you must finally be satisfied. What difference does it make?'

Rebecca's guilt had moved in to stay. *She* wasn't satisfied.

'Do you know where your brother William's car has been kept over the past several years?'

'Again. Of course. I rented a space for it. I have kept up the rent.'

'Where was the garage?'

'Again. It wasn't a garage. It was just a storage lot out in Richfield.'

'Have you been out there recently?'

'Again. No.' Her face sagged and she blew a puff of air through pursed lips. 'Can't we cover this ministerial trivia at another time, Mr Bannon? It is very late and I am very tired and my brother . . . my twin brother has died. Your cohort here picked me up hours ago; he and that other man asked me all of these same questions and more. They are all on that tape. You can listen to it.'

Kevin let his eyes drift toward Rebecca behind the mirror. His face said, she's right. We'll come back to her.

'OK, Wilma. I take it you plan to stay in the area?'

'I want to be here when they find William's body.'

On the way to Lake Vista, Kevin drove slowly through avenues cut in the squeaky cold snow. Big orange trucks with huge blades and flashing blue lights were everywhere, clearing downtown Minneapolis for the flood of Christmas shoppers due in the morning, the day after Thanksgiving, always the biggest retail day of the year. Only a few flakes still straggled down on the city.

After agreeing that Wilma must have been involved in William's escape, the conversation had faded to comfortable quiet. Rebecca let her head fall back against the headrest and closed her eyes. Schmid's trial came back. Harry Scott was asking the witness about tests. A memorably handsome man, Dr Phillips actually looked more like Montgomery Clift playing Freud than Freud himself. He had asked Rebecca for a date. At first she had accepted. On reflection she turned him down. She wanted nothing to taint Schmid's trial. Of course, Dr Phillips had waited until after the trial to call her. Still, there was the long appeal process and the goddamn newspapers would make something out of it when they found out, and they surely would.

'Dr Phillips,' Harry Scott said, 'you administered an intelligence test on William Schmid, correct?'

'Yes. I administered the Wechsler Adult Intelligence Scale as revised.'

'The results?'

'He has an IQ of one hundred and seventy.'

'What does that mean?'

'Only one person in fifty thousand has an IQ of one hundred and seventy or higher.'

'Would that be considered a genius level?'

'Genius is not really a scientific term, but yes, William Schmid's intelligence is certainly on a genius level by all standards I'm aware of.'

Kevin pulled up to Lake Vista's canopied entrance. 'What if he's not dead?' Rebecca said. 'Kevin, what if that brilliant bastard pulled off some kind of miracle?'

'I'd be more worried about that if it hadn't gotten so cold. It'd freeze the nuts off a brass monkey out there, and in that water. Chances are slim to none.'

'I hope they find the body soon,' Rebecca said.

'Big Corky told me that if this weather holds, most of the Wolf River will be frozen over for the winter in a few days. There's a lot of ice on it already.'

'It's a long time till spring,' she said.

Julie's lanky body made a ridge in the pink comforter. It had been two years or more since she had slept in her mother's bed. She must be troubled. The cop had awakened dazed when Rebecca let herself in. He said he'd stay the night on the sofa. The cop in the lobby had gone home.

'It's me, honey, I need a little room,' she said when she slipped under the comforter. Julie grunted in reply.

As tired as Rebecca was, sleep did not come. A chain of thoughts jangled through her head. Half a day ago, a proven killer who had been threatening her and Julie's life for years had escaped. Supposedly he was dead. In the horror movies that fascinated Julie so much, the killers never died easily. They came rising out of the muck. And what of this man she had drawn so near to in a matter of days? Did she want to tangle with another fragile male ego? When they had stopped for coffee earlier tonight he had had an anxiety attack when she insisted on picking up the check. It's your gas, she had said. No, it's the city's, he said. She closed the subject with, I'm paying, in the same tone she overruled objections in her courtroom. The puppy eyes had told her she was mistreating him, but he shut up and put some butter on Julie's nose. Not too bad really. Maybe this one would actually try to learn something about her, not just what worked and what didn't. If she let things develop, how would he react when she presented him with her bare brown ass and bade him spank it, and keep on even after she pleaded with him to stop. The thought got her giggling.

'Mom, what are you laughing at?' Julie was wide awake.

'Just a joke,' Rebecca said.

'Tell me.'

'Go to sleep.'

'No, tell me.'

'There was once this rabbit named Peter that lived near Mr McGregor's cabbage patch.'

'Oh, Mom, it's somethin' sexy, isn't it?'

'Why, daughter, how you talk.' She reached over and pulled Julie close to her and kissed her forehead. 'Oh, my darling daughter, you are the stars and the moon to me.'

'I love you too, Mom.'

'We have a good thing going, don't we?'

'We do, Mom, but I think you need a guy.'

'Now, why would you say that?'

'Isn't that the way things are supposed to be?' Julie's tone demanded a serious answer.

And, of course, Rebecca knew the correct one. It was no. Women don't need men. But she didn't say it. Instead she said, 'I'm not sure, honey. Let's try to go to sleep.'

Julie turned over. In a minute she was breathing evenly. Rebecca was amazed how quickly a fourteen-year-old could get to the heart of the matter. Because she wanted this man to fill some need didn't necessarily mean she needed a man. Did it? Put it this way: I want this man to fill some *want*, not need. How silly it all was. For a moment she thought of the daily overture to a soap opera Grandma Esther used to listen to. It was a question about whether or not some peasant-type girl from a little mining town in the west could find happiness with a wealthy English lord. Can a bigoted primitive Irish lummox find happiness with a black Jewish district court judge who would never admit she needed a man? Kevin barely knew her, yet his eyes said whatever she wanted he would do for her, and looking in them you could get a glimpse of something very nice, very nice indeed. Mama Julia once said, Look, if they let you see in, it's worth looking, and then she'd take a deep drag and it seemed that smoke poured from every orifice as she said, But most of them won't. They don't want you to know how weak they are. Maybe read soft instead of weak, Rebecca thought. The grin, twitching at the corners, in that sweet freckle face played on the back of her lids as she slipped off to sleep, for the moment having forgotten about the life or death of William Schmid.

16

Under the clear Dakota sky the shadows on the small town sidewalk made crisp silhouettes. William Schmid, wig and mustache carefully in place, bought a copy of the *Minneapolis Star* and a big breakfast. Sitting at the counter of the Main Street Cafe, he found the story on the first page of the second section. Divers and searchers on foot had spent a fruitless Friday. Much of the river had frozen, and further underwater operations were abandoned due to danger to the divers. The county sheriff said they would likely have to wait until spring to find the body. He had changed from the mug shot accompanying the article. Face thinner, the lines in his face deeper, he looked much older now. He was satisfied with his disguise.

The long muscles in his legs and back were still very sore, but the pain in his foot had subsided. He must have injured it on a rock in the river, or perhaps scrambling up the bank to the car in the soft rubber feet of the wet suit.

He liked the smell of the burning grease from the grill. The odor of disinfectant in his cell was hundreds of miles behind him. In a glass case behind the counter a lemon pie with three-inch meringue caught his eye. It would be good when he finished his scrambled eggs. A grizzled man in bib overalls on the next stool glanced his way.

'Nice day,' William said.

'Yep, too nice. We need that moisture they got east of here. Had a dry fall; now a dry winter, looks like.'

'I see,' said William.

The man grunted a little laugh. 'You some kinda salesman?'

'No, just traveling through,' said William.

'Goin' far?'

'West,' said William. He felt suddenly uncomfortable with the questions. He would forego the pie. Abruptly he stood. 'I will be leaving now. I wish you a very good day.'

With another grunting laugh, the man threw his hand up signaling goodbye.

Behind the wheel, William felt relieved. His manner of speaking was foreign in a place like Sisseton, now receding, with its water tower, in the rear-view mirror. Exposure to too many people could undo him. He needed to find one place and stay put until the time was right. That was the plan. He must stay on track, follow it to the letter. There was one exception. If ever he regained his freedom he had promised himself a woman, any woman. Wilma was out of reach. Another must do.

He chose to travel on paved secondary roads, his destination Aberdeen. The blacktopped highway ran exactly west along section lines for miles. In places it turned ninety degrees to the north or south, only to head straight west again in a mile or two. Lookalike farmsteads, guarded from fierce prairie winds by dense groves on the north and west, were scattered across the sun-filled countryside. Many were unoccupied, some for decades. Fall plowing had turned most of the earth to dry gray segmented by fence lines of sere brown grasses. Scattered prairie potholes were speckled black with coot and occasional flocks of ducks. Ice was forming around the edges on most.

A half-hour west of Sisseton a company of crows soared on an updraft off to the north. William had watched them glide within a few feet of his window at Wolf River. Year round, they had flown to unknown destinations, paralleling the river, north and south on a regular schedule, as though bidden by witches. In the spring they worked in pairs, one filching the eggs from songbirds' nests along the river while the expectant mother flew after the other, scolding it away. The insane were fascinated by the crows and spoke of them when the opportunity arose.

For a closer look, William headed north at the next gravel road. The Ford vibrated over the washboard surface, weaving a fabric of airborne dirt in its wake. Ahead on the left, three of the large black birds perched on the carcass of a deer lying in a field. Several others strutted around surveying the giant meal. Overhead, the watchers, flapping their glossy black wings, called out reedy warnings to those on the ground.

William stopped the car. All of them leaped aloft and joined the cawing, except one perched on the head, plucking at an eye. William withdrew the .38 from beneath the seat and aimed through the window. He pulled the trigger. And again and again and again and again and again. A loud blast over flat land quickly dissipates, but six in succession occupied all space for a few moments. William's ears rang. His target, unscathed, joined the others aloft, still cawing and wheeling in broad arcs on the air currents, waiting for the intruder to leave.

William took a deep breath of the murky prairie air, faintly redolent of the rotting deer carcass. He followed the bumpy road round the section and back to the highway. The recoil and roar of the revolver had left him with a feeling of potency. He decided he would buy a good knife at a hardware store in Aberdeen.

No more than a burg anywhere else, in South Dakota Aberdeen had the atmosphere of a major population center. Big square white homes on a grid of tree-lined streets housed retired farmers. On all sides the town abruptly ended like the shores of an island in a quiet ocean of plowed fields. Pick-up trucks clogged traffic in the center of town on Saturday afternoon. Streams of denim-clad men and their women and children flooded the sidewalks. After checking into the Frontier Motel, William found a store front cafe claiming the best in home cooking.

'Ya wanta menu?' Behind the counter a broad-hipped woman, streaks of gray in dark, pinned-up hair, didn't seem to care if he did or not.

Good, she's bored, William reasoned. 'Are you on the menu?' He got to the point. He didn't have time to cultivate a relationship.

'Kinda fresh, aintcha?' Her nasal voice was friendly, kidding.

94

'Sorry, I meant it as a compliment.'

'You're not from around here, are ya?'

'Just passing through, but I may be here for a few days. Do you like it here?'

'I've seen worse, but not much.'

'Why do you stay?'

'Where would I go?'

'An attractive person like you should have many options.' He tried his best to smile.

She touched her hair; a few strands had fallen down in front of her ear. Hazel eyes glistened through the rimless glasses. 'You got lotsa compliments, mister.'

'Frank,' William said. 'Frank Kroll.'

She squeezed his hand and held on. 'Glad to know you, Frank.' She released her grip and smiled, one front tooth slightly canted from the others.

'And I'm very happy to meet you.'

'Oh, I'm sorry, I'm Nancy. Nancy Jane Quist.' She stood more erect and straightened her red-checked apron.

From the grill a loud male voice shouted, 'Nancy, whadda hell 'appen da ya? There's three orders up.'

'Coming,' she said.

When she came back, she took his order and agreed to meet him at eight at a roadhouse just outside of town. He promised to buy her a juicy steak and she promised to teach him a new dance step. He let her believe he liked country and western.

The ceiling lights reflected from her glasses as she kept turning her broad Scandinavian face toward him while he ate his lunch. He marveled at how easy it had been. Finished, he went next door to the Coast to Coast. An affable clerk sold him a hunting knife with a broad curving blade and a coil of nylon cord. That blade does double duty for skinning, the clerk said, with a smile.

It had been years since William had been exposed to any quantity of cigarette smoke. It bit at his nostrils. As Nancy Jane promised, the music at the Sheep Shed was live. William would give the trio nothing else. An Indian, about six six, with a guitar slung from his neck, tried to sing like Hank Williams. In between he mimicked a variety of bird calls, warbling on amid enthusiastic applause. A set of drums and an electronic bass backed up the vocals.

'Do "Your Cheatin' Heart",' Nancy Jane yelled.

'But, baby, my heart don't cheat,' he yelled back. The crowd of waiting couples pulled each other close as he started the ballad.

'Ain't he great?' Nancy Jane's eyes were wide open and magnified by the lenses.

'Excellent,' said William. 'Two more,' he said to the waitress.

In the dining room they chewed for a half-hour on two T-bones before giving up and returning to the music. That afternoon William had bought a blue flannel shirt and a pair of Levis. Hey, you look right in style, Nancy Jane had said when he walked in; only thing is, to be a real shit-kicker, ya need cowboy boots.

The waitress brought two more drinks. 'You tryin' to get me drunk?' Nancy Jane giggled and squeezed William's knee under the table.

He held her hand. 'Whatever makes you happy,' he said.

'I'll bet you can make me happy,' she said.

'I hope so,' he said, and felt a surge of blood in his groin.

'But you ain't danced one dance yet.'

He had waltzed with Wilma when they were young, but he had never tried anything like the jumping around that was dancing at the Sheep Shed. He reached out with a match to Nancy Jane's cigarette. She held his wrist as she took a deep drag.

'You're kinda classy, aintcha, Frank?' she said.

No apt reply occurred to William.

'Come on now, let's give it a whirl.'

They faced each other on the dance floor. People bumped into William. Some seemed to be alone. He looked at her feet, then his. She dropped his hands and started swinging her hips. Her feet didn't move much. The Indian warbled to a strong drum beat. William started swaying side to side.

'You got it, honey. Nothin' to it. Right?'

He swayed through 'Jambalaya', 'Hey, Good Lookin' and two more bird calls. Then the Indian started crooning 'I Can't Help It If I'm Still In Love With You'. Nancy Jane pulled him up close and swayed to the music, feet in one place. Her pubic bone pressed against his penis, partially engorged in the leg of the tight denims.

'You gotta pair of pliers in your pocket?' she whispered in his ear.

'Let's go,' William said.

'Soon as this one's over,' she said with a wink.

William was waiting for her when she tapped on the motel room door. She set a half-full bottle of Seagram's Seven on the bed table with her purse.

'Honey, you get some Seven-Up and a little ice and I'll freshen up a bit.'

As he was going out the door, she called after him, 'Frankie, the ice machine's just past the office.'

As he walked down the hall, blood roared through his head. His penis, rock hard under the tight new denim, was pulled up against his stomach. He thought of the knife and cord in the drawer. He hoped he wouldn't need it. Maybe she would treat him like Wilma did, affectionately and warm. But he barely knew her. He pressed the cold Seven-Up can against his temple, hoping the headache would stay away.

Except for the glow from the open bathroom door, the room was dark when William returned. His eyes adjusted. Nancy Jane was stretched out on her back on the bed. Her legs formed an inverted 'V' under the sheet. Her head was a foot from the drawer where he had stored the cord, the gun, and the knife. The faint light glinted off the canted tooth in the broad lipsticked grin.

'Frank, honey, wanna fix me a little Seven an' Seven?'

Dutifully, he poured the whiskey over the ice, almost filling the glass.

'Hey, sweetie, don't forget the mix.'

He filled it to the brim from the green can of Seven-Up and held it out to her, spilling a little on the sheet. She raised herself on an elbow. The sheet slipped away from a large sagging breast, the circle round the nipple like a big molasses cookie. He felt his heart beating and the blood roaring in his head.

Nancy Jane took a sip and set the drink on the bed table, then her glasses next to it. William noticed the drawer wasn't closed tight. She turned back to him, the smile slashed across her wide jaw.

'Come to mama, baby,' she said. She whisked the sheet from her body.

William's eyes fell on the patch of copious dark pubic hair. Gravity pulled the flattening breasts down the sides of her rib cage.

'Well, aintcha gonna take your pants off?'

He wondered what her reaction would be to the cord. He needed to tie her in that position, so she couldn't change her mind. If she laughed she would destroy his erection. He would need time to get it back. But she might scream when she saw the cord. If he pointed the gun at her head she wouldn't scream, or laugh. He didn't want to kill her. He wasn't even sure he could. She was nice and countrified like Slim Olson. If he killed her, the police would have him in hours. Perhaps he should just leave. There was so much more he needed to do. He could never go back to Wolf River. He needed time with Wilma, and there was always the judge. Since he was a boy he had finished every project he had started, one step at a time. That was the only way. But now, desire mixed with indecision paralyzed him.

'What's the matter, honey?' On her knees, Nancy Jane crawled across the bed to him. She sat on the edge of the bed, reached out and unzipped his fly, pulled the belt buckle loose, and tugged the denims down over his hips. When she pulled his snug shorts down, his penis flopped out in her face. He would have to get the gun. Take control. He hesitated, motionless; flickers of fear and pinches of pain danced in his head. He had never had sexual intercourse with anybody but Wilma and his stepmother. None at all for more than seven years. She took the shaft of his penis in her fingers, gently milking it, inserting the head in her mouth as if it was some wonderful delicacy, so he couldn't feel her teeth. In seconds an uncontrollable electric impulse expelled the semen into her throat. She gurgled for an instant, but kept milking it into her mouth. He tangled his fingers in her thick dark hair and pulled her face against him. She kept at it, drawing it all out of him, substance and energy. His knees weakened. Nancy Jane flopped back on the bed, beckoning to him with the fingers of both hands, palms up.

'Don't I getta turn, honey?' she said.

He crawled on to the bed and placed his head on her shoulder. She rocked him with a barely perceptible motion. 'It's been a long time for you, Frankie baby, ain't it?'

She liked him, really liked him. Only Wilma had ever treated him like this. His stepmother had just used him for whatever pleased her. How will I ever leave this place? William thought.

'You go to sleep, Frankie,' she said. 'I'm off tomorrow. We got all day.'

17

On Friday Papa Nathan had insisted that Rebecca and Julie relate their separate versions of the trip to Wolf River. Later, he privately pumped Rebecca for details of what had gone before. Good the sumbitch is dead, he had said, shelving the subject permanently as far as he was concerned. For Rebecca, it wasn't so easily dismissed. When she awoke on Friday morning, elation over the extra day of vacation quickly gave way to the proximity of death, William Schmid's, as well as the other two men's. The threat to her own life lurked far in the background; the burden of culpability in the loss of three lives trapped her under the covers, pressing down, creating a tingling anxiety she had never felt before. It was the same on Saturday morning. In spite of Kevin's arguments to the contrary over the telephone that afternoon, layers of sedimentary guilt accumulated. If she had allowed the jury's verdict to stand, William Schmid would still be alive in the state prison at Stillwater. Sven Olson would be discharging his duties and looking after his wife and children in Wolf River. Thurgood Jefferson, still in his twenties, would be playing basketball in the recreation yard at the hospital. Clearly, she was responsible. You are not, Kevin had said emphatically. In this business death is part of the job. It happens, and usually to innocent people. At least this time two of the three who died were murderers. Schmid might have murdered more had he lived; same with Jefferson, said Kevin. Rebecca remained unpersuaded.

On Sunday morning Julie popped into Rebecca's bedroom, her head wrapped in a red scarf, her lithe body in a

100

bright yellow robe. 'Steaming coffee, Cheerios with peaches, a blueberry Danish and I'll get you the Sunday paper,' she announced, handing Rebecca the tray full of goodies.

'How sweet, darling daughter,' Rebecca said. 'Where's Papa?'

'He's walking round the lake.'

'In this cold?'

'It's warming up. The sun's out.' Julie opened the drapes. 'See.'

The twelfth-floor window framed a field of cloudless brilliant blue.

'It looks nice, but I'm afraid he'll slip on the ice.' Rebecca leaned forward and Julie propped up two pillows behind her.

'Do you really think you could stop him from walking round the lake once he decides he's going to?'

'I guess you're right.'

Julie assured her mother that Grandpa was dressed warmly enough. In a minute she was back with the paper.

Rebecca finished off the cereal, saving the coffee and roll for paper reading. She quickly paged through the news section, then the editorials. Already they were writing about bad security at the state hospital.

'Oh my God,' she said aloud.

Bold letters near the top of the metro section proclaimed 'ESCAPEE HAD THREATENED JUDGE'S LIFE'. To one side, William Schmid's straight-lipped mug shot flanked a smiling Judge Rebecca Goldman. Rebecca began reading the article. It continued to an interior page which it shared with an ad for a fur sale at Daytons. It was reasonably accurate, assuming Schmid was actually behind the threats, and even included a verbatim text of one of the letters. The unidentified sources were reliable, the reporter said. At that point Rebecca flipped back to the front page. Annette Rollins had the by-line. Rebecca hadn't returned Annette's calls on Friday. She wasn't ready to talk about Schmid or his trial or the Tom Phelps trial either, if that was what Annette had called about. Rebecca knew her well – she was a black sister – and even admired her as a hard-working reporter. Seven years as judge had taught Rebecca to mistrust the press generally. She often read reports of what had taken place in her courtroom that bore little resemblance to reality. At least once she had checked the trial transcript to see if she was losing her mind. Kevin's name appeared twice in the article, but he was not quoted, and Rebecca felt sure that he hadn't talked to Annette either.

Highlights from William Schmid's trial were interspersed throughout. Annette had interviewed Dr Aaron Phillips. Was Schmid's behavior consistent with the evaluation Phillips had made at the time of the trial, and did Phillips know about the letters to the judge? Yes to the first, no to the second, the psychiatrist said, and also one shouldn't be surprised when inmates as intelligent as William Schmid devised diabolical escape plans. Again, Rebecca recalled the darkly handsome face of Dr Phillips sitting in the witness box in her courtroom seven years before. She let her head fall back into the softness of the pillow, eyes closed.

Rebecca had noticed pinkish skin showing through the thinning hair on top of Schmid's head as he stared down at the table when Dr Phillips described the psychotic mind.

'Just exactly what is psychosis, Dr Phillips?' Harry Scott interrupted the flow of his witness's testimony, perhaps to make sure the jury was paying close attention.

'A person falling profoundly out of touch with reality – disorganized behavior, disorganized thoughts, disoriented perception and feelings, deteriorating personality,' said Dr Phillips, 'those are the characteristics of a psychotic, a person suffering from psychosis.'

'Psychosis is a mental illness then, I take it?' said Scott, sounding overly simplistic to Rebecca, but then she remembered Mrs Hansen, the heavy woman in the front row of the jury box. Her earlier answers to the lawyers had revealed little sophistication. Actually she had appeared too stupid to serve, but for whatever reason, neither lawyer struck her from the panel.

'Yes, it is a mental illness,' Dr Phillips replied.

'If the defendant is a psychotic, does that—'

'Objection. Assuming facts not in evidence,' said prosecutor Whitlow Strom loudly.

'Sustained,' said Rebecca.

'Put it this way,' said Scott. 'Does a psychotic person suffer from psychosis all of the time?'

'Usually not. A seemingly normal person can decline into a psychotic episode within minutes.'

'And vice versa?'

'Yes,' said Dr Phillips, 'and vice versa.'

'Have you ever observed the defendant William Schmid in a psychotic episode?'

'Objection, no foundation,' said Strom.

'How is the foundation lacking, Counsel?' Rebecca asked.

'He hasn't shown he had the opportunity to observe, or date and time, witnesses and the like,' said Strom.

'I'll overrule as to the opportunity.' Rebecca looked at Scott.

'We'll supply the rest as we go along, your honor,' said Harry Scott. Seated at his side, Schmid stared at the back of his hands, pressed flatly against the table top.

'Very well, you may proceed,' Rebecca said officiously. She was hanging on every word Dr Phillips uttered, and she felt the penetrating stare of the defendant even though it was presently directed elsewhere.

Dr Phillips supplied the details Rebecca had required, and Scott went on, 'Prior to the time you allude to, you had numerous opportunities to observe the defendant, did you not?'

'Yes.'

'And what did you observe?'

Obviously Dr Phillips had observed much, but he had testified many times on behalf of criminal defendants. He knew exactly what was expected of him at this point.

'Among other things, he was rational. He was able to converse intelligently, extremely intelligently, I should say.'

'How was he different during what you refer to as a psychotic episode?'

'He seemed to have forgotten who I was. He didn't wish to converse. When I finally got him to speak, he spoke like a child of ten or less. He seemed unduly interested in his genitals. Though he was fully clothed, he repeatedly felt himself, as though he was checking to see that they were all right – his genitals, that is. He asked for his mother several times. When I mentioned his father, he began to sob and his body convulsed. He slipped from the chair he was on and crawled under the table.'

The image of William Schmid under the table stuck in Rebecca's mind as much as any of the so-called expert testimony. But the details of the crime, the bizarre and pitiless treatment of another human being, indeed his own friend and colleague, had become an image subject to immediate recall in detail like a pop-up menu on a computer screen. Convinced of Schmid's insanity, his psychosis, Rebecca would have been wrong to let the jury verdict stand and send him to prison to mingle with sane inmates. It was well known that many psychotics did not survive long terms in prisons filled with brutal sociopaths. Now she wasn't so sure. He was brilliant. He could have been faking. But why?

Schmid had made it plain since, to Kevin and to others, that he would have preferred prison to Wolf River. He had even persuaded a lawyer from the state public defender's office to attempt to reopen the case two years after the trial. The motion alleged that Harry Scott should have argued for the lesser offenses of second degree murder and manslaughter to be included in the options the jury could convict on, not just first degree murder and not guilty by reason of insanity. Rebecca remembered the discussion in chambers, and of course it was on the record. At the hearing Harry Scott contended he had discussed it with William Schmid, and that Schmid had agreed. Scott even offered some notes he had made at the time. Rebecca wondered why Schmid would have agreed. She remembered that the testimony at trial indicated that he had lapses of memory. And Dr Phillips' testimony was still fresh in her mind. And as a practical matter, the jury would never have gone for a lesser degree of murder in a million years. She denied William Schmid's motion for a new trial and her ruling was upheld on appeal. But William Schmid had found new reasons to hate, and an additional person too: his defense counsel Harry Scott. For Scott, the acquittal by reason of insanity was a victory. Victories were what criminal law was all about, whether you were defending or prosecuting. Scott had sought to prove his case at all costs. Dr Aaron Phillips had been a priceless ally. But in the end it was Rebecca who delivered the goods, cut exactly to Harry Scott's order.

It was far past the time to haul her ample ass out of bed and enjoy Sunday. In Rebecca's adult life there had never been a time when she slept in on three straight days. She had become a creature of schedule, up every day at six, to bed at eleven when possible. She wanted to set an example for Julie. Her own life with Mama Julia had been chaotic – no schedules, no routine – and Papa Nathan was too busy at the store for more than the mildest protests. There was security in structure. Perhaps it would have been less necessary with a mate. But it served her well in law school, and as a busy public defender. Now, sitting on the bench, juggling a full calendar of cases, she couldn't imagine functioning without a complete set of routines and daily plans. Her colleagues who tried to do without struck her as abject failures, never getting court cases decided, procrastinating at every turn, making lawyers' and litigants' lives unnecessarily difficult.

She slept nude. Snapping on the ringer switch on her phone, she slid out from under the pink comforter. Against the slight chill in the room, she pulled her thick white terry robe round her. But standing upright, looking out over Lake Calhoun, didn't change the chill at her center. Stop and start traffic already crowded Lake Street. Rebecca looked vainly for the bundled-up figure of her father in the string of walkers slowly circling the lake in ones and twos. The sidewalks and streets were defined by ridges of snow left by the plows and blowers.

Death prowled her mind in spite of the starkly bright blue and white beyond the glass. When Reggie died, she had reflected on her own death. Julie's grief brought it to the top. What would happen to Julie if Rebecca somehow ceased to exist? She couldn't let it happen, at least not until

Julie had grown. She just couldn't. She put it out of her mind. Contemplation of death was for the elderly. But now her life had been seriously threatened by a locked-up lunatic who had miraculously escaped. Not so miraculously. Systems devised by human beings just didn't work that well. Overwhelming evidence appeared daily. The guilty went free to kill the innocent again, and the judge often got blamed when it was the system that failed. Airplanes guided by traffic controllers ran into each other, killing hundreds. Drunks haunted the highways in cars, killing at random. Grizzly bears in National Parks ate visitors invited by the government. All of these deaths were abstractions, footnotes to life, often buried inside newspapers. Not so with the deaths of Thanksgiving Day. Rebecca was involved. She was part of the system that allowed them to happen – no, actually caused them. Worse, this time she had interfered when she could have sat back, as probably most judges would have done, and let jury justice take its course. She had been so sure they were mistaken. She was still sure, but that was no longer the point.

Rebecca carried her tray and empty cup and bowl through the quiet living room to the kitchen. Julie had left for the afternoon with friends. The telephone rang. Probably Susan, or maybe Kevin, she thought.

'Hello.'

'Judge Goldman?' The voice sounded familiar.

'This is Judge Goldman.'

'This is Harry Scott.'

Sometimes assistant prosecutors called her at home. And cops for an order or a warrant, but defense lawyers rarely. Surprise left Rebecca searching for words.

'Are you there, Judge?'

'Yes, I'm here.' Rebecca felt the heat rising in her cheeks. Her image of Scott wasn't from the courtroom. It was from her last dream, his face in the grimace of orgasm, sweat on his forehead.

'Could I have a moment of your time?'

'Counsel, I hope this call isn't regarding the Phelps case. You know the rules on *ex parte* contacts.'

'Of course,' said Scott, 'nothing like that.'

Still, Rebecca wouldn't put it past him. She didn't think he was on anything else presently in her court. 'What is it then, counsel?'

'It's sorta personal.'

God, had he read her mind?

'I'm listening,' said Rebecca.

'I've been thinking about how the news about William Schmid must be troubling you,' said Harry Scott. 'Er . . . I find this a little difficult.'

In the ten or more years she had known Scott she had never suspected he had difficulty saying anything. Her curiosity took over. She eagerly awaited his next words, but said nothing.

He started again. 'I kind of feel like this whole Schmid business is at least partly my fault.'

'Your fault? Do you know something about his escape?'

'Oh, no. For sure no. I thought maybe we could get together and talk about it? Maybe Friday night for dinner. Or any time you're able.'

This had to be about Phelps. Rebecca's legal mind took over. 'Counsel, you have a motion before me for my recusal on the Phelps case. If I were to see you socially, that would about clinch it, wouldn't it?'

'I was afraid you would think that. This call has nothing to do with Tom Phelps. I thought I could be helpful right now and it would be an opportunity to get to know you better. I understand you are currently uncommitted.'

The dream came back, overpowering her legal mind. 'But Mr Scott—'

'Harry,' he interjected.

'Mr Scott, aren't you married?'

'Just technically. My wife served me with a petition for dissolution a couple of months ago. The jurisdiction is in Scott County.' A sigh interrupted the wistful tone. 'I guess nobody here has picked up on it. My marriage is over. There's a default hearing scheduled for the week before Christmas if we get together on the numbers. So I don't see how dinner would be out of order.'

107

'What about the Phelps case?'

'It's just another case. I could always—'

'Hardly,' she said.

'I could always have something going on in your court.'

'I think not, counsel.'

'Not what?'

'That I ought not to have dinner with you.' It wouldn't be in the good order of things, she thought, and she saw Kevin's freckle face for a moment.

'It's a great idea,' said Scott.

'I'm afraid I can't agree,' said Rebecca. Another time, another place, she thought. It might be nice.

'Is it because of the Phelps case?'

'That would be enough,' she said. As the appellate courts say, the issue is dispositive; we don't have to rule on the other questions.

'I take it you're staying on the case.'

'I didn't say that.'

'If you're not staying on the case—'

'Hold on, counsel, now you're getting close to the line that you implied at the outset you wouldn't cross.'

'Then I'll get off the Phelps case,' he said. 'I surely don't need it.'

No, but Phelps needs you, Rebecca thought. She visualized the headline: 'AMOUR DEPRIVES TOM PHELPS OF TOP DEFENSE COUNSEL'.

'You know better, Mr Scott.'

'Ah – well, most of the judges call me Harry.'

Apt correction. Rebecca knew of at least two who called him a lot of things, but never Harry. 'As I was saying, Counsel, you know better. You can't withdraw without leave of court. And no judge, particularly this one, would grant such leave without a compelling reason. What you are suggesting would never meet that standard.'

'I may have other reasons.'

'The highest profile rape case in Minneapolis history? Hardly, counsel. You'll be there. I appreciate what you said about the Schmid situation, but I'll have to deal with that on my own.' The line was quiet. She didn't want to slam the door, just close it firmly, not necessarily finally. 'Anyway, counsel, a man of Mr Phelps's public stature deserves the best.' That should do it perfectly.

'Thank you, your honor. I'm flattered, but with dozens of criminal defendants in this jurisdiction I might always have something pending before you. And most of the time I won't know which judge has been assigned to the case until after I have been retained.'

'See you in court . . . Harry.'

'Sure. Thank you. Yes, thank you very much. I'm very sorry to have bothered you at home.' Scott's voice had returned to the firm but supplicating tone that trial lawyers used on judges. And the image in Rebecca's head was now fully clothed in dark blue with a conservative tie, pale stripes on more dark blue, with a little insignia, probably Countess Mara.

'No bother,' she said.

As her first act on Monday morning Rebecca dictated an order denying attorney Harry Scott's motion that she recuse herself from *State v. Phelps*, and another setting the trial for the first business day in February, a mere ten weeks away. She put the tiny tape recorder down and swiveled her chair to face the window. Beyond the bulbous pale roof of the Metrodome, like a giant fungus in the foreground, rivulets of tiny cars trickled slowly downtown, and a picture of William Schmid's body preserved in detail by the icy waters of the Wolf River hung before her eyes. For an instant she was tempted to reach out and touch it.

18

Men less alert than William Schmid might not have departed Aberdeen having failed to assuage Nancy Jane Quist's sexual craving. But as wondrous as the workings of her mouth and body were, his continued presence in so large a town would lead to his premature capture. Death was preferable. His superior intellect allowed him no delusions about remaining at large indefinitely. But if he must die, he first meant to pursue his plan to its successful conclusion, step by step. The entire course of his adult life had been dictated by precise method. One of the psychiatrists said he had an obsessive personality. To William it made no sense that there was something wrong with finishing a job.

Last night he had momentarily forgotten about his wig until Nancy began fondling his hair as he lay on her shoulder. Before he could move away, she had realized that it wasn't *his* scalp her fingers were caressing.

'Heavens ta Betsy, you got on a wig, honey.'

'Yes,' William said. 'I have lost a great deal of hair recently.'

'You sick or somethin'? Here, lemme see.' She reached for the hair.

William jerked his head away and sat up in the bed. 'Please,' he said, 'it would embarrass me.' He thought of garrotting her with the cord if she pulled the wig off. Alive or dead, she could do him in.

'I understand, baby. Come back to mama. I won't touch your purty hair.'

During the night he found he couldn't sleep with her

body so close to him. He edged away, only to have Nancy Jane follow him across the bed. At first light, the spongy tissue of her breasts still pressed the flesh of his back and her left arm draped over his body. In one of his many fits of wakefulness, William decided he would leave town as soon as possible.

She crawled wordlessly out of the bed. Behind the closed bathroom door she gargled loudly, gagging and spitting. In a few minutes she reappeared with a cigarette stuck between the first two fingers of her right hand. Her hair was combed into a short pony tail and the nipples were inverted in her drooping breasts. In the dawn's dreary light an incongruous smile spread across her face.

'This morning I getta turn too, don't I, honey?' She stubbed the cigarette out in an ashtray.

William lifted the sheet for her. She crawled beneath it, head first.

At lunch he told her he had some paperwork he had to attend to. She should come back to the motel at six. When she was gone, he picked up the Minneapolis newspaper and a package of medium-brown hair dye at Walgreens and returned to the motel. At three he checked out and headed due south out of Aberdeen. He had done his usual methodical job. His hair was a rich shade of brown, almost chestnut, like his handsome betrayer Harry Scott. He would not soon forget his weekend with Nancy Jane. Regrettably, she probably would not forget it either.

For two hours under dismal low-hanging clouds the highway led him across a flat plain, through the tiniest of towns. As he neared Interstate 90, lamplight appeared in the farmhouse windows and he saw two hunters walking in the ditch carrying shotguns. The lights of Plankinton, like scattered fallen stars, lay across the darkened flatlands to the west. He checked into the first motel he saw.

The next morning, after breakfast in the motel coffee shop, William headed south on the same highway he had traveled the previous day. It was in this area of large farms south of I-90 and east of the Missouri River that he hoped to find a resting place. The clouds had vanished in the night and the sun still hovered low in the southeast when he turned on a blacktop crossroad heading straight west.

The sign said 'ROOK pop. 13'. The road separated a small group of buildings on the left from a grain elevator on the right. Maybe there would be information he could use in the grain elevator, William thought. Anywhere else the building would not seem tall, but in Rook it jutted above the surrounding plain like a watchtower, much wider at the bottom, tapering to a steeple-like extension under a green gable roof. High up, white letters forming 'Farmer's Co-op' were peeling off the gray weathered siding. The rest of the town withered on the other side of the highway. A black pick-up was parked beside two rusting gas pumps in front of a paintless frame building. Behind the gas station, three rundown one-story houses were strewn among a few thirsty trees. Heading into the entrance of the grain elevator, William's car bumped over a double set of railroad tracks. From the parking area he climbed the steps at the end of a loading dock. He entered a door marked 'Office'.

'Settler or savage?' Behind the counter a skinny old man in faded denims waited for an answer.

'Neither, I am afraid,' said William. Powdery dust hung in the air streaked with sunlight from the single window.

'Just joshin',' said the man. A line of brown fluid trickled from the corner of his mouth into at least a week's growth of gray stubble. 'I'm Alf Mikkelson. Spell it with two ks. What can I do fer ye?'

'I am looking for work,' said William.

'You musta took a right where you shoulda took a left.' The old man fished a box of Copenhagen out of the breast pocket of his bib overalls and his rheumy eyes looked William up and down.

Self-consciously, William looked down at his own clothes. Under his open jacket he had on a cardigan sweater over a fresh shirt, open at the neck, and the new jeans from Aberdeen. 'I have work clothes,' he said.

As though the exact spot was of prime importance, Alf carefully placed a pinch of Copenhagen against his gum behind his lower lip. 'Ain't so much the clothes, it's them pink hands and them fingernails. Gotta tell ya. From where I'm standin', ya look like a dude.'

'I assure you I am capable of hard work,' said William. 'I like the out of doors.'

'Plenty a that hereabouts.' Alf spat some brown juice into a drawer behind the counter, and ran his fingers back through his sparse silver hair. 'We sure don't need nobody. 'Sides, we only got real heavy work 'cept the weighin' and writin' up – I do that.'

'Perhaps you know someone who needs help.'

'Can't say's I do. Jist a minute.' Alf walked toward a stairway in the back of the room. The dirty overalls hung loosely on his old bones. 'Hey, Ned. You still up there?'

A voice answered.

'Guy down here lookin' fer work. You know anybody lookin' fer a hand?'

William couldn't make out the words from upstairs.

'Jeez Christ,' said Alf turning back to William. 'Farmer south a here stuck somethin' up on the board behind ya there. Week or so back.'

William wheeled round. A bulletin board covered with business cards at random angles hung on the dirty wall beside the door.

'See that piece a cardboard below the church thing,' said Alf.

William moved closer. The church of St Stephen the Martyr announced Sunday masses at 8 and 10. In the corner below, on a piece of waxy cardboard, someone had written: 'Hand wanted for chores. See Mike Bohas or call me.' The ballpoint had skipped the waxy spots and the telephone number was barely legible.

'Mike Bohas put that up there. He's one of our members. If you say it fast, sounds like boss. You can call 'im from here. If you want, I'll dial it fer ya. I got his number.'

'Please,' said William.

After a minute or more, Alf hung up. 'Let it ring a good twenty times. Mike's probably out huntin' coyotes. Mary must be gone too. She's usually around. They ain't got no

113

kids. She's probably out doin' chores or somethin'. S'only six miles, straight south a here.'

After Alf gave him the directions, William said he was very much obliged to him and was on his way.

A mile before the Bohas farm, an abandoned house slumped toward the ground in a grove of leafless trees. At least a dozen crows sitting still as decoys in the bare branches watched William drive past. The Bohas farm spread out on the west side of the road half a mile ahead. A bright metal building with a round roof descending to the ground on the sides like the top half of a section of giant pipe hunched in the foreground. The roofs of a variety of buildings stuck up behind a belt of trees like a little hidden village.

The house was a cube about thirty feet on each side under a brown-shingled hip roof with wide eaves and two or three windows above and below on the walls William could see. A woman stood on the back steps watching William's car roll into the yard.

Redhead, big-boned and fleshy, a broad friendly face, she held her hand up in greeting. William got out of his car and approached her. 'Hello, ma'am. I am Frank Kroll.' She held out her hand. 'I saw your notice at the elevator – for a farm hand.'

'Glad to know you. I'm Mary Bohas.' She pronounced the name like boss.

'I am very happy to meet you, Mrs Bohas.'

'C'mon outa the cold.'

He followed her through the entry hall into the kitchen. Mary Bohas had full hips sharply tapered to the waist and walked with a straight back. Her dark red hair fell loosely over her shoulders. The fragrance of fresh baking filled the kitchen. A half-full Mr Coffee sat beside a dish-filled sink built into the counter. A blood-streaked butcher's knife lay on a folded newspaper on the other side of the sink. Mary Bohas walked on through the kitchen, through a short hall where the door of a bathroom stood ajar, and on into the living room. Several large pieces of furniture were tastefully arranged and a spinet piano stood against the wall at the far

114

end. She pointed to an easy chair covered in a pinkish floral print and asked him to sit down. William let himself sink deep into the upholstery.

'My husband will be back in an hour or so,' she said. 'He drove over to Platte to get a part for the tractor.'

A tiny black and white bird jumped from limb to limb in a dead-looking fruit tree outside the window. Mary Bohas had the sort of skin that was easily ravaged by the sun. She sat forward on the edge of the sofa, both hands cupped on her crossed knees, the look of a woman who had spent time in places far removed from the farm.

'So you are looking for work, Mr Kroll.'

'Please call me Frank,' William said.

'Well, Frank, there's a lot of work around here. In the winter, mostly feeding cows and pigs. We have about a hundred and fifty head of cattle and a big bunch of sows. I've forgotten how many. Mike knows all the details. We had a hand for about six months, name of Lonnie. He was a drinker, but we had a keep him through the harvest. Drink or not, he was good with the machinery. Had a knack like his dad. But Mike can take care of the machinery if he's got help with the feeding.' She pushed several strands of luxurious red hair away from her eyes. 'Mike's farming about fourteen hundred acres, mostly rented. Stays pretty busy. He hated to let Lonnie go in the fall. Mike's a big hunter. Goes to Montana and Wyoming and he hunts deer and coyotes around here, sometimes geese, too, over by the river. We got relatives that come out here every opening day in October to hunt pheasants, but Mike ain't much for pheasants. He's seen so much better days – thirty years ago when he was a teenager. You like to hunt, Frank?'

'I am afraid I do not know anything about hunting, ma'am.'

'You can call me Mary. Everybody calls me Mary right off. I'd ask you about your experience and all that, but you'd just hafta go over everything again with Mike.' Her eyes fell on his hands. 'Gotta say, those hands of yours don't look like they've been doing much heavy work lately.'

'No,' he said. 'I have not been on the farm since I was

very young, but I am willing to work hard.'

'You don't talk like a farm hand either. To tell you the truth, you sound like some kind of a teacher or preacher.'

'Oh no,' he said. 'I do have an education, but I need to get away from the city life for a while, a good long while.'

'You been married?'

'No,' he said.

'Unlucky in love?'

'Something like that.' The questions made William nervous. He was afraid he would forget his answers, say something inconsistent later. They just sat there smiling at each other for a few moments. She had lovely blue eyes and a delicate turned-up nose.

'Well,' Mary broke the silence. 'I would suppose you might not necessarily want to talk about your personal life.'

William said nothing, but he felt relieved.

'How about a cup of coffee?' She stood up as she asked.

'Yes, that would be fine,' he said.

She headed for the kitchen, looked back, and stopped. 'And a fresh cinnamon roll?' Her smile showed teeth that needed some work.

'That would be very nice,' he said.

'Heavens, I forgot to ask you where you're from.'

'Milwaukee, originally,' he said.

She disappeared through the door.

A new voice came from the kitchen. Out in the yard a blue pick-up was parked beside William's car. The murmuring from the kitchen went on. Soon a hearty male laugh, followed by Mary's giggle.

A man with wind-textured skin and big shoulders encased in blue plaid followed Mary into the room. Impish dark eyes, a porch of bushy brows, and sensuous lips revealing big even teeth in an easy smile made a kind face. His powerful grip hurt William's soft hand.

'Glad ta meetcha, Frank.' Mike Bohas's words came out in a continuous laughing giggle. 'Hear you've toured Rook and still wanta live around here.'

'I need the work.'

'Well, I sure as hell need the help. One question: you ain't

116

Jack the Ripper, are ya?' More giggles.

'I assure you I am not Jack the Ripper.'

'OK. You're hired. Grab a root and holler.'

William had no idea what Mike meant, but he was pleased with the big man's enthusiasm. 'Thank you. Thank you very much. I know little about farm work, but I learn fast and I am stronger than I look.'

'We'll manage,' said Mike.

When they finished the coffee and rolls, Mike said, 'C'mon out in the yard and I'll show you the lay of the land, and Mary'll throw some lunch together. You like pork chops?'

'Very much, Mr Bohas,' said William, pronouncing both syllables.

'Call me Mike, Frank.'

'Of course.'

As they walked through the back door, Mike patted him on the back. 'One of the most important things, Frank. I'm away a lot. I need someone I can trust to look after Mary and keep her company.'

'I will try my best,' said William Schmid.

19

'Lawdy, chile, you musta been done scared outa yo wits all these years.' Face like a brown moon, Annette Rollins did her Hattie McDaniels routine. In an ill-fitting cream dress, her body looked like a snowman, getting wider as your eyes followed it down. 'Whyn't you ever tell em 'bout those awful letters? Time us darkies got together, honey chile. I sho love this view from up here.'

Rebecca laughed hysterically. 'Enough, enough,' she sputtered.

'I do declare,' said Annette, 'it's been a coon's age – oops, make that a month a Sundays – since we got together.' Then she broke into high squealing giggles, threw her coat on the sofa, and they wrapped their arms round each other.

Annette had invited Rebecca for a drink. Rebecca had declined; come to my chambers instead, she had said. She wasn't ready for anybody else's questions.

'Oh, it's so good to see you,' Rebecca said, stepping back.

'Little more to look at every time,' said Annette, her voice dropping to a lower register.

'You're not wasting away, girl.'

'It's the hog jowls and chitlins.'

'Bullshit,' said Rebecca. 'I'm sure it's the lasagne at Pronto's and those three-martini lunches. You wouldn't know a hog jowl if it bit you.'

'There's plenty here to bite.' Annette gave herself a pat on the rump. 'Sister, I'm glad you took the time today. Didn't want you to think I'd print that letter under ordinary circumstances. You know, I left calls. That damn Tolson got that letter from some dick friend of his. Course, he wouldn't

118

say. And commodious as it is, it would've been my ass if I'd tried to keep it out of the paper, me writing the article on Schmid's escape, and all.'

'Don't worry about it, Annette. You have to do your job. It would have gotten out sooner or later anyway.' Rebecca returned to her chair behind the big walnut desk and asked Annette to sit down.

'Why'd you keep it under cover so long?' Annette asked.

'The cops thought it would only encourage the writer if we published them.'

'By the way, Becka, are we on the record? Either way's fine.'

'I'd like it off. I kinda need a woman's shoulder. Susan's had her sister and brother-in-law in town for turkey day, and all weekend. Course, when anything from me goes on the record it'll be to you.'

'Fine and dandy, sister. Weep it all out to me. At least the honky's dead.'

'Yeah,' Rebecca sighed.

Annette stood up and dragged her chair round the desk to face Rebecca up close. She sat down and reached out and took Rebecca's hand in her pudgy fingers.

'I been there, baby. I've had some serious threats about things I've written. Believed some of 'em too. Cops said the same thing to me.' Her moist eyes, brown, almost black, discs surrounded by exaggerated white, fixed on Rebecca's face. 'Is there any doubt he wrote them?'

'Well, they never could prove it. Except for the first one; he admitted to that. It was handwritten. It's certain they weren't typed on his typewriter. He has a twin sister, you know.'

'I had forgotten about her until I looked up the stuff we printed at the time of Schmid's trial, and of course now she's their principal suspect in aiding the escape. If they can nail her, it's gonna be murder one for that little number.'

'They may not be able to, and if all she did is leave him a car—'

'Wait a minute, sister. Where do you think that devil got the poison?'

119

'From Wilma, I suppose, but I saw her that night. Cool as a cucumber. And I think I'd know if they had something on her.'

'I guess you would. It isn't exactly a secret that you've been keepin' company with that dick Knuckles Bannon.'

'Boy, you know everything. We've just had a couple of drinks.'

'And lunch at the Willows, and over for Thanksgiving dinner and—'

'You been talking to Julie?'

Annette dropped Rebecca's hand and her voice went up. 'Are you kiddin', Becka? I'm a crime reporter. Seventeen years. Full-fledged sob sister. This city's my beat. Nothin' happens connected with crime I don't know.'

'You didn't know about Schmid's letters.'

'Oh, *touché*. I bleed. That line sounds good, doesn't it? I heard it straight from Dorothy Kilgallen's mouth, years ago on a talk show.'

Rebecca was laughing, and Annette took her hand again. 'Isn't it good Schmid's gone for ever?' she said.

Rebecca didn't reply.

'Oh, that face. You're blamin' yourself. I knew it.' Annette began to sing, ' "She's got the whole world in her hands . . ." ' Her voice trailed off. 'That's it. I'm right.'

'A little, I guess,' said Rebecca.

'It took guts, what you did. You called it the way you saw it. My paper didn't agree, but I did, if you'll remember.'

'I remember.'

'But now we look ahead, not back, sister. Right? And with him dead it looks better up ahead. A little rhyme and a little reason.'

'If he *is* dead.'

'Now you are kiddin' me. He's frozen solid as a pimp's dick, if you'll excuse the expression.'

'Mixed metaphor.'

'Now you're gettin' with it. 'Sides, you can't be runnin' this court down in the mouth, and you got a big one comin' up, or did you take yourself off it?'

'Order's filed. I'm trying it in February.'

'Hot snot. I want to see that goddamn Phelps squirm.'

'Easy now, Annette. I don't want to talk about a case I'm going to try, OK?'

'Sho, sho, Miss Scarlett, but I'm gonna be there watchin'. Hey, you remember that NOW convention we went to down in Chicago, when you first moved to Minneapolis. You, me and Susan. What a blast. You talked to the whole hall on discrimination in the workplace. And then on Saturday night you took off with that dude who just couldn't get over your tits – who can? – and you never showed up back at the room.'

Annette hadn't brought up that incident in years.

'And hey diddle, diddle, you called the next morning and sent us home without you. You've still never told me about him. You know, with this body, I got to get my thrills vicariously.'

For the best of reasons, Rebecca had never told Annette, or anyone else. Nor would she now, or ever. The time for telling was past.

'Just a little hint, for a comrade in arms?'

'I remember, comrade. But that story stays untold. It's old news anyway. I've forgotten about it,' Rebecca lied.

'In due time,' Annette said. 'I was just thinkin', sister, y'know what I remember about that Schmid case? It was that testimony by the shrink about the amnesia. The way the devil would completely forget who he was. He mighta been fakin' it when they had him in custody, but not two years before when the department chairman had to drive to Duluth and pick him up. Y'remember, the Duluth cops identified him by the cards in his wallet. Schmid didn't know who the hell he was. And then the next day he was fine. He didn't even remember having been to Duluth.'

'How could I forget?' said Rebecca.

'And you were right, sister. Don't you forget it. You did the right thing, and there was no way you could know those dummies wouldn't take better care of him.'

'See, you're blaming too,' Rebecca said. 'They're no more at fault than I am for sending him there. A judge should know something about a facility before she commits someone to it.'

'Shit, Becka, you know better. Things often aren't what they seem. You can't know everything. You try to do what's right. That's all. Last fall I was walking down Bloomington Avenue and this brother was sitting on the bottom step in front of one of those rundown apartment buildings with a cup in his hand. I barely looked at him and I dropped a quarter in the cup. He about went nuts. I thought he was a beggar. And there he was, nice corduroy jacket and one of those expensive Persian lamb caps. Just having a cup of coffee.'

Rebecca started giggling. 'Oh, Annette, you made that up.'

'It's the gospel, sister. It happened. The brother dumped the coffee and the quarter on the sidewalk and stomped into the building. Wouldn't listen to me. I axed him to please forgive me, but he wasn't talkin'.'

Annette made Rebecca feel good. She kept things light, but she made serious points. A good friend. Far below, headlights crawled out of the city into the December night. 'Annette, my dear friend, it's time to get home to my daughter.'

Annette stood up. 'You know where to find me, I'm always ready if you need something. Next time you got to fill me in on the romance.'

In his office in the Roanoke Building two blocks away, Harry Scott pondered the news that Judge Goldman had denied his motion to remove her from the case. It was no surprise, but he had hoped he might get lucky. Not only would it be better for his client, but the obstacle to seeing Rebecca Goldman socially would have been removed. Now, she was probably pissed at him for making the motion, but last night on the phone she hadn't sounded pissed. He had plenty of experience listening to voices for something more than the words. There had been a certain positive sound in there somewhere. He wasn't ready to write the judge off yet. With William Schmid's escape attempt he had a whole new subject to discuss with her – if he wasn't on the goddamn Phelps case. But there would be another time and place, and a healthy fee from Phelps might take a little pain out of the divorce. Or would greedy Hillary, someone he would once have fought lions for, want half of that too?

His secretary Vivian's voice came over the intercom. 'Mr Phelps is here.'

'Send him in,' Harry said. Yeah, send the prick in, he thought. How to wreck a day.

Phelps's shaggy auburn hair stood out uncontrolled around the sick little smile on his florid face. 'I see you were right, counselor, the bitch is staying on the case.'

Phelps had taken away Harry's opening line. 'You heard already?'

'It's in the afternoon edition.'

'Did the paper say we're going to trial in February?'

'It said that too.' Phelps extracted a check from his wallet and dropped it on top of the papers scattered over Harry's desk. 'Here's the other twenty-five.'

Harry had asked for a fifty-thousand dollar retainer, and Phelps had needed a little time to pay all of it. Harry picked up the check and threw it in his out box. He resisted the natural impulse to say thank you.

'Sit down, Tom. I've got just a little time.'

'I know the bitch loves rattling my cage,' said Phelps. 'Those feminists got memories like elephants and some kind of secret telegraph. One knows it, they all know it.'

Harry expected sarcasm, but Phelps's attitude toward the judge would be palpable in the courtroom. It could only hurt. 'You better ease back on Judge Goldman, starting right now. I don't need any handicaps I don't already have on this one.'

'What does that mean?' Phelps was getting shapeless under the chin and when the sound stopped coming out, his mouth always twisted back into the little puckered smile.

'The rape shield law is enough weight to carry in these so-called date rape cases.'

'I thought you said you had an angle on that.'

'I do, but I'd a lot rather go after Dinah White directly. Especially with all the evidence you have about her aggressive behavior with other men, but there's no way we can do that anymore.' Harry wondered how accurate that evidence was, but he had to believe his client on this issue or there was no defense, and he had learned nothing to the contrary. Of course, he hadn't looked very hard.

'Too bad. If she had as many pricks sticking out of her as she's had in her she'd look like a porcupine.'

'In any case, I still want to interview everybody you know who has dated her.'

'You mean fucked her, don't you, counselor?'

'Not necessarily. I mean any man you know who has spent any appreciable time with her and is willing to talk to me, and the names of those who aren't. Soon as possible. I'm also getting an investigator on it.'

'What's your angle?'

'Trade secret.'

'What the hell's that supposed to mean?'

'Just what I said.'

'We're talking about my freedom here.'

'So we are. So don't start fucking it up.' Harry's tone left no doubt on the issue.

'Don't get touchy, counselor. It's your show.'

Harry didn't reply.

'Yeah, I guess if it were an election campaign I wouldn't want you telling me how to run it,' said Phelps. 'By the way, I hear you're untying the knot.'

'I'd rather not talk about my personal life.'

'You got my sympathy, buddy, I've been through it twice.'

'When can I expect the list of names and addresses?'

'Couple of days.'

'Wednesday?'

'If you say so.'

'Wednesday then.' Harry stood up.

Phelps got up and stuck out his hand. 'Shake on a winning team.'

Harry gave him a few limp fingers.

20

The scent of browning meat filled the farmhouse kitchen. William Schmid stood looking out the window. He had been there a week. This morning the first new snow came blowing in on a west wind that whistled around the eaves and stirred up little cyclones of dust mixed with white in the yard.

'Is Mike comin'?' Mary said from her spot in front of the electric range.

'Yes,' said William.

Mike had just driven the big green John Deere tractor into the round-roofed machine shed and was walking toward the house. Big boots loudly stomped off the snow and dirt in the entry porch. Mike pushed through the kitchen door, the grin on his broad fleshy face breaking into a laugh.

'Hey, Frankie, we put in a good morning. You're gettin' the hang of it.' More giggling. He threw his bright orange hunter's cap on a chair. The tips of his ears were as red as radishes and his brown eyes gleamed through a film of moisture.

Toothache-like pain pierced one of William's lumbar vertebrae. He wondered how long his body could stand the strain. He had fed all the hogs this morning, lugging full five-gallon buckets of ground corn and dumping them into the galvanized feeders from nipple level while the eager beasts milled around, banging the trough covers with grunting snouts. When he had finished, he was sure he could not have lifted one more bucket.

William and Mike took their places at the round oak table

in the center of the kitchen, the biggest room in the house. Two large stoves dominated the room, one white range where Mary did most of the cooking, and a huge old cast-iron wood-burner with elaborate scroll work and a porcelain panel on the oven door. Since William had arrived it had only been used for burning corncobs against the chill at breakfast time. Just two days before, Mary's mother had driven the sixty-odd miles from Mitchell, and the two of them had repainted the walls and ceiling an off-white. Mixed with the other kitchen smells, a faint odor of paint still hung in the air.

Mary set the bowl of meatballs buried in thick gravy in the last available space near the center of the table and took her seat with a sigh. With her elbows on the edge of the table she interlocked her fingers in a double fist and bowed her head. 'Bless us, oh Lord, in these thy gifts which we are about to receive from thy bounty through Christ our Lord, A-men.'

Mike seemed not to notice her prayer, and he reached for the mashed potatoes. William spooned out some corn, then buttered one of the big hot biscuits. Soon his plate was overloaded. Meat was part of all their meals, and potatoes at least once a day. William had never eaten in such quantity, but the work and biting air created an appetite.

'Schwann's truck was here while you were out chasin' the calves,' said Mary. 'I got five gallons of the chocolate almond bark, and the usual of vanilla.'

'You can't beat that ice cream.' Mike drew out certain syllables like cream and the con in Wisconsin. 'Right, Frankie? Have they got Schwann's back in Wis-connn-sin?'

William didn't know which question to answer so he said he wasn't sure. Mike had a massive serving of the stuff after most of his meals.

'By the way, Mary, one of them calves is cakin' up in the eyes. Better give him a shot.'

'Margaret called this morning,' said Mary. 'She says Dave's doing poorly. It's been six months since his heart attack and he still can't get back to work. They're thinking of leasing out the whole place next year. Maybe movin' into

Mitchell. She wants to know if you might be interested in that eighty this side of the railroad tracks.'

Mike chomped away at his meal and didn't look up.

'She asked if you were still eatin' all that ice cream. Imagine the nerve.'

'She don't like ice cream?' Mike looked at William and giggled.

'She says she noticed you been puttin' on weight. She says she hopes you don't get in the same pickle as her Dave. The nerve.'

Mike's deep-set eyes under brows like swatches of mink fur glanced down at his swelling stomach. 'Maybe I should get thin like Frankie.' A giggle.

'I am afraid I will gain weight on this good food.'

'Whoever's been feedin' you has been pretty skimpy,' said Mary.

'I have a high metabolism rate.'

'Can you take somethin' for that?' said Mike.

'It's not serious.'

'Oh, and y'know,' said Mary, 'Emil Kretchmer finally died.'

'That goddamn cancer,' said Mike, the perpetual smile straightening for a moment.

'He was a good friend to everybody,' said Mary. 'Y'ever lose any good friends like that, Frank?' She looked at William wide-eyed. Her red hair was twisted and tied up on top of her head.

'Yes, quite recently,' he said.

'Man?'

'Yes.'

'How'd he die?'

'Playing basketball,' said William.

'Grown man?' said Mike.

'About forty.'

'That's what I been saying. I see these guys runnin' all over in Sioux Falls. Even in the cold weather. There's even a few in Mitchell. Never saw that years ago. Maybe that's why there's so many heart attacks.'

'The way they want you to eat,' said Mary, looking at

William, 'we'd dry up and blow away. If everybody started eatin' that way we'd be outa business. All we sell is pork and beef.'

Mary Bohas recalled his stepmother to William's mind, especially the piled-up red hair. It was only physical. He remembered no kindness in his stepmother.

'Have some more meat and potatoes, Frankie,' Mike said, reaching for the bowl with a thick-fingered hand.

'Thank you, no.' William forced a smile. 'It is all very wonderful, but very filling too.'

He concentrated on the food and wasn't required to reply to any further questions. He sensed that Mike and Mary were comfortable with a person of few words.

Mike got up from the table. 'Say, Frankie, they're holdin' four sacks of supplement for me at the elevator in Rook. Will you take the truck and pick 'em up, first thing this afternoon? Make Ned put 'em in the truck. They go a hundred pounds apiece, and he won't do it unless y'tell 'im. Lazier than an old dog.'

'I will do it right away,' said William.

'Frankie, ya can take an extra hour. Y'wanta get a cup a coffee in that place west a Rook, or just look around. We ain't got no time clock here.' A giggle.

In spite of the blowing snow, William was glad to get away from the farm. As he approached the abandoned farmstead a mile north of the Bohas place, he pulled into the yard. Tall weeds stuck up out of the fresh snow. Behind the decaying house and in the shelter of the dense grove of leafless trees, tops moving in the icy wind like long bony fingers, he stopped the pick-up. He tuned in a station from one of the colleges. A pianist was playing a Chopin nocturne amid the crackling static. He let the engine idle to keep the heater going.

Two glassless windows on the back of the old house looked at him like the eye sockets in a skull. Had a father fucked his daughter and beaten his boy in this old shack? William thought back on the conversation over the lunch he had just finished. What was the point of these people's lives?

128

They spoke of death as though life mattered. He liked Mike's good nature, something like Slim Olson's. But William couldn't understand why Mike was always laughing and giggling. Was it some sort of aberration? He seemed happy most of the time. Mary didn't; she was more of a brooder. What was happy? William didn't know for sure how it felt. He remembered times of comfort, especially when he was with Wilma, when she was cuddling him and admiring him, his mind and his body, and when he had worked with Alice Wahl. What a head she had for numbers. Beautiful numbers, nearly perfect numbers. What was the point of *his* life? In elementary school he had learned college algebra. It made no impression on his father. Learning meant nothing to him. What was of true import didn't interest the boy; he had no appreciation of the Holy Spirit, no love of Jesus, Konrad Schmid had said. And then tried to beat it into him with a razor strop. Trickery with numbers would not save his soul from eternal fire. The only time his father touched him was when he hit him.

William understood the universe. Mike Bohas barely knew it existed. He sold pork and beef. That was the point of Mike's and Mary's being. As much point as anyone had in living. Food, the *sine qua non* of life. What do I sell? he thought. Students would queue up at registration to get in his classes, but *he* could not exist without Mike Bohas or the equivalent. Mike was the husband of several hundred large animals and more than a thousand acres of fertile land. To Mike pi was something you made out of pumpkins. One of William's physicist colleagues had searched for pi for much of his career, networking with a super computer that cost over twenty million dollars. He knew he would never find it. What does he sell? What point is there to his life? To find the reason was as difficult as finding pi. With the point of one's existence so obscure, why not revenge as the point?

Movement caught William's eye. Through the dirty wind-shield the shape of an owl, like a monk in a black cowl, hunched on a limb deep in the grove. In turns, half a dozen crows swooped down from higher perches to torment the solitary creature, their cries whelmed by the wind and the music.

The pick-up rumbled north toward Rook. Beneath a tide of sullen clouds the color of wet cement, the prairie undulated toward horizons hidden behind wind-swirled snow – ground blizzards, Mike had called them. Fear had taken a seat beside William. The pain, so long absent, was returning. What now? It entered his head like the throb of a primitive drum. *Hoomb, hoomb, hoomb, hoomb, hoomb hoomb.* Wilma would drive to his room near the campus and apply cool cloths to his head and massage his body, and sometimes the throbbing subsided. The psychiatrist Phillips had said it was a symptom of schizophrenia. Phillips had learned of William's recurring pain from Wilma in preparation for the trial. Now William had no medication and no Wilma. As they had planned, she would be waiting for his call tomorrow. She had always answered his call, but once she had hesitated.

He had not had his teaching job at the university very long when one night the aboriginal throbbing had taken possession of his skull. He had struggled with the telephone and finally made the connection.

'Wilma,' he said, 'it has returned.' He knew she would come.

'Is it bad?' A tearful tone in her voice.

'As ever.' The two words squeezed through a burrow of anguish.

'I will come, William, but it will be at least two hours. I promised Tom Phelps I would help him with a party function. I am due there in twenty minutes. I owe him a favor.'

'What favor?'

'Oh . . .' she had stumbled a moment, 'he helped me months ago with something. I will come as soon as it is over.'

What could Tom Phelps have ever done for his twin that William did not know about?

'If you must, you must,' William said, and hung up.

The explosions like mortar fire in his brain usurped his

consciousness. The rest he had learned from Wilma.

William's tone had haunted Wilma on the way to the meeting. She decided that Tom Phelps's needs must yield to her twin brother's. She let herself in with her own key. William lay on the bed, his head encased in a clear plastic bag snugged round his neck with a piece of cord. His eyes were closed and a faint blue cast had replaced the usual pink of his face. She tore the flimsy plastic and forced his lips apart with her tongue. She blew air into his mouth and pinched his nostrils shut. In seconds he coughed and she drew back, looking down into the eyes that had just opened in a stare, each one piercing each of hers as though their function was more than vision.

'Oh, William, my darling, what have you done?' she said.

He seemed incapable of speech and for moments there was nothing but his icy blue eyes.

'Say something to me, William.'

His face contorted to an awful grimace. 'Who are you?' he had asked.

The pick-up continued on its course toward Rook. Inside, the man with the throbbing brain tried to remember his purpose. Oh yes, today it was to fetch four sacks of supplement. A truly transcendent purpose must await its proper time. *Hoomb. Hoomb. Hoomb. Hoomb. Hoomb.*

21

As darkness descended over the city outside her window, Rebecca scribbled notes for a quick memorandum denying a stupid motion for summary judgment. A judge's loneliness had fostered a sanguine reaction to a tap at the door.

'It's open. Come in,' she trilled.

Henry Wheatland, squarish balding head on beefy shoulders, his hand on the knob, pushed the door open and advanced one shiny black wing tip into the room. 'Too busy to talk to an old pal?' Gritty words from a throat rinsed in decades of Jack Daniels.

'Of course not.' Rebecca got up and moved round her desk. 'Come in and sit down.' Trepidation replaced the conditioned flicker of pleasure that had followed the gentle tap on the door. Henry Wheatland, a churlish old party power, had sat on the state Supreme Court for four or five years, resigned for an ill-advised run for Congress, and a couple of years ago had moved to the city to accept an appointment to the district bench. The Governor, in his infinite lack of wisdom, could think of no other place to put him.

'We need to chat, you and me.' He dropped into the gray sofa without waiting to be asked.

Uh-oh. Talking to Henry Wheatland was never enjoyable. Certain groups couldn't be trusted; they wanted to seize power for their own purposes. Individuals were conniving. The opposition was infiltrating. Rebecca returned to her chair. 'What about?' she said lightly.

'Becka, I was wondering why you were so all fired anxious to stay on this Tom Phelps thing.' He began to tap a cigarette out of the pack of Camels.

Only close friends called her Becka, but that was small offense coming from this black belt asshole. 'Judge Wheatland, I don't allow smoking in my chambers,' she said, determined to gain the initiative, plus she couldn't stand the smell the next morning. 'I hope you understand.'

'Oh heavens, forgive me. You haven't got a little nip in the cabinet, perchance?'

'Sorry, no,' said Rebecca. Without tobacco or booze, maybe this would be a short talk.

'About Phelps?' he said.

'Did you read my memorandum?'

'My clerk read it.'

'There was simply no material cause alleged by the defendant to support a claim of bias. They had already passed on one judge as the rules provide. I believe it's my duty to prevent defendants from going down the list until they find somebody they think is favorable to them.'

'I guess you're not favorable to them?'

'Judge Wheatland, I'm not favorable to either side, or unfavorable. Isn't that the way it's supposed to be?'

'What about the Governor's affidavit?'

'The Governor was mistaken.' Wheatland should know that's not a rarity, Rebecca thought.

Wheatland wiggled forward to the edge of the sofa and clasped his knees with long-fingered liver-spotted hands. Elbows encased in dark gray flared like the wings of a hawk. Set under shaggy brows the same flinty gray as the sparse hair slicked back from a high waxy forehead, his steely eyes betrayed no humor. 'Tom Phelps thinks you're out to get him,' he said, and his eroded face said, so do I.

Like bees in a hive, thoughts buzzed around Rebecca's brain. Easy, girl. Remember, keep it win win as long as you can. Who does this sonofabitch think he is? 'I'm sorry he feels that way. It's not true, Judge Wheatland.'

He shook his head, wobbling the rosy wattle hanging under his chin. The lipless mouth pursed. 'I just don't know why a bunch of old friends have to have so much unnecessary trouble.'

She had to ask. 'Does his defense counsel know about your coming here?'

'That clown, Scott? Indeed he doesn't. I don't trust those lawyers far's I could throw 'em. Might use it against me sometime.'

Harry Scott had gotten Wheatland reversed on the first major criminal case that had come before him in this court. From that same trial Wheatland had brought charges against Scott – alleged disrespect. The ethics committee had let him off with a mild letter. Rebecca felt relieved that Harry Scott wasn't in league with Henry Wheatland.

'I can't understand why Phelps is so worried about me. He gets a jury trial.' Rebecca immediately regretted allowing herself to be drawn into the substance of the matter.

'You know, my dear, especially in these so-called date rapes, the judge has a great deal of control.'

He was getting at the rape shield law.

He went on, pushing his granular voice through a resisting throat. 'There will be important rulings on who can testify, and what about, and so on and so forth.'

'I have tried rape cases. I know the law fairly well. I think it's quite clear.' There was something wrong with defending herself to this man. He wouldn't listen anyway.

'Let's get down to brass tacks, Becka. Holiday's comin' up. Interest in the case will die down for a while. After the first of the year, you can reconsider, ask the chief judge to replace you.'

Not in a thousand years, you sonofabitch, came out as, 'It just wouldn't be right, Judge Wheatland. I can't do that. Does he want a man, is that it?'

'No. To calm that fear in the female populace, I think the chief would step in and assign the case to a woman.'

An alarm went off in the hive. Cadwallader. They want to get Phelps to Cadwallader. He'd waive a jury and she'd find reasonable doubt and Phelps would walk. For Christ's sake, Phelps has fucked Cadwallader. He got her appointed. 'Are you thinking of Judge Cadwallader?'

'Whomever the chief judge might choose.'

'As long as it's not me.' To hell with the win win, Rebecca

thought. 'Phelps got Cadwallader appointed.'

'Why, I think that's a very unkind thing to say. The Governor uses his own judgment in these matters, and he has an excellent advisory committee.'

Hacks like you, Rebecca thought, with their hands on somebody's purse strings. She stood up. 'I don't think we should continue this conversation, Judge Wheatland.'

'Calm down a minute, my dear, just hear me out.' He covered his mouth and hacked into a yellowish hand-kerchief.

Rebecca didn't reply, but sat down, knowing she had not heard the worst. Her eyes fell on the framed reproduction of the original Bill of Rights on the wall behind Wheatland. His little hawk eyes bored in with ferocity from square fleshy sockets.

'Becka, I hoped it wouldn't have to come to this, but you know politics. Strange bedfellows and all that crap.' The ferocious face melted to a wide grin followed by a little heh-heh laugh. Her tight mouth prompted him to continue without pause. 'You know I'm pretty close to Chief Judge Waterbury, and he understands politics. The Governor appointed him, same as you 'n' me. And you know he controls who does what around here. Why . . . let me say it as simple as I can, Becka. You stay on this Phelps case, I got a purty good idea who's gonna fill the vacancy on the family court this spring. Whoever it is is gonna be dividing property and listenin' to just how bad it gets for those sad people for a long time. For a very long time, Becka. I think that's a foregone conclusion. Everybody's gotta take their turn, my dear.' Wheatland reached in his pocket, pulled out the pack, tapped out a Camel and lit it. He let his body sag back in the sofa and blew a long stream of smoke at Rebecca. 'You seem to forget how you got here, hon. Now you gonna take the easy way or the hard way?'

Rebecca stood up again, 'Judge Wheatland—'

'Hold it there. I don't want an answer now. Take advantage of the time you have. Don't be too quick. I'll call you after the first of the year.' For his size, he was up quickly

135

and out the door before Rebecca could decide what to say next.

On the other side of the Government Center in the prosecutor's office, Dinah White and Assistant DA Barbara Bird plotted to undo Tom Phelps. Out the window over Barbara's shoulder, Caesar Peli's magnificent Norwest Bank Building, offset upper stories illuminated like a crown, dominated the foreground of downtown.

'We got our fourth call yesterday in this office,' Barbara Bird said, highlights glinting in her blue-black hair.

'What's her name?'

'Jean Daugherty.'

'Doesn't ring a bell.'

'She goes way back. When Phelps was Sigma Chi at the University. She says he sucked her in with the same playful dodge. Promised not to hurt her. Tied her hands and feet to the posters of his mother's bed. He was stark naked when the sound of the automatic garage door opening in the basement scared him and he untied her and put his pants on.'

'Jesus. He hasn't changed in twenty years, the bastard.' Sepia-skinned Dinah White was still angry, but calmer than when she last visited the prosecutor's office. She had the habit of continually moistening her puffy lips with the darting pink tip of her tongue.

'Apparently not. Ms Daugherty claims she remembers it as though it had just happened. She says he was going to rape her, no doubt about it, but when his mother showed up, he claimed he had just been trying to scare her. She's eager to testify. Sounds even a little too eager.'

'Will they let her?'

'It's up to the judge.'

'What do you think?'

'Knowing Rebecca Goldman, I don't think so.'

'Why'n hell not?'

'She'll reason that if he was just trying to scare her, it would be terribly unfair to him to let it in. And it's a long time ago. Boys will be boys, you know, that kind of thing.'

'How about the three who called before, and my two calls?'

'Where there's actual penetration or some kind of harm, I think there's a better chance. But I don't think that's what it's gonna come down to, sister.'

'Spell it out, Barbara.'

'It's gonna come down to your word against his, unless he's got some witnesses we haven't anticipated.'

'I don't know who the hell that would be. You said just 'cause I mighta slept with somebody it's not relevant to this case, right?'

'That's what the rape shield law says.'

'And?'

'We gotta believe Judge Goldman will uphold the statute.'

'Both of the women who called me want to come into court. One says Phelps has affected her whole life.'

'We'll sure interview anyone who contacts us. Whit Strom wants to win this one. We haven't gotten him out from behind that desk in five years, and he's comin' out for this one. But like I say, the ball game is likely to be decided by what the jury hears from your rosy red lips and, of course, Phelps's too, if he testifies. You know he's not required to say a word.'

'I know,' said Dinah White.

22

The Farmer's Co-op elevator stood stark and alone against the gusts of December wind. The pick-up truck rolled to a stop beside the loading dock. Through the ground blizzards beyond the railroad tracks and the highway, Rook remained only scattered shadows. The unremitting throbs of pain in William Schmid's skull drowned out the wind and the idling V-8. His eyes stared straight ahead through the windshield, seeing nothing. *Hoomb. Hoomb. Hoomb. Hoomb.*

Someone knocked on the driver's side window, opaque with steam. 'That you, Mike?' It was Alf Mikkelson's voice. Then his face peered through the windshield. 'Oh, the new guy. I'll get Ned to throw those sacks in the back. Just hang on a minute. This wind'd like to blow me clear outa here.' The face disappeared.

In a couple of minutes the truck sagged slightly under the weight of the first sack of supplement. Then three more. Somewhere down the tracks in the storm the 4:15's whistle wailed through the wind.

A strange voice in a country twang: 'They're all loaded. You got plenty time to get crosst the tracks 'fore that freight gets here.'

William's foot depressed the clutch and pushed the stick shift into first. The truck made a wide turn to where the driveway crossed the railroad tracks. Far to the right the headlight of the locomotive punctured the storm. A west wind carried the blatant whistle ahead of it. The pick-up stopped astraddle the tracks, the train's headlamp a glowing point growing larger on the frosted glass of the passenger side window. The warning whistle blasted a continual staccato. Primeval pain throbbed in William's head. His hand reached forward and turned the ignition off.

'Mary, this is Alf Mikkelson at the elevator. Lemme talk to Mike . . . When will he be back? . . . Geez, it won't keep. There's been a little accident down here . . . No, nothin' too serious. I don't know what happened, but the four fifteen hit your truck . . . Oh, geez no, just barely, shoved it about ten, fifteen feet sideways down the track. The train was fixin' to drop a couple cars on the siding . . . No, I don't think he's hurt much, can't say the same for the truck, prolly ain't worth more 'n junk now . . . He's holdin' his head bent way down and he hasn't said a dang word . . . No, even when he pulled in to pick up that supplement, he never said a dang thing . . . He's sittin' here on the bench but I don't think it'd do no good to give 'im the phone. He won't say a dang thing . . . OK, we'll be here waitin'. I'll see if I can get some hot coffee in 'im . . . Watch them roads. It's lookin' purty icy out there, but not too bad. Gettin' dark awful early. Time you get here, they should have the crossing clear.'

Alf Mikkelson's words were meaningless to William. A new spasm stabbing at his neck united with the throbbing in his skull. The scent of coffee reached his nostrils. Two dirty boots breached his line of vision, still fixed directly on the floor.

'C'mon, Frank, try a little a this. It'll make ya feel better. Don't worry about that old truck. Mike was about ready to trade it anyway. This way he'll be ahead on the *in*-shurnce.'

Alf's words were mere noise in William's grinding brain. The boots moved away; the coffee aroma lingered behind.

'Ya kin lead a horse to water, but ya can't make 'im drink,' said Alf. 'Mary'll be here ta gitcha in a few minutes.'

William stared at the floor, his elbows on his knees, his head cradled in his hands.

Minutes later, after a puff of cold air preceded her through the door, Mary's voice filled the room. 'Oh, poor Frankie. Not to worry. Are you OK, Frankie?'

Her chilled fingers touched his forehead. Wilma? He jerked his head up. Long red hair hung loose about the face. It was the bitch. How did his bitch stepmother find him? He dropped his head, eyes again on the floor.

'Frankie, are you hurt?'

It wasn't the bitch's sound. He listened. He tried to ignore the explosions in his head. The cool hand touched his forehead again. It lifted the wool cap from his head, and petted his hair, just as Wilma had done. The words became more distinct.

'Frankie, should I call the doctor?'

A face and an image of the white jacket with 'Perlman' embroidered in red thread on the pocket merged in William's mind. Not sure why, he shook his head in the negative. She sat down beside him on the bench. The flesh below her hips squeezed out against him. Her arm extended across his shoulders just below the tender spot in his neck.

'Can't you say anything, Frankie?' Her voice was soft, worried.

'He ain't said a word since we led him in here,' said Alf.

'You can hear me, can't you, Frankie?' She pulled him against her.

It felt good.

'Will you come home with me now, Frankie?'

Mary's soft voice soothed, like Wilma's, like his real mother's must have sounded when he was born. His head nodded its assent.

Mary stood up. She reached down and tugged gently on the hand that was supporting his head. 'C'mon now, Frankie,' she said. 'Let's go home.'

He let himself stand.

'S'pose Mike'll be there when you get back,' said Alf Mikkelson.

'I doubt it,' said Mary. 'He went coyote hunting with that darn Kenny Speer.' She pronounced it as the Germans would: Schpeer. 'You know where they go when they get cold.'

'I s'pose I do,' said the old man. 'Over to that saloon in Geddes?'

'You know those guys, Alf. And you know how Mike gets when he goes out with Kenny – stinkin', stinkin' drunk.'

William's shivering body soaked up the hot air of the over-heated farm kitchen.

'Here now, Frankie, let's get that stuff off.'

In front of the big cast-iron stove she helped him with his cap and jacket. Then she held his hand and led him up to the second floor. The bare treads of the narrow stairway creaked under their weight. A pinkish glass ball hanging from the ceiling lit the upper hall. They passed the door of Mike and Mary's bedroom on the left and the bathroom on the right. In the dark of his bedroom at the end of the hall, William sat down on the double bed. The thumping in his head continued unabated. He hadn't said a word since she'd come to the elevator for him. She turned the switch on the bed-table lamp. In the light a picture of Jesus watched from the wall above the headboard. Out in the yard, accompanied by the whine of the wind, the feeder lids dropped heavily as the hogs withdrew their snouts from the troughs.

William dropped his eyes to the floor and cradled his head in his hands. Mary left the room and walked down the hall, her shoes tapping gently on the hardwood floor. In a minute she returned. 'Take these aspirin, Frankie. The way you're holding your head, it must be hurting something terrible.'

He didn't respond. Her cool fingers pressed the tablets against his lips. They became powdery in his mouth. He raised his head and sipped from the glass. One of the tablets stuck in his throat. He reached out and took the glass and drained it, dislodging the pill. As he raised his head, he saw Mary's swelling bosom. The silver medallion resting against the white skin at the scooped neck of her dress redirected a beam of lamplight to his eye. She stood stock still. William stared at the medallion and the beam of light.

'What is it, Frankie? What do you see?'

He stared at the silver stab of light. It moved slightly with the rise and fall of her breathing. His hand came up toward her throat.

She took a step back. 'Frankie, what do you see?'

His hand fell back. The muscles of his face softened. The source of the beam suddenly faded to a disk of gray metal, its quiddity of light gone. His head throbbed.

'Frankie, you must lie down and relax. Let the aspirin work.'

A tear leaked from his eye.

'Oh Frankie, you're crying.' She stepped toward him and wrapped both arms round his head.

Wilma. Wilma. The woman softness lulled the grinding of his brain. The drumming receded some.

She freed one arm and stroked the back of his head, smoothing his hair, letting her hand slide down over the tenderness of his neck. 'Frankie, won't you please say something? I'm very worried. What's happened to you?'

It wasn't Wilma speaking to him, but it was Wilma's body he smelled. William stretched his arms round the woman and held on tightly as the drumming receded.

'That's better, Frankie, you're coming back to life.' She reached back and gripped both his arms and gently tugged at them to free herself.

But William persisted in his embrace, his arms locked firmly round her. Her body stiffened slightly. She leaned back, trying to withdraw her breasts from his face.

'Frankie, you must lie down now.'

He held on, hearing but not heeding, craving the softness of the breasts beneath the thin satiny fabric, inhaling the smell of her body, the smell of Wilma.

'Frankie, you must lie down now.' She spoke more sharply. When she reached behind her with both hands to pry off his fingers, her shoulders drew back, thrusting her breasts forward, two pillows embracing his face. Her strong farm woman's hands and arms finally loosened William's grip. She stepped back.

His arms fell to his sides. Again the lamplight flared from the silver medallion. William focused on the light. Slowly, Mary's right hand moved to the medallion as William stared. She tried tilting it slightly, testing the effect. William's eyes remained transfixed. Her fingers manipulated the medallion,

142

moving its beam across his face, no other movement but the bright point of light. Then she bent her knees, dropping into a crouch, steadying the reflected beam of light into William's eyes. She slowly moved the beam down and toward the head of the bed. He felt his body list steeply to one side. He let his head and shoulders sink to the firm mattress. Now, still in a crouch, Mary moved steadily toward his feet, fingering the medal to keep the light in William's eyes. Her hand grasped his slim ankles. She lifted his legs on to the bed, one at a time. Standing up, she moved toward the head of the bed, the beam still in his eyes. After switching off the lamp, she sat down softly on the bed beside his upper body. She gently pushed on his shoulder. He let himself roll over on his back. Hands, grown warm, reached out, their fingertips resting lightly on his temples. They began a circling motion, slowly rubbing the pain away. Wilma. Oh Wilma. The drumming passed away beneath the dexterous fingers. The female smell was William's last sensation as he drifted into quiet sleep.

23

Two weeks after the visit from Judge Henry Wheatland, Rebecca and Kevin met to eat at a crowded Applebee's just down the street from her building. Through the frosty window by their table a multi-colored galaxy of Christmas lights signaled the season. Huge piles of snow surrounded a parking lot full of cars. Columns of exhaust rose into the eleven below zero night. A fat-faced little waitress poured a splash of white wine into Kevin's glass.

He passed the bouquet under his nose, then took a sip. 'Tastes like Ripple to me,' he said.

'Oh you!' said the girl.

'No, it's just fine, m'dear.'

She filled Kevin's glass then Rebecca's and was gone.

Kevin raised his glass. 'To the holidays.'

Rebecca clinked hers to his and added, 'And a little peace of mind.'

'Devoutly to be wished but seldom achieved by cops or judges,' he said.

Looking at his squarish face, the faint freckles and laughing eyes, Rebecca felt a lightness in her chest. She resisted the compulsion to reach across the table and touch his cheek. Instead she took a folded sheet of paper out of her purse and handed it to him. 'The latest. Henry Wheatland means to keep his promise.'

Kevin mumbled through it. 'Memo, to Judge Goldman, from Cletis Waterbury, Chief Judge. This is to notify you that you are being considered for the position of Judge of the Family Court being vacated by the retirement of Judge Boyer.'

'I would rather sex chickens at a hatchery,' said Rebecca.

'The old fart's a hardball player. Everybody knows that.' Kevin took another sip of wine. 'But he's in a hardball league, Becka. Maybe we can throw 'im a few curves.'

'I don't know what. I can sic Annette Rollins on him in the paper, but these guys are immune to the press. And Wheatland doesn't come up for election until he's reached mandatory retirement age anyway. Speaking of elections, Midge Gobol called me.'

'Who she?'

'Party Central Committee for years. Old buddy of mine. Anyway, she says that some of the smoke-filled room guys have decided to get Jason Delong to run for my judgeship next election.'

'Delong'd be tough to beat. He looks like Billy Graham and thinks like a Baghdad rug merchant. Every union in town owes him.'

'You're telling me,' said Rebecca. 'He'd be impossible to beat. I know they told Midge 'cause they knew she'd tell me right away. They want me off this Phelps case bad.'

'You could always give in.'

'I don't shave, but I still look in the mirror. You wouldn't want me to give in, would you, Kevin?'

'No. I guess I wouldn't. Whatever you want is what I want.'

Above the already loud cacophony of voices, a group started singing 'Jingle Bells' at a table in the back.

Kevin went on, 'You're not gonna let this ruin your holidays, are you?'

'Hannukah was always important to my grandmother Goldman. But my mother almost ignored it.' Her voice went flat. 'And Papa was so busy feeding the Christians during the season, he was hardly ever home. Mama insisted on giving Christmas presents, so I still get Julie a Christmas present. I suppose your family was big on Christmas.'

'Faith and begorra, me mother spent the whole rest of the year planning for Christmas. Four boys and two girls. Took a lot of planning. Funny, though, never expected much. Got way more than we thought we would. Every year. Pop wasn't draggin' down much from the mine. Anyhow, we're not going to let a few little difficulties wreck December for us.'

'God knows,' said Rebecca, 'the weather does a good enough job of that. Either no sun for weeks on end, or when it does come out it's below zero. I thought Milwaukee was bad.'

'By the way, where's my pal tonight?'

'She's out at Wayzata with her friend Monica. They hit it off right after Julie started Breck this past fall. Julie says Monica's family have an outrageously large house right on the lake.'

'She's a great kid,' said Kevin.

'Y'know it's been close to a month and she's still asking questions about Schmid. She thinks he might have got away.'

'The kid's got a good imagination.'

'And there's a writer from Minneapolis-St Paul magazine wants to do a story on the letters.'

'No harm in that, I guess.'

The waitress arrived with their stir fries. They ate quietly in the noisy room for a few minutes. Kevin was the first to speak.

'You aren't still worrying about Schmid?'

'I'll feel better when they find the body,' said Rebecca.

An hour later Rebecca unlocked the door to her dark apartment. Among the bills and greeting cards she had retrieved from her box in the lobby was a business-size white envelope without a return address. Unusual. Even before she removed her coat she snapped on the foyer light, shoved the other envelopes under her arm and tore open the letter. It was neatly typed on cheap white paper. She glanced to the bottom. It was signed 'an interested citizen'.

Dear Judge Goldman,
    One can only suspect that you insist on staying on the Phelps case so that you can railroad him. Everyone knows that the feminists have always hated Tom

146

Phelps, and now you see this as your opportunity to get him. You leave me no alternative. I have learned how your ex-husband died. Somehow the public has overlooked the exposure of you and your child to AIDS. This would make interesting copy. If you are still on the Phelps case come January 5, I will notify the newspaper. I am sure it will make fascinating conversation among your daughter's upper-crust colleagues at Breck school.

Oh Jesus Christ! Now they're dragging Julie into it. They had both been tested three times. The last time three years ago, eleven years after she had had any sexual contact with Reggie. Several doctors had assured her they had nothing more to worry about. It was almost certain that Reggie hadn't been exposed to the virus until after the divorce.

Rebecca hung her coat in the closet. In the living room she dropped on to the sofa without turning on the light. A full moon hung in the cold sky over Lake Calhoun. The fragrance of the popcorn Julie had made the night before lingered in the room. Rebecca felt the tears coming. Thoughtful people sometimes spent lifetimes attempting to divine a purpose to their existence. Not Rebecca. There was no question, not the least ambiguity. Her purpose was to nurture and protect Julie Regina Smith, the light and love of her life. If she really believed this was her purpose, had the time come to withdraw from the Phelps case, to protect Julie?

Was it that simple? This question might come up again. Might? It would. But Julie would be older, maybe through high school. Rebecca knew the district bench would bring controversy. She was used to it. Actually thrived on it. Lawyers live for controversy. But had she ever given any real thought to how her own career might affect Julie? What is protection? And from what do you protect?

The tears had dried up. Rebecca was processing the problem much as she would a decision to be made on one of her cases. To protect a child from every unfriendly possibility was to protect the child not at all. Adolescents must experience the negatives. They must learn to deal with them as they arise. Such things aren't learned from books. One must feel pain, and accept it. It all came down to where you drew the line. Obviously, she would never allow her daughter to wander through the city at night to learn the pain of rape. But ridicule and gossip came with the territory of a young woman, especially a young black woman in this culture, with ambition, whose mother was a judge. Rebecca reflected back on the process. What were the inputs she used in decision-making as a judge? Evidence. One must first hear all the evidence. In this case she had heard only her own ideas. Julie must be heard. In a custody case, all judges would want to hear from a child of Julie's years. She would talk to her after the holidays.

24

A chaotic and formless sleep, full of unclear images and portentous shadows descended upon William Schmid's brain. At least his enigmatic dreams were without pain. Now, he sank in billows on a mammary sea grasping at dangling tendrils of coarse hair – probably red, but his dreams only hinted at color. Gummy nipples protruded from dark aureoles. Somewhere among them a spot of intense light beckoned, coming and going like those beacons on towers that warned away pilots in the dark. From nowhere came ranks of base ten numbers; then, glimpses of the face of Alice Wahl. The numbers were replaced by his stepmother's slitty eyes above bulbous breasts that became thighs meeting at the crevice of her vagina, all dissolving into clots of coarse pubic hair. Craving Wilma, he searched the corners of the dream screen but could find no trace of her. The blinking beacon returned, superimposed on the benign smiling face of Mary Bohas looking at him through smudgy glass. William awakened to the small dark room. Mary Bohas was sitting on the edge of his bed, her silhouette back-lit by the hall light beyond the open door.

'Mary, is that you?' he said. Lying on his side, he raised his head and shoulders, then braced himself on his elbow.

'Yes, it's me, Frankie. Those are your first words in hours and hours. Except I thought you said Wilma or something like that a couple of times in your sleep. Why wouldn't you talk before?'

'I am afraid I do not remember why.' He fought to orient himself, to recall coming into this room. He remembered only their lunch and stopping up the road at the old

Anderson place and the crows and the owl and the virtuo-so's rendition of the Chopin. Nothing since then. How did she come to be sitting on his bed? As if by instinct, he reached toward her neck with his free hand. His fingers touched metal.

'Oh, you remember my medallion?'

He didn't. 'Yes, I do,' he said.

'I'm glad you remember something.'

'Where's Mike?' he heard himself ask.

'He's still out with Speer. It's after one in the morning.'

'How long have I been sleeping?'

'I don't know for sure. Maybe four hours. Does your head feel better?'

'Oh yes, my head is fine.'

'It must have been terrible before.'

He remembered no pain. 'Oh, sometimes I get severe headaches.'

'I think the aspirin helped.'

'Yes, I'm sure it did.'

Outside in the faint whistling of the dying wind the Bohas dogs commenced yapping.

'That's probably Mike. Finally come home,' Mary said.

She stood up and moved toward the rectangle of light behind her, hesitated a moment then returned to the edge of the bed. She leaned over. First he felt the cool touch of her fingers on his face, then the warm moisture of her lips on his forehead.

'Good night, Frankie,' she said. 'I'm glad you're feeling better.'

'Thank you very much. Yes, thank you very much,' said William. She closed the door behind her. Outside, in the South Dakota blackness, the dogs stopped barking.

After Mary left the room he fought frantically to conjure forth something of what had happened the previous after-noon and evening. Nothing emerged. Suddenly, he heard the raised voice, but not the words, of Mike Bohas. It was the first time William had heard anything but Mike's pleasant monotone. In between, Mary's soprano was barely audible. William strained to sort the words from the wind.

A few came through: truck . . . little bastard . . . fucking train . . . can't get hands. The voice fell to a level below any chance of William hearing. They would hear his feet if he moved to a better vantage point.

The door at the bottom of the stairs creaked open. 'Quiet now, don't wake Frankie,' said Mary in a stage whisper.

'I s'pose he'll—'

'Quiet,' said Mary.

William lay in the dark, listening. Their feet creaked up the stairs. Their bedroom door closed. After a few scraping sounds and two flushes of the toilet, Mike's voice danced through the darkness, falsetto sputtering drowned by the wind. Then Mary's voice above the wind, shrill, angry: 'You keep your hands off me. The only time you touch me is when you're drunk!'

For a long time William waited for more. There was nothing but the silence and the wind, and when the wind lapsed, the metallic clunking of the hog feeders. The ten-hour gap in his life plagued him. At intervals a steadily growing light glowing through frosty glass appeared on the black screen of his brain. Once or twice the bright blinking light from his dream faded in and out. He remembered the testimony of Dr Phillips. Goddamn Scott had pressed so hard for the so-called insanity defense. It's a way to win, he had said. But winning meant nothing to William. He wanted his punishment limited. It should have been no more than second degree murder. He knew he had not planned to kill Alice. If the case had been presented correctly, the jury would have understood. But no, Scott knew best. According to Tom Phelps, Harry Scott was supposed to be the very finest defense lawyer. And Wilma said she knew Tom would know best. It was Tom Phelps who had persuaded Scott to take the case. Hard Head Harry Scott, Phelps had called him, as if he was some kind of friend of his. William never knew why Phelps had been so helpful. Total blank spots in the memory when taken together with everything else were symptoms of the paranoid schizophrenic, Dr Phillips had testified.

Later, in the darkness of the small room, William felt a

tingling in his groin and a craving for his sister and for the feel of another human being's flesh. He turned over on his stomach and reached out to the bed table. From the drawer he withdrew the knife. He closed his fingers tightly round the bone handle. With his other hand he found his hardening penis.

25

Shaggy auburn hair framed Tom Phelps's face on the silk pillow case. Lying on his back his face didn't look so fat and jowly. A trumpet riffed on the stereo as Wilma's fingertips glided through the profusion of hair on his chest. 'William is alive, you know,' she said.

Startled, he raised his head off the pillow to look at her face. Her head was propped up by one arm, her elbow planted against his rib cage. Her eyes remained focused on his thick torso. 'Baby, that's a nice thought for Christmas Eve, but it's hardly likely.'

After a downtown dinner they had returned to Phelps's apartment. Now, she let her slim fingers wander into his navel. She turned her head and her blue eyes widened. Her dark blonde hair hung long and loose over her shoulder and on the upper part of her arm. 'I talked to him yesterday,' she said, her tone flippant.

'At a seance,' he said with a little laugh. Phelps resisted the impulse to sit up. He didn't want to break the mood and she had to be teasing him. She had seemed unusually ebullient at dinner, the first time in a month that she had even smiled at him. Her smooth hand glided back up across his chest. The musky fragrance of recent sex permeated the bed, the taste on his newly-grown mustache.

'No, not at a seance, my sweet. On the telephone.' Her voice had turned serious.

'What the hell are you talking . . .' He started to push himself into a sitting position. But her hand had reached his neck and she pushed him back down and pressed her index finger gently against his lips.

'Let me tell you, Tommy,' she said.

He felt the fine hairs on his neck and upper arms move on their own. His whole body tingled. She rolled on to him and settled her nude form on top of his, full length. Straightening her arms, she pushed herself up above him with her knees on either side of his hips. Some slack flesh drooped from the bones of her face, making her look older. Her eyes, fixed on his, seemed to have retreated into their little nests of flesh.

'He didn't drown, Tommy,' she said. 'He is alive. I heard his voice just yesterday. Of course, I knew he was alive when there was no mention of finding the other car.'

Other car. Phelps didn't know what she was talking about.

'It was all arranged. He would call me on December twenty-third. There's a cubicle with a direct line in the law library at the railroad. I made sure it was locked yesterday morning. Then I went in there on my break at ten. He was always so precise. The phone rang at five after. And it was him. He sounded good.'

Phelps had been so goddamn glad Schmid had died in the escape. For many reasons. Especially since he had provided Wilma with the fucking cyanide. He never knew how she intended to use it, but who would believe that? He just couldn't resist her. Others had come and gone, but Wilma was always there ready to ply her skills. She had written the book on sex. Phelps knew she didn't really care a lick about him. But she delivered, and she seemed to hate every other man in the world except her dear brother. The psycho sonofabitch. Phelps lay still, dumbfounded. Did he even want to hear any more?

'He said he was fine. And he's going to call me again.' The loose flesh drew back in a broad smile, showing bright teeth and her upper gums.

Her nipples brushed his chest as she let her body slide down along his and dropped her head into the hollow of his neck and shoulder. He had loved the abundance and texture of her hair, but now he barely noticed the strands that fell over his face. 'Where the hell is he?' Phelps blurted.

'He didn't say.'

If Wilma knew, she probably wouldn't tell him. She lied with impunity. Goddamn. If he hadn't gotten her the cyanide, this would be his ticket out of the rape mess. He could give them both Wilma and William and he could plea bargain his way to a suite at the Ritz. But with the cyanide in the picture he could forget a plea bargain. Maybe he should talk to that hotshot Scott.

One breast compressed against the side of his chest. 'What *did* he say?' Phelps asked.

'I told him I would go to him, but he said no. He said that his time was soon up, that he would see me soon, but that he wanted to get them before they got him.'

'What does that mean?' Phelps asked.

'He means to kill the judge and maybe Harry Scott. He's obsessed with the idea. He won't listen.'

Phelps decided to test her. 'Maybe you should call the cops.'

'I would die before I'd turn my brother in,' she said into the side of his neck.

'We've gotta think this thing through,' said Phelps. Images and thoughts passed through his mind like a video tape on fast forward. After he had heard about the escape and the two murders, neither one of them had ever mentioned the cyanide. But it inhabited Phelps's mind like a mantra, an unspoken element in all their talk and all their intimacy. Rape was one thing. He had gotten away with several . . . but murder . . . The same feelings gripped his body and fluttered around his insides as the time when he had flown home in a lightning storm. The plane had bounced around like a leaf in the wind. Many of the passengers were yelling and puking, and cups and food were flying around the cabin. For a few minutes death had lurked just minutes away. But that had all subsided with the coming of smooth air. Now, would the fear ever go away?

'There's nothing I can do,' said Wilma, 'unless he lets me go to him. Then maybe I can take him far away. Maybe another country . . . Tommy, could you get some money?'

'Of course,' Phelps said, grabbing for any reprieve.

'It's very unlikely that I can dissuade him from coming here, but if I could, we would need a lot of money.'

'I'd get it some way.' He truly didn't know how, but he meant what he said. 'When is he going to call again?'

'The Wednesday after New Year's. He wants more information.'

'What kind of information, for Christ's sake?'

'I've been watching Rebecca Goldman. Some of her comings and goings.'

'Wilma, don't, please don't.' The panicky sensation prickling his inner core, having subsided for just seconds, returned in full measure. 'And what possible benefit—'

'William wants to know the details of her movements.'

'My God. If you get involved, they'll put you away for ever.' Involved. Shit, she's already involved. In it up to her ass and so am I, Phelps thought. She had to have been in on that escape. At least the cyanide. Felony murder. If someone died during the commission of a crime, all involved were charged with murder.

'He's my brother, my beloved brother,' Wilma said. 'I have argued with him, but I am all he has. And what he wants me to do, I must do. And you must know, I'm already involved. You gave me the cyanide.'

The word was finally uttered. The first time since the escape. As he had done every day since, Phelps remembered the bold face type: TWO DIE OF CYANIDE POISONING. A lot of money. Jesus Christ, she had set him up to draw him into the whole thing. Felony murder, him as well as Wilma. It wasn't just doing her a favor. She had wanted him in. She had been thinking about the money all along. She could have got the cyanide herself. You could get it from any jeweler. Just that one fucking pellet. Thank God he had picked it up in Chicago. He had almost asked Bill Backus for it and Bill was a party regular; Bill knew that he and Wilma were tight. The cops would have been knocking on the door the day the article on the escape hit the newspapers.

'Sure, I understand, William means a lot to you,' Phelps said. He had to be careful.

'More than anything,' she said.

Just visible in the dim light, a tiny spider crawled across the ceiling. He should never have got that crazy prick that job at the university. But Wilma hadn't asked much. Everybody wanted something from the Governor's right-hand man. It was the least he could do for her. She had provided him with every conceivable pleasure for years. She never saw anyone else. Funny though, the students had loved Schmid's classes. The department head had even called and thanked him for the referral. Now he needed to get her the money and keep that psycho away from the city. Fat chance. The cops must be watching her every move. But why should they? They thought the sonofabitch was dead. Everybody thought he was dead.

Phelps let Wilma pull on his jaw and turn his face toward her. She kissed him lightly on the lips. The record on the stereo had stopped. Phelps lay absolutely still, his mind racing, the demons skittering around his insides. Her kisses stirred him not in the least. He felt as if he'd had his last hard-on. He might as well hear the details. 'What did you mean when you said "the other car"?'

'We left another car a few miles downstream from Wolf River,' Wilma said.

'We!' Phelps shouted.

'I couldn't move all those cars around by myself.'

'Then the cops must know there were at least two people involved beside your brother. Who the hell helped you?'

'My stepmother. But don't forget they don't know about the car that was parked down the river.'

'Where is your stepmother now?'

'She's been living in Eau Claire for the last several years. She keeps house for some old man.'

'Have the cops talked to her?'

'I don't think they know where she lives. A few years ago I told Dr Perlman – he was William's psychiatrist at Wolf River – I told him she was alive.'

Phelps got out of bed and headed into the bathroom.

Wilma raised her voice over the sound of his tinkling stream. 'He wanted to ask me some questions about

William's relationship with our stepmother.'

Back-lit by the light over the bathroom sink, Phelps stood in the bathroom door, pulling a robe on.

'What'd you tell him?'

'William had warned me never to talk about our step-mother with Perlman. I told him that I had told everything to the psychiatrists when William's case was tried. He should check the records. I told him it was upsetting to me to dig up the past, and of course it was.' Wilma had taken a sitting position against two large pillows pushed up against the head of the brass bed, just the bedsheet over her knees.

Phelps lit a cigarette.

'Tommy, you know what the smoke does to me,' Wilma said.

'I'm sorry. I forgot. I really need one. I'll go out on the balcony.'

On the balcony, Phelps shivered and pulled the thick terry robe tightly round him. There was a gentle breeze from the south and it was warm for Christmas Eve. Close to forty. The streets far below were almost empty. Usually you could see thousands of cars moving all over the city this early in the evening. He sucked hard on the cigarette and edged up to the railing and looked straight down. From thirty floors up it could be over in an instant. He had stood in this exact spot and thought about it the night he was released on bail after his arrest for the rape of Dinah White. But not seriously. He could beat the White thing. The only glitch had been that goddamn Rebecca Goldman. With Judge Amy Cadwallader on the case, it would be in the bag. With the Governor's suspension lifted he'd be back at his old job the day after the trial. But old Goldie. He had always wanted to get in her pants, and she wouldn't even pass a cordial word with him.

Now, the rape case seemed like a hundred years ago. He was looking at murder. His whole future, even his very life, depended on the whims of that psycho Schmid, and his twin sister lying thirty feet away, waiting for him to finish his cigarette. He lit another and glanced down thankfully at the sheepskin slippers Wilma had given him for Christmas.

William Schmid would be very displeased if he knew he had been fucking his sister for almost ten years. Wilma had always said not to let William get any idea they were at all close. He was very jealous, she said. Now Schmid was coming to town to kill Goldman and Harry Scott. If Goldman were dead, I wouldn't need Scott, Phelps mused. But in a second it occurred to him that Scott might be more important now than before. The whole escape episode might eventually envelop him in a cyanide mist of his own. He would need the best lawyer he could find.

Phelps looked straight down again. It was as though he was already falling. All that remained was the collision with the ground. But that was not for him. At least not for now. He meant to survive and didn't intend to give up his place at the Governor's right hand without a fight. But what control did he have left? It was all up to Schmid, or even Wilma, or Goldman, or Scott, or some fucking jury. One thing was sure: he might survive the rape case intact, but no way could he survive being implicated in the Schmid escape and attendant murders. Even if he found Schmid and killed him, there would be Wilma and maybe even the fucking stepmother. But Wilma and her stepmother had a lot to lose too. What *was* certain was that William Schmid needed to be dead.

Phelps heard the movement of the sliding glass door. 'Aren't you getting cold out here?' Wilma said.

He realized he was shivering. He turned to see her standing naked in the open doorway.

26

Kevin had spent Christmas up north with his mother. Rebecca missed not seeing him for almost a week. Since the eerie trip to Wolf River on Thanksgiving Day, rarely a day had passed when they hadn't at least talked on the telephone. They had met for lunch and dinner and drinks several times. She had taken him to a play at the Guthrie and he had invited her to a Christmas party where she was the only person present who was not either a cop or married to one. Best of all, he and Julie had become truly fond of each other, even though she persisted in calling him Knuckles. Hasn't Knuckles made any moves on you yet, Mom? Julie had asked just last night. What's the matter with him? Rebecca told her it was none of her business, but admitted to herself that she was a little surprised at Kevin's reserve in such matters.

Kevin had spent much of December working with the State Crime Bureau's investigation of the Schmid escape. He was convinced that it was Wilma who had dropped the car for Schmid, and he had questioned her twice since Thanksgiving night. All they could prove was that she had apparently kept it in running condition and paid the annual storage and license fees. Was there a law against that? she had asked.

The car Schmid crashed into the Wolf River had been moved to a police garage in St Paul. With three days left in the year, Rebecca had accepted an invitation to spend her evening with Kevin looking at the wreck. He had been over it before, but this was the first time with a Chevrolet mechanic.

'Judge, meet Tony Lombardo,' Kevin said.

'Rebecca Goldman.' Rebecca held out her hand. 'Glad to—'

'Knuckles has told me a lot about you, your honor.' Tony looked like Klinger in *MASH*, the same black frizzy hair and hawk-like nose. 'It's a pleasure.' He held out a dirty hand and snatched it back. 'On second thought, we better skip the handshake tonight.' He wiped both hands futilely on his coveralls.

Rebecca felt the heat in her face that she feared references to Kevin talking about her would always bring. Listening to his inventory of her anatomy as she had hidden behind the door wasn't something she would forget.

'Tell Judge Goldman what you told me on the phone,' said Kevin.

'Better I show you,' said Tony.

Rebecca thought of him in a pink evening dress, the last garment she had seen Klinger wearing in *MASH*. She and Kevin followed him to the car, illuminated by floodlights on tripods at each corner. It was a dark green station wagon. There were long scrapes through to the bare metal along the driver's side and the hood was buckled almost double.

'We've gone over this thing for the last week in minute detail,' Kevin said, pushing the dark forelock back off his forehead. 'The idea is to come up with something, anything connecting it to Wilma on the day of the escape. You know she doesn't deny having contact with the car over the years, so her prints wouldn't prove a thing. But we didn't find any prints other than William Schmid's anyway. Everybody with any connection to that storage lot has been questioned. Nobody saw the car leave. I suppose they were all home for Thanksgiving.'

'Did you find anything?' Rebecca asked.

'Well, I don't know, but there's one thing that's a little strange.' Kevin looked at Tony and motioned toward the car. 'Show her.'

Tony pulled open both doors on the driver's side and dragged the floodlights in close. 'See, the back of the driver's seat is broke.'

Kevin stepped back and let Rebecca get her head in the back door on the driver's side. The back of the driver's seat lay down almost flat against the rear seat. Rebecca drew her head out of the car. 'Couldn't the impact have broken the seat?'

'Well, your honor,' Tony said, 'all the force should have been to the front. The sergeant tells me, and you could tell anyway by looking at the front end, that the car plowed through the railing and dove down into the river head first, I mean front end first.' He was squinting against one of the floodlights. 'The driver's body would have flown forward against the seat belt which I guess was hooked up 'cause he didn't crack the windshield. He did crack the steering wheel a little, but that was probably 'cause he was squeezin' it very tight, like this.' Tony extended his arms toward Rebecca, his two clenched fists slightly canted toward each other. 'Ya follow?'

Rebecca nodded.

'For the seat to have broke in the crash like that, something would have had to push back on it and shear off the bolts that hold it in the upright position. In this kind of a wreck there wouldn't be much impact against the seat by the driver's body because it's getting jolted forward. See what I mean? And none of what was left of those bolts or nuts were in the car.'

'Couldn't they have fallen into the river?'

'It's possible,' said Kevin, 'but an expert has looked at the car. He thinks the car moved around a lot in the current. He says big rocks made those gouges on this side and the car settled on the passenger side. He says that Schmid's body went out the driver's side window or otherwise the door opened and shut while the car was in the river. It's not too likely that those broken bolts and nuts would have all gotten out of the car. As a matter of fact, there were a couple of other bolts and nuts lying around loose that were still in the car.'

Rebecca asked the same question she had asked that night and many times since. 'Kevin, couldn't he have swum to shore and crawled up the bank?'

He gave her a patient look. 'It was below zero. Another expert said soaking wet he would have died in a few minutes. There was no shelter anywhere near that he could have gotten into, and even if there was, it would have had to be heated or he would have died anyway. The current is swift. Our guy calculated that he could not have reached shore before the first bend two hundred and seventy-five yards downstream.'

Rebecca's heart raced. She could remember how cold she got standing on the bridge in a heavy coat for five minutes.

'And of course,' Kevin said, 'the sheriff had men combing the banks for a half-mile downstream within an hour. But the clincher is the weather. Old Wojihowsky saw the car go through the rail with Schmid in it, and there was a light dusting of snow on the bridge with no foot tracks around.'

Rebecca had heard it all before. It stood to reason Schmid had drowned, but she remembered what Julie had said: I'll believe he's dead when I see the body.

'And the next morning search teams combed the river banks for miles,' Kevin went on.

'But it snowed a lot that night,' said Rebecca.

'I know,' said Kevin.

'It would have covered everything up.'

'Yeah, it would.'

Rebecca looked back at Tony. 'Did you find anything else?'

'Nothing out of the ordinary.'

The Minneapolis night skyline loomed off to the right as they crossed the I-94 bridge over the Mississippi. Rebecca had never learned where St Paul ended and Minneapolis began. It was snowing again and traffic had slowed to a creep. Although Kevin had tried to change the subject several times, they were still rehashing William Schmid's escape.

'No matter how you cut it,' Kevin said, 'after a month all we've got is Wojihowsky's eyewitness statement and the unusual condition of that seat. It's embarrassing.'

'And still nothing on how he got the cyanide?'

'You'd be the first to know, but there's no doubt in my mind he got it from Wilma. Other than the attorney who handled the appeal three or four years ago, she's the only visitor he ever had, and it's hard to believe there's any chance a hospital employee might pass cyanide to an inmate. But not impossible. And, of course, a visitor of another inmate could have brought it in. It would take a thorough body search to find one capsule. Even then you could miss it. We have methodically checked all visitors and employees who have had access to the hospital within the past year.'

'What next?'

'I guess the hospital employees' union or organization or something is planning to post a substantial reward. That might bring somebody out of the woodwork. By the way, Becka, any news on the Wheatland thing?'

'We're less than six weeks to trial in the Phelps case, and nothing has changed. The die is cast. I'm heading for family court and then all the way out at the next election. They'll spend the money to do it. Annette Rollins tells me Jason Delong likes the thought of running against me.' The whole idea gave her a miserable feeling.

'You could always give 'em what they want,' Kevin said.

'Not really. Even if I were so inclined, which I'm not, I couldn't function as a judge again. Worse is how I'd feel about myself. And how my daughter would feel about me.'

'You told her about the threatening letter?'

'She didn't consider it a threat. "Let them tell everybody," she said. "I loved my daddy and there's nobody can change that," she said. Julie wouldn't stand for me caving in.'

'I got an angle,' Kevin said. 'Might come to nothing.'

'What're you thinking about, Sergeant?'

He didn't reply. The windshield wipers cut neat arcs across the white glass.

'C'mon, Kevin, tell Mama what's going on in that manly head.' It was the most intimate tone she had ever used on him.

'Not just yet.'

She was surprised when he pulled up under the awning at Lake Vista. She had thought he would head into the visitors' parking. He turned toward her. The eyes were talking again. Give me a little space on this one. I really care what happens to you.

'I thought we could have some coffee,' she said. 'I bought a German chocolate cake.'

'I've gotta see somebody before it gets too late.'

She unsnapped her seat belt and leaned across the center console, her hand pressing against the back of his head. Pulling his lips down to hers, she held him there for several seconds, then quickly jumped out of the car. She leaned down and looked back in the door. 'I never did like bucket seats,' she said.

27

The gray days of Christmas had come and gone from the Bohas household without leaving much joy in their wake. Mike and Mary had presented William with a new pair of buckskin gloves. He thanked them extravagantly and apologized for not having got them something in return.

Mike had gone coyote hunting with Speer several more times, staying out very late. Sometimes on the morning after, the dun carcass of a coyote would be hanging in the machine shed, its fur deep and thick and lovely to the touch. Two days after Christmas the two of them left early in the morning on a hunting trip for elk near Yellowstone Park, hundreds of miles to the west. There was a special season for the huge creatures because the snow was so deep they were in danger of starving. As Mike took his rifle from its cabinet in the entry hall he asked William whether he could handle things around the farm for about a week. He ended with a little giggle. William said he was sure he could. He had already told Mike several times before.

Moments later, just the tail lights of Mike's new truck were visible as he headed out of the yard to pick up Speer. A light touch on his shoulder made William jump and catch his breath. Mary had come up behind him.

'You startled me. I did not know you were up. It is not yet five.'

Her carroty red hair hung loose around the shoulders of a green and white gingham robe. She had touched up her lips with a bit of rose gloss. She looked as if she had been up for hours, but she hadn't come downstairs to say goodbye to Mike.

'Well, he's on his way to pick up that darn Speer,' she said. 'I don't like that man.'

William chose not to reply.

'Frankie, do you want a cup of coffee? Mike left some on the stove.'

'That would be nice,' he said.

'And I'll fry you up some eggs and some links. OK?'

'OK.'

'You know, Frankie, your mustache is growing out nicely. You look so distinguished.'

William stammered a thank you and sat down at the round oak table. No matter how much dye he put on his mustache, he couldn't get it as dark as his hair. A little of Mary's mascara had done the trick. He would have to get a tube of his own.

Soon the fat was crackling in the pan. He loaded his coffee with sugar and a little milk. It tasted good and the warmth in his stomach countered the chill. The corncobs burning in the old cast-iron stove were just starting to heat up the large room. With her back to him in the gingham and with her long red hair she looked like his stepmother had thirty years ago. Except now it was nice to know that his father would not be stomping into the room looking for his breakfast.

The day broke warm and sunny. William drove the immense green John Deere to the place where Mike stored hay for the winter season. The big round bales, flat on two sides, weighed about half a ton each. A pincers-like attachment on the front of the tractor grabbed the bale in its mechanical jaws. William drove it over to the cattle yard. Almost a hundred cows stood behind the gate, loudly lowing in antici-pation. After dropping the bale over the gate, William let himself inside. With a pitchfork he separated the tightly compacted hay. Then he spread it out across the frozen mud, roughly textured with the hoof prints of the heavy animals. The condensation from their breath collected in little clouds that quickly disappeared in the light breeze. He inhaled great lungfuls of the cold air laced with the acrid smell of fresh manure. William's back ached and his nostrils filled with dust from the hay. Yet there was a certain pleasure in feeding these gentle brutes, their amber and white bodies illuminated by the rising sun.

They crowded close to munch the freshly spread hay. A group of younger ones fenced in on the other side of the barn bellowed in protest. To satisfy their hunger William began the procedure all over again. When he was done, it was time to feed the hogs, as he had been doing every day since he arrived almost a month ago.

The hog feeding was his regular job. It sapped his strength, but he approached it with resignation. He stopped for a moment in the shed out of the growing wind. The vast winter whiteness of the South Dakota plain reached toward the horizon to the south. Without Mike scurrying around the yard, he felt a serenity and a certain worth. William had always been a student or a teacher or an inmate. He had never really worked enough to make his muscles burn and to blister his hands and feet. He found the pain completely tolerable, so different from the intolerable pain that had been his life. If this one morning, this one day, could represent the whole of his existence, he thought he could accept it. If for some reason Mike did not return, he could imagine staying here with Mary. Perhaps if enough time passed Wilma might even come to visit. Perhaps all concerned would go on believing he was dead. But Mike *would* return and he would not keep him as a farm hand. None of these farmers would. William had overheard enough giggling comments about his weakness and his ignorance of their ways. But Mike was wrong. William knew he could pull his own weight in this environment, given the time.

He could rebuild one of the wrecked farmsteads that dotted the landscape for hundreds of miles. He would make it the finest house anywhere. He might even get a wife to live there with him and they could raise cattle and hogs and even children. And he would build a huge stone fireplace covering a whole wall and he would go to the river bottom and cut firewood and keep a fire blazing all winter. If only they would leave him alone. He knew he could do it and a lot more.

He picked up the heavy pail and emerged from the shed. Mary was coming across the yard in her woolen jacket, checked in red and black like one Slim Olson used to wear in the spring.

'Frankie, wait a minute. Let me help with the hogs.'

'The pails are way too heavy for you,' William said.

'Let me just help you with the ones you carry.' She grabbed hold of the steel handle.

Grunting hogs with log-like black backs milled around the feeders, clunking the lids with their noses. When they dumped their last pail, the sun had climbed almost as high in the southern sky as it was going to that December day.

'Frankie, you have earned a good lunch and I mean to give it to you,' Mary said. 'You come on in now and relax. Maybe you'd like to watch some television while I cook.'

'There is more work to do,' said Frankie.

'It'll keep until this afternoon or even tomorrow. You don't have to work yourself to death while Mike and that Speer are out loafing.'

In her sweet soprano she sang 'Oh Come All Ye Faithful' as he followed her to the house, the two black and white border collies sniffing at his heels.

She took his jacket and sat him down in the living room and turned the TV on for him. 'Now you get comfortable,' she said, as she handed him the remote control.

William flipped through the channels and stopped at a Sioux Falls newscast. The talking head didn't reach him as he stared at the ceiling, again thinking of having his own house and his own woman, one just like Mary. He thought of his telephone call to Wilma just three days ago. How she had pleaded with him to let her come to him. Of course, they would be watching her. Even if they were totally convinced he was dead, they would be watching her. They would try to punish her for her complicity in his escape. The tangy fragrance of a frying pork chop drifted into the room. He must wait until he was ready, but not too long. For today, he was content to be what he was.

'Soup's on,' Mary called.

William dragged himself out of the big soft chair, his joints and muscles stiff and sore. In the kitchen he washed his hands in the sink and sat down. Mary had set out her good china. The center of the round table was covered with steaming dishes: potatoes, carrots, pickles, biscuits, a boat of gravy, a leafy salad, a casserole of green beans and mushrooms, and a platter of pork chops. No one, not even Wilma, had ever laid out a meal like this just for William Schmid.

She leaned over his shoulder to pour his coffee. Her long hair gently tickled his ear. She had set her place just partway round the table from him. She bowed her head to say grace and William watched and thought she was beautiful. She rose from her chair to hand him each dish of hot food and to insist he try everything. She had a surprise for him when he was finished, she said.

William ate with relish. They talked about the morning's chores, and the cows and the hogs, and how William planned to have the whole machine shed picked up and organized by the time Mike returned. But William was mostly quiet.

The subject of Speer deepened the vertical groove between Mary's eyebrows. 'Kenny Speer spent twenty years in the army right out of school,' she said.

Although William had been in the same room with him more than once, Speer had never said a word to him. William liked it that way.

'Mike and him were friends in high school. Kenny would come round now and then over the years when he was home on leave, but they never exchanged one letter. Then two years ago when he comes back he starts hanging around Mike like he'd never been gone. Mike just dropped his other friends. He used to do a lotta things with Eugene and Sonny. They're nice guys, good family men. But they weren't drinkers and Mike likes to drink with Kenny Speer. They got in trouble in high school for drinking. Then Mike goes twenty years with hardly more than a beer now and then and a little wine at Christmas. Maybe some harder stuff at weddings. But nothing like the last year, especially the last few months. After he got that job on the blasting crew, Kenny had lots of extra money to spend, with his army pension and all. Seems like he's spending it all on booze and running around. Takin' Mike with him whenever he can.'

'Blasting crew?' said William.

'Yes, I guess in the army he learned all about explosives, nitro and dynamite, that kind of thing. Mike says he keeps cases of the stuff in his barn. Like ta blow the whole farm away, Mike says, if he ain't careful. Damn fool. I can't say as I'd care much.'

Mary ignored her food, but William ate heartily. Dynamite. He remembered studying the principles, how explosives worked, what made them do what they do. They were hard for the layman to come by. For most kinds, he thought, you needed some kind of a permit to buy and store them. He paused to look at Mary's face, the smoothness of her pinkish skin, the fullness of her lips. Her eyes met his whenever he permitted her the opportunity. He wished she would smile like she had so many times this morning. But her anxious face indicated she had to talk about Speer.

'And one of the worst things about the man – you know how dirty and smelly he is – he's always walking right in without even knocking, even when Mike's not here, even when he *knows* Mike's not here. Like that day Mike went to pick up his new truck and you rode along to drive the car back. I heard Mike on the telephone. He told Kenny that you guys were going to Mitchell to get the truck. An hour after you're gone he shows up here. I was upstairs hanging those new curtains and up he comes. I didn't hear him on the stairs. I concentrate so hard when my mind is on something I'm trying to do right. I almost jumped right through the window and I says, Kenny you scared me half to death. I wish you wouldn't do that, and he just laughs and leans on the door and tries to start a conversation. I just went in the bathroom and locked the door. I stayed in there until I heard him go down the stairs. Then I saw him get in his truck and go. Now, Frankie, you eat another pork chop.'

She reached over and dropped it on his plate. 'I told Mike as soon as he got home. He just laughed and said Kenny don't mean no harm.' She paused, looking at William, apparently expecting some comment.

He couldn't afford to have anything negative he might say about Speer repeated to Mike. But anger did intrude on his good feelings of the day. 'This is the finest meal anyone has ever prepared for me. I thank you very, very much.'

He got his smile. 'Oh, you're so entirely welcome, Frankie. I think it's been nice having you around here, and you try very hard in your work. You deserve good food. Maybe I can put a little weight on your bones.' She giggled and stood up and went to the refrigerator. When she turned round she had a pie in her hands with meringue a couple of inches high. 'You told me lemon pie was your favourite so here you are, just for you.' She set the whole pie on his plate.

The pleasing odor of baking had found its way up to his room late the night before. 'Thank you, thank you very much,' said William.

After they had eaten their pie and drank more coffee, Mary asked him to join her in the living room. She sat down at the piano and he stood behind her. Her splendid hair flared out over her shoulders. She began to play from Chopin. William was amazed; the notes flooded the room like a gentle waterfall. In the background, the wind had picked up and whistled in the crevices of the window. In a few minutes she stopped and turned to look up at him.

He reached out and touched her hair. 'The music was very beautiful, and you are very beautiful,' he said. He felt his face redden. 'Now I must get out to the machine shed.'

William went to bed before nine. They had a meal of left-overs. Later, Mary had again played the piano. There was little talk. Now, he lay in the dark too tired to think about the next phase of his plan. He mused about how he had hoped there would be a basketball backboard so he could stay fit. His muscles burned from more exercise than he had ever had. The Chopin played in his head. How could

Mike risk the affection of this lovely woman? What was Speer's appeal? How could it be worth it? But what does it have to do with me? he thought. Again, he saw the fine home built with his own hands, the blazing fire, the children, and acres of cattle and hogs and a wife. This time the wife was Mary Bohas and the house was filled with lovely piano music. Then sleep.

Later on in the night – William had no idea what time it was – Mary came into his room and slipped beneath the quilts beside him. Her nude body was warm and soft and smooth. She stayed there with him until from somewhere out in the yard they heard the rooster crow.

28

A kiss from a fairytale princess had banished all fear of rejection from Kevin Bannon's busy mind. He savored the taste of the residue of Judge Rebecca Goldman's lipstick. Her full lips had felt as soft and warm as he had thought they would. The car behind him blinked its lights. He was barely moving. With the huge piles of snow and parked cars along the curb, traffic was piling up behind him on Lake Street. He stepped on the accelerator, then pulled into the next available parking space. A fresh blanket of the relentless snow covered everything except the wiper's arcs on his windshield. After a short search through his pockets he dialed a number on the car phone.

'And whom may we please tonight?' a breathless feminine voice answered.

'Sergeant Bannon calling.'

After a perceptible pause, 'Oh, Knuckles, I thought I was going to have to go out in this awful weather.'

'No, I'd like to come over.'

'Business or pleasure?'

'You know better, Doris.'

'Should I have my attorney present?' No longer breathless.

'Hardly.'

'When?'

'Fifteen minutes.'

'I'll buzz you in.'

Doris Elmore lived downtown in the Towers. Somebody had scratched a nasty groove in the rich wood lining the elevator. Kevin punched nineteen. She was waiting with the door open in a high-necked lavender dress, elaborately embroidered across the upper bodice. He had seen her several times over the years, mostly at the courthouse, once or twice in the station, and he was in on a petty collar where she was involved. With a vice record filling three cards, she had successfully commercialized her gigantic breasts, double H cup, she claimed. With make-up and bleach she looked quite spectacular and top-heavy, to say the least. Supposedly, she hauled in two fifty a trick and, although not on the social register, some of her clients were quite well-known.

'Sergeant, you're looking great, but somehow lipstick doesn't become you.'

Jesus Christ, he had forgotten. He felt the heat in his face. She would never let go of this. 'Just a little goodbye kiss, Doris.'

'She must have been going away for a long time.' As if out of thin air, she produced a Kleenex.

Rubbing his mouth, he walked past her and dropped into a striped sofa. Her apartment was tastefully traditional, predominately green.

'Come in and sit down,' she said sarcastically, but not unfriendly. 'And whatever brings you out in this snowstorm?'

'Minnesota is one long snowstorm,' Kevin said. 'I got a problem.' He ran his finger along the inside of his collar as if to stretch it.

She took a seat in a leather wing chair. 'What's that got to—'

'Nothing to do with you, but you got a problem, too. Right?' She didn't answer. He glanced at her awesome bosom. She smiled. 'I've still got pals in vice, and they tell me you got a real problem, enough to make a felony, and wreck a very lucrative enterprise.'

'I asked you if I should have my attorney present.'

'No need, Doris, this has all gotta be off the record, but you and I both know you got a problem worth a little talk. Even in a snowstorm.'

Kevin got up and snapped on the TV. He waited for the picture, then set the volume uncomfortably loud.

'Good God, Knuckles, the neighbors'll bitch.'

He backed it off slightly. 'We'll only be a minute.' He picked up a chair from the dining room and set it down in front of Doris's knees with the back closest to her. Then he straddled the chair with his legs, his forearms crossed on the top of the back, bringing his face within a foot or two of hers. CNN blared.

'Sergeant, you actually think I might record what you have to say?'

'No harm in being careful.'

'That works both ways.'

'Let's get to it, Doris. I heard a little rumor that Hank Wheatland has a breast fetish, that he's been known to partake of your delights.'

'A lot of people have.'

'I'm only interested in Wheatland.'

'Now, if I knew a judge that well he'd be able to take care of my problems, right, Knuckles?'

'Wrong, Doris, and you know it. He wouldn't want anyone, not anyone, especially cops, to know about his little proclivity.'

'That being the case, Sergeant, if I knew about his – what did you say? – proclivity, and he didn't want anyone to know, and he was a good partaker of mine, as you put it, why would I tell you about it?'

'Because I can solve your problem.'

'How?'

'You don't want to know the details. It will just go away.'

'That would be nice.' A Chevy commercial loudly proclaimed its trucks were better than Ford's. 'What do I hafta do?'

Rebecca smiled at the security camera attached high on the wall of the elevator. She giggled out loud when she remembered the smear of lipstick she had left on Kevin's mouth. Would he remember to wipe it off before he encountered anyone? It would be hilarious if he stopped at police headquarters.

Her apartment was dark and empty. Julie wasn't home.

176

Rebecca snapped the light on in the white kitchen. There was no note. No calls on the machine. What made her think of William Schmid's car and the broken seat? She didn't like the subconscious connection. I've told that kid to keep me informed, she thought.

She picked up the phone and called Monica's. Her mother answered. She's not here, Judge Goldman. Hasn't been all evening. Monica's up in her room with her school-work. Rebecca didn't know who else to call. It was going on ten. Only then did she realize she was trembling. She was still holding the mail she'd picked up downstairs. She opened the one without a return address. It was a copy of the one she'd received a couple of weeks ago about Reggie's death with a little note suggesting she shit or get off the pot. Fuck you, you creep, she thought. You don't know my daughter. No doubt the writer was associated with Wheat-land, if it wasn't Wheatland himself. But where was Julie? She thought of calling Kevin, then decided to give it until ten thirty. Then she spotted it on the floor: one of those yellow post-its with tiny handwriting: 'Mommy dearest, we had a meeting for the class play. I'll be home around ten. J.'

Rebecca heard the click of the lock in the foyer. If she hadn't seen the note just then she would have jumped all over Julie before she'd had a chance to explain. Why are you always quickest to attack the ones you love the most? Precisely because you do love them so much, she thought. These anxieties could affect her performance on the bench.

When her beautiful daughter with her perfect bronze skin and her long perfect legs and her perfect face walked in, Rebecca threw her arms round her and held back a sob. 'Oh, Julie, I love you so much.'

'Geez, Mom, what brought that on?'

'I was a little worried. I didn't find your note until just now. They don't stick well on refrigerator doors, especially that pebble grain.'

The telephone's raucous jangling penetrated Rebecca's sleep. Suddenly wide awake, she was scared. She must have forgotten to turn the ringer off. She believed all news good or bad would wait until morning. When Julie wasn't home she didn't turn the ringer off. But Julie was home. At first there was no sound at all. Then the whispering voice, maybe familiar, maybe not: 'How can you sit on any rape case or is it that you just want to get Phelps?' Rebecca hung up, switched off the ringer and lay back and stared into the blackness.

Maybe she shouldn't sit on rape cases, but she honestly thought the rapists tried in her court in the past had been given fair trials. Two out of four had been acquitted. There were events in every judge's past that could engender bias. It was a judge's duty to rise above her own experience and apply the law. Not just apply the law, she thought. But apply it with compassion. Any good judge must have compassion. Corny was the best. He was known for his compassion. Would Tom Phelps be treated with compassion? He probably had problems that she would never know. Perhaps he was an entirely different person from the one he projected. Sleep would be a long time coming.

Rebecca thought back on the pleas yesterday morning. In the Tremain case the defendant's lawyer Jim Winkler had walked out shaking his head. He was a fine lawyer. He would not have let her see him shaking his head if he had not been genuinely offended. She had doubled the guidelines on his client, eighty-four months instead of forty-two. Even though he hadn't physically hurt anyone, he had scared two women half to death. They would be affected for life. But should she have doubled the guidelines? The pre-sentencing report didn't really justify it. The defendant had stood there so blankly, like a zombie. And those penetrating blue eyes. God, how scared those women must have been. Killer eyes. He had never killed anyone. There were no assaults on his record. He had been convicted of false imprisonment. Why did she think of him as a killer? Why could she feel her heart beat now? Schmid. He had Schmid's eyes. This guy got double the guidelines because he had Schmid's eyes.

First thing the next morning Rebecca dictated an order

reducing Tremain's sentence to the guidelines and had it hand-delivered to Jim Winkler's office without explanation. When lawyers got what they wanted, explanations were unnecessary.

Rebecca felt out of sorts and sleepy. In fifteen minutes a trial was beginning in her court. The issue: whether the defendant homeowner would be required to remove a wall that had been erected seventeen years ago on what he thought was his property line. Pretty dry stuff, but infinitely compelling compared to the divorce cases she would be hearing after the conclusion of the Phelps trial. And for the rest of her judicial career, apparently to be much shorter than she had hoped.

29

Mike Bohas and Kenny Speer arrived home a day before they were expected. With Mike away, the days had passed swiftly. The weather had steadily improved. William had worked hard and Mary had helped. She had fed him prodigally and played more Chopin and other wonderful music. The first four nights that the hunters were gone she had stayed in William's bed until morning. After that she was afraid they might come home unexpectedly. Mike would kill us if he found out, she said.

The evening of Mike's homecoming Mary broiled inch-thick slices of the elk's tenderloin. Mike had wanted to invite Kenny Speer over to eat with them, but Mary said if he did she wouldn't cook and she wouldn't eat.

'I'll have another one of them slices of that meat, Frankie,' Mike said. 'How do you like it?'

'Very good,' William said. He had never tasted anything better.

Mary picked at her food. Mike didn't seem to notice. His face was wind-burned and he had a scabby fever blister on his upper lip. When they had finished, Mary served vanilla ice cream covered with chocolate sauce. Before Mike took his first bite, the telephone rang.

'Hello,' Mike barked. 'Oh, for heaven's sake . . . That bad, huh? Fer cryin' out loud . . . What'd the doctor say? . . . Fer cryin' out loud . . . I just got back from huntin'. Went clear out to Yellowstone with Kenny Speer. Got my elk . . . Listen, Nancy, I'll call and make reservations now. Tell John I'll see him by this time tomorrow . . . Yeah . . . Yeah . . . Yeah . . . OK then. 'Bye.' He looked at

Mary; his big face sagged to a frown. 'I'll be darned. John had a heart attack. Nancy says they think he'll pull through, but he wants to see me.'

'Oh no,' Mary said. 'He let himself get so heavy. You better go right away. With Harold gone, you're the only brother he's got.'

'Will you go with me?'

'Frankie's not ready to take care of this place alone, Mike.'

'Kenny Speer could help out.'

'He'd do more damage than good around here. If you ask me, he already has. No. I'll stay; you go. It's you John wants to see, and when you get a plane ticket on short notice it costs a whole lot.'

'OK,' said Mike.

'Didn't you think we did a pretty good job last week?' said Mary.

'That's for sure,' said Mike. 'Thanks again, Frankie. Think you can stand it for a few more days? Not more'n three days.'

'I am sure I can,' said William. Excitement rose in his chest in anticipation of more time alone with Mary.

'Mike, your ice cream is melting,' said Mary.

As William finished his chocolate sundae he pondered where his involvement with Mike's wife would lead. He vowed to enjoy it while he could, but he knew it would all be over very soon. There was no life for him in the Bohas household, or anywhere else. He hadn't forgotten his plan, or his resolve to bring it to a successful conclusion.

Early in the morning Mike left for Sioux Falls where he would catch a plane for Kansas City. With Mary's help, William tore into his feeding chores with vigor. At lunchtime she prepared him a feast which he quickly devoured. As he was finishing the meal, she stood behind him and kneaded the muscles of his neck with her strong hands. When she invited him to her bedroom, he was ready for her before he reached the top step.

She quickly undressed and dived on to the unmade bed face down. Laced with the shadows of winter tree branches,

181

Mary sat down on the edge of the bed. 'What about it, Kenny?'

'What about what?'

'You know my marriage will be over if you tell Mike. We've been married for twenty-one years.'

'I always thought you were too high-falutin' for this country.'

'This is my home, Kenny.'

As they spoke, William pulled his pants on without objection from Speer. Even if he said he wouldn't tell, could Mary actually trust this malevolent creature? William wondered. Of course, it was that or be out of here by tomorrow night. In any event, this was no longer a place of refuge for a fugitive.

Mary was still talking. 'I will make your life much better, Kenny. I'll see that you get fed properly. And it will only hurt Mike if you tell him.'

Mary's desperation angered William. Perhaps she was just buying some time. Maybe he should take her with him. He had never seriously considered it and it wasn't a decision to be made in the span of a day or two.

'I'll have to think about it,' said Speer.

'Will you call me?'

'No, you come over tomorrow.' The row of uneven stained teeth came into view. 'And don't bring this with you.' He jerked his head toward William standing in the corner next to the window. Speer turned quickly and went out the door leaving a dirty palm print on the casing. His feet were heavy on the stairs. Mary, draped in the sheet, and William, in just his pants, stood before the window and watched him drive out of the yard in his rusty green pick-up.

'Oh, Frankie, what will we do?' Mary bowed her head into her open palms and began to sob.

William had no experience with comforting. He sat down beside her a little distance away. 'I am very sorry,' he said.

She looked at him, her eyes overflowing. 'It's not your fault. I let this happen. I wanted it to happen. There's been no warmth here for a long time. Two years or more. Ever since Mike started coming home drunk. Ever since that awful Kenny Speer retired from the army.'

The two of them sat staring out the window. William silent, Mary softly sobbing.

'Frankie, you'll have to go. There isn't much time. Speer will tell Mike as soon as he gets back. If he knew where he was he might call him and tell him now.'

'What will happen?'

She stopped sobbing and caught her breath. 'I know what Kenny Speer is going to say to me tomorrow.'

William looked at her face, waiting.

'He's going to say that he will keep this quiet if I have sex with him. He has always leered at me, letting me know. He touches me whenever he can.' She drew in a breath and her shoulders heaved. 'Mike says oh, he don't mean no harm. But I know better. I hate him.'

'What will you do?' William asked.

'I don't know. I'll have to think this through. I have no one to talk to but you, Frankie. And you'll be in danger if you stay here. These guys have guns.'

It occurred to William that either Mike or Speer could kill him and no one would ever know, except Mary; not even Wilma. He would only be a memory to Rebecca Goldman, and Harry Scott. They would assume that the river had claimed him for ever. He could not let that happen. But he was not ready to return to Minneapolis. An important aspect of his plan was the passage of time, to lull his targets into a sense of security that would make them vulnerable. Only then would he have an even chance of success.

The ringing of the telephone downstairs startled them. 'Frankie, I can't talk to anyone now,' Mary said. 'I need to think.'

'I will leave for a while,' William said. He picked up his shirt and underwear from the chair and walked down the hall to his room. The telephone rang and rang, at least about twenty times, before it stopped.

The scene with Speer was the most stress he had felt since the day the train hit the truck. He lay still, looking at the ceiling, waiting for the pain. If it came, Mary was in no frame of mind to help. He remembered waiting for the pain in the past. Perlman had said that sometimes thinking it was coming might have been what actually brought it.

About an hour later, the telephone started ringing again. This time it stopped on the third ring. Mary must have gone back downstairs. William hadn't realized he had been sleeping. His dream had already slipped away, but he remembered the idea he had been working on when he was awake. He felt strangely calm. There was a gentle tap-tap on his door.

'Please, come in.'

There was a distant look of despair in Mary's eyes.

'That was Mike. John died. I've got to go to Kansas City for the funeral. I have to leave tomorrow morning. First thing. Oh, Frankie, I'm scared to death. And I feel guilty worrying about myself when John just died.'

'I'm sorry,' said William. He swung his legs round and sat on the edge of the bed. She remained in the doorway.

'And Frankie . . .'

'Yes?'

'When I didn't answer the first time, Mike called Kenny Speer.'

William's jaw muscles tightened.

'He didn't answer either. Mike wants me to tell John's friends. He had a lot of friends around here. Almost everyone knew John. He was one of the best ball players they ever had in the whole county.'

'If you tell other people, Speer will find out,' said William in a matter-of-fact tone. 'Then he will know where Mike is.'

'Mike wanted me to call Kenny right away. I said I would; otherwise, Mike would have called him himself. I suppose he might anyway.'

'Speer might not tell Mike what he saw,' said William. 'He might wait until tomorrow to see what happens when you visit him.'

Her grief-contorted face looked unpersuaded. 'Oh, Frankie, I'm afraid. My life has been unhappy, but it's been a life. I'm so afraid.'

She stepped into the room and William rose and drew her

into his embrace, her soft hair falling loosely over his hands. He could think of nothing else to do or say. He had some sort of duty to this woman, an obligation. He had never before felt an obligation to any person, except Wilma. He liked the feeling and he liked the sense of reciprocity. Before he left here he would do what he could to help Mary. But he must be extremely careful lest he make matters even worse for her. He needed time to think, to develop his idea into a foolproof plan. Perhaps it was too late. His plan must contain a way to gauge whether Mike Bohas already knew their secret. Mary's head seemed to relax on his shoulder and her breathing settled into a regular cadence. It was as though his thoughts had become her thoughts and his calm had become her calm.

'Do not call anyone tonight,' he said. 'Wait until morning. I have an idea.'

She stepped back and looked into his face. 'What idea? I have to leave first thing in the morning.'

He ignored her first question. 'Make up a list of names and telephone numbers. I will call them all before noon.'

'OK, Frankie. I'll go get ready.'

30

The case about the misplaced wall was even more boring than Rebecca expected. The good news was that it would be over in two days, maybe less if she got lucky. There was no jury. In equity cases – where the plaintiff asked the judge to make the defendant do or not do something, rather than pay money – there was no right to trial by jury. It was all up to the judge. Accordingly, Rebecca tried to give every bit of evidence her complete attention. The two lawyers trying this case made it difficult. They were the kind Warren Burger had given speeches about when he was Chief Justice of the United States. Before Rebecca became a judge herself, she had resented Burger and his speeches. Who was he to criticize trial lawyers? He hadn't made that great a record himself. He got on the bench the way most of them had, including her: good political connections. He helped deliver the 1952 Republican Convention to Eisenhower. When they named a library after him she had thought it was absurd, like naming a bridge after Ted Kennedy. But over the past few years she had begun to think old Warren had hit the mark. Half the lawyers that appeared in her court were incompetent.

A witness droned on about some erroneously located surveyor's stakes. Rebecca fought to stay awake as hard as she had fought to go to sleep the night before. The Phelps case and all its problems had taken over her mind for weeks. Now a broken seat in William Schmid's car was claiming another share of her consciousness.

'Your honor, may we approach the bench?'

What the hell for? Rebecca thought. 'Mr Zillincloss, you

can speak from your seat. There's no jury and no onlookers in here.'

His long thin face took on a hurt look, but he droned on. Rebecca looked at her clerk with an expression that said, pay attention, you're going to have to help me on this one.

To Zillincloss she said, 'The objection is overruled. This is a bench trial. I'm going to hear the testimony. Let's keep things moving.'

She had made the decision. Why did she have to keep rehashing? She was staying on the Phelps case. It was the right thing to do. That was the only issue to be considered. She had tried rape cases before in an unbiased way. If it eventually cost her her seat on the bench, so be it. Phelps and Wheatland had access to power and they intended to exercise their clout. There was no question about that. Wheatland had taken to ignoring her in the hallways of the courthouse. Even the chief judge had looked at her with a little smirk in the elevator this morning, as if to say, you stupid girl. And then she thought of Kevin and the lipstick and she could feel herself smiling while her clerk administered the oath to somebody. She quickly returned to a serious demeanor. What had Kevin meant about an angle? He better be careful. Politics could reach its ugly arm into the police department too. Annette Rollins had left a message on Rebecca's machine to watch the morning paper's gossip column. She had clipped it, and reread it now as the witness testified he had told the defendant fifteen years ago that he thought the fence was built in the wrong spot. Under the by-line C.J. – she was one of the sisters – the third paragraph read: 'You all know that certain judge who's been criticized as being anti-police. Well, guess what? She's lately taken to entertaining one. Let's hope she doesn't skin her knuckles.' Rebecca had to bite the inside of her cheek to keep from howling. She wondered if Annette had put C.J. up to it. She heard her clerk clear her throat.

'Yes, Mr Zillincloss, we will finish this trial tomorrow if we have to stay in session until midnight. But I urge you two attorneys to get your heads together and resolve this matter. For now, we'll recess for lunch. Let's get started this afternoon at one thirty sharp.' Rebecca stood up and walked quickly out the door behind the bench, the black robe fluttering in her wake.

On her desk was a note to call Kevin. The first thing she said to him was, 'You see the morning paper?'

'At least five guys tore it out and put it on my desk.'

She imagined his broad ruddy face with the hint of freckles and the grin twitching around the ends of his tight-lipped smile. 'I think it's funny,' she said.

'What about your policy against fraternization with the cops?'

'I make exceptions.'

'I'm honored.'

'Did you leave that call to discuss my non-fraternization policy?'

'No, I wanted to invite you to dinner.'

'Do you still want to?'

'I'm not sure.'

She thought of asking him about the lipstick. Instead she said, 'I've got a hankering for Chinese.'

They agreed to meet at the Nankin at six. Rebecca had a feeling this would be a big night and she hoped the case of the misplaced wall would settle.

Tom Phelps was on a mission. He stubbed out the fortieth or fiftieth butt for that day in the ashtray on his desk. Since spending Christmas Eve with Wilma he had thought of little else than her psycho brother. His best hope was to come up with enough money for Wilma to persuade him not to come back to Minneapolis and then see that he became very dead sometime, somewhere, before the police found him. That was a long shot, but to have any chance at such an outcome, he had to find the money quickly – before William called Wilma again on the Wednesday after New Year's. Phelps had more than one possibility for the money, but the source he liked best might be the same place he could get Schmid disposed of, maybe Wilma too. But Schmid for sure, if he came back to the city and those boys found him before the cops did. The union had plenty at stake in Phelps's future.

He had shown them what he could do in the capitol. He lit another cigarette and went out into the hall to catch the elevator. At the pay phone in the lobby, he dialed a number.

It rang just once. 'Local 1411,' said a hoarse male voice.

'Clyde Magus, please.'

'Who's callin'?'

'It's personal,' said Phelps.

'Hold on. See what he says.'

An FM station playing 'Back Home Again In Indiana' cut in.

Then the voice, 'He'll be right witcha.'

'Thanks.'

More music.

'Magus here.'

'Clyde, it's Tom Phelps.'

'Tommm-mee bay-beee. Long time. Jesus fucking H. Christ, them newspapers been killin' you.' Magus had the smooth voice of an anchor man but the syntax of an eighth-grade drop-out.

'I gotta talk to you, Clyde.' Phelps was abrupt. 'Quick.'

'So talk, Tommy. Great to hear from ya.'

'It's gotta be private, Clyde.'

'OK, OK. Anything you say. Ain't I always ready to help a pal, specially a stand-up guy like you, Tommy?'

'Yeah, Clyde, that's what I figured. Why I called.'

'So where you wanna talk, Tommy?'

'How about takin' a steam at the club?' Phelps hoped he hadn't offended Magus. On this one he couldn't chance a wire. Even if it was his mother.

'So you wanna get naked, Tommy.' The syrupy voice took on a little edge.

'I'm scared, Clyde.'

'Whatever you say, buddy. Ten tonight?'

'I'll be there waiting,' said Phelps.

'Bring the Governor along,' said Clyde, laughing loudly as he hung up.

Rebecca knew she would not lose any weight eating the Nankin's great duck, but she ordered it anyway. Kevin had chow mein. She ridiculed his choice. He said he loved it, that it had been the principal dinner treat when he was a kid. Despite that bit of banter, he was unusually quiet. She knew he was holding something back. Then he spat it out.

'I wasn't going to say anything. I wanted it to be a special night, but you have a right to know right away, I guess.'

His tone jolted her like the telephone ringing in the middle of the night. 'What on earth—'

'Wilma Schmid *has* been following you.'

'Oh my God, I told you I saw her when I came out of the courthouse garage that time.'

'I know, but—'

'I didn't really believe it was her,' said Rebecca.

'We've been tailing her off and on, hoping to get a lead. It's been only in the past couple of days that our guy realized she followed you in yesterday morning and then home last night before I picked you up. He got hold of me just before I left to come here, and she was parked by Lake Vista.'

'Do you think she's dangerous?'

'We think she helped poison two people with cyanide. That should be good enough to make the all-star team in the dangerous league.'

'Of course,' said Rebecca.

'I'm worried about you.' The fine little horizontal grooves in Kevin's forehead deepened. 'We're thinking of putting a fulltime tail on her, but I'd feel better if you were armed.'

'Me armed? You gotta be kidding. I've never shot a gun in my life, and I couldn't kill a person if my life depended on it.'

'How about Julie's life?'

The question flew into her heart like an arrow. 'How do I get a gun?' she said. 'And how do I learn to use it?'

That had been an hour ago. Now, she followed his tail lights on the way to his apartment on East Franklin, near the Mississippi. Tonight would be the first time she had seen his place. As she followed his car into the parking lot outside his building, she thought how hard it must have been for Kevin to bring up the subject earlier. She had a feeling he had special plans for her. So much so that she had arranged to have Julie stay at Monica's. The plaintiffs had settled for some kind of a land swap to settle the case she was to finish tomorrow. She didn't even have to get up early. But of course she always did.

When Kevin snapped the light on in his apartment, Rebecca was surprised. On the long wall in the living room was an inviting over-stuffed sofa. The decorator cushions matched the blue print of drapes. She almost hesitated to step on the champagne carpet. 'Wow!' was all she said.

'You like it?' Kevin asked with a smile.

'I love it.'

He showed her through. The bedroom displayed the same panache as the rest of the apartment. The bed was covered in the same print as the living room drapes, with a pile of little white pillows. Kevin took her hand and led her back to the sofa.

'My compliments to the decorator,' she said. 'Who was it?' The woman's touch was unmistakable.

'It doesn't usually look this good,' said Kevin, ignoring her question. 'I kinda spruced it up for company. You sit down. I'll get the drinks.'

She sank into the soft sofa and listened to the tinkle of glasses in the kitchen. He came back with two snifters of brandy. She passed hers under her nose. 'Hmmm, cognac.'

'Courvoisier,' he said.

He sat down on the edge of the sofa, turned toward her and held his cognac up. 'To the light at the end of the tunnel,' he said.

After the delicate ring of the crystal, she said, 'May it shine brightly.'

Kevin took a sip and set his drink on the glass cocktail table, then reached out for hers and placed it next to his. He leaned over for the kiss and Rebecca reached out and pulled him to her, then wrapped her arms round his head and met his mouth with her open lips. It had been a long time since she had felt passion surge through her whole body. Too long.

★ ★ ★

193

When Clyde Magus walked into the steam room at the Athletic Club, Tom Phelps was alone, sitting on a towel waiting for him. Streams of sweat ran down his face. Another towel was draped across his lap.

'Tommy, how are ya? Look, no wire.' Clyde let the towel round his middle drop to one side. His uncircumcised penis peeked out of a dense thicket of black hair. He spread the towel out on the tile beside Phelps and sat down.

Phelps ignored the antics. 'Thanks a whole lot for coming,' he said.

'What are friends for?' said Clyde. 'Hey, listen, Tommy, I got a nice broad waitin' for me.' He held out his hands, palms up, fingers cupped.

'I'll be as quick as I can,' said Phelps. 'I got multiple problems.'

'Yeah,' grunted Clyde, his black curly hair already damp.

'I need fifty big ones.'

'A little loan?'

'I don't know how I'll ever pay it back, but I can do you some favors.'

'Not no more you can't.'

'I didn't rape that bitch, Clyde.'

'Yeah.' Clyde was absently rubbing his muscular chest. His entire body was lightly covered with black hair.

'They can't convict me for something I didn't do. And the day this is over I'm back in the capitol. The Governor has assured me.'

'You payin' somebody off?'

'In a way.'

'You know, I'm in deep shit and so is the local if anybody gets hold of a deal like you're talkin' about. Course if you're payin' somebody off so's you get back in good in St Paul, it's probably a good investment for us.'

'That's what I thought,' said Phelps.

'You payin' off the judge?'

'Don't ya think it's better, Clyde, that you don't know what I'm doin' with the money?'

'Yeah, maybe you're right.'

'Anybody asks, I'm desperate. I got big legal expenses.'

'I'll talk to the boys. But I gotta tell 'em there's good interest on this loan. You're gonna get back in good in St Paul. That's gotta be a sure thing.'

'It's a sure thing,' Phelps lied.

'Shit, man, it's gettin' hot in here.' Clyde's body was covered with beads of water. 'Hardly need to come in here to talk about a little loan.'

'There's more,' said Phelps.

'Oh, yeah? What more?'

'I need a guy killed.' Until he heard himself say it, he hadn't been sure he would be able to put words to the thought.

'Holy shit, I see why we're sittin' here cookin'. I ain't in the hit business, Tommy, you know that.'

'I don't know anything about the hit business,' said Phelps. 'But I heard from a reliable source that if it was a good cause, there were some guys you know who could put me in touch with the right people.'

'You don't want that lady judge hit, do ya, Tommy? There ain't nobody I know that would wanna touch that with Mussolini's dick.'

'No, no, nothing like that. I'm talkin' about gettin' rid of a criminal who can ruin a lot of people's lives. He's a fucking killer himself.'

'Are the cops after him?'

'Yeah, but they got no idea where he is.'

'And you do?'

'I'm gonna know soon.'

'Sounds a little dangerous. I take it you don't want him talkin' to the cops?'

'Something like that.'

'You doing this for a friend?'

'Yeah. Can it be handled?'

'I'll have a guy call ya. His name is Leroy. You don't have to talk to him in a steam bath either. But don't talk to nobody else. Just Leroy.'

'What's it gonna cost?'

Clyde shrugged his shoulders. 'Five, maybe ten large. All depends.'

Rebecca lay with her head on Kevin's shoulder. She drew her knee up and stretched her leg across his thighs. She pulled him even closer with the arm she had draped across his chest. Her breasts pushed tightly against his side. 'Mmmmmmm. This feels so good,' she said. The film of moisture covering her body was evaporating in the cool, dry air of the room. Their vigorous activity had knocked the comforter on the floor. She was loath to move out of her lovely position for the seconds it would take to pick it up and cover them.

He read her mind. 'Gettin' a little chilly?'

'A little. You?'

'No, not me. Want me to get that quilt?'

'Ooooooh. I don't want you to move.' She let her hand run down across his stomach to his crotch where she gently cupped his genitals. Although her image had been with them all evening, Rebecca was pleased that they hadn't let Wilma Schmid break up the party.

31

William Schmid had spent a sleepless night listening to the cold wind and thinking. After they had a cup of coffee together, Mary left around five for Sioux Falls on her way to John Bohas's funeral. William poached two eggs and ate a piece of toast smeared with home-canned raspberry preserve. He hadn't bothered to light a corncob fire in the big stove. His time was limited. Not long after seven thirty the cows would begin bawling for their hay. His dark blue jacket felt tight over the thick black sweater. He put on a navy watch cap and headed out the door.

Yesterday's sun had melted most of the snow in the yard, leaving it sticky underfoot, and the south wind carried the scent of cow manure. As always, the hogs were banging the lids on the feeders. In the machine shed he found a long piece of 1½-inch pipe and clamped it in the vice. With one of Mike's hacksaws he cut off a piece thirty inches long. Last week, when he was cleaning up, he had stored a spare belt used with power takeoffs on tractors in a drawer along the wall. It was made of pliable rubber about two inches wide. He cut off a piece four feet long. With rubber electrical tape he anchored it to the longer exposed portion of the pipe already clamped in the vice. He wound the rubber snugly round the pipe down to a spot about ten inches from the other end. He secured the loose end with the electrical tape and cut off the excess. He opened the vice and removed the finished product, gripping the bare steel end. Then he headed back to the house. There was no hint of light in the east. One of the dogs barked at something in the dense grove to the north.

Inside, the warmth felt good. His bare hands were icy from the contact with the cold steel. In his room he found the buckskin gloves he had been given for Christmas. From the drawer in the bed table he withdrew the cord, the hunting knife, and the .38 revolver. He dropped the cord and knife in one large jacket pocket and the gloves and gun in the other. In the kitchen he grabbed a dish rag from the sink. The clock on the stove said 6:00. In the back hall he put on a pair of Mike's rubbers, pulled on the gloves and headed out the door.

Remembering his experience at the river, he took the time to put tire chains on his rear wheels. He turned right out of the farmyard. The headlights played along the piles of snow left by the plow. All that was visible across the dark miles of landscape were the solitary security lights indicating farmsteads that were still occupied. The heater was blowing cold air. He turned it off. The chains jingled along the frozen road. At the Horst place a mile south, where William turned left, someone turned a light on behind a drawn shade. He proceeded very slowly on the narrow rutted road past a deserted farmhouse on the right until he had gone two miles to the east. Ahead in the distance, like a beacon in a darkened sea, he spotted the security light in Kenny Speer's yard.

The headlights found an old shed sagging to the ground as William pulled his car into a turn-out a quarter mile before he got to the Speer farm. He lifted the rubberized pipe out of the back seat and started down the road. He would walk the last quarter-mile to Speer's house.

Off to the south a coyote howled, a clear, pure sound like one of the small pipes on a great organ. William barely noticed. He plodded steadily up the center of the road, his mind carefully sorting details.

Speer's security light was fixed to a tall wooden pole in the center of the yard. Its glow illuminated the white faces of a few cows gawking at the intruder from behind a fence. William had been here once before, with Mike. The house was a small one-story affair only about seventy or eighty feet back from the road. Black tar paper showed through in many places where the gray asbestos drop siding was broken. Speer's rust-covered truck was parked near the back steps. A bumper sticker said EAT BEEF. William noted with satisfaction that Speer's German shepherd Prince was nowhere to be seen. Lamplight shone forth from the first-floor windows and the pleasant smell of burning wood settled down from the chimney. A radio played somewhere inside. Before mounting the steps to the back door, William laid the rubberized length of pipe on the ground in the shadow of the stoop.

At the very first knock the dog went wild with barking, followed by vigorous scratching on the inside of the door. Moments later it opened a crack.

'Who is it?' It was Speer's voice.

The barking continued. William was just a silhouette against the brightly lit area behind him.

'It is Frank Kroll. I have a message for you.'

'Oh, ya do, do ya? God dammit, Prince, *shut up*! Mary knows she damn well better come up here herself. Nothin' you say is gonna do any good.'

'The message is not about Mary,' said William.

'Who's it about then?'

'John.'

'John who?'

'John Bohas,' said William.

'What about John, for Christ's sake? Whyn'tchu call on the phone?'

He didn't know John was dead. He hadn't talked to Mike. 'The telephone is not working. May I come in?' said William.

'Oh, awright, but make it snappy. She knows I gotta be to work by eight. Shoulda come herself. She ain't here when I get back tonight, I'm telling Mike what I saw soon's he gets home.' Light flooded the doorway as it opened. The dog slunk behind Speer's legs, growling. Speer turned and walked from the vestibule into the kitchen. 'Get in here, Prince,' he snarled.

William followed the two of them into a well-lit kitchen with dirty colorless walls. There was nothing cooking on the old black iron farm stove, yet the room smelled of burnt fat. Speer and the dog stopped in front of the stove and turned to face William, standing across the room, just inside the door. He had the .38 in his hand, leveled at Speer's chest.

Speer took a step forward. 'You little . . .'

William moved his arm to the right and down and carefully shot the dog in the head. Prince collapsed. Blood oozed from between his eyes, a few drops fell on the worn linoleum. The loud report rang in William's ears.

Speer stood still, wide-eyed. He had shaved the black beard, perhaps in anticipation of Mary's visit.

'I will shoot you in the heart if you do not do exactly what I tell you to do,' said William evenly, his voice betraying no emotion whatsoever. The clock above the stove said 6:38. The dog's bowels had evacuated and the rank smell of canine feces filled the room.

'Prince was a good dog. Why'd ya hafta go shoot 'im?' Speer whined.

'You gave me no alternative,' said William. He looked around the room and backed toward the kitchen table, the .38 in his right hand pointed at Speer's chest eight feet away. Empty beer cans stood randomly on every flat surface. William dragged a chair across the room to a point behind Speer, beside the stove. Speer's head slowly turned to watch, but his body remained stationary. 'Remove all of your clothes,' said William.

'What the hell for?' Speer's voice shook.

'I am going to shoot you in the heart unless you remove your clothes.' William drew the hammer of the .38 back with his thumb, the clicking noise clearly audible.

Speer sat down on the edge of the chair and began untying his boots. William eased the hammer back into the safe position. He withdrew the cord and knife from his jacket and laid the knife on the front edge of the stove. Speer removed his shoes, then stood up and shed his green plaid shirt, letting it fall on the floor between the chair and the dead dog. After he unhitched his belt and let his pants fall, he said, 'Underwear too?'

'Yes,' said William.

200

Speer sat back down on the chair, his tanned arms and face in stark contrast to the whiteness of his body. He started to cry, his bulky shoulders quivering. On the radio a soprano sang 'America The Beautiful'.

Still holding the gun, William pulled both of Speer's thick wrists behind the back of the chair and wound the cord round them three times, not so tightly as to permanently mark the skin or interfere with circulation. The nails on Speer's long fingers were clogged with dirt. William deftly knotted the rope with a double half-hitch.

'What're ya gonna do to me?' Speer's voice was quaking.

William pulled the remaining long end under the seat of the chair and tied each of Speer's ankles to a leg of the chair. With the hunting knife he cut the remaining cord into two pieces and tied the two chair legs closest to the stove to two of its heavy cast-iron legs. Then he went back over each knot, checking for any slip-ups. Urine spread out over the seat of the chair and dripped on to the floor. Satisfied with the knots, William walked through the untidy living room to the bathroom. The bathtub was old-fashioned cast iron with claw-foot legs. A picture of Jesus praying in the garden at Gethsemane hung above the tub. William shoved the rubber plug into the drain hole and turned on the water, testing it with his finger, adjusting the faucets to obtain bathwater temperature. Then he urinated in the toilet.

He walked back into the kitchen and pressed the muzzle of the .38 against Speer's temple. Speer closed his eyes tightly.

'Open your mouth,' said William.

Speer obeyed. William pulled the dish rag out of his pocket and fed it into Speer's mouth, taking care not to choke him. The sound of an automobile engine came from the yard. Cat-like, William bounded over to the window and peered round the sash, careful to keep his shadow off the shade. Morning light under a gray sky revealed a red and yellow Schwan Ice Cream truck parked in the yard. He recognized the driver walking toward the door with two gallons of ice cream under his arm. With quick steps William crossed the kitchen floor to the vestibule. He quietly slid the primitive locking bolt into position just before the driver knocked. William stood behind the door considering his alternatives. If he killed the driver, he would have to leave the area immediately. It made sense only as a last resort. He waited. Again the knocking. The doorknob twisted and the door shook against the bolt. William edged back to the window. The driver walked to the back of his truck and replaced the ice cream. Then he stood looking at the house. William remained perfectly still, wishing he had turned the kitchen light off when he had finished tying the knots. If the driver looked through the crack between the shade and the sash he would see Speer tied to the chair, stark naked, his terrified eyes open wide, his mouth filled with a rag. William drew the .38 out of his pocket where Speer could see it. The only sound was a low voice on the radio, then the crunching of the driver's shoes in the crisp snow, drawing nearer to the house with each step.

The driver spoke. 'Shit, snow's two feet deep under that window. Kenny's probably sleeping off a drunk anyway.'

The sound of the crunching steps receded from the house. William peeked round the curtain as the driver climbed into the cab. The engine gunned and the truck lumbered out of the yard. The clock above the stove said 7:10.

William hurried back to the door, slid the bolt, and opened it a crack so he could see the road. Then, out and down the two steps. He picked up the rubber-wrapped pipe and returned to the house. Stepping over the carcass of the dog, he moved to a point behind Speer's chair. Speer twisted his head to see him, his eyes pleading. William leaned the pipe against the stove, and pulled the .38 out of his pocket. He pressed the muzzle against the back of Speer's head. 'If you turn your head again. I will pull the trigger,' he said. He put the .38 back in his pocket. With his right hand he grabbed the bare end of the pipe then wrapped the fingers of his left hand round the remaining portion of bare steel. He hefted it to a horizontal position behind Speer's head, like a batter waiting for the pitch. Speer could see William's shadow on the wall. William moved the pipe up behind Speer's head, holding it steady for a moment. Speer emitted a series of tight grunts like the last turns of a car engine when the battery is running down. William drew the pipe back very slowly, keeping his eye on the back of the head, his shadow in his peripheral vision. He brought it forward again almost touching Speer's dense black hair. Satisfied, he drew it back further and brought it forward firmly, with some speed, but not too swiftly. *Thwuck.* The rubberized part of the pipe made solid contact with Speer's skull. His head flopped forward, chin resting on his chest. William pressed his fingers against the front of Speer's neck under his drooping chin. There was a steady pulse. Blood seeped through the hair on the back of his head.

William leaned the pipe against Speer's hands, still tied behind the chair, then strode into the bathroom. The tub was almost full. He turned off the faucets, pulled his jacket off, threw it on the floor, pushed up his sweater sleeve, reached in and pulled the plug. After about six inches of the water gurgled down the drain, he replaced the plug and kicked his jacket under the sink.

Back in the kitchen, William felt Speer's pulse. Thready, but perceptible. He loosened the chair's two side legs from the stove. With the chair tilted backwards, like an Indian travois, he pulled the chair, little by little, toward the bathroom. Immediately, he noticed the drag marks on the old linoleum. He pulled the rag out of Speer's mouth and tore it in half. Using the remnants of the cord, he tied the pieces of rag under and round the two back chair legs. Again, he started pulling the chain. The rags worked. There were no marks. Speer was heavy, but William found new strength.

Eventually, he had Speer sitting next to the bathtub, two-thirds full of lukewarm water. William retrieved the hunting knife from the kitchen and cut the cord that bound Speer to the chair.

William moved to a point in front of the chair, then placed one foot on either side of it. He bent forward and got a grip on Speer's torso under the armpits. With a heave he shoved Speer into the bathtub. Waves of water splashed on the floor and soaked William's shoes and pant legs. Speer came to rest with his left leg, from the knee down, dangling over the edge of the tub. William flipped the foot into the water. Speer's head was resting against the sloping end of the tub, his face just above the water line. A low moan emanated from his mouth, and his eyelids moved. William kicked the chair out of the way and moved to the head of the tub. He shoved down hard on the top of Speer's head with both hands. Speer's eyelids sprang open. His pupils were dilated like black yolks in frying eggs. His mouth opened for air, but all it got was water. Then it emitted a large bubble that popped to the surface. Both legs kicked feebly. William held Speer's head down with all the force he could muster. A string of bubbles trailed to the surface from Speer's nostrils. The terrified eyes widened. The mouth emitted another bubble. More bubbles from the nose. The legs stopped moving. William gingerly withdrew his hands no more than an inch and waited. Speer lay still, his eyes open. William ignored the ringing telephone.

There was still much to be done. He flushed the toilet and put the lid down. He retrieved Speer's clothes from the kitchen and threw them on the top of the toilet seat. The blood from the wound on the back of Speer's skull formed a pink halo round his black hair, loosely floating out from the scalp. His open mouth exposed long yellow teeth.

William glanced in the mirror over the sink. Along the parting in his hair the bare bulb's glare disclosed a lightening at the roots. His mustache covered his upper lip, looking thick and masculine. Droplets of water speckled the lenses of his glasses. He put his jacket on and picked up the knife, the gun, and the pieces of cord. Then he untied the rags from the two back legs of the chair and put the pieces in his pocket. He carried the chair back into the kitchen. From the radio the strains of a favorite hymn: 'When The Role Is Called Up Yonder'.

He carefully examined the wound on the dog. It had bled very little. He rolled the dog over and ran his fingers through the fine black and brown hair of the head and neck

204

area. There was no exit wound. Good, he thought. The bullet remained in the dog. He sat down in the chair and laced on Speer's much too large boots. From the scene in Mary's bedroom, he remembered Speer's big feet. He picked up the rubberized pipe and walked out the back door and across the yard. The cows behind the fence were lowing. When he got to the road he began to run toward his car. The sun, a barely visible silver ball veiled in the morning haze, hung low in the eastern sky.

His underwear was drenched with sweat and he was sucking in deep breaths of the cool air when the engine turned over and started. To avoid leaving tire impressions in the yard he parked in the road in front of Speer's driveway. He opened the trunk lid and left the motor running.

When he entered the house, he left the door open. In the kitchen he edged up to the dog and dropped into a deep squat, almost sitting on his heels. He slid his arms under the dog and heaved, barely able to lift it. On wobbly knees he carried the big dog out to the car, dumped it in the trunk and slammed the lid. He looked down the rarely-used road in both directions. Nothing unusual. He opened the rear door of the car and returned to the house. The bathroom floor was very wet, but he reasoned Speer's slipping in the tub would have splashed at least that much water on the floor. Back in the kitchen he cleaned up the dog feces and urine from the linoleum and wiped off the chair he had used. The clock above the stove said 7:50. The cows would be getting hungry. As he left the house the telephone began ringing again.

He headed across the farmyard past the security light pole to the old barn. Only a few splotches of red paint still stuck to the weathered siding. Expecting a meal, the watching cows began to low more vociferously. He opened the barn door and looked around the dirt-floored room, dimly lit by a few broken windows. A beat-up motorcycle leaned against a post. In the corner to his left boxes were stacked against the wall. Intrigued, he moved closer. Speer's cache of dynamite. Beyond imagination. One stray deer hunter's bullet could make the entire farmstead and everything on it disappear. The corrugated boxes were about two feet wide, a foot and a half deep and a foot high. On the top of each in big orange letters the words DYNAMITE, HIGH EXPLOSIVES were imprinted. On the side, ATLAS was printed in orange. Below that in black, the letters I.I.D. were printed across an orange diamond-shaped sticker. William lifted one of the boxes. It weighed about fifty pounds. There were eleven cases. He decided to take five.

He loaded the dynamite in his car, one case at a time. On the last trip across the yard he brought a box of fuses and blasting caps. His back seat was packed so full he could barely shut the door.

Wearing Speer's big boots, William retraced his original steps through the yard, stepping on each track he had made earlier with Mike's rubbers. He left the boots in the vestibule and appropriated an old pair of Speer's shoes from the bedroom closet. He returned to the car carrying his own shoes and Mike's rubbers.

William headed his car toward the rising sun. At the next mile corner he turned north paralleling the Bohas road, three miles to the west. In the second mile, another of the ubiquitous abandoned farmsteads stood just off the road on the right. An almost impenetrable tangle of briars and other undergrowth snarled through the trees on the north side of the rundown buildings. Ahead and behind, the road was clear for as far as William could see.

He stopped the car on the side of the road opposite the edge of the grove. An expanse of snow about fifty feet across blocked his path. Kenny Speer's big shoes might slip off his feet, William thought. Putting his own shoes and the rubbers back on took still more time. He opened the trunk lid and struggled to get hold of the dog. He finally hoisted it out of the trunk. To avoid leaving drag marks or blood streaks, he carried the body, one deliberate step at a time, through the knee-deep snow. When he reached the under-brush, he plunged in holding his head down, chin against his chest, relying on his glasses to protect his eyes. A briar scratched his face and he decided he was far enough into the brush to afford the concealment he sought. He dropped the dog.

On the way back to the road he stepped in his original tracks with the vivid M over W monograms. At the car William looked back. A pair of crows had landed in the tallest tree. Perhaps he should have taken the dog back to the Bohas farm and burned it, but in the depth of winter there was little chance the dog would be discovered. By the time he turned back to the west at the next mile corner he had put it out of his mind. A half-mile down the road he met a red pick-up heading west with several sheep standing in the box. The driver waved. William waved back.

Back home, the farmyard ensemble of white faces clamored for fresh hay. William removed the chains from his tires. Then he got a can of gas from the shed and carried it to the rusty oil drum beside the garage. On top of the accumulated kitchen refuse and papers he dropped his bloody gloves, the pieces of cord and rag, Mike's rubbers, the belting he had wrapped round the pipe, some gunny sacks that he had laid under the dog, and Kenny Speer's old shoes. He doused the pile with gasoline and lit a match, jumping back from the small explosion. Flames and inky smoke from the burning rubber leaped out of the top of the drum.

He went back to the car and moved the five cases of dynamite and the fuses and blasting caps to the trunk. He took the trunk key off the ignition key ring and slipped it in his wallet.

In the house he threw his jacket in the washing machine and drank two glasses of water. The kitchen clock said 8:53. He sat down at the kitchen table and called the three numbers Mary had left. They would spread the word about the funeral, she had said. He made a mental note to touch up his roots later on that day. Now, it was time to get the chores done.

32

The morning after her first visit to Kevin's apartment, Rebecca called Sports and Courts to check out a membership. She wanted to tighten up her stomach muscles. Since Julie was born they'd been looser than she liked. Last night, Kevin's hand on her spongy tummy had made her wish she had done something about it a long time ago.

It had been years since she had actually engaged in sexual intercourse – or gotten laid as she would have said to Susan. Oh, and a white guy, Susan would say when she heard. Jewish or not, white father or not, Rebecca's caramel skin labeled her African-American. In the United States of America in the twentieth century, no African-American could be completely indifferent to color. That was for future generations to achieve. She had experienced both black and white men. She had no preference. Reggie had taught her almost everything she knew about the finer points of sex, but she set much greater store by her own intuition. That certainly seemed to have worked last night.

It had been so long it was almost like another first time. The real first time had been in Reggie's Greenwich Village walk-up with a Billie Holiday record playing over and over again and a baby screaming its head off on the other side of the wall. Rebecca had been scared and nervous and she hadn't known what she was doing. Of course Reggie knew. But this time she did know, and it was quiet, only some water running through pipes in the wall. She had learned to let herself feel. There was no pain. Just the ultimate awareness of closeness. Later, on the way home, she had pushed back her hair and caught the scent of him and herself on her hand. Deep down at her woman's core she had felt the electrical thrills all over again, like the after-shocks of an earthquake.

She was glad the hiatus was over. Having found the right man, the liquid feel of fulfillment oozed through her body. How did *he* feel? Tempted to call, she thought better of it. She meant to tend the relationship like a prize rose. Brittle male machismo still made her jumpy. It infested the court-house. The trial lawyers were the worst, but the cops weren't far behind. Kevin had a mild case, but still needed some treatment. Those wonderful innocent eyes. She remembered what Mama Julia had said about men's eyes. Kevin let her see in and he cared about her as much as any man ever had, including Reggie. She hadn't kidded herself about Reggie. He respected her and he cared, but he had never allowed her to become *the* important part of his life. That spot was reserved for his music. With Kevin there was room at the top. She saw his face, the determined set of his jaw, the twitchy little grin. Was she falling in love? Would she die for him? She couldn't die for anyone but Julie. She would never forget the ultimate purpose of her existence. The neat bonus was the way Kevin and Julie got along. Julie looked forward to his every visit. When's Knuckles coming over? I haven't seen him for ages, she'd say. So little time had passed since their lunch at the Willows. It had been only about six weeks since she got the last letter. What a rock Kevin was in that regard. And that lovely apartment with the woman's touch. What had happened to her? Might her own gain be another's loss? Other than his childhood and a mention of an early short marriage, they had never talked about his past. There hadn't been that much time.

At the very end last night, after he'd finally got up and pulled the comforter over them, they lay side by side on their backs looking up into the flickering candlelight. It was the time when smokers light a cigarette. Neither had made a sound for a few minutes. He reached for her hand and she moved a little closer.

Kevin rose on one elbow, his face only a shadow. 'Thank you,' he said.

'My pleasure,' she replied and giggled.

'You know you make me very happy,' he said. 'If I was God I would be so proud to have created you.'

There must be hope for a man who could say that. Getting up and going home had made her feel a little melancholy. It would have been nice to spend the night in his bed, but somehow she wasn't ready. Kevin hadn't pushed it either. What would it be like a year from now? Would she be fixing his breakfast? Would Julie be asleep in a nearby room?

After kissing Kevin good night, thoughts of Wilma Schmid had returned. Rebecca had turned the key in the lock of her dark, empty apartment at two in the morning. Driving through the midnight streets she had watched her mirror as much as the road ahead. The ordinary sounds of the night hadn't seemed so ordinary. What possible interest could Wilma have in following her? Like her brother, was Wilma mentally out to lunch?

Seven years ago at the trial, after Wilma had told the jury how her father had substituted himself for her brother William in an ongoing incestuous relationship, every eye and ear had awaited Harry Scott's next question.

'Ms Schmid, did you tell any adult about what was happening to you?'

Wilma's mouth had tightened. 'He hurt me,' she said. 'It was not like it had been with my brother. We were still children. My father hurt me. I told him I was going to tell one of my teachers.'

'What did he say?'

'He said that no one would believe me. They would take the word of a minister of the gospel over some evil child who had been fucking her twin brother.'

'Did you tell anyone?'

'No.'

'Did you think that you wouldn't be believed?'

'It was more than that.'

'Please explain for the jury,' Harry Scott said.

'I had a cat, a big white cat. His name was Teaser. He was the only possession I had that meant anything to me. One

210

day, after I had threatened to tell, my father told me to go out to the garage with him. When we got there I saw Teaser hanging from one of the rafters. His white coat was covered with blood. His throat had been cut. My father said that if I told anybody that he was having sex with me he would do the same to my twin brother William.' Wilma's face was gray and hard as stone, her voice filled with hate.

A woman juror burst into tears. Rebecca called a recess. As bad as it had been for Wilma, no evidence had come to light that she was unbalanced. Since that awful day, she had been promoted more than once at the railroad and she had become a hard worker for the party. She was even close to Tom Phelps. According to Kevin, Wilma had spent Christmas Eve in Phelps's apartment. Rebecca wondered if she would show up at his trial.

Later that afternoon Kevin watched Wilma Schmid pull out of her downtown parking lot on to Tenth Street going east. Kevin followed. Her brake lights blinked on and off in the late afternoon traffic. She turned right on Second Avenue South, then right again on Eleventh. She stopped to wait for the light at the Nicollet Mall. She took LaSalle south to Franklin and Franklin to Hennepin, then south on Hennepin. Just before Twenty-sixth, she pulled over to the curb. Leaving two or three cars between Wilma's car and his, Kevin pulled in about a hundred feet behind her. She just sat there with the motor running; clouds of vapor from her exhaust obscured the back of her car.

It was after six. Hennepin Avenue had become a conveyor belt of lights when Wilma's car merged back into the flow of traffic. Kevin followed. She eased up to the bumper of a white Buick that had stopped for the light on Twenty-eighth. Kevin was behind her. Just as he had expected, the car in front of Wilma's was Rebecca's. Wilma stayed right behind the Buick as it weaved in and out, working its way through the stop-and-go winter rush hour. After Rebecca's car disappeared into the garage at Lake Vista, Wilma continued on round the lake, Kevin on her tail. When she turned into the driveway of her home in Richfield, Kevin was still with her. He quickly jumped out of his car and was waiting beside her door when she opened it.

'Good evening, Ms Schmid,' he said. As she stood up, he kept his face close to hers.

'Sergeant Bannon,' she said. 'What are you doing here?'

'I've been right behind you ever since you left your parking lot downtown.'

'What on earth for?'

'You know damn well what for, and either you invite me in out of the cold, or we'll take a ride back downtown to talk about it.'

'Come in if you must,' she said. 'I have nothing to hide.'

'That remains to be seen,' said Kevin.

She opened the back door of the little stucco bungalow and they stepped into the warm interior, faintly redolent of heating oil. From the back hall they climbed two steps into a small pink kitchen. There was an apartment-sized electric range, a cupboard with a sink built into the counter and an old refrigerator. A table and two chairs were shoved up against the wall under the window. She offered Kevin one of the chairs and held out her hand to take his coat, then carried it into another room. Having removed her coat, she returned wearing a two-piece dark suit with a red scarf.

She sat down in the other chair and pulled it up to the table. An old black and white photograph of the Matterhorn hung on the wall above her head. 'So talk,' she said.

'Obviously, you have been following Judge Goldman,' Kevin said.

'It's a free country.' She hadn't taken off her gloves and she was fidgeting with her keys.

'Do you mind telling me why you are following her?'

'Perhaps because you have had some fools following me.'

'We've investigating a double murder,' said Kevin, 'and we will do anything that needs to be done to further that investigation, including the use of surveillance.'

'Perhaps I am conducting an investigation of my own,' said Wilma.

'And what are you investigating?'

'That's my business.'

'Not necessarily. I think there is good reason to believe you are the person who typed and sent a threatening letter to Judge Goldman in November.'

'Now you're bluffing, Sergeant. If you had anything but a guess, you would have searched this place a long time ago. And I've seen your eyes darting around since you came in the door. I assure you, you won't see anything in my kitchen.'

'C'mon, Wilma. Now that your brother's dead, why don't you get on with your life? He was the crazy.'

'You don't really want me to get on with my life or you wouldn't be harassing me.'

He took a flyer. 'Wilma, if you gave William that cyanide thinking he was going to commit suicide, the law would probably deal very leniently with you. We could put this whole thing to bed and you *could* get on with your life.'

'I know nothing of any cyanide,' she said. 'And, Sergeant, I believe I have a right to a lawyer if you are questioning me about a crime. Shall I call Mr Scott?'

'No need. But I suggest that harassing a district court judge may get you into serious trouble. If you don't stop, you're going to make a mistake along the line and I'm going to nail you.' He tried unsuccessfully to suppress the anger in his voice. His stake was becoming more and more personal. Department policy barred cops from working on cases where they had a personal interest. No matter. They wouldn't get him off this one with a SWAT team.

'Sergeant, you quit following me, and I will quit following her.'

'Don't hold your breath, lady.'

After Kevin left, Wilma waited an hour, then headed back downtown. She let herself into the railroad building with her own key, exchanged pleasantries with the night guard, then took the elevator directly to the law library on the eleventh floor. The cleaning crews were out in full force, but she was able to lock herself in a cubicle and use the telephone. After at least a dozen rings her stepmother answered.

'It's Wilma. I need to talk to you, Mother.'

'I was just helping Mr Carlson with the bedpan. I thought the phone would stop before I got to it.' She was breathing hard, her voice hoarse and squeaky.

'Mother, William will be calling again next week and I am worried.'

'Have the police figured out what we did?'

'Mother, don't say things like that. Mr Carlson may hear you.'

'He is down the hall swimming in shit and he can't hear anything anyway. What is it? Why did you call?'

'William is bound and determined to come back here. He is still obsessed with the idea that that woman judge and his lawyer did him in.'

'So what can you do about it?'

'I have arranged to get some money, quite a lot of money. He could go a long way away, maybe get started at something else. Eventually, I could go with him.'

'What about the judge? William never gave a damn about money.'

'If she were already dead, he wouldn't come back.'

'Oh my God, Wilma, you're crazy. What're you going to do? Just walk up to her and shoot her?'

'Whatever I do, it has to be soon. I can probably stall him for a while when he calls, but he'll be wanting to get on with it. He is convinced that he has only a short time to live.'

'He isn't the only one.'

'What is that supposed to mean?'

'Those tests. Remember those tests I told you I was getting at the clinic?'

'You said they were nothing.'

'I didn't think they amounted to much.'

'Well, what were they?'

'This Dr Hakim, he's that dark-complected one. Remember? Some kind of an Arab or something.'

'Yes, I remember, Mother.' She didn't.

'Anyway. He thought they oughta check that dark blood I been passing.'

'You didn't tell me about any blood.'

'Wilma, just listen and I'll tell you. They ran a buncha

214

tests. Biopsies and stuff like that. I got cancer, Wilma. All over the place. I asked him right out how much time I got. He said he wanted to do another test. I said forget it. How much time? Three months, he said. No more than four.'

Wilma felt no emotion whatsoever. Her stepmother was going to die and William was going to die. That would leave her with Phelps who might be going to prison. It was only William she cared about. All the better that the old lady would soon be dead. That would make one fewer with direct knowledge of her complicity in the murders at the state hospital. But she needed her stepmother's help again. Wilma realized she was taking too long to respond. Her stepmother had three or four months to live. 'That's terrible, Mother.'

'It's terrible for Mr Carlson. That's who it's terrible for. They'll stick him in a home. I have been taking care of him twenty-four hours a day for years, his every little wish. He's eighty-five and his father and uncle lived to be almost a hundred. His mother, a hundred and one. I do everything he wants. I mean everything, Wilma, even you-know-what.'

'I'm so sorry, Mother. Now remember, dear, if you call me at home, or maybe even my phone at the office, the police are probably listening.'

'Reason I didn't call you yesterday was I was thinking about Mr Carlson and I decided last night.'

'Decided what?'

'I'm going to take him with me.'

Late that evening Julie answered the phone at their apartment. 'It's Knuckles, Mom! Sounds like he's on something.'

Before Rebecca hung up they had made elaborate plans for New Year, beginning tomorrow, the last day of the year. He *had* sounded manic, game for anything she wanted to do and full of ideas of his own. At the end of the conversation he said he was going to wait until the stroke of midnight tomorrow to tell her but it couldn't wait. What on earth are you talking about? she asked. I love you, he said, and hung up.

Rebecca turned the last light off and settled into the

customary blackness of her bedroom, never more wide awake. In the distance a siren penetrated the night. The sound of somebody's misery. She thought again of the white cat hanging from the rafter. And Wilma. And William Schmid's body trapped under the ice in the Wolf River. And the broken seat in his car. And she thought of the gun and she wished Kevin would hurry up and bring it to her. She wanted to learn how to use it.

Her wakefulness sharpened her senses. The tiny details of each little shadow. Each individual wrinkle in the sheets. Sounds she usually didn't hear were everywhere. If a cockroach walked across the carpet she thought she would hear it. All of this awareness made it even more clear that she couldn't really protect herself or Julie from resolute evil. In spite of her effort to focus on the rapidly unfolding wonderment of her new relationship, it was this grim reality that kept her awake until past two in the morning.

33

New Year's Day had come and gone unnoticed. Yesterday, the day of his morning mission to the Speer farm, the telephone rang repeatedly. William ignored it. Callers would assume he was outside working. That evening he did answer Mike's call. William told him everything was going just fine on the farm. Mike said that they would be home tomorrow night. Now, William expected them to return in a few hours. Mary should be pleased that there was no longer any danger of Kenny Speer telling Mike what he had seen in the bedroom.

After lunch, while a few snowflakes the size of quarters came spinning out of the steely sky, William chose to continue the job of tightening the fence round the hogs. One of the biggest and blackest bristly sows insisted on rooting in the ground wherever he placed his foot. A month ago he would have given this brute wide berth, but he had come to understand their nature much better. No doubt hogs were more intelligent than cows. Yet he found their odor and habits repulsive. He wouldn't choose to be a hog farmer. The big sow nudged him in the thigh when he kneeled to replace a staple in one of the posts. He rapped her smartly on the snout with the staple gun and she ran squealing away.

William looked up to see a county sheriff's patrol car roll into the yard. It stopped near the back door of the house and the driver got out, making a move toward the door.

'Sir,' William shouted, not loud but his loudest. The feeder covers clanked in the background.

The deputy waved. 'You holler?' His dark down coat was

open, partially covering a tan uniform.

'They are not at home,' William shouted.

The deputy walked toward William. 'When are they comin' back?' The two black and white collies tagged along, sniffing at his feet. He wore high-heeled boots, the tops hidden under the narrow pants. With his rabbit-fur hat he looked like a Russian cowboy.

'Tonight.'

'Happen to see a big German shepherd runnin' around here?'

'No, sir,' said William. Perhaps he is searching for Prince, he thought.

The deputy reached a point right outside the fence, within a few feet of William. His face was as red as raw meat. 'New around here, ain'tcha?'

'Yes, yes,' said William, raising his right shoulder just enough to feel the reassuring weight of the .38 in his big jacket pocket.

'Ya don't sound like no farm hand.'

'No, sir,' said William.

'Where ya from?'

'Wisconsin,' said William.

'I got relatives back there. Around Cumberland some-place. You know where that is?'

'I think so,' said William. 'I am from much further east.'

'Where might that be?'

'Near Sheboygan.'

'I heard of it, I guess, but I ain't been there,' the deputy said. 'That big old sow is kinda sneakin' up on ya there.'

William felt the friendly poke of her snout against his jeans followed by a jarring push behind his knee. He reached out to steady himself on the post, then turned round and banged her on the snout with the staple gun. She let out a squeal and retreated.

'Well, I see ya know how to handle them hogs,' the deputy said. 'You tell Mike to call me down at Lake Andes soon as he gets back. My name's Blitzko. Ivan Blitzko. OK?'

'OK,' said William.

'What's yours?'

'Frank,' said William.

'Frank what?'

'Frank Kroll.'

'Good to meetcha, Frank.' Without offering his hand, Ivan Blitzko turned and headed for his car. Radio voices crackled when he opened the door. In a few seconds he was gone.

The darkening sky poured forth millions of the big flakes. With his carcass frozen solid under a thick blanket of snow, the crows and coyotes would lose interest in Prince, and William's tracks from the road to that old overgrown shelter belt would disappear for ever. Maybe.

Even though he had buried his brother that morning, Mike Bohas had a smile and a giggle for William when he walked in the door. Mary's rosy face had faded and her tired eyes were undershot with gray. Tiny red lines spread out across the whites. She had no smiles for William, but from her husband's demeanor there could be no question that the episode with Speer remained a secret. William gave an account of exactly what he had done since they left, except, of course, his trip to the Speer farm. When he was finished he said he had almost forgotten, but a deputy sheriff named Ivan Blitzko had stopped by and asked Mike to call him as soon as he got home. 'It'll wait till after we eat,' Mike said.

Mary hurriedly heated up some beans and frankfurters. When it was time for his ice cream, Mike began to tell William about the death of his brother. 'Y'know, when I got there John seemed just fine. We was really glad to get together 'cause we hadn't seen each other for two years. Him and Nancy went to Europe last summer, so we didn't get together like we always used ta – y'know, after we got all the plantin' done in the summer. Well, we was just settin' there talkin' and he had to tell me this story. He said there was this old guy workin' as a wrangler out in Wyoming someplace and the boss bought a real high-priced bull and when he got the dang thing home it wouldn't do nothin'. Seemed like it just didn't give a dang about any a the cows. Well, I guess they paid about forty thousand for it and the boss was really kinda pissed off 'bout the whole thing, so he called the vet. Well, the vet said he'd come out that afternoon and take a look and the boss said, you come on ahead, but I gotta go into town – for some dang thing or another. Then when he hung up the phone, he asked that old wrangler – I guess he was over ninety years old – he asked him if he could look after things and show the vet where the bull was and all that kinda stuff. So the old guy says, yep, he could. And the boss says he would call later on to see what happened because he was going to stay over-night in town. Ya know out there in Wyoming it can be a three-hour drive to town. Anyways, the vet showed up and the old guy helped like he said he would. Then later on that day the boss called and asked if the vet got there, and the old guy says, yep, he did. An' the boss says, well, what's the vet do? And the old guy says, well, he took a little bottle out of his bag and he rubbed some of the stuff in it on the bull's gums. Then what? says the boss. Well, that dern bull busted right through the fence and serviced the first cow he saw and he just kep' on a going till he serviced every cow on the place and then kep' on going and serviced every cow clear to the Nebraska line, and the boss says, for cryin' out loud, what was in that bottle? And the old guy says I don't know, but it tastes just like vanilla.' Mike laughed and laughed while his ice cream melted in the dish.

Mary didn't even smile, and William didn't really get the joke because he was thinking so hard about other things. He did force a little grin. He never ever laughed out loud anyway.

Mike went on. 'Well, we were just settin' there laughin' at that story and all of a sudden John starts kinda chokin' and his eyes rolled right back up to the top.' Mike rolled his eyes as far up as a conscious human being could. 'And he just lay back down in the bed and Nancy ran to get somebody down the hall there in the hospital. Time they got back – just a minute or so – he was gone. At least he died with a smile on his face. That ain't too bad, I guess, huh?'

'No,' said William. 'That is not bad.'

While they finished their ice cream, William glanced at

Mary several times. Her face looked lost. She hadn't eaten anything.

'Well, I better call Ivan,' said Mike. 'See what he wants. Maybe wants me to partner with him in that pitch tournament over in Geddes. But I awready told Kenny Speer I'd play with him. Maybe I should check the water for them calves first.'

'I have already finished with that,' said William.

'Well, that's good, Frankie, real good. Ya don't hardly need me around here any more, I guess.'

'Thank you,' said William.

Mary started picking up the dishes. Mike seemed not to notice her anguish, but it preoccupied William's mind. When she turned from the sink to walk back to the table, he caught her eyes. There was nothing there.

Still in his place at the table, Mike reached back for the cordless telephone on the cupboard. 'Might as well try him at home first.' He dialed and waited. 'Hello there, Ivan. Mike Bohas callin' . . . Ya, I heard you was here . . . Oh no! For cryin' out loud, what happened? . . . The bathtub . . . Slipped in the damn bathtub . . . Oh, for cryin' out loud.'

Mary came to life. 'What on earth's happened?'

Mike covered the phone with his hand. 'Kenny's dead. Slipped in the bathtub. Yeah, Ivan. I just buried my brother this morning . . . Ya, thanks, Ivan . . . Y'never know . . . Oh sure, we'll be there. That'd be good . . . The dog? You'd think he'd a been right there. He followed Kenny around like a calf . . . I s'pose it's real hard on Edith if she found 'im and all . . . For God's sake, we were just huntin' elk together in Montana last week. I got a five point . . . OK. That'll be fine. I'll be here. Anytime after the funeral's fine. That'll be two for me this week . . . Geez, you're right, they say things come in threes . . . Ya, I wonder what's next. Ya . . . Ya . . . See you tomorrow then . . . G'bye.'

Most of the color had drained from Mike's face, one tear slid down each of his cheeks. Mary sat back down in her place at the table, her face full of fright and awful questions.

William got up from the table. 'I will leave you two alone,' he said. 'I am sorry, Mike.'

'You don't hafta go, Frankie,' said Mike. But William continued through the door into the living room and sat down on the sofa. The voices in the kitchen remained clearly audible.

'I'm so sorry, Mike. I know Kenny meant a lot to you.'

'It's just one of those things.'

'What did Ivan say about the funeral?'

'Tomorrow, I guess, in Lake Andes.'

'What else did Ivan say?'

'I guess he just slipped. Musta been standin' up in a bathtub full of water and slipped and hit his head on the tub, then drowned.'

The telephone rang.

'Ya, this is Mike . . . Ya Edith, sure I'll be there early . . .'

William sat in the dark listening to the long conversation between Mike and Kenny Speer's sister Edith. People make such a thing over death. As if it only happens to an unlucky few.

The corncobs burning in the big stove warmed the kitchen early, but it was quiet around the breakfast table. William felt uncomfortable. They invited him to the funeral but he declined, saying he could be most helpful at home doing the chores. Mike thanked him profusely. Mary seemed to be avoiding his eyes. Could she possibly suspect he was involved? Not likely. She was merely distraught over the multiple deaths.

After Mike and Mary left for the funeral, William tore through the chores. Because of the morning feeding he had told Wilma not to expect today's call until eleven thirty. To speed things up he cut the quantity of hog feed by one-third. For one day it would make no difference and no one would be the wiser, except perhaps the hogs themselves. He had read somewhere that in zoos they often skipped a day's feeding for certain species. At eleven he wheeled out of the yard and headed for a truck stop seventeen miles north where he could make a telephone call in relative privacy.

Wilma picked it up on the first ring, her voice filled with excitement. William assured her that he was in good health, that he had not had a headache for several weeks, that farm life agreed with him.

'You're working on a farm?' she said.

'Just as I planned,' he said. 'But it is soon time for me to return to the city.'

Her voice was hurried. 'Is it really necessary, William? I have an idea. I can raise several thousand dollars—'

'I do not need money,' he said.

'You didn't let me finish. We can go somewhere where they will never find us.'

'There is no such place,' he said. The operator asked for more coins. William complied. He went on, 'Besides, Wilma, you know I have important things to do. Promises to keep. When you wrote those letters for me they were not meant to be empty threats.'

'But they will kill you, my sweet.'

'They can only do that once.'

'I wish you wouldn't say such things. I wouldn't have helped you escape if I had known it would mean losing you for ever.'

William didn't believe her for a moment. She had never refused to help him when he had asked. 'Wilma, I am coming back, and I will need your help.'

'William, please think it over. We could maybe have a life somewhere.'

'There is nothing more to say on the subject. My plan has worked perfectly and I intend to see it through to the end. Have you been watching Judge Goldman?'

'Her daily routine is amazing, only the smallest variations. She passes the same points at the same time each day, at least four times out of five. It's taking a lot of my time.'

William listened calmly, if not patiently. Wilma went on about Bannon coming to her house. When she was finished he said, 'What about the child? Are you keeping account of her habits?'

'I took some vacation time and got her routine down while you were still at Wolf River. I know her school habits. She's very active coming and going, and she spends a lot of time, even overnights, with a friend who lives right on Lake

Minnetonka, near Wayzata. I have every one of her usual destinations marked on a map. Same for her mother. The daughter is more active and gets around more than the mother. But William, this is so unnecessary. We can have a life—'

'I am pleased that you have done a thorough job on these people. I take it the child has no idea she has been watched.'

'No, William, there's no chance she knows.'

'Keep it that way.' The operator came on and William made another deposit in the pay phone. 'When the time comes, they will not be able to protect any of them from someone who is willing to die.'

'Oh William, don't leave me alone.'

'You will not be alone. You have your work.'

'I will be alone.'

'Wilma, where did you intend to get the money you spoke of?'

'I think I can borrow it from Tom Phelps.'

'I thought he was going to prison for rape. Stay away from him. Now I must hurry,' he said.

'Don't hang up, William.' Wilma sounded frantic.

'I must. I have no more coins. I will call you at this same time three weeks from today. I will be coming soon after that. Find out what you can about my lawyer, Mr Scott, Goodbye, Wilma.'

'William, please.'

Late that afternoon the sun made a brief showing. William poured shelled corn into the grinder while Mike tried to keep the motor running. It cast a long shadow across the rough, textured earth of the yard to the spot where Ivan Blitzko had just parked his patrol car.

'Hey, Mike, you havin' trouble?' he yelled above the noise of the sputtering motor. Today he was out of uniform, but the rabbit-fur hat was still on his head with the ear flaps hanging down.

'Aw, I think the dang plugs are all gummed up,' Mike said. 'We're about done here for today anyhow.' He shut the engine off.

'This clear sky, it's gonna get colder'n hell tonight,' Ivan said.

'Yep, I s'pose,' said Mike, the blaze-orange hunting cap cocked back on his head, his bare ears bright red. 'I guess you met Frankie here.'

'Yeah, we said hello yesterday,' said Ivan. 'Looks like he's been helpin' out around here a lot.'

'Past couple weeks I dunno what I'da done without 'im,' Mike said. 'Quite a bunch turned out for Kenny's funeral.'

'Yeah. Teachin' school all these years, Edith's got a lotta friends all around this part of the country. I just come from the Speer place. There's a guy come all the way down from Pierre to look the place over.'

'What could he be lookin' for?' said Mike.

'Well, Sheriff Bettendorf asked him to, I guess. When a guy dies in a funny way like that they like to check things over. Edith was over there too.'

'Ya,' said Mike, 'she saw a lotta Kenny, specially during the holidays. She used ta bring 'im them punkin pies he liked so well. She took it purty hard.'

'Y'know it's really goofy,' said Ivan, 'the way that dog lit out. Don't make sense. Edith says that dog never even left the yard. Y'know they had 'im neutered last year because he was chasin' all over the place. Since then Edith says Prince never left the yard.'

'I know,' said Mike. 'I never seen him but in the yard, or mostly in the house, to tell you the truth. Since he bit that guy a coupla years ago, Kenny kept 'im pretty close.'

William stood there listening and shivering.

'Frankie, you go ahead in outa the cold, tell Mary I'll be in in a minute.'

Without a word, William headed for the back door of the house. Before he was out of earshot, Ivan said, 'Awful quiet guy, ain't he? Maybe a little spooky, huh?'

'Aw no,' Mike said. 'He's a good guy. Not really cut out for this hard work, but he tries hard.'

Once inside the door, William began looking for Mary. He ran upstairs. Her bedroom was nearly dark in the winter afternoon light. She was standing by the window looking out over the yard where Mike and Ivan were still talking. William said her name.

She whirled round abruptly. She couldn't have been startled. She saw him come across the yard and she must have heard him run up the stairs. She looked better, but there was tension in her face. She had brushed her long red hair and it spread out softly on her shoulders.

'Are we not indeed fortunate?' William said.

'But he's dead, Frankie. That's not right. It can't be fortunate that Kenny Speer died in that awful accident.'

'Everybody dies,' said William. 'He was going to tell Mike what he saw in this room.'

'I don't think he really would have,' she said. 'I made him a fair proposition. He wasn't a nice man, but he was no fool. Mike was his only friend and I think he would have spared him the heartache.'

William moved closer. Through the window behind her, Mike and Ivan were walking toward the house, talking animatedly. 'You would never know for sure,' William said, 'and Speer was not a compassionate man. He would have held it over you, made demands on you.'

Mary's face softened and she stepped forward and pressed her cheek against the collar of his jacket and held on tightly. In a minute the back door slammed. William pulled away and went to his room.

34

Kevin walked down the dimly lit corridor in the basement of the Commercial Building, Rebecca's left hand firmly clasped in his right and a case holding two revolvers and a hundred rounds of .38 Police Special ammunition in his left. On the green steel door at the end of the hall the word *Range* was stenciled in large white letters. With a key from a ring in his pocket Kevin let them into a room with pale green concrete walls, dominated by a tan steel cabinet with floor-to-ceiling doors and a matching steel table. From behind another steel door came the muffled reports of gunfire. Kevin signed his name in a log book on the table and took two sets of ear protectors from the cabinet. They looked like oversize earmuffs, but the earpieces were covered with hard green plastic. He put one set on his head and showed Rebecca how to adjust hers.

'Nothing complicated about that,' she said as she fitted hers to her head and over her ears.

Kevin opened the door into the white glare of the shooting range. Big black-lettered signs entitled RANGE RULES were fixed to each of the long side walls. Off to the right a tall man was shooting at a black and white target about fifty feet away. Even with the ear protectors Rebecca thought the shot was too loud. The man's arm bounced sharply up and back from the recoil. With a little wave of one hand, he acknowledged Kevin's presence then fired again. 'He's shooting a .44 magnum,' said Kevin. 'That's one of the biggest handguns. Just firing it can injure your hand if you're inexperienced.'

227

'No thanks,' said Rebecca. 'Hey, isn't that what Dirty Harry used?'

'That's the one. Clint Eastwood was aiming it at that guy's head when he said "Make my day", but I've got something a little more practical in here.'

From the case, Kevin extracted a small stainless steel revolver. Grasping it by the barrel, he held it out to Rebecca. 'This is called a snub-nose revolver,' he said. 'The barrel is only an inch and a half long.'

Tentatively, she gripped the wood-covered stock. The banging of the .44 magnum continued every few seconds, just twenty feet away. The acrid odor of burning gunpowder filled the room.

'That little honey is made in Brazil,' Kevin said, 'just right for a lady. How does it feel?'

'OK I guess.' She held it out in front of her and pointed it down the range.

'Revolvers are the safest of all handguns because to fire them you have to either draw the hammer back or put significant pressure on the trigger. Let me show you how it works,' said Kevin.

She handed it back to him.

'This is what we call the cylinder.' He pushed a release on the side of the gun and popped the cylinder out on its hinge. 'You can put five thirty-eight cartridges in these holes.' He snapped the cylinder back in. 'You can fire it rapidly by just pulling the trigger hard like this.' He pointed the revolver down the range and pulled the trigger several times. Here, you try it.'

Rebecca did. It felt like a cap gun from her childhood.

'Or,' said Kevin, holding his hand out for the gun, 'you can fire it single action. Keep your finger off the trigger and draw back the hammer with your thumb like this. Then very gently squeeze the trigger.' He demonstrated. 'See, that way you can hold the gun much steadier because it requires far less pressure on the trigger to fire it. Here, try it.'

She did. The hammer fell. 'Oh, I see. That's real smooth.'

'You got it.'

Kevin retrieved a target from the cabinet under the

counter and clipped it into the target holder. Then he cranked the target hanging from the holder on its cable about thirty feet down the range. He picked up the gun and inserted five cartridges in it from a handful he had taken out of his pocket. He held the gun up in his right hand and grasped his right wrist with his left hand and fired. He fired four more times at intervals of about one second. Then he handed the gun to Rebecca and cranked the target back to where they stood. He had hit the bull's-eye with four of the shots. The other was a fraction of an inch outside.

'Wow!' said Rebecca.

'You can do the same with a little practice,' said Kevin. He handed her five more cartridges.

Rebecca opened the cylinder. 'How do I get the spent ones out?'

'Just push that little extractor rod,' said Kevin, pointing.

She pushed it and the five empty cartridges fell on the floor with a tinkling sound.

Kevin bent down and picked them up. 'We just throw them in these cans.' Then he handed her five live rounds. As she inserted the cartridges in the cylinder, he started cranking a fresh target down the range.

'See ya, Sergeant,' yelled the guy with the .44 mag just before he walked out the door.

'Now, your honor,' Kevin said, 'give it a try. Fire one at a time, single action. Line the front sight up between the rear sights so it's level with them. In other words, imagine a straight line across the top of the front sight and the two sides of the rear sight. Then put the front sight at the six o'clock position on the black bull, so it looks like the bull is sitting right on the top of the front sight. Now, this is the part I like.' He got himself in position behind her with his chest pressing against her back. He reached round her and guided her left hand up to grasp her right wrist. As the gun in her hand moved in spite of her effort to steady it, he cupped her formidable breasts in both of his hands.

'Kevin! You stop that! I can't hold it steady as it is.'

He backed off, laughing. 'No one can hold that front sight perfectly steady. Think of the bull as a moving target and try to anticipate when that front sight is going to be on six o'clock. The idea is to squeeze the trigger so that it fires when the sight is on six o'clock on the bull. You don't attempt to hold the sight on that spot constantly. It can't be done.'

With the gun extended in front of her as Kevin instructed, Rebecca eased it up to eye level. The thumping of her heart gained speed. She drew back the hammer. As she squeezed the trigger, she closed her eyes. With the bang came the force of the recoil in her hands. She opened her eyes. Kevin was looking at the target through a spotting scope. 'How'd I do?' she said.

'I'm afraid you missed the target.'

Rebecca didn't mention that her eyes had been closed at the moment of truth.

'Try again,' said Kevin.

She fired.

'Hey, good, you hit the target down in the right-hand corner. That's a start,' he said.

'A start,' she said, and fired again.

They stayed for more than an hour. On the last target, Rebecca got two of the five in the black and all five in the target.

'Way to go,' said Kevin. 'Most of those would have stopped a man, if not killed him.'

Rebecca shuddered. 'How about a woman?' she said.

On the way home they stopped for pie and coffee at a diner near the parking lot. Ensconced in a booth with no one else in the place but the waiter, and probably a cook in the back, Rebecca felt safe for the moment. It was a high like when she opened a Christmas present that was exactly what she wanted. 'You know, Kevin, I'm going to take this gun home and keep it in my purse just as soon as you complete the paperwork, but there is a story I have to tell you first.'

'Shoot,' said Kevin. 'No pun intended.'

She giggled. 'This story is part of the reason I hesitated in the first place, I think.'

'The suspense is killing me.'

'When I was about fifteen living in Milwaukee and Papa's business was going great guns – no pun intended . . .'

'Cut that out.'

She giggled again. 'Anyway, he was almost never home, and he started getting kind of antsy about leaving Mama Julia and me home alone late at night, so for her birthday that fall he bought her a gun.'

'Did she learn how to use it?'

'I don't remember just what she learned, but I do remember there was a minor crime wave in our area right about then, so she started carrying that little gun in her purse. It was a German gun, an automatic, I think.'

'Maybe a .380.'

'Maybe. Anyway, Christmas that year Papa bought her a brand-new car, a four-door Ford. Mama was so excited when he showed it to her she wet her pants.'

Kevin was hanging on each word. She just loved those intense eyes of his.

Rebecca went on, 'So it was still during the holidays, and she was taking some gift back or going to a sale or something at this big shopping center near our home. On her way out she was walking across the shopping center and she saw two men getting into her new blue four-door Ford. She ran up to the car just as the man on the driver's side pulled the door shut. She reached out and opened it and shoved the gun right in the guy's face.'

'Uh-oh,' said Kevin.

' "Get out of my car," she yelled at the guy. "You too," she said to the other guy. So they both got out and she herded them round the back of the car. And then,' said Rebecca, 'instead of calling the police – I guess she didn't have the necessary permit to carry the darn gun so that might have been why – she leaves the two guys standing behind the car and jumps in behind the wheel. When she stuck her key in the ignition, guess what? It didn't fit. It wasn't her car.'

'Jesus Christ,' said Kevin. 'Talk about getting over-extended.'

'Her car was in the next row, and a few stalls down.'

'What in hell happened?'

'Some lengthy apologies and a few free dinners as Papa's guest at the club. And Mama got rid of the gun.'

'That's quite a story,' said Kevin. 'Only point your gun at somebody you are actually willing to shoot right then, for whatever reason. You don't shoot someone for simply stealing your car. Right?'

'Right.'

'The corollary to that rule,' said Kevin, 'is that if something happens that makes you point the gun, you shoot. No second thoughts. Got that?'

'I think so,' said Rebecca. She thought of a piece of lead tearing through someone's flesh, perhaps ending their life.

Traffic sprayed Wilma's windshield with slush as she headed east on I-94 to Eau Claire into the glare of an unbroken line of oncoming headlights. She had followed a convoluted route through the twisting streets on the east side of St Paul to make sure no one was following her. William pre-empted all other thought. When she hung up after his call yesterday she knew it was up to her to save him. His return to the Twin Cities meant certain death.

Mr Carlson lived on the edge of town in a stand of tall winter-bare elms that made his house look even smaller than it was. From inside came the yipping of a small dog as Wilma stepped on to the sagging floor of the unlit front porch. The porch light blinked on and the door to the house opened. Her stepmother's frail voice directed her to come in. Wilma followed her through a short dark hallway. In the shadows ahead, the dog continued its crazed yipping. 'Shut up, Maggie,' Wilma's stepmother said listlessly.

The living room was papered in a faded floral design that clashed unmercifully with her stepmother's flowered shapeless dress. The nondescript fuzz-ball of a dog had changed its tune to a simpering whine. The old woman bent over and picked it up.

'Sit down, Wilma,' she said and motioned to an easy chair. She dropped on to the sofa, her face haggard and old, beyond repairing with make-up. She still dyed her sparse hair red, but at least an inch of gray roots showed. The dog settled contentedly on her lap.

'Cloris, did somebody come?' a weak old voice called out from a room in the rear.

Cloris ignored him.

'Just as well he doesn't know I'm here,' said Wilma.

'Who's there?' the voice called again.

'Just a woman collecting for the Red Cross,' Cloris bleated with great effort.

'Fuck the Red Cross,' he yelled back, hoarse and rough like a whiskey throat.

'He's getting pretty difficult,' Cloris said. 'Not that he's changing. He's been that way for years. It's me. I'm getting weaker fast.' Her voice was just above a whisper.

'I'm sorry, Mother,' said Wilma.

'There isn't much time, not very much time at all. I need some of that stuff William used on that prison guard.'

Wilma hadn't quite known how to broach the subject she had driven all the way to Eau Claire to talk about. Now Cloris had given her the opening she needed. 'I can get that for you,' Wilma said.

'Good. Get me three pills. One for Mr Carlson, one for me and one for Maggie.' At the sound of her name, the tiny dog looked up.

'Fine, Mother,' said Wilma. 'But I need you to do something for me first.'

'There isn't much I can do anymore.' Cloris's eyelids sagged. Moisture had accumulated at the corners of her mouth.

'I want you to help me save William's life.'

'What in hell can I do?' Cloris wiped the back of her hand across her chin.

'You can help me kill that judge he hates.'

Driving home after dropping Rebecca at Lake Vista, Kevin wondered if he was doing the right thing in arming her. A public advocate of gun control, she had taken to the whole idea much more readily than he had expected. Now, he was joined with her in two battles: one against a very tangible enemy, Judge Henry Wheatland, surrogate for Tom Phelps; the other against no more than an apprehension, the unpredictable and possible lethal behavior of multiple killer William Schmid's surviving twin sister. With regard to Wheatland, he was pursuing a positive course that, at least theoretically, could result in a solution. What should he be doing about Wilma Schmid? He had the power to assign permanent surveillance on her, but he'd be questioned at the highest levels of the department. It wasn't even his primary jurisdiction. The murders of Slim Olson and Thurgood Jefferson had occurred outside Minneapolis. But William Schmid had been his prisoner and the letters were delivered in Minneapolis. Now, the word was out around the department that he was seeing Judge Rebecca Goldman. If he wasn't, would Wilma Schmid get a permanent tail? The answer was no. He had to live with that. But if he couldn't do something about Wilma now, he would at least give it his best in the battle with that sonofabitch Wheatland.

When he got back to his apartment he called Doris Elmore and as he waited for her to answer, he imagined her double H breasts bouncing as she hurried across the lush carpet to the phone.

'Hello.' The little voice belied the Titaness behind it.

'Doris, it's Kevin Bannon.'

'You caught me in the bath,' she said.

'I should be so lucky. Do they float?'

'That's for me to know and you to find out.'

'Doris, I've been waiting to hear from you.'

'He's coming over tomorrow at noon.'

'Wonderful. Are you all set? Don't forget that little felony lurking in the bushes downtown.'

'And don't you forget our deal, Mr Big Detective.'

'I won't forget,' he said.

35

Barbara Bird in jeans and Saturday morning sweatshirt introduced herself to an anxious looking young woman in the lobby of the County Attorney's office. Even in the casual attire, five-foot-ten Barbara looked like an African princess. She had shining anthracite hair and skin as dark and rich as black walnut.

'Dinah White is anxious to meet you, Melody,' Barbara said. 'She's waiting in my office. I'm so glad you could come in.'

'Like I told you on the phone, Miss Bird, I'm not sure I want to get involved.'

'Well, we can at least talk about it a little,' said Barbara. 'Right in here.'

Dinah White, her slim face dominated by wonderful wide-set eyes, stood up when they entered the room.

'Dinah, this is Melody Sanford,' said Barbara. 'Melody meet Dinah White.'

Dinah held out her hand. Melody took it meekly. Behind them through the wall of windows the IDS Tower and the Norwest Bank Building reached toward the bright sky through the cold, dry, January air. Barbara dropped into her chair. Dinah and Melody sat in chrome chairs straight across the desk from her.

'As I've told you, Dinah, Melody is an old friend of Tom Phelps,' said Barbara.

'I wouldn't really say we were old friends.' Melody's hair was dyed jet black and permed in a mass of curls on top. Her lips were a kind of magenta against her chalk-white skin. Perhaps she had been beautiful once, but she had taken on extra weight and she wore one of those blouses that hung straight down from her breasts to hide her stomach. 'Miss Bird says he raped you,' she said to Dinah.

'He did,' said Dinah. 'But it's my word against his. We need other voices to help put him where he belongs.'

Melody looked at Barbara. 'You say you got my name from Marlene Mays. How'd she know about me and Tom?'

Dinah answered for Barbara. 'I knew her through Democratic Party activities. She said Phelps told her about you when she was going with him.'

'She get raped too?'

'Not exactly, but close. Well, I shouldn't really say. It would be up to her to tell you what happened,' said Dinah.

'What'd she say Tom said about me?'

'He implied you were a little kinky in your tastes.'

'What the hell did he mean by that?'

'I don't know. I just assumed coming from him it was a lie. I figured you probably dropped him and that's what he told people to save face.'

'Can I smoke in here?' Melody asked.

Barbara nodded her assent.

After a couple of drags, Melody said, 'I don't think I want to get involved in this. I've got enough problems.'

'Maybe you could think it over,' said Barbara.

'Yeah, I'll think it over,' said Melody, but the impression was clear. She wasn't going to help them.

'Can you just tell me this,' said Dinah. 'Do you know of any other women who've had trouble with Phelps, or even any other women who've gone out with him?'

'I know one. She's one of those, what'ya call 'em, activists in the Democrat Party. Sue Klein. She's the one who introduced me to Tom. She brought me to one of those caucuses and we went out for drinks after. Then he called me, and you know how it goes.'

'That's just it, Melody.' Dinah's large eyes flashed, her voice razor-edged. 'I do know how it goes with Phelps. And I know Sue Klein.'

'You can't really forget her,' said Melody. 'She's six foot two.' She stubbed her cigarette out and stood up. 'I gotta be going. I'm really sorry I wasn't more help.'

'Can I tell Sue you gave me her name?' Dinah asked.

'I wish you wouldn't,' Melody said, looking at Barbara. 'I'm sure you're smart enough to think of something without using my name, right?'

'I'm sure we can,' said Barbara.

Both Dinah and Barbara assured Melody that they were very grateful to her for coming downtown on a Saturday morning, and Barbara said she looked forward to hearing from her soon. When the door closed, Dinah said, 'She's scared shitless.'

'I'm not sure that was fear,' said Barbara. 'She maybe likes the guy. Just didn't want to tell us.'

'Nobody likes the guy. I'll bet his mother hates his guts.'

'We haven't got a solid commitment from any of them yet.' Barbara stood up and walked over to the window. 'And I don't know if we can gamble on getting even one of them to testify when the time comes.'

'That may be a little pessimistic,' said Dinah. 'I think Marlene Mays will come through. She's just got to work through the idea that it's going to do her in politically. I think it's the opposite. If she doesn't, the feminists will hate her for it.'

'You might have a point there. The Phelps case is becoming a cause célèbre with the feminists. We already have a file full of letters of encouragement. Whit Strom thinks he has a lot on the line here. Remember, it's going to be the first case he's tried himself in almost five years.'

'I appreciate him going to all the trouble on my behalf, but are you sure he's up to it? I think you could eat him alive, Barbara.'

'I'll be right there next to him and, Dinah baby, he isn't doing this just for you.' Barbara leaned forward, her voice ardent. 'He wants to get this guy Phelps. Whit thinks Phelps and his like are ruining the party. Whit's up to it. He's a very able lawyer. No reason to believe he can't handle this case, but both sides will be ready and competent. The evidence should determine the winner. I just wish we could come up with at least two women who would testify about lover boy's

237

propensities. I think one might be worse than none.'

'Why do you say that?'

'An awful lot of men – a good chance even one or more of the jurors – knows one woman out there with an axe to grind. I think Harry Scott would make an awful lot out of that.'

'There's another thing we need to talk about, sister,' said Dinah. 'There's somebody working awfully hard trying to find men who have slept with me who are willing to talk about it.'

'I told you there'd be some of that going on,' said Barbara.

'What about the goddamn rape shield law?'

'Rebecca Goldman will enforce it, you can be sure. Nobody's going to be able to testify about your sexual proclivities.'

'Then what are they up to?'

'I wouldn't hazard a guess,' said Barbara Bird. Not out loud, at least, she thought.

Monica's mother, Denise Clark, had invited Rebecca and Julie over for Saturday afternoon snowmobiling on Lake Minnetonka and the two mother-daughter couples were having a blast. They tore across Wayzata Bay at sixty per, two to a sled. Even Rebecca knew that was well over the speed limit for that busy lake. She could see the heading: DISTRICT COURT JUDGE ARRESTED FOR RECK-LESS SNOWMOBILING. She put it out of her mind. This was too much fun to worry about banalities. The weather had cooperated. They had started out under clear skies in the late afternoon, then watched the spectacular sunset. Now they were slicing through the dusk following the beams of their headlights. The lights of other machines sped around in the dark like fireflies on a summer evening. It was anything but summer. At these speeds little blades of icy wind cut through the cracks around their face masks.

With a wave of her arm, Denise made a wide turn and headed for home on the west side of the bay. Julie sped after her. Rebecca held on tightly in the seat behind her. Monica's father had a bonfire blazing in the yard when they got there.

Denise took her mask off. 'Rebecca, would you rather we build a fire inside in the rec room? Dan says it's down to ten above.'

'Whatever the girls want,' said Rebecca.

'Let's sit out here for a little while,' said Julie, her voice loud and enthusiastic.

Several sections cut from a thick log and set on end encircled the fire for seating. The four of them sat down, gazing into the flames. Pods of snowmobiles roared by on the lake. There was a rule that kept them from running too close to the shore.

'OK, you guys, Monica and I have a question for you. We've been discussing it for a while,' said Julie. 'Right, Monica?'

'Right.' Her voice was small and sweet.

'Shoot,' said Rebecca.

'Mom, how do you know what to do?'

'I don't understand,' said Rebecca. 'About what?'

'About important things,' said Julie. 'You know, when you have to make a decision whether or not to do something. How do you decide?'

Monica's little voice added, 'We learn all sorts of things like math and Spanish and stuff, but not how to decide things.'

As the fire heated their faces and the frosty air cooled their backs, the girls waited for an answer. Had anyone in all her life ever asked a more profound question? Rebecca wondered. 'You want to take first shot at that, Denise?' Denise Clark was a psychiatrist.

'I don't want to dodge the question,' said Denise from inside her parka hood, 'but I'll defer to your honor, for the time being.'

'Well,' said Rebecca, 'when I have to make a decision I think of the pluses and the minuses of my various options.'

'How do you tell whether something's a plus or a minus?' Julie asked.

'Sometimes that can be difficult. But first I look for anything about the option that's just plain wrong. Is it

239

immoral, or illegal? That sort of thing. Of course, if it's illegal that makes it easy.' She knew that was a cop-out. 'But often it's unclear whether something is wrong or not, but almost always my conscience gives me a pretty strong nudge one way or the other.'

'But Mom,' said Julie, 'how do you know for sure when it's your conscience?'

'Maybe experience. From the time we first begin to understand the world, even a little bit, we store up bits and pieces of information from our parents, or religion or that sort of thing.'

'Do you really use all that stuff when you make a decision?' asked Monica.

The fire crackled and snapped while Rebecca pondered. 'I'd like to think I do.' The flames illuminated Denise's face. She was watching Rebecca intently. 'Chime in, Denise,' Rebecca said.

'What you say is true, but I'm afraid most of us aren't that analytical. I think that most of what we do is out of habit. And many of those habits we've borrowed from parents or friends, or society at large.'

'Then don't you just keep making the same decisions over and over again even if they're mistakes?' Julie asked.

'Out of the mouths of babes,' said Rebecca.

'What's that supposed to mean?' said Julie.

'That young minds are sometimes wiser than old ones,' said Rebecca. 'But Denise is right. We should all ask: is this my decision or have I borrowed it from someone else?' Rebecca felt obligated to give a truthful and useful answer whenever a child asked an important question. 'Another approach you might use,' she said looking directly at Julie, 'is to think about what you want to accomplish. Then ask yourself what exactly you have to do in order to reach your goal.'

'That sounds awful hard,' said Julie.

'I agree,' said Rebecca, feeling inadequate and ineffectual.

'Let's go inside and roast the wieners,' said Monica.

'Now that's a good decision,' said Denise and laughed a lovely melodious laugh.

Rebecca liked her. On the way in she said, 'Denise, it would be nice if you called me Becka. All my friends do.'

After the wiener roast, Denise gave Rebecca the tour. The house had been built by Denise's grandfather in the twenties on a hillside overlooking the bay. The neighborhood was an enclave of industrial money, mostly milling and electronics. The descending generations had often entered the professions, in the Clarks' case, surgery and psychiatry.

The lowest level of the house was divided into servants' quarters, laundry, games rooms, including a bowling alley, an indoor pool and spa, and the big recreation room with a massive stone fireplace. From there Denise took Rebecca to the main level. The elevator opened on to a dazzling grand foyer where a crystal chandelier hung from a lofty frescoed ceiling. Rebecca guessed that it cost more than she had earned in her entire life. The floor was Italian marble and a wide staircase with marble balustrade curved its way up to the next level.

They strolled on into the main drawing room furnished in blue Louis XIV with magnificent oil paintings – portraits and still lifes – lining the wall in ornate gilt frames. Vast oriental rugs were strategically placed on the marble floors. Denise knew the origin of everything and Rebecca was captivated by her narrative. They moved from room to room, twelve or more on the first floor plus four or five bathrooms. The highlight was the rosewood-paneled library of thousands of volumes. One floor-to-ceiling bookcase was balanced on a motorized pivot. Denise removed a book from the adjacent bookcase and pushed a button. The wall of books turned on its pivot revealing a windowless den hidden behind it. In this secret chamber, about twelve feet square, Dan Clark kept a free-standing cabinet of sporting rifles and shotguns and a glass-fronted wall cabinet containing several handguns. Rebecca spotted a small stainless steel revolver like the one Kevin had given her. She wondered if the guns were loaded. A roll-top desk and a couple of leather-covered chairs were the only other items in the room.

From the gracefully curving staircase, the chandelier

looked even more magnificent. On the next level there were at least eight bedrooms, each with its own bath. Massive closets concealed passageways with hidden stairways leading to rooms on other levels. As on the main floor, splendid paintings and sculptures were everywhere. Denise ended the tour on the second level, waving off the third with, 'It's pretty musty and dusty. We rarely ever go up there any more. There's a lot of old furniture and family junk up there, sixty years' worth. Monica's totally persuaded that it's haunted.'

Julie had been on the third floor – she called it the attic – several times and said it would be a good place for a slumber party. With Monica's talk of ghosts, Rebecca didn't think such a party would last much past midnight.

On the way home, Rebecca and Julie chattered nonstop about what a great evening it had been. Rebecca thought of Denise's grandfather's handsome but stern face in the giant portrait hanging in the main dining room. It reminded her of the portrait of Charles Evans Hughes, every lawyer's apotheosis, that hung in the Bar Association building on Vescey Street in New York. She wondered what Denise's grandpa would have thought had he known that seventy years hence two Negro women would be the guests of honor in his grand household.

When Rebecca made the left turn from Highway 101, another car made the same turn. For the eleven or twelve miles they traveled on Minnetonka Boulevard, the same car remained behind them. From time to time, another car or two pulled in between, but eventually turned off. The original car followed them toward the garage entrance to Lake Vista. When they turned in, it continued on past. Rebecca was trembling. Would Julie notice? On the way to the elevator, Rebecca hefted the extra weight in her purse and repeated to herself: 'If I have to use this gun, I will use it, no matter what.'

36

The last thing William needed was a January thaw. According to the radio, the temperature had climbed to fifty-nine in Rapid City two hundred odd miles to the west of the Bohas farm. While the three of them ate lunch, the thermometer next to the back door had already hit forty and the sun was smiling down warmly all across the South Dakota plain. As he watered the calves, he considered moving the remains of the dog to a better hiding place after dark. He rejected the idea, reasoning that if he were seen he would be clearly implicated in Speer's killing. Assuming someone found the dog's body, the investigation would heat up; but the authorities would have a long way to go to connect him to the crime. As a boy, William had always wanted a German shepherd.

Late the next afternoon Ivan Blitzko returned yet again. Mike and William had just loaded a wagon with manure for spreading. A cluster of high white clouds was blowing in ahead of a stiff northwest wind. The temperature was dropping as quickly as it had risen.

Blitzko's rabbit-fur hat was in place, his face redder than ever. 'Mike, you ain't gonna believe this.' He gave William a look, acknowledging his presence. 'We found that damn dog. Somebody plugged 'im 'twixt the eyes.'

'For cryin' out loud,' said Mike, and pushed his blaze-orange cap back on his head.

'Yeah, he was layin' in the shelter belt north of the old Jedlicka place. A big buncha crows was flappin' around in them trees. I'd stopped in to old Mrs Porter's place lookin' for 'im yesterday. Today she called and said she figgered there was sumpin' dead back in there. Sure as hell, there was old Prince, picked over purty good. Somebody just walked in there and dumped 'im in the brush.'

'Got any idea who done it?' Mike asked.

'Shit, no.'

'Coulda been somebody he was botherin',' said Mike. 'Ya know he could get pretty nasty, at least he useta.'

'Without this thaw, we'd never a found 'im till spring probably,' Ivan said. 'It looked like whoever lugged 'im back in there was wearing those overshoes with the Ms over the Ws; we found some tracks under the melting snow.'

'Them's from Monkey Wards,' said Mike. 'I useta have a pair. Don't know what become of 'em. They're still around here someplace.'

'The state wanted us to bring that dog clear to Pierre for an examination because Kenny died and all, but Sheriff Bettendorf said nothin' doing.'

'Whadya do with 'im?'

'We took 'im to that vet over at Armour. He cut 'im open and found the bullet. I saw the dang thing, and ya know what? It ain't a rifle slug. Joe Bettendorf says it's either from a .357 magnum or a .38 Special. Same bullet works for either one a them.'

'Who the hell'd shoot that dog with a pistol?'

'You tell me,' said Ivan. 'A dog runnin' loose like that, you'd think sure as anything if a guy's gonna shoot 'im he'd use a rifle.'

'In between the eyes with a pistol, you gotta get awful close to 'im,' said Mike.

'An' he'd hafta be standin' still,' said Ivan, 'an' if he's standin' still, why'd a guy wanna go shoot 'im anyhow?'

'Beats me,' said Mike. 'Whadya think of all this goofy stuff, Frankie?' He turned to William with one of his giggles.

William just shook his head and shrugged his shoulders.

'Anyway,' said Ivan, 'now the guy from the state says we gotta seal off the house. I guess they're gonna look it over some more. We put up some stakes with that yellow police tape across the driveway.'

'You mean they think maybe it wasn't an accident?'

'I was the first one there after Edith, an' it sure looked like an accident to me,' said Ivan.

'Geez,' Mike said. 'Who'd wanna hurt Kenny anyway?'

'He had kind of a mean streak, ya know,' said Ivan. 'He knew how to tee a guy off.'

'Aw, not enough for somebody to kill 'im,' said Mike.

'Like I said, it looked like an accident to me. By the way, did you know Kenny had six cases a dynamite in that old barn? Coulda blowed half the county to kingdom come.'

'I thought he had more'n that,' said Mike. 'Musta used some up, I guess.'

'Say, Mike,' said Ivan, 'Joe Bettendorf asked if you'd come in and talk to 'im cause you knew Kenny better'n anyone else around here 'cept maybe Edith, his sister.'

'Why don't I go down there right now? I can be home by supper.' Mike headed for his pick-up. 'Frankie, tell Mary I'll be back by seven.'

'Yes, sir,' said William.

Mary had perked up over the last couple of days, apparently reconciled to the idea that she need not feel guilty benefiting from Kenny Speer's death. Still, there had been no opportunity for intimacy between her and William since Speer had walked in on them more than a week before.

William found her sitting on the sofa in the waning light, watching *The People's Court* on television. When she saw him she said, 'Oh, I guess it's about time I get supper on.'

'There is no hurry,' said William. 'Mike has gone to town. He said he would not be back until seven.'

'What were they talking about?' She looked up at William.

'I did not pay any attention,' William lied.

Mary patted the sofa beside her. 'Sit down, Frankie.' She picked up his hand and held it in her lap. 'I've missed you these last days,' she said. She reached out and with gentle pressure on his jaw turned his face to her. She looked directly in his eyes, her face framed by her soft red hair. Voices from the television prated, unnoticed.

'It will soon be time for me to leave,' said William.

'Don't go. It's a shame, but with Kenny gone there's no reason for you to leave.'

'I have things I must do.'

'What things?'

'Private things.'

'Oh, Frankie, how can anything be private from me? I have never been so intimate with anyone, not even my husband. We always did it in the dark.' Her face formed a hopeful smile.

'It is not important for you to know.'

'Everything you do is important to me.'

She did not fit into the plan. But her warmth these past weeks had added something William had never known before, even with Wilma. Wilma was warm and loving, but she often treated him like a needy child. With Mary it was man and woman. The headaches hadn't returned. He thought of the giant fireplace and the burning logs and the acres of shiny black cows, Mary sharing it all with him. 'Do you want to go with me?' he said.

'Leave here? Leave Mike?' Her voice had gone up a level.

'Yes,' he said. He could hear her playing Chopin. He could taste her luscious meals and her luscious body.

He kissed her. Her soft lips parted, moving in a desperate rhythm, her arms wrapped tightly round his neck. She released him and leaned back on the sofa with her head propped against a cushion on the end. Light from the television flickered over her body. She pulled her skirt up round her waist. Wisps of coppery hair protruded where her silky white panties met her bare thighs. William was filled with desire, but he was conscious of the dirt and odors clinging to his pants and hands.

'I must go wash,' he said.

She held out her arms to him. 'No, no,' she said, 'I don't care at all. I want you now.'

He dropped down on his knees and pulled her panties down, leaving them hooked round one of her ankles, then plunged his face into the wetness of her vagina. Time became irrelevant.

An hour later the dogs began barking loudly. They had

246

turned the television off and were both completely nude. Mary leaped up from the sofa. The security light in the yard, diffused by the curtain panels, vaguely illuminated her body. 'That might be Mike coming. I've forgotten all about dinner.'

William was buckling his belt when he heard boots in the entry hall. He hurried up the stairs, leaving Mary to put the best face on the situation she could. There were no lights on anywhere in the house.

'Hey, anybody home?' It was Mike's voice. William listened at the top of the stairs.

'Oh, I'm in here, Mike. I fell asleep on the sofa. Frankie told me you wouldn't be home till seven, so I thought I'd have a catnap and I slept right through. I'm sorry.'

'Aw, no harm done,' said Mike. From the top of the stairs William saw the light go on in the living room.

'I'll fix something to eat right away,' she said.

William checked his clothing, then started down the stairs. He knew what was coming next and he wanted to see Mary's face. The two of them were standing in the middle of the living room. Mike still had his orange cap on.

'Mrs Porter was drivin' by the old Jedlicka place over east and saw a bunch a crows flying around in that shelter belt on the north side. So she called the sheriff. Darned if they didn't find Kenny's dog in there. Y'know, that big black German shepherd. Dead as hell. Somebody shot 'im right between the eyes with a pistol.'

'Heaven forbid,' Mary said, her face and tone totally unwary. 'Who would do a thing like that?'

'They ain't got a clue, I guess, but they think maybe what happened to Kenny wasn't an accident.'

Mary looked at William. Their eyes met. She looked away quickly. 'Not an accident? My God,' she said.

'Ivan says the guy that carried that dog back in the brush on the Jedlicka place had Monkey Ward overshoes on.'

'How on earth do they know that?' asked Mary.

'They got them bottoms on 'em with the M over the W. He left some tracks in the snow. You know I got a pair around here somewhere.'

247

William stood silent, thinking about his revolver lying in the drawer upstairs. It wouldn't do to have Mary come upon it. But whatever happened, he meant to take her with him, one way or another.

37

Cloris Schmid, William's stepmother, drove west on I-94. It was Friday night and Wilma had come to Eau Claire to take care of Mr Carlson and the little dog Maggie while Cloris went to Minneapolis for the weekend. Wilma had made it plain enough. Just kill the judge, she had said. Get up close to her and aim the gun right at her heart, in the middle of the flat part of her chest just above her breasts.

A car behind her blinked its lights and she moved over into the right lane. Her old Dodge was doing just fifty-five and the traffic on the Interstate passed her frequently. For Cloris it would be her first killing. Ever since her husband Konrad Schmid died, and before she began taking care of Mr Carlson, she had been a lawbreaker: petty thief, embezzler, arsonist, child molester and any other behavior that brought her what she wanted at the time, and involved little or no real aggressive behavior on her part. Murder would be different, but the stakes were high. She didn't want to go through the death throes of cancer; she wanted an easier death. A cyanide pill like Wilma had smuggled into Wolf River would do nicely. But, more importantly, Cloris needed the pills to give Mr Carlson and her dog Maggie an easy death before she took hers. Those pills were in Wilma's purse right now back at Mr Carlson's house in Eau Claire. All Cloris had to do was kill Judge Rebecca Goldman. The murder of the judge would not only accomplish Cloris's ends, it would give Wilma what she wanted and, most important of all, it would save William's life.

Cloris was very fond of Wilma. After all, Wilma and Mr Carlson were the only two people in the world who cared a whit about her. And she didn't know how much Mr Carlson would care about her if she didn't give him a blow job at least once a week. He had drawn up a will leaving the house and his other meager assets to her. Thinking William was in prison for life, Cloris had an Eau Claire attorney prepare a will for her, leaving whatever she had to Wilma. Tonight she wondered what would happen to everything now that she and Mr Carlson were going to die at the same time. Maybe she should leave a note and make it plain that he died first. Maybe she should even let a day go by in between.

She had always thought it so strange that William was the twin who ended up in prison. Sure, she guessed William must be nutty as a fruitcake, but he was always such a good little boy. Now that darn Wilma, she might be his twin, but you sure couldn't say she was a good little girl. She was always in some kind of mischief from the time she started school. She cheated in her work, even though she was the smartest one in the class, except William, of course. She took other kids' stuff and stole jewelry from their parents. She was the one who got the sex thing started between her and William. She always did anything William asked. She needed one person in the world to love her and that was William. She told those headshrinkers at William's trial that she was her father's favorite. Her father couldn't stand her, although he couldn't keep himself from fucking her. It wrecked Cloris's sex life with her husband. To think he thought he was the only one screwing Wilma. She must have had at least half the boys in the high school.

Killing that cat was one of the worst things Wilma ever did. She made out in court that Konrad had killed the cat. It was all over the papers. That was a laugh. She had that cat for four years and then she wanted a poodle dog like this other girl had got for her birthday. Konrad said she couldn't have both a cat and a dog, so she killed her own cat with a knife, cut its throat and hung it up in the garage to scare William. William cried for two days. Then Konrad bought her a poodle dog.

Cloris was heading down the long hill into Hudson where

the interstate crossed the Saint Croix River from Wisconsin to Minnesota. For all her faults, Wilma was still the only person in the world who ever called her on the telephone just to talk a few minutes. It would be nice if she could do one last thing for those twins and kill this judge. If they caught her in the attempt, Wilma had promised to give the pills to Maggie and Mr Carlson, and then later give one to Cloris in jail. That should be easy enough; she hadn't had any trouble getting one into William when he was locked up.

Wilma had given Cloris a Minneapolis map with the judge's apartment building marked on it. Wilma said Rebecca Goldman was always home at one time or another over a weekend. Cloris should check by calling first. Wilma had got her number somehow. Cloris would read over the other instructions in the morning in her motel. She was getting very tired and she didn't dare take another pain pill until she got off the highway.

Back in Eau Claire, lying on the sofa with a pair of rubber gloves on, Wilma thought enough time had gone by to get on with it. It was not a pleasant place to while away the hours. The house had the stink of the very sick. Mr Carlson had been sleeping ever since Cloris left. Now he had woken and was calling out in his crackly voice.

'Cloris, where the hell are you? I shit my diaper again.'

Wilma got up off the sofa and walked down the hall to his bedroom at the back of the house, the fuzz ball of a dog trailing at her heel. The smell of the load in his diaper met her halfway down the hall.

He yelled again. 'Cloris, where . . . Wilma, what the fuck are you doing here? Where's Cloris?' His face was hidden behind a bushy silver beard but his brown eyes were alive and full of sparks.

There were two windows in the room covered with tightly closed dirty Venetian blinds. The head of the hospital bed was slightly elevated.

'She had to go out for a while. I told her I would look after you.'

251

'Must be quite a while. She goes for two, three hours and leaves me here alone.' Under his mouth the beard was stained with drool.

'It may be a little longer than that. She'll be back later. Here, let me help you with that.'

'Oh, you wanna get a look at a real hunk a meat, haah.' He pulled his nightshirt up revealing a pale green disposable diaper held in place by Velcro straps. His bluish thighs were almost as thin as his calves.

Wilma's arms were strong. She raised his spindly legs up as if he was a baby and removed the diaper. She took it into the bathroom, flushed the contents down the toilet and threw it into a can under the sink. She came back with a wash cloth and a towel. She swabbed the crease of his buttocks, his testicles and the entire pubic area. When she got to his uncircumcised penis, she smiled at him and gently squeezed.

'That feels purty good,' the old man said. 'How's chances of a blow job?'

'Now, if you be a good boy we shall see how good I can make you feel.' This will be easy, she thought. She opened the door of the small clothes closet. Several garish neckties hung under an old felt hat. She selected four and put the hat back on the nail. She went back to the bed and grasped his penis and moved it a little.

'What the fuck are you doin' with those neckties?' Mr Carlson croaked.

She massaged his penis until it evidenced some tumescence. 'Mr Carlson,' she said gently, 'if you want me to take you in my mouth, you must let me tie your hands and feet. Otherwise I would be afraid how you might react. You might hurt me.' She winked at him and flashed her broadest smile, a considerable effort for Wilma.

'Shit, Wilma, I couldn't hurt a fucking fly. But listen, sweetheart, if you're going to give me a real good blow job, you can cut off my hands and feet.'

'That's my boy,' she said.

In a minute or two she had both feeble wrists and both feeble ankles tied to the bed rails.

'Do it to me, baby.' The words barely wheezed out through the tightness of his excited throat.

Wilma quickly pulled the pillow from beneath his head and pushed it down hard over his face. His weak protest was almost totally muffled in the pillow feathers. His head moved from side to side and his back arched, immediately fell back, then arched again. She threw her chest on top of the pillow and bore down with her whole body weight. Urine squirted out of his penis. There was one more faint grunt. Somewhere on the floor the little dog whined. In a minute or so Mr Carlson's body relaxed completely. She lay on top of him for perhaps another two minutes and then got up and put the pillow back under his head. The sparks had gone out of his eyes.

She put a fresh diaper on the body. Then she untied the four neckties and hung them back in the closet. She bent over and picked up the tiny dog and took her into the bathroom. She lifted the toilet seat and plunged the small head under the water and held it there until the frantically struggling little body went limp. She put the dead dog in a plastic bag, put on her coat and hat in the living room, picked up the bag and her purse and went out the front door. Once in her car, she took off the rubber gloves and put them in the bag with the dog.

Heading east on I-94, she thought that she had done the right thing; her stepmother would be happy to know Mr Carlson and precious yippie little Maggie were dead. Perhaps it had not been quite as comfortable as the cyanide would have been, but Cloris would never know the difference. When someone finally found Mr Carlson, they would assume he had died naturally, and even if they didn't, there was no reason whatsoever to suspect her. And Cloris would never tell. If she was still alive to have the question put to her, she would be locked up. She sure would never get out of the city if she put a bullet in the judge. She probably wouldn't even try. By this time tomorrow night, Rebecca Goldman will likely be dead, Wilma thought. Wouldn't that be wonderful.

Later that night Wilma checked into a hotel in Madison

253

over two hundred and fifty miles down I-94 from Minneapolis. She was there to attend a self-improvement seminar that lasted all weekend.

In a baggy gray wool sweater Annette Rollins waddled toward Rebecca's table at Applebee's, a newspaper under her arm, an angry, defiant look on her face. 'Becka, have you seen the editorial in my newspaper?'

'You look ready to spit fire. I haven't had a chance to read the paper yet.' Rebecca was ready for a fun dinner with one of her favorite people. She had no desire to read more tripe in the *Tribune*.

As best she could, Annette squeezed her large bottom between the arms of the small chair. 'That sanctimonious bitch. Writin' in my paper. Y'all read this,' she said. Her voice retained vestiges of growing up in New Orleans twenty-five years ago. 'You'll puke.'

'Do I have to?' said Rebecca.

'I think you better, hon.'

The paper was folded open to the op-ed section. Annette pointed to one of the editorials in the unsigned column down the left edge of the page. The first line was in bold face:

TIME TO STEP ASIDE

Until now District Court Judge Rebecca Goldman has steadfastly refused to remove herself from the Phelps case, standing on the principle that to do so would be tantamount to permitting judge shopping in the criminal court. She further contends that there has been no showing of bias or of any reason whatsoever that she would not be able to conduct a fair and impartial trial of Democrat pol Thomas Phelps. We have applauded her position, just as we applauded her appointment, and just as we have applauded many of her rulings protecting the rights of the accused in the face of widespread public outcry. But in view of the most recent revelations regarding some of the actors in this unfolding drama, we can no longer support Judge Goldman's decision.

It has been reported recently in this newspaper that defendant Tom Phelps has a longstanding, more than just friendly relationship with Wilma Schmid, twin sister of recent escapee and mass murderer William Schmid. Wilma Schmid has been questioned several times in connection with her brother's escape. There is no question that her brother's escape was assisted, and in almost two months the police have mentioned no other suspects. It was also reported in this paper and fully corroborated that Judge Goldman had received one or more threats in the form of letters, ostensibly written by or on behalf of William Schmid. Wilma Schmid has also been investigated in regard to this crime, the lead investigator here being none other than Detective Sergeant Kevin Bannon. Judge Goldman does not deny that she and Bannon are close friends; rumor has it they are more than that.

Rumor normally should be given short shrift in public or private matters, but in an area as sensitive as criminal justice we believe, and we have been told by the bar itself, that even the appearance of impropriety is unacceptable. Therefore we think the Phelps-Wilma Schmid-William Schmid-Goldman-Bannon imbroglio no longer passes the smell test. Judge Goldman should remove herself. Another rapidly circulating rumor at the courthouse is that if she doesn't, Chief Judge Cletis Waterbury will intercede.

Rebecca felt very tired. She looked across the table at Annette who was ordering two extra dry martinis from a gray-haired waitress with a very young face.

'Make that just one,' Rebecca said. 'I don't feel like drinking tonight. Maybe I should get off the case.'

'Like hell you should. If Phelps goes free, it should be a jury that lets him off, not Judge Amy Cadwallader who screwed him to get the job. You're the only one that can keep that from happening.'

'But just as it says in here, Waterbury has the power to take me off. So can the Court of Appeals.'

'Then let them do it.' Annette's eyes blazed. 'At least you won't be the one to put the screws to the woman in this case. The victim Dinah White should get a fair trial too. She won't with Cadwallader.'

'All so true,' said Rebecca, 'but I'm so tired of this shit. And even Julie is involved. They're going to reveal how Reggie died.'

'Oh Jesus,' said Annette. 'Well, they always say Harry Scott will find any way to win.'

'There's no way he's involved with any of this,' Rebecca said. Then, swearing her to secrecy, she told Annette of Scott's telephone call to her the Sunday after Thanksgiving. She had turned him down, but she hadn't slammed the door, she said. 'He is a very nice man. And very good-looking,' she added.

For the rest of the evening they batted the issue back and forth across the table like a shuttlecock. When it was time to go home, Rebecca said, 'If Waterbury calls me in, I'm not going to fight him, but I just might resign.'

Annette leaned over the table. She spat the words in Rebecca's face. 'Don't you dare resign. Look where we are, sister. Just look at us, leather coats, fancy hairdos, top jobs in Mr Male Whitey's private little world. We didn't get here by quitting. We got here because Mr Whitey knew people like you and me don't quit, hear?'

'I hear you, Annette, and I love you,' said Rebecca. 'I'm sure looking forward to one more quiet weekend before it all blows up.'

In another part of the night, Kevin's telephone woke him at eleven-thirty.

'Bannon here.'

A little-girl voice. 'Knuckles?'

'Yeah.'

'This is Doris.'

He was finally awake. 'Yeah, Doris. You got it?'

'I got it.'

'I'll be right over.' He jumped out of bed and started looking for his socks.

38

Cloris Schmid had stopped in a budget motel on the I-494 bypass just south of Minneapolis. Sleep had come very slowly to her confused mind. In the beginning, one of the powerful pain pills was all it had taken to assuage the pain, then quickly bring sleep. Last night, sleep came only after interminable waiting and thoughts of impending death.

She finally slept for about four hours and when she awoke the illuminated face of the radio alarm said 5:44. Even before she tried to move, a shaky feeling crawled through her arms. She lay on her back for several minutes thinking about what was ahead of her. To actually kill a person, or even try, seemed beyond her mediocre talents.

She hoped she could eat, and keep it down for a little extra strength. There were sandwiches to take in the car, goddamn baloney and Velveeta. She meant to get a hot breakfast at a Perkins or a Denny's. How she loved to have somebody else cook.

She snapped the lamp on. The dirty yellow emptiness of the cheap room made her feel terribly alone. She wished she was back home with Maggie and Mr Carlson. Maybe this whole idea was stupid. It would be horrible to die in jail. Wilma had assured her that couldn't happen, that if she was caught she would get good hospital care for her last days. And Wilma promised to bring her the pill that would release her from all her pain.

Typewritten on the long sheet of yellow tablet paper that Wilma had given her were Judge Goldman's address, apartment number, telephone number and license plate number. The judge drove a white Buick Century and she usually wore a brown leather coat. When it got real cold she wore a navy quilted down coat, below the knee. Her hair was medium length, dark brown, with reddish highlights in bright sun. She had full lips and her skin was tan. She was about five foot six and she weighed about a hundred and thirty-five. A full face color picture was stapled to the lower right corner of the paper. It appeared to have been clipped from a magazine. Pretty, Cloris thought.

She swung her legs over the edge of the bed and used her hands to help herself up. Pain flared somewhere around her liver and the large muscles of her back were tearing in a thousand places. Short shaky steps transported her to the bathroom. Sitting on the toilet, she washed her pain pill down with a couple of swallows of water, then remembering Dr Clancy's warning against dehydration, she drank the whole glass. It hit her stomach with a jolt. She was supposed to take the pill with a meal, but she couldn't wait.

She took the gun out of her purse. It was bluish-black. She didn't even know what you called it. She thought it was some kind of a pistol. Wilma had shown her how to load it and unload it. But she wasn't sure she remembered. It was loaded and ready to fire, Wilma had said. All Cloris had to do was push the safety from ON to OFF with her thumb. Then the gun would fire eight times as fast as she could pull the trigger. Practice aiming it with the safety on, Wilma had said. Cloris aimed it at the head of a child in a picture on the wall right in front of her, no more than four or five feet away. The barrel waved unsteadily. She had never fired a gun before in her life. Wilma had said she should get as close to Judge Goldman as she could. If she was more than five or six feet away, she would likely miss or just wound her. William would still come to finish the job. That was what they wanted to avoid at all costs.

It was after seven when Cloris stepped out into the chilly morning. The sun was just coming up behind a row of trees on the edge of the parking lot. Her steps had lengthened and some elasticity had returned to her back. She would have a plate of bacon and scrambled eggs and then she would see if she could find Rebecca Goldman.

★ ★ ★

Rebecca woke at six thirty. When she remembered it was Saturday morning and there was no reason to get out of bed, she pulled the comforter over her head and settled back down into a deep sleep. The Harry Scott dream occurred again. As always, he whinnied when he came.

When she awoke again at eight thirty and looked at the clock, she was elated. Almost never could she steal an extra hour, let alone two. She giggled at the funny feeling of guilt brought on by the thought of the dream about Harry Scott intertwined with the image of Kevin Bannon devoted to her for life — or at least so he had said to her in his bed a few nights before, as the throes of passion were subsiding.

She put on her robe and padded through the apartment to get the paper. As she was about to open the door, she remembered the peephole. Kevin had been drilling it into her head. Always look through the peephole before you open the door. It was just good sense for all city dwellers, he had said. She looked. She just caught a glimpse of the back of a brown wool coat moving down the hall toward the elevators. She didn't recognize it. There were four apartments on her floor, including her own. She hadn't remembered seeing any coat like that this winter. It could be anybody. Especially on Saturday. She opened the door, stuck her head out and looked up and down the softly lit halls, carpeted in green tweed. She saw nobody, so she stepped out of the door, snatched her paper, and jumped back in and locked the door.

Julie had spent the night at Monica's. In the dim morning light the apartment seemed empty without her, but Julie always had a great time at Monica's. She loved to explore the attic. Not long ago Julie and Monica had found boxes full of clothes from the twenties: button shoes, spats, derby hats and straw sailors, and those little round hats that covered a woman's whole head except her face. The girls had dressed up and posed. They got some great snapshots. Julie was heading for show business. She could thank Reggie for those genes. Rebecca picked up the kitchen telephone on one ring. She said hello twice, then heard it hang up on the other end.

In spite of everything, Saturday morning stretched out pleasantly before her. She would have a leisurely breakfast, just an English muffin and coffee. No listening to Pettiford calling the court to order, no tedious lawyers pressing petty little advantages. She would read a little in *New York Magazine*. She had subscribed ever since she was at NYU. Even though she almost never got to see the plays he reviewed, she looked forward weekly to John Simon's caustic wit. She still missed the Village and the energy she had felt in Manhattan. What she didn't miss was the filth, especially when the wind blew and whipped it round your face.

At eight thirty Cloris Schmid found a parking place on a side street where she could see the front entrance built into the corner of the Lake Vista building, as well as the garage door on the side. She was so close, the cream-colored brick walls rose up out of sight above the top of her windshield. She counted balconies on the front corner up to twelve floors. That would be where the judge lived.

On the way to use a coffee shop telephone a block away, Cloris complied with the last of Wilma's carefully prepared instructions. She tore them into small pieces and threw them in a sidewalk trash can. On the phone she heard a voice she presumed was Rebecca Goldman's say hello, then hung up and walked slowly back to the car. The snow piled up along the curb was dirty, but it extended clean and white across the lawns and among the trees of the park-like neighborhood. As she settled in behind the wheel to watch, she thanked God for the warming weather. It was supposed to get up to somewhere in the thirties. A stream of cars moved slowly in both directions on the thoroughfare running along the side of Lake Vista.

Maybe the watching and waiting would make time slow down. She had the radio tuned to a golden oldie station. She tried to recognize the singers. The only one she had guessed so far was Bing Crosby singing 'Would You Like To

Swing On A Star.' Cloris had met Konrad Schmid during World War II when that song was popular.

The first hour disappeared. Nothing can slow time down when there is so little of it left, she thought. What a place to spend one of your last days. William had always marveled at how stupid criminals were. Cloris understood; she was a criminal and she must be stupid to be sitting here.

Two hours. Still no sign of Rebecca Goldman at the front door, or the white Buick coming out of the garage. One thing Cloris knew. She had to get her here at Lake Vista. She wasn't up to following her in the city traffic. If the judge left in her car, she would just wait until she returned. Wilma said that on a weekend the judge would eventually come out through the lobby. They had discussed the possibility of going up to the apartment on some pretext. Wilma decided it wouldn't work. Cloris started her engine to run the heater for a while. She guessed another singer right: Kate Smith singing 'God Bless America'. Any dummy would have gotten that one, Cloris thought.

As the day wore on, many people appeared on the sidewalk, some in a hurry, some strolling along, enjoying the sunshine. A patrol car with two cops in it stopped right next to her and gave her the once over. She tried to smile at them. They both smiled back at her and then bumped into the car in front of them. That got their attention in a hurry. The pain in Cloris's abdomen seemed to have connected up with the one in her back.

It was almost eleven before the sun had moved far enough west in the southern sky to flash some rays in Rebecca's kitchen. She sat at the table and looked out into the glare and across the white lake. Somebody was fooling around with an ice boat, but there was barely enough wind to get it moving. The ringing of the phone evoked a quick pang of anxiety. At least this time there was a voice on the other end. Denise Clark said the girls were skating and she was headed into town. Would Rebecca like to have lunch with her at Applebee's? Great idea, Rebecca said. At least she would want to talk about something other than the Phelps trial, only a little more than a week away. Denise said she would be there in an hour.

Cloris had been sitting in her car for almost four hours. The aching at her center had demanded another pill. She followed it with a bite from a bologna sandwich. A finger of pain shot down her left leg. She had to stand up. Just as she opened the door on the driver's side, she saw the brown leather coat and the highlight in the dark hair. Rebecca Goldman was walking out of the front door of Lake Vista. A woman in furs and piled-up dark hair was with her. They started walking directly away from Cloris. She grabbed her purse and started after them. A fast-moving car narrowly missed her. She hurried on. A car moving in the opposite direction in the far lane hit his brakes and waved her across. When she climbed up on the curb on the other side, the two women were a couple of hundred feet ahead of her. She doggedly followed, feeling the weight of the gun in her purse. They were walking faster than Cloris and she felt weaker with each step. They turned right into a shopping center full of cars and people. She lost sight of them, but plodded on. She was very tired. She stopped and leaned up against the plate-glass window of the first building at the entry to the shopping center. She took deep breaths, hoping to get her strength back, but it was no use. She should not have hurried after those young women. She felt dizzy. All the people and traffic were spinning around her head. She felt herself slipping down the glass.

'My God, Becka. That old woman is falling down,' said Denise, bringing her hand to her throat as women do. She wore a white turtleneck under navy cashmere.

Within three feet of their table an old woman with stringy red hair sticking out from under a stocking cap had been leaning on the window and seemed to have lost her balance. Two men were helping her get up.

'It looks like she's got all the help she needs,' said Rebecca.

The old woman appeared to have regained her senses and

was talking to the men. One reached down and picked up her purse. He gave it a little heft as though he thought it was unusually heavy. She held out her hand for it. They took hold of her upper arms and, one on each side, led her down the sidewalk toward Lake Vista.

'Becka, are you all right?' Denise asked, her gray eyes concerned.

'I was just thinking. That bright red hair . . . and there was something in that face. I felt like I knew her from somewhere.'

'You looked far away.'

'My mind talk has been working overtime lately. I suppose you run into that sort of thing in your practice. Hey, that's a great idea; tell me a little about your practice, you know, what it's really like to be a shrink.'

'I imagine you see some of it in court,' said Denise.

'I sure have, but they're always talking about some pretty far-out characters.'

'In my line of work far-out characters are not that unusual.'

They ordered salads and spent the next two hours talking about psychotherapy and many other things, not the least of which were their two darling daughters.

When the two nice gentlemen had escorted Cloris back to her car, they asked if they could call somebody for her. No, she said, she was fine now, and she thanked them again and they were gone. There was no point in sitting here and freezing. If those two women came back to the building, they would be inside before she could get out of her car. She had a better idea. According to the radio, the temperature was supposed to reach the forties tomorrow. If she could get a good night's sleep, she would sneak up a little closer to her quarry. Wilma said the judge sometimes walked round the lake with Julie on Sunday mornings.

39

Kevin called Rebecca late on Saturday afternoon to cancel their date for the evening. He didn't tell her why, just said it was important police business. He hoped she would understand. Naturally she did. She and Julie would go to the movies, she said.

Henry Wheatland was the why. When he had returned his call, Kevin had told him that he needed to see him on a matter of the utmost urgency. How long would it take? Wheatland had asked. Probably not over an hour, Kevin said. Wheatland agreed to come to Kevin's apartment at seven.

At five to, the buzzer from the security lobby sounded in Kevin's apartment. He pushed the release and a couple of minutes later he watched through the peephole as Judge Henry Wheatland approached his door and knocked.

Kevin took an affable tone. 'Come in, Judge, good to see ya.'

'Hank to you, and all other good cops,' said Wheatland. He took a dark fedora off his balding head and sailed it on to the sofa. 'Say, nice place you got here, Knuckles. Who's your decorator?'

'How about a little juice of the grape, your honor?' said Kevin.

'Brandy'd be fine. I guess we're not standing on formalities here.' He threw his coat next to his hat and dropped his big frame into the remaining space on the sofa. 'Been a long time, Knuckles. Fact is, you got me out of a dinner date with a couple I can't stand. Teetotallers. Wife's mad, though. She wanted to see that play at the dinner theater that's about to close. Been runnin' for ages. What the hell's the name of it?'

'*Driving Miss Daisy*,' said Kevin. He handed the judge a small snifter, half full of brandy.

Kevin sat down in a wing chair and set his drink on the end of the glass cocktail table in front of the sofa. Wheatland leaned forward and set his empty snifter near Kevin's. When Kevin refilled it, Wheatland sank back into the white leather sofa. He spoke as though his vocal cords were covered with stucco. 'I hear you've got yourself a new girlfriend, Knuckles, old buddy. Mighty pretty one at that. Kinda stubborn though.'

'Think so, huh, Judge?'

'Yeah, and I'm hopin' that's what this little confab is about.' With liver-spotted hands he set his drink on the table, this time with a splash left in the bottom. 'You know I've always done right by the police. When I was in the legislature you guys didn't have a better friend in St Paul.'

'That a fact, Judge?' said Kevin.

'Now, Knuckles, there's a lotta party pressure on this Phelps thing.' He pulled his dirty handkerchief out and blew his big red nose. 'Some say it could bring the Governor down, or at least wreck his chances for re-election next fall. He's been a good Governor.'

'There's those who'd give you an argument on that.'

'Oh, I know he acts a little stupid from time to time. What Governor doesn't? But it's important he be re-elected, right, Knuckles?'

'If you say so, Judge.'

'Fact is, Tom Phelps is not too bad a guy either. Don't know why that girlfriend a yours got such a hard-on for him.'

'Judge, Phelps is a schmuck and you know it,' said Kevin.

'Oooo, hit your soft spot, did I? That why she wants to stay on the case? You don't like Phelps?'

'She never asked me if I liked that asshole. And I never told her.'

'Whatever. Knuckles, you got me out on a January night for some good reason. Let's hear it.' Wheatland drew a big cigar from a pocket in his maroon cardigan and began groping in his pants pocket, presumably for a match.

'I want to show you something,' said Kevin. He snatched the remote control from the end of the cocktail table. On the far wall the TV came on, the Discovery channel. A big male lion was trying to mount a female. She snapped at him.

'Fucking female for ya,' said Wheatland.

The picture abruptly changed to a bedroom, really a bed. A vast silky pink spread covered a king-sized mattress. A row of big frilly blue pillows reached across the top of the entire TV screen. Kevin glanced at his guest's face. The abundant age lines deepened. A nude woman with a head full of peroxide curls sat down on the edge of the bed, gigantic breasts hanging down, not nearly as far as Kevin had thought they would. Doris Elmore said, 'C'mon, honey, whatcha waitin' for?' in her little-girl voice.

'That's . . .' Wheatland's whiskey voice started up, then shut down abruptly, as an erect penis, seemingly floating in space at a slight downward angle, intruded from the right edge of the picture. Doris touched the end with her tongue, then took a full helping. Then she reached out and drew Henry Wheatland into the picture with one of her hands on each cheek of his flabby old ass. She dropped back down on her back and propped up her bottom on one of the blue pillows. Her breasts slid partially down the sides of her rib cage, leaving an impressive amount still in place on her chest. She spread her legs for the camera, revealing a mat of reddish pubic hair. Wheatland crawled into position between her raised knees. After fumbling and murmuring for a minute, he began grunting and pumping in the missionary fashion, his senescent testicles dangling and swaying in the foreground.

Across the room from Kevin's TV set the lipless mouth in Wheatland's exsanguinated face hung open. The cigar remained unlit between his fingers.

'Seen enough?' said Kevin.

'Shut it off,' said Wheatland. Like a ventriloquist, his lips barely moved. 'How much do you want for it?'

'It's not for sale,' said Kevin. 'Besides, I have a hundred

copies. Let me give you the drill . . . Hank.'

Wheatland leaned back into the sofa, apparently ready to listen.

'First, if there is any more heat of any kind put on Rebecca Goldman from anywhere within the government, judicial, legislative or administrative branches, this tape will be released to the print and electronic media. This week Cletis Waterbury will announce that he has decided that Judge Goldman was properly chosen and there is no legal or ethical impediment to her serving as trial judge in the Phelps case. If not, each member of the district bench will receive a tape in the mail. I hope you get the point. She stays, and I don't mean in the family court, or you go, and it's hard telling how far you go. You and I both know it's pretty damn far. Another thing. The production might be a little less professional, but I think this tape could be as intriguing to Mrs Wheatland as *Driving Miss Daisy*.'

Wheatland's blanched face just stared at Kevin. Then he mumbled, 'Who else has seen this?'

'Just Doris and me,' said Kevin. 'One last point, Judge. Any harm comes to Doris Elmore, even if she slips and falls on the ice, everybody gets a tape.'

Wheatland spoke again, in a gravelly whisper. 'What about after the trial? After the Phelps thing is over?'

'We'll talk about it then. As you say, you been a friend to the cops. We got something to talk about.'

Wheatland struggled up out of the sofa, hat in one hand, coat in the other.

'Any questions on procedure, you better call me,' said Kevin. 'I'm sure you don't want to make any mistakes. And by the way, your honor, Rebecca Goldman knows nothing of this tape or that Doris Elmore even exists. Keep it that way. *Capice?*'

Wheatland's grizzled head made a barely perceptible nod, his pupils tiny dots in watery eyes.

The next morning, just before nine, Cloris Schmid parked her car in the exact same spot she had yesterday. Sharp-edged shadows lined the snow and the climbing sun had already driven the temperature into the thirties. Minneapolis was in for a wonderful winter Sunday. Wilma had told her not to risk a telephone call on Saturday night, but about eight she had tried anyway. No answer. Wilma must have gone out for a while and turned off the ringer on the telephone by Mr Carlson's bed. Maybe he had just slept through the ringing. She had had nothing to report anyway, but she hoped she might hear little Maggie barking in the background.

Cloris drew in several deep breaths before opening the car door. The last pill had dulled the spike of pain driven through her navel to her spine. She didn't expend the energy required to walk the block to the coffee shop to telephone. She just assumed the judge was in the building. Anyway, there was nothing else to do but wait. When she stood up, the sciatica ran down her left leg like a current of electricity. Shakily, she stepped out into the street, her heavy purse dangling from one hand. The cool air felt clean and bracing in her nostrils. Sunday morning traffic was light. It occurred to her she should have a cane. She wouldn't have fallen down yesterday if she had had a cane. The longer shadows crossed the pavement and folded upward on the cream-colored brick side of Lake Vista. Sun glinted off the cars passing through the intermittent shade. When the street was clear, she walked across, one tentative step at a time. Only one car had to slow down for her. She stepped up on to the curb on the other side and crossed the sidewalk to the east wall of Lake Vista. She rested against it for a minute or two. Energy-wise, she was way ahead of yesterday.

From where she stood near the first window on the lobby, she could see the backs of people leaving the building. They stepped from the lobby on to the sidewalk just round the corner from where Cloris waited. This morning in the motel, she had again practiced pointing the gun at the child's head in the picture. Her hand had been unsteady, but Cloris reasoned that from where she stood today she could get so close it wouldn't make much difference.

268

The Sunday paper completely covered Rebecca's queen-sized bed except for the spot she occupied. Quickly perusing each section, she assigned them to separate piles according to a priority rank for her morning reading.

Julie stood at the window looking out over the lake. 'Mom, Monica's teaching me how to skate. She's had scads of lessons. She makes perfect figure eights.'

'Denise and I had a great time too.'

'Wouldn't it be neat if you became best friends with my best friend's mother?'

'We're already good friends.'

'But I mean best friends,' Julie said impatiently.

'I'm afraid Susan will always be my best friend. We go back a long way. How's it look out there?'

'Super. Best day of the year so far, I bet.'

Rebecca had already read a small article in the local news section speculating that on Monday Cletis Waterbury would be assigning a new judge in the Phelps case. She wanted to get the damn case out of her mind for this beautiful Sunday with her beautiful daughter. 'Let's fix a great breakfast. Then take a nice walk round the lake,' she said.

Twelve stories below, Cloris leaned against the bricks absorbing the intense rays of the sun. For a few moments she turned her back to the sunlight and the street. Huddled up closely to the wall, her shoulders hunched, she dipped her hand into her purse and dropped the gun into her right-hand coat pocket.

Numerous people had come and gone from the lobby since she had taken up her post, none in the least resembling Rebecca Goldman. Cloris focused mainly on the lobby, but she also kept track of the cars exiting and entering the garage half a block down the street. The only white car she had seen was a station wagon.

Most of those leaving the lobby either turned right, as the judge had yesterday, or headed directly across Lake Street to the shores of Lake Calhoun. Cloris interrupted her vigil at intervals by gazing out over the lake. She remembered walking round it with Konrad on a Sunday many years before. It was summer and sail boats skittered along ahead of the wind and the beach on the other end of the lake was packed with bathers in brightly colored swimsuits. She had looked good in a swimming suit in those happy days when the twins were still toddlers. She wondered whether Konrad would approve of what she was doing, one last effort to help the twins, especially William who hated her so much. He hated her over the sex thing. What was so bad? She wasn't even his real mother. And when Konrad turned his attentions to Wilma, it seemed OK for her to have a little fun with William. William had even wanted it sometimes, she had just got too demanding about it. It seemed like she never was able to do the right thing. Still, she thought, it had been better to keep it in the family.

She watched the back of a woman step quickly through the lobby in a leather coat, but it was black and she was a bleach blonde. Cloris leaned against the bricks. If she had been standing where she was now she might have got to Rebecca Goldman yesterday when she left the building with the woman in the fur coat.

The temperature continued to rise as the morning wore on. A man walked by wearing only a sweater. Weariness began to permeate Cloris's cancer-ridden body. Even as she lay in wait to kill, she was flooded with self-pity. She might never see another beautiful winter Sunday. If the judge didn't come out soon, she would have to swallow another pain pill.

After a last gulp of orange juice, Rebecca cleared the breakfast dishes off the kitchen table. Julie emerged from her bedroom brushing her hair. Opening the sliding glass doors of the living room, she walked out on the balcony. She stood at the rail looking out over the lake, then turned and called back, 'Mom, it's so nice, we could probably wear sweaters.'

Rebecca appeared in the door in her brown leather coat. 'No, I think I'll wear my coat. Maybe you should too.'

'I'm going to wear that ski jacket you gave me, the light one.'

★ ★ ★

It was going on noon. Trembling seized Cloris and the pain down her leg was going wild. Maybe she should take the goddamn gun and shoot herself in the head with it. No, she needed to last out this one day. Do what she had promised to do. Do something right for a change. She sensed movement in the lobby. She saw their backs. The brown leather coat, the dark brown hair. A young girl in a jacket. Cloris moved forward to the corner of the building. The door was just swinging shut behind the two. They stood on the curb looking out over the lake, waiting for a break in the traffic. Do something right for a change. Bent over from back spasm and pain, Cloris shuffled forward until she was only five or six feet behind the brown leather coat. Do something right for a change. 'Judge,' she squawked as loudly as she could. She thumbed the safety off and raised the gun. The brown leather coat turned abruptly toward her. Cloris kept her eyes on the bulge of the breasts and pointed the gun just a little higher at the flat part of the chest and squeezed the trigger. The little automatic bucked in her hand and she squeezed the trigger again and again and again. The crackling reports of the gunshots startled her, and she looked up at the face, frozen in fear. The girl in the jacket stood shrieking, her hands to her temples. Cloris stared at the face and dropped the gun to her side. Another shot went off into the sidewalk. Something was terribly wrong. The face. The face was pinkish-white like her own. It wasn't the face in the picture. It wasn't the face of Rebecca Goldman. The woman in the brown leather coat dropped to her knees, then flopped over, her head only inches from Cloris's shoes.

The gun fell from her hand. She tried to run to her car. She tripped on the curb. The last thing she ever saw was the tasteful understated grill of a dark green Jaguar.

Julie was coming in from the balcony when they heard the shots. She ran back to the railing and looked down at the sidewalk just as the dark green car sent a woman flying out on to Lake Street. 'Mom, did you hear those shots?' Julie screamed. 'Somebody shot a woman down by the front

271

door! She's wearing a leather coat like yours! And a car hit a woman. Oh Mom! It's awful.'

They sounded like fire crackers. Four or five. Rebecca ran out on the balcony and looked down. Traffic on Lake Street had stopped. A woman with red hair lay in a weird position on the pavement, as if her back was hyper-extended. Straight below in front of the lobby door another woman lay face down in a brown leather coat.

Julie's voice sounded out of control, keening. 'Ooooooooooh. Oooooooooooh.' Finally, she spoke. 'Mom, I saw the car hit the woman.'

Rebecca ran back into the living room and grabbed her binoculars out of the desk drawer. Back at the railing she tried to focus on the face of the woman in the street, but it was obscured by the men kneeling around her. Rebecca held steady. When one man moved, she saw the face in detail. It was the same woman she had seen fall outside Applebee's yesterday. She swung the glasses back to the figure on the sidewalk encircled by a crowd. A gun lay beside her head. A young woman in a pink jacket knelt next to the fallen woman, repeatedly turning her face from the woman to the onlookers and back to the woman. A siren sounded in the distance.

She was judge of the district court. She must go down there. 'Julie, would you please stay here and make good notes of everything you see and have seen.' Rebecca handed her the binoculars.

Julie started to argue. She wanted to go with her mother.

'No arguments,' said Rebecca. 'Don't forget to make the notes. I'll be back soon.' She grabbed a plastic bag in the kitchen.

The elevator stopped on almost every floor. When it reached the lobby, Rebecca was packed into a corner behind a huge man in a pajama top. The air was full of sirens. She pushed her way through the group surrounding the woman in the leather coat. Two men looked as if they were going to roll her on her back. 'Don't touch her,' Rebecca said with authority. Then she bent over and pushed a pencil through the trigger guard of the automatic,

272

gently lifted it into the plastic bag and put it back on the sidewalk.

'I felt her pulse. She's alive,' said one of the men.

Rebecca recognized the pretty face of the young woman in the pink jacket, but she couldn't put a name to it. An older woman had her arm round her.

Some blood trickled out from under the victim's right shoulder into a low spot on the sidewalk. Rebecca took her coat off and laid it over the woman as the first police officers burst through the circle.

'She was shot about five or six minutes ago,' said Rebecca.

'There's an ambulance coming right behind us,' said the taller of the two cops.

'I put the gun in the bag,' said Rebecca. 'I didn't touch it, and I don't think anyone else has.'

One of the sirens wound down just feet away. A team of paramedics rushed through the crowd with a litter and sophisticated-looking equipment, followed by a third cop.

'The old woman in the street is dead. Did anyone see what happened?' he said.

'My daughter saw the car hit the red-haired woman,' said Rebecca. 'She's up on the balcony. I'm Rebecca Goldman.'

'The judge?' said the cop.

'Yes.'

The medics were heading for the ambulance with the woman on the litter, unconscious. Somebody handed Rebecca her coat. Blood dripped from one sleeve. The young woman in the pink jacket was alongside the litter. 'She's my mother,' she said. 'Will she be all right?'

A voice said, 'We'll do our best. Get in. You can ride along.'

With the three cops, Rebecca stood looking after them. 'The girl there in the pink jacket. She probably saw the shooting,' Rebecca said.

A cop started after her.

'Leave her alone,' Rebecca said. 'She won't forget.'

40

The police wanted Julie to go with them downtown and make a formal statement, but Rebecca vetoed the idea. 'We'll make some notes. Maybe she can come in tomorrow,' she said. 'This experience today has been too traumatic. She needs time to calm down a little.'

With the awful world on the other side of the locked door, Rebecca let herself fall into the big blue and gold striped sofa and held her arms open to Julie. She snuggled in close and pressed her head against her mother's neck.

'Mom, why would that old lady shoot that woman who lives on the seventh floor? You know, her daughter, the one in the pink jacket, gave me a ride to school one morning.'

Rebecca had an idea. It was growing with the speed of one of those buds opening on stop-action photography. She believed in being honest with Julie, but this was still just an idea. She'd wait for a little while.

'I don't even know her, honey,' Rebecca said, 'so I don't know why anyone would shoot her.' When she had seen the old red-headed woman's face yesterday it had kindled a faint spark of recognition, but nothing more. The woman from the seventh floor, Mrs Graham, had been wearing a coat like her own and her hair was just a shade lighter. But Mrs Graham was white, as white as people get, that ultra-fair pinkish skin that burns so easily in the sun. How could anyone have mistaken her for me? Rebecca's mind had put words to the thought. Was Mrs Graham lying on some operating table somewhere because that old lady mistook her for me? What was she doing outside Applebee's yesterday? Had she followed us?

'I wonder if she's still alive,' said Julie.

'Let's hope and pray,' said Rebecca.

'Hey, Mom, I'm gonna go call Monica. I've got to tell her about it.' Julie's voice was going up the register.

'Calm down, honey. You go ahead and call Monica. Then come back in here. I want to get exactly what you saw down on paper. OK?'

'OK, Mom.'

Rebecca knew it would be an hour. 'Remember, you get any bleeps for incoming calls, I've got to take them.'

She turned on the TV. They were just doing a news brief on Channel Four. Mrs Jane Graham was fighting for her life at Hennepin County Medical Center. Her daughter was an eyewitness. The shooter remained unidentified. Julie Smith, the daughter of Judge Rebecca Goldman, was an eyewitness to the automobile accident that took the life of the shooter. 'Shit!' said Rebecca out loud. 'Shit!' This kind of involvement with violence was something a fourteen-year-old could do without.

Channel Four resumed its coverage of a basketball game and Rebecca turned the set off. She got up and walked over to the window. It was business as usual. The traffic flowed easily on Lake Street. The anonymous afternoon walkers inexorably circled the lake, most unaware that ninety minutes ago murder and mayhem had intruded on the lovely day. But Rebecca was acutely aware. If it had been her walking through the lobby door at that moment, Julie might now be an orphan. A brace of crows did a bank and turn a few feet from the glass, ending in a long glide into the top of a tree near the corner, across the street from where Jane Graham had fallen. To Rebecca the idea of her own death had never before borne any resemblance to anything real or concrete. Now it cozied up close, intimate, ominous. A chill ran down the bones of her arms like cold water in a pipe. Was this what fear really felt like? She had never before had cause for this kind of fright. This must be that level of fear only once removed from the fear that can never be described, the fear felt by passengers in an airliner instantly split open by a bomb, the fear felt only by those who take the feeling with them to their death.

Rebecca turned from the window. Julie's playful smile beamed forth from her latest school picture, framed in silver on a shelf in the wall unit. The immediate chill of the fear gave way to a desolate disquiet that coated her body like a rash. One of those sensations you knew wouldn't go away very soon. This room she had loved through most of the years of Julie's growing up and all her years on the bench had been her secure haven, far above the busy streets – a full security building, as the real estate agents say. Jane Graham, if she lived to utter another word, might dispute that description. Was there a safer place? Certainly none that Rebecca knew. Not here in Minneapolis. Was it time to pack up and leave, go underground? She would never consider such a response if it were not for Julie. But if this shooting was in any way connected to Wilma Schmid, there could be more to come, perhaps more carefully planned, more carefully executed. Perhaps successful. This apartment, brick and mortar, wood, fiber, and furniture represented everything material Rebecca had worked for and earned over her lifetime. Was that even a consideration? Strangely, it reminded her of a conversation with a witness in her courtroom weeks back. The subject had been breast cancer. 'Y'know, Judge, I've had this lump in my breast for about six months,' the woman said. 'Surely you've seen a doctor,' Rebecca commented. 'Not yet, Judge, I've got to get some insurance first,' had been the reply.

Kevin smeared some mayonnaise on a piece of dark bread as the first step in building a Swiss cheese sandwich. He was grabbing a quiet Sunday at home. Rebecca was going to drop by tonight. The telephone rang before he got his first bite.

'Bannon here.'

'Sergeant, a guy down here at the station says he wants to talk to you in person. Gives his name as Odmar Woji-howsky.'

'Who the hell is he?'

'Says he's from Wolf River. You would know him.'

'Oh, that Wojihowsky.'

'Sarge, how many Wojihowskys do you know? Says he remembered somethin' he thought you'd wanna hear.'

'Got any idea what he's talkin' about?'

'Says he needs to talk to you in person. I think he wants to show you something.'

'I'll be there in twenty minutes.'

Kevin remembered Wojihowsky as a nice old guy, a little the worse for wear. He had said there was something strange about Schmid, but he couldn't put his finger on it. Kevin ate his cheese sandwich as he guided his car through light Sunday traffic.

'Mr Wojihowsky, good seeing you again.' With outstretched hand, Kevin approached the old man sitting in his office.

'Call me Woody,' he said and got up and took Kevin's hand in a bone-crushing grip that went with a set of miner's shoulders. He had a few hundred long silver hairs left that he combed straight back over the pink skin of his scalp. Thick glasses magnified pale blue eyes. 'I been meanin' to call ya, Sergeant, but then when I knew I'd be comin' down to the Cities, I thought I'd wait and talk to you in person.'

'Fine, I'm glad you did. Why'n't you pull that chair up a little closer to the desk here,' Kevin said. 'Good. Now, what can I do for you?'

'I hope I can do something for you. Anyhow, couple a weeks back my wife rented this damn fool video. Something about the knights of the round table, that kinda stuff. King Arthur and all that shit. Anyhow, I'm sittin' there watchin' it. She paid the two dollars, just as well watch it. Anyhow, this knight or whatever ya call it takes this big steel helmet off and he's got some kinda thing on his head goes over his ears.' Wojihowsky motioned around his head with his hand. 'An' it comes down on his forehead a little bit, covers up all his hair and even comes up a little on his chin. I guess it's kinda to protect his head from the helmet he wears when he jousts or whatever the hell you call it. Anyhow, it got me to thinkin' about that fella Schmid that drove the car into the river on Thanksgiving. Ya 'member, I told ya I got a look at his face, but there was somethin' about the guy.'

Kevin nodded, his eyes fixed intently on Wojihowsky.

'I just couldn't pick it up again in my mind's eye. But when I saw this knight, I says to Beatta, that's my wife, I says I think that Schmid had one a them things on like that there guy on the video. I was bored stiff with the movie, so I dug up the picture Beatta had clipped outa the Sunday paper of this Schmid and I took a pencil and I shaded around his picture.' Wojihowsky pulled an envelope out of his jacket pocket and handed it to Kevin. 'And sure 'nuff, I remembered clear as anything that was what Schmid looked like when he darn near run over me.'

Kevin pulled the picture out of the envelope. The hair moved on his scalp. A wet suit. 'A goddamn wet suit,' he said out loud. 'Woody, he had on a wet suit.'

'What the hell's a wet suit?'

'It's a neoprene rubber suit, maybe an eighth of an inch thick, that divers wear in cold water. Covers everything watertight except their face.'

'He musta knowed he was a goin' into the water.'

'That's for damn sure. That was no accident. He meant to drive that car through that railing.'

'You mean maybe he ain't dead?'

The weather played right into his hands, Kevin thought. He was speeding away from a murder. It wasn't unlikely that he might lose control in all the ice and snow and poor visibility. 'Yeah, Woody, maybe he's not dead.'

A cop in uniform tapped on the window in the office door. Kevin waved him in.

He stuck his head and big ruddy face round the door. 'Knuckles, did you know there was a shooting this afternoon at Lake Vista? Some woman took a handful of slugs in the chest.'

Kevin began drawing in his breath in the middle of the statement. 'Was the victim identified?'

'Yeah, a woman named Graham.'

Kevin blew all the air out. 'White woman?'

'I don't know.'

'Who's on it?'

278

'Dickstein. I think he's back in. At least he was.' The cop closed the door.

Kevin thanked Mr Wojihowsky and told him he'd keep him posted. Don't worry about it, Woody said. I'll read the papers. A second after the old man was out the door, Kevin called Rebecca. Julie answered.

'Hi, Knuckles. Let me get off the line with Monica and I'll go get my mother.'

Rebecca came on the line, 'Hi, Kevin. I suppose you've heard.'

'Just now. Do you know anything about it?'

She described everything that had happened in the minutest detail. Kevin interposed a question here and there. She finished with, 'I don't feel very safe here any more.'

'I can understand that,' he said, 'but it may all be a coincidence. It might be a domestic.'

'I forgot to tell you,' Rebecca said. 'Yesterday I saw the woman who did the shooting.' She described what she had seen through Applebee's window.

Kevin thought maybe she was mistaken. There was no question, she said. She had looked at the woman's face through the binoculars. It was her. She asked him to hurry and find out what he could about the old woman. She was sorry she wouldn't be able to come over tonight. She couldn't leave Julie alone. And, she thought, romance was out of the question. All her emotions had melted into a molten pot of fear.

Kevin hurried down the marble-lined hall in the basement of the old courthouse to Miles Dickstein's desk in Homicide. Dickstein was the best looking cop on the force, dark wavy hair, big mustache but neatly trimmed. He was going to night law school.

He knew very little so far, he said. The Graham woman was still alive, hanging by a thread. We got no motive, not even a theory of a motive, he said. The shooter had ID in her purse. They had a folder on her; petty criminal, last offense twenty years ago. They had found the car she was using just a couple of hundred feet from the scene, Wisconsin plates registered to Olaf Carlson, a guy living in Eau

Claire. Same address as the one on the shooter's driver's license. 'He doesn't answer his phone,' Dickstein said. 'We sent the local cops out to check on him just a few minutes ago.'

'What's the shooter's name?' Kevin yelled.

'Cloris Schmid,' said Dickstein.

'She had no motive to shoot the Graham woman,' said Kevin. 'She thought she was shooting somebody else.'

'What the hell are you talking about?' said Dickstein.

Kevin told him.

41

At the big round table in the Bohas kitchen William Schmid savored the chocolate chip ice cream, one small spoonful at a time. Mike had already finished his bowl, three times the size of William's, and was paging impulsively through the newspaper, a creamy smear on his chin.

'Sure a lotta shootin' goin' on in them cities,' said Mike. 'See here in Minneapolis where a woman shot another woman. Don't hear that too often.'

'Can I see that?' said Mary. Her hair was pulled back tightly from her face and rolled into a knot at the back. Her skin looked paler and a mark in front of her ear a little darker than usual. William thought she looked older, almost somber.

'Take it,' said Mike, 'I gotta check the water on them calves, then I'm goin' to Geddes. Pitch tournament starts tonight.' He wiped his chin with the back of his hand. 'Frankie, that chocolate chip's damn good, ain't it?'

William nodded. Aspiring to a smile, he was unsure whether he had achieved it. He marveled at the persistent good nature of the man, the ebullient spirit. He had speculated that it was forced, unreal, hiding a more sinister self, like many of the other men who had passed through his life. The back door slammed. Mary's eyes rose above the paper and met William's. They hadn't been alone for more than a few minutes since the day the corpse of Kenny Speer's dog was found. Tomorrow William would make his last call to Wilma. Within a week he must be on his way to Minneapolis.

'Read this weird story,' she said, passing the newspaper across the table.

William rarely bothered to look at the Sioux Falls *Argus*. Before he was imprisoned he had always believed newspapers were a waste of time.

The headline was near the bottom of the page: 'MINNEAPOLIS WOMAN CLINGS TO LIFE'. Somebody named Graham had been shot. Cloris Schmid. No one else would have that name. Dyed red hair. His stepmother was dead. His name was in the article. She had tried to kill the judge. Her employer of ten years found dead. Wilma had been questioned. Said she knew nothing. Mary must not sense any reaction. He handed her the paper. 'It is indeed a strange story,' he said.

The engine in Mike's pick-up started. Mary went to the window to watch it drive out of the yard. Framed by the window in a pullover sweater with a white scarf at the neck, the thick brown wool accentuated the swell of her breasts. The news of his stepmother's death still reverberated in William's skull. He had to have time to think, but now was not the time. This was Mary's time. William was moved to get up from the table and take her in his arms, but a slight cramping around her eyes and the level line of her mouth held him back.

'Frankie,' she said, 'I know you had a gun in the bed table by the wall. I haven't wanted to bring it up, that I had snooped in your drawer. Right after the truck was hit by the train in Rook. You acted so strange that day.' One hand went to the silver medallion hanging from her neck. 'I was worried. Then after, when I got to know you better, I wished I hadn't snooped in your drawer.' Two short vertical lines formed between her eyebrows.

William thought she might cry.

'Then,' Mary said, 'when they found the dog over at Jedlicka's and it had been shot with a pistol, I thought of the gun in your drawer. The next day I looked again. To be honest, I wanted to see if it was what Ivan Blitzko had talked about. A .38 or magnum or whatever. I thought it might say on it. Anyway, when I opened the drawer, it was gone.'

Sadness sagged through her face. Or maybe it was guilt,

William thought. No one had ever been ashamed of violating *his* privacy.

'After that I looked high and low for those rubbers of Mike's, the ones from Montgomery Wards. I know I had just seen them in the back hall. Just before Mike left for Kansas City. They're not here anymore, any place, Frankie.' She stopped talking for a while, as if she was gathering energy to go on. The only sound was the banging of the hog feeder lids.

William hadn't said a word since she had begun. But he had already planned for the moment she might ask him pointedly about Kenny Speer's death. He had decided what his answer would be. For the first time in his life he had the confidence to believe a woman other than Wilma could love him, without imposing conditions. There was even a chance she would leave with him. Afterward, when he was gone for ever, she could even return to the farm. Mike would take her back. Any sane man would. William knew he could not leave here without her.

The state's investigation was ongoing. Ivan Blitzko was apparently out of the loop. At least he had brought no more news. Someday an investigator might drive up in the yard to question William. When that day came, he must be gone for good.

Mary lowered the window shade and came across the room. She stopped behind William's chair and rested her hands easily on his shoulders and began kneading the muscles at the base of his neck. He felt lightened, reassured.

'Frankie, did you kill Kenny Speer?'

What if she picked up the telephone and called the police when he answered her question? Mary was one person he could not hurt. Again, the certainty of her love buoyed him. 'I did,' he said.

Her hands dropped from his shoulders. He stood up and faced her. She stepped back a step, her eyes locked to his.

He spoke in his way, choosing each word and turning it over in his mind before allowing it to pass from his lips. 'The threat he made was totally unacceptable. There was no doubt that he would attempt to use you in the worst way. I believe it was inevitable that he would eventually tell Mike what he saw.'

'But how could you kill a person, any person, even one as despicable as Kenny?'

'I did what I thought had to be done. I did it to protect you.'

The last caused her eyes to overflow. 'That's what I feared most,' she said. 'That I am part to blame.'

'You are not in any way responsible. You had no control over what I did. You did not even know I planned to do it.'

Her tears ran freely, streaking her face. She stepped forward and put her arms round his neck and her head on his shoulder. 'I would never believe I could love someone who could kill a person,' she sobbed.

He tipped her face up to his and kissed her. The rhythmic passion of her lips wiped away all doubt. With his lips still touching hers he said, 'You must leave the day after tomorrow.'

She pulled free of him and stepped back. 'I'm not sure I can, Frankie. I do love you, but I couldn't kill someone for you. I don't think that means I love you any less, do you?'

'Of course not,' he said.

'I don't know if I can do it to Mike. Leave him. He's been good to me,' she said. 'I need to think.'

William stepped forward and took her hand and led her to the sofa in the living room where they played out the same scene they had the night Mike surprised them with news about finding the dog.

Sexually spent, William climbed the stairs to his own bed about nine. In minutes he was asleep. His last waking image was his stepmother lying dead in the street.

Hours later he awoke suddenly. Had he heard a woman shout or was it in his dream? Then Mary's voice penetrated the darkness.

'Mike, I've never seen you this drunk.'

Mike's reply was an indistinct jumble. William crept quietly to his door and opened it a crack. From their bedroom down the hall came an indistinct colloquy. Clearest were Mary's words repeatedly asking him to leave her alone. 'Never get laid,' was the only audible coherent phrase from Mike. The crack of open hand on skin was distinct, then another. Mary said, 'Please stop,' and sobbed. The bathroom door slammed, followed by the clicking turn of the old-fashioned skeleton key in the lock. After a time, raucous snores rumbled down the hall from the bedroom. William crawled back under the blankets and waited. He heard the turn of the bathroom lock, then the faint squeak of the hinges on his door.

'You awake?' came the whisper.

'Yes.'

She slipped beneath the quilt and huddled against him, the wetness of her face against his. William held her for a few minutes. Then he said, 'You must go back there now. He is asleep and you will not be in any danger. In two days you will be gone from here.'

The following morning under dull skies Mike and William worked through the chores with hardly a word. Without Mike's usual congenial banter, the work seemed to take longer, the air seemed even chillier. Later, when they broke for coffee around nine, William asked for a couple of hours off. Then he headed north for his last call to Wilma.

She picked up immediately. 'Oh, William, the horror of what's happened.'

'I have read the papers,' he said. 'It was a stupid idea. You were a fool to try such a thing. She could have been valuable to me, to us. And the police must be a step away from arresting you. But I do not want to talk about that now. I am leaving for Minneapolis, as early as the day after tomorrow.'

'William, don't come. They'll kill you before you have a chance to get to that woman.'

'They think I am dead. Of course your botched assassination attempt will make it more difficult for me. I will need a place to stay.'

'What can I do? They will be watching my every move.'

'Probably nothing. I'm sure they have your line tapped at

home. If they learn of the telephone you are on now they will tap that line also.'

'No one has seen me on these calls.'

'You are assuming. You cannot be sure of that. Do not assume anything. Do you understand?'

'I understand.'

'I need all the information you have gathered, especially on the daughter.'

'How will I get it to you?'

'Put it in the mail, no later than tomorrow, to Frank Kroll, general delivery, Mankato, Minnesota.'

'That's very close to home. I'm scared. I can get plenty of money. You can go in the other direction and forget about the judge.'

'You did not forget about the judge.'

'Obviously, if she were dead, there'd be no reason for you to come back here.'

'I suspected as much. I am amazed that the old bag tried.'

'She did it for you, William. She loved you.'

'Be very careful with that mail,' he said. 'I do not want to meet the police at the post office.'

'Don't worry. I'll drop it in the mail at work.'

'I will call you four days from now. Same time. I have devised a somewhat different plan. I will not be alone.' Immediately, he was sorry he had told her.

'Not alone? My God, William, who's with you?'

'It is not important now.'

After Wilma hung up, William called the Bohas farm. Mary answered.

'It is Frankie. Do not say my name.'

'There's no one here. Mike's outside.'

'Good,' said William. 'You have decided?'

'Yes,' she said.

'Will you go?'

'I don't want to stay here if you go. I'll go with you.'

'I am glad,' said William. 'I have had to change my plan somewhat. It is very important that you act normally until you leave.'

'After last night, he won't expect me to act normally.

286

That's the first time he ever hit me.'

She is right, William thought. No need to worry about her demeanor. He went on and explained his plan to her in detail. He could visualize her face nodding as he spoke into the telephone. She would get on with her part this afternoon, she said.

As he drove back to the farm across the flat open prairie, the little whirlwinds of powdery snow partially obscured the highway. He wondered if she would have made the same decision if Mike had not hit her last night. It was not only a break for himself; it was a break for Mary. Now, in view of the assault, Mike's first ever, her leaving would be for good reason. If she should decide to come back, Mike would welcome her with open arms. I must take care not to make a criminal out of her, William thought.

42

On Monday morning Rebecca's lower back complained of the sagging mattress she had slept on last night at Susan's. When she entered her chambers, lying on top of today's files was a pink telephone message slip asking her to call Cletis Waterbury. This is it, she thought. As far as the Phelps case is concerned, Judge Rebecca Goldman is history. Then she noticed the time in the corner of the slip: 4:55 p.m. The call had come in right after she had left last Friday afternoon. She picked up the phone and got Waterbury's clerk. He was ready for her. 'Judge Waterbury asked that you disregard his message to call,' said the clerk. Rebecca was puzzled. Why doesn't that corrupt asshole get it over with? she thought. It no longer meant anything to her anyway.

She took a rag out of her bottom drawer, along with a bottle of furniture polish. Dabbing a little on the rag, she polished the dark walnut, banishing the fingerprints she had spotted in the reflected morning sunlight. Everything was relative. Just yesterday, a deadly serious murder plot against her had failed by pure chance. If Jane Graham had left her apartment just fifteen minutes later, it would have been her own chest that was drilled full of bullet holes. How could the Phelps case seem important this morning? When Kevin had told her the old woman's name, Rebecca's life had changed. Just as it had changed when she was admitted to law school. Just as it had changed when she walked in on Reggie and Voytek Milanowski. Just as it had changed when Mama Julia died. Just as it had changed when she was appointed to the bench. Just as it would have changed if the bullets had hit her.

She had known there would be no sleeping Sunday night without help. She had called for a prescription and picked it up on the way to Susan's house, where she and Julie had borrowed the guest bedroom. Tonight she was going with Kevin for more practice on the shooting range. Of course, yesterday the gun would have been of no value to her whatsoever. Jane Graham could have been wearing two six-guns in her belt like Wyatt Earp. There would still be just as many bullet holes in her chest. Nevertheless, Rebecca intended to go on carrying the little five-shot revolver in her purse. If Julie were harmed, she would find and kill the bastard with her own gun. In spite of such solemn thoughts, she laughed at herself. She had carried the banner against capital punishment. Minnesota had been on the cutting edge, abolishing the death penalty more than eighty years ago. That fact had influenced her decision to settle here in a community of advanced civilized thought, but the blacks and whites of philosophy could become a confusion of muddled grays to a worried mother. Now she thought it possible, given sufficient cause, that she could hunt a person down and kill him.

She took a call from Kevin. He wanted to know all about her night, and Julie, and whether their plans for this evening were still on. She would be there. Julie was moving in with Monica. Rebecca was the target. It made sense to get Julie out of the line of fire. The conversation turned to Cloris Schmid. Yesterday, the assumption had been that she was killing for her own motives, or, at the worst, those of William Schmid. The letters sent in his name had all described his unequivocal intent to kill Rebecca. A deranged stepmother, on the brink of death, might have wanted to implement the wishes of her stepson. Not your everyday motherly act, but plausible. Today Kevin had another possibility.

'We know Wilma and Tom Phelps are close,' said Kevin, 'and we know how much he wants you off his case. Do you suppose that somehow Wilma got her to try to get you?'

'That's crossed my mind,' said Rebecca, 'but it won't fly. Waterbury's ready to take me off the case. It was in the paper yesterday. Everybody in the courthouse knew it.' She told Kevin about Friday's call that was canceled this morning. The lemon fragrance of the furniture polish still teased her nose.

'Somebody over here said Waterbury has scheduled a press conference for two o'clock,' said Kevin. 'They always notify our PR department when a judge has got something to say about a criminal prosecution.'

'That is strange,' said Rebecca. 'Even Waterbury would give me the courtesy of letting me in on it before he makes an official announcement.'

'I think I'll walk over and take it in. Would you like that?'

'Hey, I'd love it. Will you?'

'Consider it done, ma'am.'

In his downtown apartment, Tom Phelps got a call from Wilma. 'We need to talk. I'll meet you at a quarter of twelve where the skyway crosses Eighth into Twin City Federal.'

Phelps was horny. 'Whyn't you just come up here, hon?'

'Got to work. There's a board meeting this afternoon. I have to sit in with my boss. I can take an hour and a half, that's it. I'd kill at least half of that getting to your place and back.'

'All right, I'll be there,' said Phelps.

Peter's Grill, redolent of frying burgers and corned beef, was a longtime favorite for a quick lunch in downtown Minneapolis. Rows of dark wooden booths with red cushions ran along three walls, with a double row running through the center. Tom Phelps asked to be seated along the wall. There were young secretary types having lunch in the booths on either side. Phelps kept an eye out for any other eavesdroppers, although the combination of clamorous luncheon patter and their own hushed conspiratorial tones made it difficult for them to hear even each other.

'Tommy, I need that money,' Wilma said.

'Hold on, baby. We gotta talk about what happened yesterday to your loving stepmother.'

'But Tommy, I've finally persuaded William not to come.'

'Wilma, turn your head more to the wall so somebody can't read your lips.' He was jumpy and kept looking around the room for watchful eyes. Either one of them could have a tail. If Wilma didn't, he would be surprised.

'You guys ready to order?'

The new voice startled Phelps. He didn't even look up. 'Reuben,' he said, 'and coffee.'

'Same,' said Wilma.

'Now what the hell happened out at Lake Vista?' Phelps said, as soon as the girl left.

'What makes you think I know anything about it?'

'Goddammit, Wilma, if you expect me to cough up fifty big ones for your brother to play with, at least give me the fuckin' facts.'

'You don't have to get angry, Tommy. Cloris didn't want William to come back here and get himself killed. She figured if she did the job for him he would stay away.' Wilma's face looked as if she thought Phelps didn't believe her. 'It's true, Tommy. She told me herself. She was dying of cancer anyway, had only a month or two to live. She had nothing to lose.'

'How did that Carlson guy she lived with get so dead?' Phelps asked.

'That I don't know,' said Wilma.

'You weren't involved?' Phelps was skeptical. 'You were gone the whole damn weekend.'

'No, not unless involved includes just knowing that she might try to kill that judge. And I'm glad I was gone. As I told that handsome detective, I was in Madison at a seminar.'

She must have known the old lady was making her move on the weekend, Phelps thought. 'What detective?' he asked.

'Miles Dickstein,' she said. 'If Cloris had gotten the right woman, I would think it would have made you happy.'

'I don't know,' said Phelps, talking into his coffee cup. 'I'm not into murder.'

Her face said, what do you mean you're not into murder? You're in it up to your big pink ass. But her lips said,

'Tommy, I need the money. When can you get it?'

'Before the week's over,' he said. 'How do you want it?'

'Can you get cash?'

'Maybe.'

'Cash'd be fine. Five hundred hundreds.'

'Does that mean I can stop worrying about your crazy brother coming back here?'

'You can stop worrying,' she said.

At five to two, Kevin sat down in the back row of Cletis Waterbury's crowded courtroom. Judges rarely gave press conferences. This one had even allowed TV cameras and multiple microphones. Henry Wheatland must have been persuasive, Kevin thought. God only knows what he has on Waterbury. They're both rotten old political hacks. If Waterbury intended to take Rebecca off the case, he'd try to keep it low profile. He certainly wouldn't announce it at a press conference. Kevin felt as if he had just assembled a complicated machine exactly as the instructions prescribed and he was about to plug it in to see if it worked.

Waterbury, without his robes, in a plain gray suit and red tie, entered the room by the back door and took a seat behind the bench. 'Thank you all for coming,' he said. People who hadn't been watching him for twenty years would suppose the intense redness of his face was caused by a noose drawn tightly round his neck. Kevin knew he put away a fifth or more a day. Waterbury went on, 'I have had so many inquiries on the subject of the upcoming trial of the case of *State of Minnesota v. Thomas Phelps* that I thought I could answer them all by calling this one short press conference. I will make a brief statement. I don't think questions will be necessary.'

A reporter from one of the TV stations sitting in front of Kevin said 'Bullshit' so loudly, Waterbury probably heard it.

Waterbury began reading from a single sheet of paper he held in one hand: 'The counsel for the defendant in the case I mentioned, as well as the various members of the public, have asked me to review the assignment of Judge Goldman to the case. I have made such a review and read all the documents related to these requests. I have decided that there is no evidence of any kind to indicate that Judge Goldman would be unable to protect the defendant's constitutional right to a fair trial. Therefore, no other judge shall be assigned to the case, and the case will begin on schedule next Monday.'

Before Waterbury could take another breath, the guy in front of Kevin leaped to his feet and said, 'Very reliable leaks coming out of here over the past several days have indicated that you had decided to take Judge Goldman off the case. What changed your mind?'

'Nothing,' said Waterbury. 'I hadn't made up my mind.'

'Aren't we supposed to expect the truth from our judges?' the questioner asked in a sarcastic tone.

'Of course,' said Waterbury.

'Then why aren't we getting it?'

Kevin was beside himself with glee.

'I can have you removed,' said Waterbury. His face shading to purple, he turned to his bailiff sitting at a desk up against the wall under the clock. The black man in a tan deputy sheriff's uniform looked back blankly.

'I will go voluntarily if you will tell me the truth,' said the questioner.

'I have no further comment,' said Waterbury, heading for the door.

Another voice shouted, 'Who have you talked to regarding your decision?'

The door slammed shut.

Becka will love it and she can see it on the news, Kevin thought. Wistfully, he wondered when, or if, he could ever tell her he had brought the whole thing off single-handedly. Of course Doris Elmore helped, but she didn't really have any choice in the matter. The elation evaporated with the thought that in a couple of hours he would have to break the news of Odmar Wojihowsky's refreshed memory. Distracted by the news of the shooting at Lake Vista, it wasn't until Kevin was falling asleep late last night that it dawned on him. The broken driver's seat in the escape car: Schmid had wanted the seat back out of the way to make room for an oxygen tank on his back. If a car had been dropped for him downstream and he had drowned or frozen to death, it would have been discovered. Unless his stepmother had been waiting for him. It was better than fifty-fifty the sonofabitch was alive. Had he been the one who put his stepmother up to Sunday's shooting? Goose flesh kept breaking out on Kevin's upper arms. There was no time for fooling around. They had to find this psycho. Now.

In another part of town on Monday evening a completely different type of meeting in regard to *State v. Phelps* was taking place. Four people participated, all women.

Sue Klein, over six feet tall and honey blonde, led a frightened looking young woman by the hand. Two women, already seated in the upscale contemporary living room, jumped to their feet. 'Allow me,' said Sue, 'to present an old friend of mine, Melody Sanford.'

The slim strawberry-blonde with a Candice Bergen look held out her hand. 'I'm Marlene Mays. We met several years ago at a party caucus or something.'

'Yeah, I think I remember you,' said Melody. She nervously tapped the fingertips of both hands together.

The other woman extended her hand. 'I'm Jean Daugherty.' Her dark hair was down over one shoulder in front and her dress looked expensive.

'I mixed up some martinis, Melody. Like one? Or anything? Maybe a Scotch?'

'No thank you. I really don't care for anything.' Melody sat down on the front edge of the chair. A loose cardigan hung straight down from her large breasts. Her jet-black perm shone under the track lighting. 'I would like a cigarette, if you don't mind.'

'Go right ahead,' said Sue. 'I'll find you an ashtray.'

'Thanks,' said Melody. 'Thanks very much.' She looked relieved, as if permission to smoke was a reprieve from a death sentence.

Sue Klein surveyed her own lanky form in the wall mirror. She poked at her piled-up hair with both hands, then sat down on the sofa beside Marlene who was asking the gorgeous Jean about a sapphire ring she was wearing. Jean and Melody occupied the two chairs opposite the sofa. Three martinis rested on an oriental cocktail table in their midst.

'Now that Melody's here, I guess we can get down to the reasons we got together,' said Sue. 'As we have discussed on the phone, we all fall into the category, God help us, of former associates, for want of a better word, of Tom Phelps.'

'Associates?' said Marlene with a laugh. 'I think dupes might be better.'

'Whatever,' said Sue. 'As I think you three may have done at first, I promised myself I would stay out of this case. Thinking more about it, I've come to believe we women have an obligation. And, I gather, you three tend to agree with me or you wouldn't be here.'

At the police shooting range, Rebecca squeezed off five double-action shots.

'All in the black,' said Kevin. 'Let's go, I don't want you to get better than me.' There was no one but them in the big, brightly lit room. Kevin's smile and clever remarks couldn't hide the tension in his face. An alloy of lingering fear mixed with doubt had settled into Rebecca's stomach. But she had been coming to terms with it. There was a reasonable chance that Cloris Schmid had been acting on her own, and if there was someone else involved, it was, in all likelihood, Wilma. They could keep an eye on Wilma. At least that was what Kevin had said. But on the way to the range Kevin had related the details of Wojihowsky's visit and his subsequent conclusions about the broken seat back. All this had stepped her fear up to the ultimate level, opening a window to a clear vision of her own death. William Schmid, who everyone had assured her was dead, was now very likely alive. The image of the last typed letter materialized in her mind: 'You will get the same as Alice got. You can bank on it. The only question is when.' Yes, Rebecca thought, the only question is when.

Rebecca sat down on a padded bench behind the firing

line, leaned back against the wall, and drew in a deep breath. The burnt gunpowder odor bit at her nose. Kevin had been pushing for her to have a fulltime bodyguard and to take another residence where it would be harder to get at her. He took a seat next to her and reached out and picked up her hand.

'Listen, love,' he said, 'it's still possible Schmid is deep-sixed in that frozen river.'

'No,' she listened to herself say, 'he's too smart. His stepmother picked him up downstream somewhere that night.'

'He hated his stepmother. Their history was clear.'

'All the more reason for her to make amends,' she said.

'If you really believe that, Becka,' Kevin said, 'it's time for you to get out of sight until we find him.'

'That could be years,' she said. 'We begin picking a jury in the Phelps case in less than a week. After what I've gone through to uphold a principle, I have to see that trial through to the end. That's no longer open to argument.'

'What about Julie?' Kevin asked.

'When I told her Schmid might be alive, she reminded me what she had said when we drove to Wolf River on Thanksgiving.'

'What was that?' Kevin asked.

'She said she would believe he was dead when they found his body.'

'OK,' said Kevin. 'I have a serious proposal and I want you to give it some thought before you respond.' He looked her dead in the eye.

'And it is?'

'Promise you will keep an open mind. Just like you do when you start a new case.'

'Let's hear it.'

'Promise?'

'I promise.'

'Becka, with Julie living at the lake with Monica, the logical place for you, at least till we find out if Schmid is alive . . . the logical place for you is with me.'

'Live with you?' The pitch of her voice went up a notch.

'Would that be so bad?'

'No, Kevin, that would not be bad at all, but it wouldn't be appropriate now.'

Ten minutes later in his car heading for Rebecca's parking ramp, Kevin said, 'You broke your promise.'

'What do you mean?' Rebecca asked.

'You said you'd keep an open mind.'

'Maybe you're right,' she said.

43

January was not giving up easily. Skin exposed for only seconds felt the sharp teeth of the north wind. Mike Bohas crossed the yard in the heated cab of the big green John Deere tractor bringing a bale of hay to the calves. He turned his head with its blaze-orange cap to watch Mary pass behind him in the blue Chevy, headed for the road in front. William, lugging a pail of mash for the hogs, waved as she passed a few feet away, her red hair tied up in a scarf. She puckered her lips and blew him a kiss. William quickly looked back toward Mike, but he was too far away to see anything. The Chevy headed north toward Rook and was out of sight in a few seconds. The cawing of a flock of crows in the shelter belt behind the house blended with the persistent clunking of the hog feeder lids and the whistling of the wind.

Later in the morning when William was helping him hook a wagon to the tractor, Mike asked, 'Frankie, you got any idea where Mary was headed? She didn't tell me she was going any place.'

William just shook his head. Minutes later they went in for their morning coffee break. An envelope on the kitchen table was addressed simply, 'Mike'. He opened the envelope as William poured two cups of coffee. Mike's custom was to drink down one hot coffee and pour another. Today, he ignored the steaming cup. Looking at the single sheet of paper, his eyes moved from word to word in jerky motions. William sipped his coffee and removed a Danish from under the Saran wrap on the plate Mary had left for them. Mike's eyes came to the end, then jumped back to the beginning to begin the process again.

When he finished the second time, he let the paper fall to the table and stared straight ahead at nothing. Finally, he took a sip of the cooling coffee. 'Read it,' he said to William, and he gave the handwritten letter a push. William picked it up.

Dear Mike,

I have left you. I am not sure whether I would ever be willing to come back. I ask you please not to try to follow me or even get in touch with me for at least one month. I will let my mother know that I am all right. You two get along fine, so I have no objection in your talking to her. I am taking $10,000.00 out of our savings. I inherited more than that when Uncle Howard died, so you should have no objection. There has been no warmth between us for a long time and I need some time away from the farm to think about my future. I may stop and see Nancy in Kansas City, but I would appreciate it if you would let me tell her I'm coming in my own time. I will get in touch with you in a month or so. Say goodbye to Frankie for me.

Love, Mary.

William slid the letter back along the table. 'I am sorry, Mike.' When he heard his own words, he realized he actually felt compassion for the big friendly man whom he had come to respect, especially for his willingness to do whatever it took to get a job done right. Determination would be what most people called it. But it was something different, something to do with belief. William went back out into the yard, leaving Mike alone with his misery.

With Mary gone, William picked up the mail from the box mounted on a post out by the road. Mary must be halfway to Sioux Falls by now, he thought. The box was full of junk mail and bills and the morning edition of the *Argus*. A headline caught his eye near the bottom of the front page: 'CHARLES MIX COUNTY DEATH RULED ACCI-DENTAL.' He stepped into the machine shed to read the short article.

'After an investigation by the state Crime Bureau, officials have ruled that the death of a rural Charles Mix County man, Kenneth W. Speer, was an accident. Because the dead man's dog was found in the area with a bullet hole in its skull, law enforcement officials decided Speer's drowning in his own bath tub merited further investigation. No other evidence was uncovered to indicate his slipping and hitting his head was anything but an accident. Investigators concluded that the dog must have been shot by someone in the area annoyed by its presence.

It seemed too good to be true. William was not totally persuaded. Perhaps the article was a plant to instill a false sense of security in the killer. But that was very unlikely.

William dropped the mail on the kitchen table. Even with Mike's footsteps moving across the floor upstairs, the house seemed empty. It must seem even emptier to Mike.

That evening sitting on the sofa after supper, William brought up the article about Speer.

'It makes more sense that it was an accident,' said Mike, looking at William. 'Like I told Ivan, ain't nobody mad enough at Kenny to go and kill 'em.'

In the next instant William's face took up the whole television screen. His hair was lighter and there was no beard or mustache. William held Mike's eyes. 'I think you are right, Mike.'

The anchor man was talking about William '. . . police think he may not have died in the river.'

William picked up the remote control without taking his eyes off Mike's face. 'Kenny Speer would not provoke someone to kill him,' said William. He switched channels. Some woman with three chins bent over and spun the wheel. It stopped on BANKRUPT.

Twenty-four hours later they were again resting on the sofa after the evening meal. Since she had left, Mike had been avoiding any direct mention of Mary. 'Times like this a guy wonders if it's all worth it,' he said now. 'At least there's no

300

crop in the field. If it wasn't winter, she wouldn't have left.'

William remembered a song Slim Olson had liked about some farmer whose wife left him when there was a crop in the field. He wondered if Mike had heard the song. There was another man involved in that song too. An antsy feeling of discomfort teased William, a feeling entirely new to him. It was remorse. He felt remorse. He remembered the prosecutor in his trial almost seven years ago saying to the jury, the defendant Schmid has shown no remorse. It was true. He wasn't sure then how remorse felt, but he was sure now. He was feeling remorse. The telephone rang. Mike made a move to get up.

'I will get it. I am expecting a call,' said William.

Mike was preoccupied. He had probably forgotten that William had never received one telephone call since he came to the farm. William picked up the phone in the kitchen. 'Hello,' he said loudly, as if he had a bad connection. 'Yes, Mother . . . Yes, Mother . . . I will talk to Mr Bohas . . . I will leave right away if it is all right with him . . . Goodbye, Mother.'

Back in the living room, he said to Mike, 'That was my mother calling. I called her yesterday to check on my father. He is ill and getting worse. She wants me there.'

'Well, you better go. I 'member when my dad died. It was tough around here. Yeah, Frankie. You go right ahead. There's not that much work this time a year anyway. Maybe you can come back in the spring.'

'That would be nice,' said William. 'I hate to be the cause of problems.'

'No problem, Frankie,' said Mike. 'You go ahead, any-time you're ready. I'll be fine.'

The next morning William examined his face closely in the medicine chest mirror. His beard was two inches long, his mustache was full but lighter than his evenly-dyed dark brown hair. The clear specs completed the image. He would put a little mascara on the mustache from time to time. He looked nothing like the picture he had seen on TV. He doubted that even Wilma would recognize him. He wondered what clue the police had discovered to doubt his death by drowning. He would find out from Wilma when next he called her.

He had loaded his car last night, except for the small bag he held in his left hand. Mike was already in the kitchen. Bacon crackled in the pan. Mike handed him a piece of toast and said, 'Good morning. Your money is in that envelope on the table.'

William would miss the wonderful food. Before he came to the Bohas farm, he had no idea what a significant human pleasure eating could be. With his toast he wiped his plate clean of the runny egg yolk. The time had come to leave. He told Mike how grateful he had been to find the work when he needed it.

'Now, you come back, Frankie,' Mike said. 'I meant what I said. You're a fast learner.' He smiled and let a little laugh slip out.

As he drove out of the yard, a wave of sadness swept over William. For a few moments it seemed less important to kill Rebecca Goldman. But it was the culmination of a plan that had been years in the making. And his life was almost over anyway. He would not submit again to a locked-up exist-ence. He felt like a train speeding down a track, knowing the bridge over the gorge was out but not even slowing down. And Mary belonged on this farm. She had helped make it what it was. She and Mike would work things out after he was dead.

The Minnesota River was second in importance in Minne-sota only to the Mississippi. From Big Stone Lake on the South Dakota border it ran southeast for two hundred miles, then it turned abruptly northeast for another hun-dred miles where it dumped into the Mississippi within the metropolitan area of Minneapolis-St Paul. On the hills overlooking the river, at precisely where it turned northeast, industrious Midwesterners had built the city of Mankato. It was in Mankato that William planned to rendezvous with the only person who had ever loved him the way women love men, and from Mankato he would launch the final phase of his plan of retribution.

302

Mary was waiting for him in room 141 of the Red Roof Inn. For William, seeing her and the two wide beds and closing the door on the dark and the cold was like getting into a spaceship bound for another galaxy. Though his intellect warned him of the ephemeral nature of this secure place, his body allowed the tension to begin to subside. He was at least one day ahead of schedule. There was no need to hurry. This night would be theirs, and there would be other nights. More than forty years after his birth he was just beginning to understand the full breadth of the human organism's capacity to feel. Until now the flowers of feeling that sprang from the soil of relationship had never existed for him, except in the twisted mutations he had nurtured with Wilma.

For the rest of the evening he wanted no discussion of the past or the future. Tonight, he would soothe his love. She was tormented by the guilt of having left Mike alone on the farm. He, too, felt sorry for Mike, he said. But Mike had made many choices in his life. A warm, sensual, physical nurturing relationship with Mary was not one of them. We must live with the consequences of our choices, William argued eloquently. He knew something of consequences. The enthusiasm for his logic flared out of his newfound feeling of passion. She deserved what he was able to give her now, he told her. When her tears gave way to smiles, then giggles, they melted together in an amalgam of flesh and breath that William had never dreamed existed. Much later when she fell asleep in his arms, he had visions of going on somehow to a life with his love. In the inky dark room the vision gave way to the overwhelming weight of oppressive reality. They would make him pay for Slim and Thurgood and Alice. Alice. Briefly, she had begun to bring to the surface something unidentifiable within him; perhaps it was the germ of awareness. Then he had killed her. Killing her had made no sense. Sometimes William actually believed he remembered killing her. He had listened to so much discussion of it at his trial – the medical examiner, the psychiatrists, the police. But the fact remained. Even under hypnosis he had not been able to remember. When Alice had come into the lab that day, the headache had already begun. The pounding in his head had blocked out everything that happened later. The jury hadn't believed him. Even Judge Rebecca Goldman, who had decided he was a lunatic, had not believed him when he said he didn't remember.

In the morning when William had to do the things people do in the morning, he was embarrassed. Mary tried to make him feel at ease. You use the bathroom first, she said. I'll lie here awhile. A little later, she picked up the continental breakfasts in the lobby and brought them back to the room. As they sipped their coffee and munched on croissants, William decided it was time to give her an idea of what was ahead. But only an idea; he meant to keep her in the dark about the realities.

'My darling,' he said, his hands shaking with anxiety, 'this time with you has been the best time of my life. Even if it does not last much longer, it will certainly be the only thing in my life worth remembering.'

'Don't talk that way, Frankie. We can have a long time together,' Mary said.

He smiled at her and shook his head. 'In a few days,' he said, 'I must go to work on a very important task that I have been planning for a long time.'

'Do you still think you can't tell me?' she asked.

'I cannot tell you. There is no question about that.'

'You've already told me that you killed Kenny Speer; what can be worse?'

'I should not have told you. I am sorry, but no one will ever claim you were involved, or even know about Speer's death.' He recounted for her the article in the *Argus* reporting that the police had decided Speer's death was an accident. 'So you see,' he finished, 'there was no need to tell you about it.'

'Then we can go back to the farm if we want to, together.'

'Hardly,' he said. 'There is no place there for me, and I will not be able to in any event.'

She cajoled and played with him, grabbed at his ribs and

tickled him. 'So tell me, Frankie, what is it you must do now?'

'I do not wish to talk about it any more,' he said. There must never be any question of her involvement, he thought. 'I am getting some mail here today or tomorrow. Until then we can just enjoy our freedom,' he said.

She stopped playing and looked steadily into his eyes. 'Frankie, I need to ask you a question.'

Her red hair floated loose around her sweet face, her gaze gentle and loving. Yet he dreaded any questions. With all their intimacy at the farm, there had been no questions about his past. He feared she would expect answers, and be hurt when they weren't forthcoming. He said nothing.

'Frankie, are you married? You don't have to tell me, but naturally I'm curious. It wouldn't affect the way I feel. After all, I'm married. I only left my husband's bed two days ago.'

'No,' he said, 'I am not married.'

'There must have been a special woman in your life at one time or another.'

'None really. Only my sister, and when I was a boy my stepmother.'

'Oh, Frankie, you are such a wonderful lover. I thought surely there must have been someone special.'

'No, you are the first woman I have ever loved the way a man loves a woman.'

'Then we mustn't let it slip away. What could be so important to be worth losing what we have?'

'If there were any way possible, I would take it, but there is not.'

'There must be,' she said. An eye overflowed and a tear ran down her cheek.

He bade her lie down beside him on the unmade bed. He stroked her hair for a long time and told her he loved her again and again. Lying on her back, she began to sing Ophelia-like, in a very high pitch. 'Frankie, Frankie, my love, I love Frankie. Frankie, Frankie, my love, you must never leave me.' She went on and on, mixing words and humming and trilling. He thought again of the vast farm of his dreams, with the herds of black cows and the big logs burning in the fireplace. What made it all impossible had begun that day with Alice Wahl. It had begun with an event of which he had no memory whatsoever. Now, he had another to kill, perhaps two, and it would all be over.

Mary reached for the telephone. 'I should call my mother,' she said.

'No, not from here, and not today. When we leave Mankato you can call from a pay phone,' said William.

'What difference does it make?'

'We cannot be sure Mike is not already looking for you. It would upset my plans if he found us. We might stay here a few days.'

'I would just say to my mother I'm all right, don't worry.'

'No, no call for now. I am sorry, but we must not take such a risk.'

Mary's face looked troubled, but she dropped the idea.

44

Barbara Bird, tall enough to kiss a cloud, skin as black as a queen of the upper Nile, opened Whit Strom's door and barged in without knocking. 'Chief, great news. At least three of those women are going to testify against Phelps. Sue Klein and Marlene Mays both called me, and Jean Daugherty called Dinah White. I've got an investigator meeting with them today. She'll have her reports ready by five.'

'All three come through in one day?' Strom, his expression skeptical, passed his hand over his bare scalp. It felt as if it had been waxed and polished.

'Dinah's been working on them pretty hard, you know,' said Barbara.

'What about Melody what's-her-name?'

'She's still doubtful.'

'Don't forget, Scott's got a right to notice on this new testimony.'

'Hey, Whit, I wasn't born yesterday. I'll walk the Spriegel notice over to him this afternoon, with the reports,' Barbara said. 'He'll probably want more time.'

'Don't give it to him. Goldman will give him a hearing before the trial starts. But she'll let these ladies testify, I'd bet on it.'

'Hallelujah!' cried Barbara Bird. She would like to see the look on Harry Scott's face when he read the Spriegel notice this afternoon.

In the basement of the old courthouse, across Fifth Street from the Government Center, Kevin leaned back in one of

Miles Dickstein's office chairs with his ankles crossed, his black wingtips resting on the corner of Miles's desk.

'I'm startin' to feel pretty silly about Wilma Schmid,' said Kevin. 'I've never had a case where I've been more sure that I've got the right person. I can't seem to get one little break.'

'I'm with ya,' said Miles, smoke spurting out of his nostrils. 'No way old Cloris Schmid didn't have help fucking up that shooting out at Lake Vista. It had to be her darling daughter Wilma, but that whole weekend she was in Madison, Wisconsin. She must have driven right by Eau Claire on I-90, but so far we can't put 'er in that old man Carlson's house at all. Snowed like hell that night. And no motive for that one either. All she does is smile at me and answer all the questions, nice and controlled like.'

'All the puss smile at you,' said Kevin. 'Must be nice. What you're sayin', and with what I know went down in Wolf River, is that broad is involved in killing four people, counting Cloris, five if the Graham woman dies. That's more than we've got on her brother, the psycho. And she's walkin' around smilin' at our homicide dicks.'

'Nothing on your scuba theory?' Miles lit another cigarette.

'Those things are gonna kill ya, Miles. We've walked her picture into every dealer within a hundred miles of here. I'm asking for help in Milwaukee and Chicago and we've contacted all the mail order houses.'

'Knuckles, she mighta bought the stuff used, from a private party.'

'We had a kid check all the ads over the past three years and call the sellers. Still nothin'.'

'Course, you don't know he used a tank.'

'He used a tank all right,' said Kevin. 'And we been checkin' out the cyanide. No luck there either. You can get it from a jeweler.'

'Yeah, I'm not doing any better. We been working on the gun. I doubt if Cloris bought it. Figure she mighta got that from the daughter. All dead ends.'

'I got another angle,' said Kevin. 'Talked to Whit Strom this afternoon, he's prosecuting Phelps. Tom Phelps may know a hell of a lot. He's been fucking Wilma, off and on, mostly on, for years – at least that's what I'm told by one of those reliable sources.'

'Doesn't that case start Monday?'

'Yeah. I asked Strom if he'd turn him loose on the rape charge if Phelps could give us Wilma Schmid on multiple murders.'

'What'd he say?'

'No problem. He said he didn't have a sure winner anyway.'

Tom Phelps drove his Corvette through the night around the lakes and up and down side streets to make sure he didn't have a tail. Wilma's car, lights out but exhaust spewing white clouds of vapor into the icy air, was waiting where she said she would be in the crowded parking lot of the Mount Olivet Lutheran Church on Fiftieth and Knox. In a deep crouch, she ran through two rows of cars to his Corvette. As soon as she hit the seat, the Corvette jumped forward and out of the parking lot. Phelps handed her a man's hat to wear and headed back downtown to his garage, his eye on the rearview mirror.

'Did you take in a service with the Reverend Youngdahl tonight?'

'I didn't really have time, Tommy. Are they following us?' She twisted round in her seat and looked back.

'Don't see anything unusual but there are headlights everywhere.'

'They were there, at the church,' she said. 'It looks like it worked.'

'Anything for love,' he said, and screeched the Corvette round a corner and down a dark side street one block and quickly round another corner. 'Looks clear,' he said.

'You got the money?'

'Wilma, baby. I told you I had it on the phone.'

'I'm just nervous, Tommy. Where is it?'

'At the apartment.' He took a right and was back heading north in the traffic on Lyndale.

'I thought you were bringing it.' She looked out the back window again.

'We'll bring it with us when I take you back. Relax, baby. I need some of what you've got.'

'You always do.'

'Not always. Just mosta the time. C'mon, lighten up.'

Not much over an hour later, the musky scent of their coupling still fresh in the air, Phelps told her about a call he had received from Harry Scott. 'They'll drop the rape case if I help them convict you of murder, honey.' As soon as he said it he wondered if it was a mistake. Wilma remained silent, staring at the ceiling, strands of her dark blonde hair spread out across her face. The only light in the room was what spilled through the open bathroom door. 'I told Scott to tell them I had nothing they could use, that it was crazy to think you could be involved in killing somebody.' He had been tempted to ask Scott about the cyanide problem but thought better of doing it on the telephone. 'He said you are being investigated by four law enforcement agencies. Two here, two in Wisconsin.'

'Tommy, is Harry Scott going to try to get you immunity?'

'Immunity from what?'

'From being prosecuted for helping me help William escape?'

'That wasn't brought up. He has no idea I helped you. Push comes to shove, I had no idea I helped you until I read the paper.'

'Who'd believe that?' said Wilma.

'Wouldn't you tell them the truth?' Phelps asked, trying to sound ingenuous.

'Who'd believe me?' said Wilma.

'Why are we talking like this?' said Phelps. 'I'm not telling anybody anything. I'm going to beat the rape case, and I'd hardly go in hock up to my nose to borrow fifty grand for you if I was going to turn you in.' He didn't mention the real reason he got that money. He was scared shitless of a visit from William Schmid and didn't tell her that Harry Scott had said he'd got a Spriegel notice from the prosecutor's office. They had three different women ready to testify that he had done things to them similar to what Dinah White had accused him of doing to her. Judge Goldman had set a hearing immediately prior to the trial to decide whether the testimony was admissible. Scott already had the investigative reports. They didn't look good, he had said.

'You sound pretty confident,' Wilma said.

'I got a good lawyer, and he's got an angle and I'm still working on one of my own.'

'What's that?'

'I want to work on it a little more. I'll tell you if I put it together.' Phelps swung his legs over the side of the bed and pranced naked toward the open door of his closet, feeling a little self-conscious that Wilma was getting an eye-level view of his over-sized pink pimpled ass.

He returned with a brown paper bag and dumped the contents over her pelvic area, fifty neat little packages of ten one-hundred dollar bills. 'From what I've read about Ben Franklin,' Phelps said, 'he'd love to know that five hundred pictures of him now repose atop one of the finest pussies in the western hemisphere.'

Wilma sat up in bed staring at the pile of money. 'Thank you, Tommy. I'm impressed.'

'Impressed enough to give me my favorite?' He moved slightly toward the head of the bed, poking his semi-rigid penis toward Wilma's mouth. She pushed the money away, dropped her legs over the side of the bed and sat up, eye to eye with Phelps's organ. She gave him his favorite.

When she had sucked him dry he dropped face down across the bed. In a few minutes he began to snore like a car engine starting, then cutting out every few seconds. Wilma kicked his leg. 'Tommy, don't go to sleep. You have to take me back to the church.'

'I'm so tired, baby.'

'Come on now, Tommy, let's go.'

'How you going to get that money to your brother?'

'Better you don't know those kinds of details.'

'If I don't get my job back with the Governor I gotta pay that money back. Every dime.' Phelps thought it was worth whatever it cost if it meant he would never see William

311

Schmid again. Getting murderous Wilma out of his life for ever would be a bonus. Leroy, Clyde Magus's connection for getting people killed, still hadn't called. Even if he did, Phelps had no idea where he'd get another ten grand. How did he ever get mixed up with these psychos? The answer stood before him pulling her pantyhose on long graceful legs, then harnessing her full breasts into her bra. 'When are you leaving to meet your brother?' Phelps asked.

'Soon, but now they're watching everything I do. They're not only investigating me, they hope I will lead them to William. Bannon is convinced he's alive.'

'Do you have any idea what changed their mind?'

'No,' said Wilma.

The next morning Wilma went to the law library at the appointed time. A man she had never seen before walked through the door right after she did. He stood looking at the stacks of books along both walls, then walked over to the maroon-bound United States Code Annotated. The phone in the usual cubicle would ring in three minutes. She walked over to where he stood. 'Can I help you?' she asked.

'No, I'm fine, need to do a little research,' he said. He was under thirty and was wearing a nicely tailored navy pinstripe suit. He carried nothing, not even a legal pad.

'I don't believe I've seen you in here before,' Wilma said.

'I'm with a law firm down on the thirteenth floor. Just started.' He smiled broadly. 'Kinda glad to get the job, to tell you the truth.'

It was less than two minutes until the ring. Do not assume anything, William had said. 'I'm sorry,' said Wilma, 'but I have to have some ID or something. Only tenants may use the law library. I'm sure you understand. Do you have anything with you? Perhaps a business card?' She had one minute, ten seconds until the ring.

'Everybody has always said I have an honest face,' he said.

'You do, sir, but the rules are the rules. I'm afraid I'll have to call security,' said Wilma. She walked into the cubicle and closed the door behind her. She grabbed the phone on half a ring. She whispered into the phone. 'I'm afraid I was followed in here. Call back at eleven thirty.' There was a click, then the dial tone. She punched in the numbers for security. 'Gilda, there's some guy up here in the library has no ID. Better send Clayton up.'

She left the cubicle. There was nobody in the library. She looked out in the hall. Nobody. She got on the elevator and pushed thirteen. On thirteen she walked the full length of the hall. There were two insurance companies, an ad agency and a firm of CPAs. No lawyers. He must be a cop. She had no other way of communicating with William. If the cop had heard that ring, they would certainly monitor that line but it would take them a few hours to set it up.

She took the elevator back up to twenty and went into her office, waited a minute or so, then put on her coat and got back on the elevator. In the lobby she ran out the door to Sixth Street and jumped into a cab. She told the driver to take a left on Marquette. She looked back toward the entrance to the building. The pinstriped guy from the library had just stepped on to the sidewalk, his coat over his arm and his breath blowing clouds of vapor into the five above air. She ordered the driver through the traffic with clipped commands. Left here. Another left. She finally guided him into an alley behind an old sooty structure across the street from her building. She handed him a five, then ran up a few steps on to a loading dock. Inside, she went down a flight and into a dingy brick-lined tunnel under the street. In the basement of her building she entered the elevator and got off on seventeen. She was back in the library cubicle at eleven twenty-four. It would be the longest six minutes of her life.

Five blocks away, at police headquarters, Kevin took a telephone call.

'She gave us the slip again,' the voice said.

'Shit,' said Kevin.

'We'd need six guys to stay tight on her.'

'I know it's tough, Randy,' said Kevin. 'We just gotta keep trying.'

'I think I might have something worth checking though, Sergeant.'

'Shoot,' said Kevin.

'I think she either got a phone call or was going to get one on a private line in the railroad law library.'

'You mean the line's separate from the switchboard?'

'I'm not sure. I'll have to check it. But in the county law library they have some phones for lawyers to use that don't go through the county switchboard. I gotta hunch that's what this is. It's in one of those little rooms the lawyers can use for privacy.'

'You got any idea where she went?'

'I think she got in a cab. I took a chance and ran down the street after this one, but I couldn't catch up with it. It took a left on Marquette, then another left on Fifth.'

'How long ago?'

'Good half-hour.'

'Randy, after you lost sight of her, if she took another left on First Avenue she coulda been goin' right back to the railroad building.'

'Godamn, Sarge, I'll call ya.'

'Where are you?'

'In the Government Center cafeteria. I was gonna get a sandwich.'

'We got anybody back at the railroad?'

'No. Lucas is with me.'

'Great,' said Kevin. 'Get your ass back there quick.'

'Right, Sarge.'

'And Randy, check that line. If it's not comin' through the switchboard, get all the in-coming calls for the last thirteen weeks.'

'I'll get back to you as soon as I can, Sarge.'

'You do that.'

William's call came precisely at eleven thirty. When she heard his voice, Wilma said, 'We must hurry. They will be tapping this line very soon.'

'You should have been more careful,' said William, 'but it does not matter, I will be there soon enough, and they have no idea where. No one would recognize me; not even you. Have you got another number I can call?'

'I found a pay phone that you can call in on,' she said and gave him the number.

'If I need to talk to you I will call the number on days of the month divisible by three,' he said, 'at six thirty p.m. Do not let them follow you. Best would be to have a new number each time.'

'I'll try,' she said. 'Did you get the material I sent to Mankato?'

'Thank you, I did. Are you still involved with that Phelps character? I see his trial is about to start.'

'I see him on occasion, William.'

'How much does he know? Do not hide anything from me. Your freedom could be at stake.'

Wilma felt compelled to answer honestly. She had always deferred to William's superior intelligence. 'I promised him I wouldn't tell you, but he got me the cyanide.'

'That was a major mistake. You must be very involved with him. Sexually, I think. Is that true?'

She didn't answer.

'We have little time, Wilma. You have not been telling me everything. They will use him against you. You must realize that. Does he know I am alive?'

'That's how I was able to get the money I promised you.'

'I told you I did not want any money. You have been a fool. But you must not give him the idea you have told me.'

'I don't plan to see him again, William.'

'Do not lie to me. You have been seeing him for ten years. He is your accomplice.'

'He thinks I'm taking the money to you. He doesn't expect to see me again. That's the truth, William.'

'Days of the month, divisible by three, at six thirty p.m. A new number each time. Perhaps you can evade them. One last thing, Wilma. If something should slip up, check for general delivery in your name at the Camden post office. Goodbye, and thank you for all you have done for me.'

She heard the dial tone before she had a chance to say goodbye. She should have lied to him about Phelps. What if William got to him? Phelps has suspicions he hasn't even dared bring up with me, she thought.

★ ★ ★

Two hours later Kevin took another call.

'Randy here, Sarge. We just got a recorder on that line. I got permission from the head of the legal department at the railroad. Lucas checked with the phone company. There's been quite a few long-distance calls to that number over the last thirteen weeks. Maybe more'n just Wilma Schmid using it. We're still calling some of the numbers. But two came in today from a pay phone in Mankato, the last one at eleven thirty. She was just coming out of the library when I got back there about eleven forty.'

'You call the Mankato police?'

'I called you as soon as I knew. No other calls look helpful, right off. There are two unexplained ones from the same truck stop on I-90 about halfway between Mitchell and Chamberlain out in South Dakota. Lucas is going to check all the lawyers in the building. See if they know anything about those calls. But I think the only thing worthwhile are today's two calls from Mankato. I bet a week's pay she took that call, but shit, it coulda been from anybody.'

'I think it was from William Schmid,' said Kevin, feeling the hair move on his upper arms. He wished Rebecca would take a long trip.

'Could be, Sarge.'

'Anyway, good work, Randy. See if you can keep a tight tail on her again. Tell the guys on the other shifts that I'm especially interested in what telephones she might be using.'

Kevin disconnected, then called the Mankato police and the highway patrol. He had kept his theories about the wet suit and the oxygen tank to himself, but he had put an APB out on William Schmid the day after Wojihowsky came in.

Later, he sat staring at a gravy spot on his fly. It was still possible that the deadly sonofabitch was lying well-preserved by the numbing water at the bottom of Wolf River. Every reporter in town was howling because Kevin wouldn't say why he thought Schmid might be alive.

45

William Schmid and Mary Bohas, driving their two cars in tandem, left Mankato on Highway 169 minutes after he had completed his telephone conversation with Wilma. Calling back at eleven thirty had been a calculated risk, but if he hadn't it was possible he would never have been able to make contact with Wilma again. Leaving the great plains behind, they followed the Minnesota River valley up and down hills and through stands of tall winter-naked trees. An hour and a half's driving in light traffic, carefully observing the speed limits, brought them to the outskirts of the Minneapolis-St Paul metropolitan area. William made a left turn across a bridge over the frozen river into the old town of Chaska, enveloped in recent years by urban sprawl. When William was a boy his Uncle Walt used to take him fishing for catfish in the river above the town.

After dropping Mary's car in the municipal parking lot, William pulled up in front of a drugstore. Mary went in for a newspaper. William studied the street ahead and watched his side mirror. A black and white patrol car stopped beside him and tapped the horn. William touched the hardness of the .38 in his coat pocket. The driver's side window of the patrol car came down. William opened his and met the cop's eyes.

'Say there,' yelled the cop, 'didn't you see that fire hydrant?'

'No, I am sorry,' said William. 'I will move. I am sorry.'

Mary was opening the door and climbing in. The cop waved and drove off. A block further up the street they stopped and went into a cafe.

★ ★ ★

It was Kevin's first visit to Harry Scott's office in the Roanoke Building. He and Miles Dickstein followed the receptionist down a short hall. When the door opened, Scott was standing behind his desk, the trademark little elliptical smile that juries were said to love fixed firmly in place. Tom Phelps got up and offered his hand when Kevin and Miles had shaken Scott's.

Finished with the Minnesota ritual of talking about the cold weather, Scott looked at Kevin. 'As I told you on the phone, Sergeant, I had already discussed with Mr Phelps his helping you in your investigation of certain other events and he told me he knew of nothing that could conceivably be helpful to you.'

Kevin nodded slightly and waited for more. After all, Phelps was sitting there. He had taken the trouble to come in to hear him out. And Scott was a busy man.

Scott continued, 'By the way, gentlemen, do you mind if I record this session?'

'We might accomplish more off the record,' Kevin said, 'but if you insist, we can do it any way you want.'

'No, off the record will be fine. Now, as I was saying, Mr Phelps doesn't think he can help, but we are ready to listen. There's only one full day plus the weekend before the trial begins. It would be nice to avoid it. But I've got to say at the outset, if you are investigating other crimes that you think my client might have some knowledge of, *any* knowledge of, we've got to have an agreement, on the record, that my client will be immune from prosecution for any of these crimes.'

'That's asking a lot,' said Kevin.

'I don't know if it is or isn't,' said Scott.

Kevin noticed the 'Thank you for not smoking' sign on Scott's cherrywood desk and knew Miles Dickstein was suffering. 'Whit Strom's willing to take a misdemeanor plea of some kind on the rape case,' said Kevin, 'anything short of an outright dismissal. You know there'll be a major public outcry if that case isn't tried.'

'No doubt,' said Scott.

318

'Strom's even willing to get the Governor involved, make sure Mr Phelps gets his job back if he helps us – helps us substantially, that is. The Governor would like to see the Schmid twins off the street too.'

'You really must want this woman bad,' said Scott.

'We think she is involved in four killings,' said Kevin. 'Five if Jane Graham dies.'

'In any event,' Scott said, 'I don't see how we can do anything without a guarantee of immunity.'

'Well, if we're talking immunity, I'm sure the Governor would want out of any deal like the one I just suggested. Obviously, if Mr Phelps is involved in these murders, there's no way the Governor would promise anything,' said Kevin.

Miles piped up, 'Might make a difference, Sarge, if we had some idea what Mr Phelps could give us.'

'That's true,' said Kevin. 'I'd recommend to Whit Strom that Mr Phelps be guaranteed complete immunity if he can give us Wilma Schmid on premeditated murder. That could be on either the guard and the inmate at Wolf River, or that old guy in Eau Claire. Or, for that matter, on Jane Graham, God help her, if she dies.'

Scott looked interested. Phelps's eyes were on some workmen suspended on the side of the Marquette Inn across the street. Kevin continued as though he was thinking out loud. 'On the other hand, Whit Strom knows, and I know, that we're gonna nail this broad eventually. Nobody's gonna kill four people in this jurisdiction with us knowin' she did it and get away with it. Maybe not tomorrow or the next day, but we're gonna nail her, and when we nail her she's gonna take everyone else with her that's involved. I guess that would include anyone who thought they needed immunity now.' Kevin stared at the side of Phelps's bushy head until it turned toward him. Kevin knew fear when he saw it and he saw it in Tom Phelps's eyes.

'I guess we at least got some cards on the table.' Harry Scott punctuated his statement with the little smile. 'I don't want you fellas to get the wrong idea. I'm not saying my client needs immunity. I'm not saying he needs anything. I doubt if Strom can prove a case of rape – legitimately.'

'What the hell does that mean?' asked Miles.

'Oh,' Scott showed a couple of teeth, 'things aren't always as they seem.' He stood up. 'Now, gentlemen, my client and I need to get to work. We've got a case to try.'

Kevin felt the chance of a deal slipping away. Phelps knew way too much. He was in up to his ass. The Governor wasn't going to welcome him back if he got out of a murder case by squealing on his accomplice. If he wanted to return to his seat of power in St Paul, he needed to beat the rape case and hope Wilma somehow slipped through the net.

Late that afternoon, Harry Scott leaned back in his leather chair and gazed at the lit windows across the street. He took an ashtray out of his drawer and put a match to a Havana that one of his drug-pusher clients had given him. He loved the smooth nutty flavor and allowed himself one cigar a week. It was the first time he had talked to Kevin Bannon in years. This was the kind of man who appealed to Rebecca Goldman, the lucky bastard. That night on the phone, she didn't slam the door in my face, he thought. Maybe after the Phelps trial. If only he could win it outright. With no appeal to keep the goddamn case alive, he could give this guy Bannon a run for his money where Rebecca Goldman was concerned. Money. That was another problem.

The telephone ringing in the front lobby persisted. Everybody must have gone home. He punched the speaker button on his phone. 'Law office,' he said.

'That you, Harry?'

'Yeah.'

'Chet Ronning here.'

'Oh, hello, Chet. I was just thinking about you and the fucking money. I've got a big trial coming up. My divorce is going to have to wait a couple a weeks.'

'Harry, two weeks from now or a year from now, your wife isn't going to take what we have put on the table. I just can't make it work, Harry. If you want to avoid a trial on the value of your practice, and you want to keep your pension plan intact, you're going to have to come up with another hundred grand. That's it. Period. Paragraph. This lawyer of hers ain't no hay-shaker. He's read the Flynn case.'

'Shit, Chet, I can't afford it right now.' Some woman took her brassiere off in a brightly lit room in the Marquette Inn across the street.

'You gotta afford it. You're just running up the fees, hers and yours. Go to the bank.'

'That's easier said than done.'

'Do you want the case tried?'

'No. See if you can buy a couple more weeks. If they read the paper, they know I'm tied up on this Phelps case.'

'I'll see what I can do.'

William and Mary had a busy afternoon. They responded to some ads in the paper for houses for rent on the outskirts. By seven in the evening, about twelve miles west and a little north of Wayzata, William found what he was looking for. Near the end of a dead-end gravel road with no other homes on it, the house was set into the side of a hill. A long, straight driveway headed into a double-wide garage door that opened into the basement. After they had blasted through a couple of snowdrifts, a woman had waved them up a flight of wooden steps to an open deck extending across the front of the house. She couldn't have been much over fifty. Her eyes were magnified by thick glasses in pink frames that turned up at the corners. The mister, as she called him, had been forced to retire because of heart trouble. This had been their dream. A house in the country, by itself, on a good-sized tract of land, with lots of woods. But he had died just before Christmas. She was going to stay with her son and daughter-in-law in Phoenix for a few months. They could have it month to month, a minimum of three months, she said. Her friend Alice said she should be sure to get a security deposit. Such a nice couple, she doubted that she needed it.

William gave her eight hundred dollars for a month's rent in advance and a security deposit of five hundred. In less than a month he expected to be dead, and Mary would be on her way back to the farm.

They could move in tonight, the woman said. She'd go

stay with her daughter until she left for Phoenix. William told her they would be back by ten, he wanted to go shopping for a snowmobile and pick up their other car. Don't you bother, she said. Chester's is sitting right down in the garage on a trailer. An Arctic Cat. It's five or six years old, but there's hardly any miles on it. His heart, you know. You're welcome to it while you're here. There's a snow blower down there too. You can use it to clear out the driveway. My, you have beautiful hair, she said to Mary.

46

On the morning of the third day of the trial of *State of Minnesota v. Thomas Phelps*, Rebecca's paneled courtroom was a buzz of blended voices. The hundred or so spectators were packed into five rows of seats with an aisle down the center. Immediately in front of them was a low balustrade with a gate that swung both ways.

Bailiff Henry Pettiford, handsome, with dark bronze skin, dressed in his neatly pressed tan sheriff's deputy uniform, had just called attention to Rebecca's arrival, ordering everyone to stand. Rebecca asked the congregation to be seated, said good morning to the lawyers, then to all of the rest assembled. After spending the first day and part of the second selecting a jury, Dinah White had been called to the witness box. She described how Tom Phelps had playfully bound her wrists and ankles to the bed. In spite of her protests, he had mounted her in the carnal fashion and had his way with her, including an ejaculation of semen into her vagina. Rebecca knew a medical witness would later testify that said semen had originated within the bulky, pinkish body of the defendant. Dinah White's testimony was vividly recounted in this morning's edition of the *Tribune*.

At Rebecca's request, Henry Pettiford brought the jury in. Eight women and six men followed Henry down the center aisle. They took their seats in two rows of green leather swivel chairs, situated in a railed-off box against the wall, to Rebecca's left.

Rebecca greeted the jury and took command. 'Yesterday we completed the direct examination of Dinah White. Mr

Scott, you may cross-examine. Ms White, you are still under oath.'

Harry Scott, navy pinstripe, dark wavy hair and little smile in place, leaned back in his chair behind the counsel table closest to the jury. Tom Phelps sat beside him in a similar dark suit. Bald-pated, gray-clad Whitlow Strom and Barbara Bird were whispering at the other counsel table.

Her slim sepia face dominated by large, marvelous eyes, Dinah White took her seat in the witness box. It was elevated and attached to Rebecca's raised bench on the side nearest the jury.

Scott asked a series of innocuous questions that took most of an hour, the witness spitting back the answers almost before the questions were finished. Dinah White appeared confident, perhaps even a little smug. From past experience, Rebecca knew witnesses being cross-examined by Harry Scott didn't remain smug for long.

Scott narrowed his focus. 'Ms White, do you make a habit of spending the early morning hours in hotel rooms with members of the opposite sex?'

'No,' she said.

'But it's a fact, is it not, that the sexual intercourse you spoke of yesterday on this record did not take place until two thirty a.m.?'

'Yes.'

'And of course you were there in Mr Phelps's room alone because you wanted to be?'

'I don't understand the question.'

'Up to the point where you were tied to the bed, you could have left the room at any time.'

'I'm not sure.'

'Did you try to leave the room?'

'No, not until I was tied up. Then I tried to get loose.'

'You didn't scream, did you?'

'Yes, I screamed.'

'Loud enough to hope to get help?'

'Of course, I hope—'

'The rooms on either side were occupied by sleeping guests, were they not?'

'Yes, but—'

'None of those people heard you, did they?'

'I'm not sure—'

'You are aware, are you not, that the people in those rooms have been interviewed by investigators working for the government?'

'I guess—'

Whitlow Strom leaped to his feet, his waxen head reflecting the overhead lighting, his face a pink hue. 'Objection. Counsel is not letting the witness complete her answers.'

'Overruled,' said Rebecca.

'And isn't it a fact that you are a crusader for political causes?'

'Objection, irrelevant,' said Strom.

'I'll tie it in, your honor,' said Scott.

'Overruled,' said Rebecca. 'The witness may answer.'

'That's true,' said Dinah White.

'And aren't you known in some circles as Dynamite Dinah White?'

Dinah White looked at Rebecca, then at Strom and didn't answer.

'Did you hear the question?' Scott asked.

'Yes, but what's that got—'

'I ask the questions,' said Scott. 'Please answer it.'

'Yes,' she sighed.

'Now Ms White, didn't you acquire that sobriquet because you have shown a talent for leading factions that are trying to shout down people you disagree with?'

'I don't know for sure how I got the name.'

'Is it your contention that you were unable to scream loud enough to be heard?'

'Apparently. I screamed as loud as I could and no one heard me.'

Scott looked at Rebecca without expression. 'With your permission, your honor, I want to play a video tape for purposes of impeaching this witness.'

Rebecca looked at Strom.

'Of course I object, your honor. I have no idea what's on the tape.'

'Approach the bench,' said Rebecca.

Whitlow Strom, lanky Barbara Bird, who Rebecca thought was one of the most beautiful women she had ever seen, and Harry Scott gathered closely in front of the bench. The court reporter fingering the Stenotype in front of the witness box cocked her curly blonde head, straining to hear. 'Mr Scott, what is on the tape?' Rebecca asked.

'It's a tape made by WCCO-TV showing the witness leading a shout-down while a person is attempting to address a political convention on the issue of abortion. At one point she is yelling a solo at the top of her lungs. You could hear her from here to St Paul.'

'This is the first we have heard of this tape, your honor,' said Strom.

'We just obtained it last night after we heard the witness testify yesterday that she screamed her head off on the night in question.'

'That's not a fair characterization of her testimony,' said Strom.

Barbara Bird chimed in, 'If there is anyone on this jury that's opposed to abortion, this tape could be highly prejudicial.'

'Let's not forget who's on trial here. It's my client, the defendant, whom we must be most careful not to prejudice, your honor,' said Scott.

The fox has done it again, Rebecca thought. 'We'll take a fifteen-minute recess,' she announced to the whole court.

She retreated with her clerk to her chambers. 'Tess, take a lesson. You want to be a trial lawyer. You are seeing the best there is in action. Believe it. I know what's on that tape. I've seen Dinah White in a frenzy.'

'How did they get it so quickly,' Tess asked, 'if they didn't have it already, as Mr Scott said?'

'Somebody was up all night studying tapes in that TV studio. Phelps has the clout to get the access and you can bet your last dollar that they found one to show Dinah at her worst, or best, depending on your point of view. It occurred to Scott yesterday, when she said she had screamed. He knew those adjoining rooms were occupied by people who had told

326

the investigators they had heard nothing.'

'How are you going to rule?' Tess asked.

'You tell me. This is one you can bring up in law school. Strom will argue that there is insufficient foundation because Scott hasn't established how soundproof the room actually is. I'm sure Scott hasn't had time to get expert testimony on that question. That's the issue, foundation. But if I keep it out, there's a good chance I get reversed on appeal. The prosecution can bring in testimony on sound-proofing on rebuttal, if they have it.'

'Aren't those women going to sink Phelps anyway?' Tess asked. 'Harry Scott didn't put up that big a battle when Strom moved that they be allowed to testify under 404(b).'

'He knew that testimony was coming in. We're the most liberal state in the country for allowing testimony on prior acts in these rape trials.'

'I can't help wonder,' said Tess, 'why somebody didn't hear her if she was screaming.'

'Maybe she wasn't. Maybe she was too scared,' said Rebecca, remembering a time long ago.

'I don't think I'd ever be too scared to scream,' said Tess.

'Probably better I let the tape in,' Rebecca said.

Back in the courtroom, with the jury still out, Rebecca asked Whitlow Strom if he had a formal objection to the use of the tape.

Strom began a rambling objection citing Scott's inability to lay a proper foundation without which the tape would be probative of nothing. As Rebecca listened to him, her breath caught in her throat. She met the eyes of a man who had taken someone else's seat in the front row directly behind Tom Phelps. He had not been there before. He had not been in her courtroom during this trial, or ever, for that matter. She looked away from him, and she wouldn't look back. It had been a dozen years, but she would never forget his face, the sweet smile, the sensual lips, the dark wavy hair, the fair skin, the innocent blue eyes that had become mocking and then ruthlessly evil as he raped her the same way Tom Phelps was supposed to have raped Dinah White.

Graydon Williams, son of some bigshot industrialist. She

had met him at an N.O.W. convention in Chicago with Annette Rollins and Susan. She had never told one person in the entire world that she had been raped. Annette and Susan knew she had spent the night with him. But she had been too embarrassed to tell them what had happened. She had been so drunk, she hardly realized the guy was tying her up. Now, had he come to embarrass her again? He had some kind of job in Washington, in the administration. Even if the sonofabitch was a friend of Phelps, as he must be, he could only hurt himself if he admitted he raped her. Of course, the statute of limitations had long since run. He would be safe from prosecution. When had Phelps first learned she had been raped? Had he known all along? Probably not. He certainly hadn't told Harry Scott. He wouldn't be a party to this stunt.

Rebecca suddenly realized that the courtroom was quiet. It had been quiet for a time. She didn't know how long. She had heard very little of what Strom said. 'The objection is overruled,' she said. She was grateful that she had made her mind up in chambers, or she would always wonder if the face had affected her decision.

The defendant, Tom Phelps himself, pushed the table that the TV monitor and VCR were on to a position easily seen by the jury. Rebecca stepped from behind the bench and stood beside the jury box.

The tape began to play. Dinah White was standing on a chair yelling and waving her arms to encourage others to join her. 'CHOICE!' she screamed. 'CHOICE! CHOICE! CHOICE!' Others took up the chant. When Dinah White apparently became dissatisfied with just the yelling, she began to blow a shrill whistle, like the ones used at basketball games. Others followed her lead. Rebecca moved toward the TV set.

Whitlow Strom rose to his feet. 'I object to anything further. She didn't have a whistle in the hotel that night.'

'Sustained,' said Rebecca as she turned off the TV.

Rebecca invited Monica's mother Denise to bring something to eat for lunch in her chambers. She had only wanted an update on Julie, but as it developed she needed somebody to talk to.

'I trust everything is going just fine,' Denise said as she set a Thermos and a large box down on Rebecca's desk. After she had thrown her mink on the red leather sofa, she extracted a feast from the box: fancy crackers and a paté, smoked turkey, a spectacular green and bean salad, and little goblets of chocolate mousse. 'Let's dig in,' she said.

Rebecca had once thought the time had passed for telling anyone about her experience in Chicago, but now the time had come again. Between a few bites of the gourmet lunch, she let it all splash out, together with a plenitude of tears. Denise, her black hair parted in the middle, cut stylishly short just over the ears, listened silently, only picking at the food.

When Rebecca was finished she said again, 'I was drunk. You know, Denise, I have never been drunk since. Not even close. And now the sonofabitch who did it is sitting in my courtroom smirking at me, as if he and Phelps think it will somehow work to their advantage.'

'How do you know that Phelps brought him?' Denise asked.

'I just assumed it must be Phelps. They want me to believe that if he doesn't win, they're going to use the fact that I was raped on appeal. To show I couldn't possibly give a fair trial to someone accused of rape, especially someone who was raped in the same way.'

'Don't you think it's a bluff?' said Denise. 'If this Graydon what's-his-name is assistant secretary of something or other, it isn't likely that he would come forward with that kind of a story.'

'But there he sits,' Rebecca said.

'Could you call it a day?' asked Denise. 'Sort of regroup?'

'No way. What I'm going to do is see that this defendant gets a fair trial. Now let's eat this great layout you brought.' Telling the story had been a great relief.

'In spite of the gall of this Mr Phelps, the trial must be quite interesting,' said Denise.

'Now that I've finally awakened to what this trial is really about I guess you could call it interesting.'

'I'm not sure I understand,' said Denise.

'I thought this case was about rape,' said Rebecca. 'It's not. It's about politics. Plain and simple. On the one hand the alleged victim represents the left-wing of the party, the group that is used to getting its way on the so-called causes of the day. The defendant represents the more moderate or pragmatic element of the party, the group that puts together the coalitions required to maintain power. Phelps is a guy that the Dinah Whites of the party would love to get out of their way.'

'Are you saying that it's possible that Dinah White set up her own rape?'

'Denise, can this be doctor-patient?' Rebecca asked earnestly.

'I don't see why not.'

'Send me a bill,' said Rebecca seriously. 'If she was indeed raped, I think she probably did set it up. If I thought that the evidence supported that as a reasonable alternative theory, I would dismiss the case. But I have to go by the evidence presented here. I can't rely on what I know from my experience and what I learn outside the courtroom.'

'You have a tough job ahead of you,' said Denise.

'Not really. I think it might be the jury who has the tough job ahead. You know, when I first got this case, I was so excited. I knew all the hoopla that went with high-profile criminal cases and I was swept away with it. Then I became a little doubtful, but when it became obvious that they were using political pressure to knock me off the case, I decided to be a bulldog. Hold on with my teeth. Then simultaneously with winning that fight, some crazy person almost kills a neighbor of mine, thinking she's me. Against that, this trial is no longer of any relative importance, Denise. Julie came within fifteen minutes of maybe becoming an orphan.'

'By the way,' said Denise, 'there was a news report this morning that her doctors have declared Jane Graham out of danger.'

'Praise the Lord,' said Rebecca. 'That makes my day. To hell with Graydon Williams.'

Before she left, Denise went on about the great time the girls were having, living like sisters. Rebecca took just a little consolation from the fact that Cloris Schmid had made no attempt to hurt Jane Graham's daughter, who she must have thought at the time was Julie. When one has nothing else to grasp, one grasps at straws.

That afternoon Harry Scott continued the siege of Dinah White. She denied all his leading questions that suggested she had ulterior motives for getting Tom Phelps convicted. But the idea was planted firmly in the jurors' minds. By the end of the day, Rebecca thought that the jury would never convict Tom Phelps on Dinah White's testimony alone. But there were more witnesses coming, and they apparently didn't like Tom Phelps any better than Dinah did.

47

Exhilarated, William shot across Lake Minnetonka's snow-covered ice like an arrow from a bow. The powerful Arctic Cat growled fiercely beneath him. His third night out, he was ready to set the next phase of his plan in motion. Headlights on other snowmobiles dotted the lake. He came quite close to some as he raced over the ice toward Wayzata Bay into the edge of the north wind. Rebecca Goldman's daughter had been spending many evenings with her friend who lived in the Clark mansion. Last night, through the vast windows facing the lake, William had spotted her face, unmistakably black among the white, with his binoculars. Much of the planned privacy of the lake-front homes was lost with the falling of the leaves. Local law prevented the snowmobilers from operating too close to the shoreline, so residents seldom bothered to draw the drapes on the windows facing Minnetonka's great winter vistas.

William played a game of patience. During the day he examined the Clark estate with binoculars. Like a French chateau on the hillside, the monolithic main house dominated the wooded estate. At night no light came from the structure attached to the north end. William assumed it was a large garage, with perhaps unused living quarters above. Wilma had seen no evidence of live-in servants, but from its size William reasoned that there had to be at least one or two. It would be much easier if there were none. Most of the main floor was lit up through the evening. Lights flicked on and off in the lower level and the second level. Only on the first night had he seen a light in one of the windows of the dormered top story.

As he had reckoned for months, he had a full week ahead with no moon. Seven days of relative darkness, though the broad expanses of snow still reflected more light than he would have liked. He planned to observe the movements within the house from six to eleven each night, as long as it took, moon or no moon. He had hit upon the ideal cover. His landlady's deceased husband Chester had left ice fishing equipment in the garage. Through his binoculars, unknowing anglers had taught him the rudiments the first day. Now he would observe the Clark home in the guise of an ice fisherman. He had even bought a fishing license in the name of Frank Kroll of Sheboygan, Wisconsin.

When he had pushed his face plate up to look through the binoculars that first night, the icy wind had numbed his skin. Tonight, he wore a ski mask with just holes for his eyes and mouth. He kept the binoculars inside Chester's snowmobile suit, so they wouldn't fog from his breath. He had borrowed a pair of Chester's pacs and he wore long underwear and a turtleneck. He stopped his machine straight out from the brightly lit windows of what he supposed was the living room, if mansions have living rooms. With a hatchet he broke open the frozen-over hole that he had bored through two and a half feet of ice the night before. A few dead minnows floated in a small bottle that he withdrew from an inside pocket. He impaled one on a hook and dropped the line down through the hole. With his back to the wind, he sat on the snowmobile as though it was a bench. And watched.

It could be a long wait, but William was not new to waiting. He had languished in the locked cell at Wolf River for years, watching crows cruise on the air currents above the river. He would not be going back there. He would die with the .38 in his hand. In the Clarks' dining room four people sat at the table eating. No sign of a maid. One of the faces was black.

To the east, red and white lights moving horizontally were the only evidence of the steady procession of cars that passed over the Highway 101 causeway, separating Wayzata Bay and Grays Bay. The hum of their engines was occasionally obliterated by the roar of a nearby snowmobile. Sirens came and went in the distance, and halfway through the evening the flashing light of a police car raced down the main street of Wayzata, the village built on the northwest corner of the bay.

Sometime after dinner William saw the man go to a closet near the front door, just visible beyond the dining room. He put on a winter coat and disappeared, then reappeared for an instant in one of the windows to the right. Minutes later the tail lights of a car moved out from behind the black hulk of the garage and on up the curving driveway. If he saw the two adults leave together, he would make his move. If he ran out of time, he would make his move in any event.

Cold began to seep through the layers of clothing. If the temperature fell any further, on future nights he would need warmer clothes. In the shadows of his mind, crackling logs blazed in a stone fireplace. Herds of sleek black cattle roamed the prairie. Mary played a Chopin nocturne. He could have been a wonderful farmer. He could have done anything he aspired to do. A whole squadron of snowmobiles roared toward him. His pulse quickened. The glaring eyes of their headlights surrounded him.

'You catchin' anything?' a teenager's voice yelled.

'No luck tonight,' said William.

Their engines came back to life. With a mighty din they sped off toward Wayzata. At ten minutes to eleven he succumbed to the thought of Mary's lush body waiting for him in their bed. He would return again tomorrow night.

48

S *tate of Minnesota v. Thomas Phelps.* Day four. In spite of
the presence of Graydon Williams's smirking face in the
courtroom, the shadowy Wilma Schmid and the ghostly
incarnation of William Schmid somewhere outside,
Rebecca had managed to get through yesterday afternoon's
cross-examination of Dinah White with judgely aplomb. In
view of the video tape showing her screaming her lungs out
like a champion Arkansas hog caller, the newspaper reports
belittled Dinah White's testimony as self-serving. The prosecution would depend heavily on today's witnesses.

Whitlow Strom, in brown this morning, bare dome as
pink and shiny as ever, called Jean Daugherty to testify for
the state. She approached the witness box with a quick but
graceful prance, placing one foot precisely ahead of the
other. Her dark hair was swept round to one side, falling on
the front of her left shoulder. She said, I do, in response to
the oath and smiled graciously. After a series of background
questions, Strom asked her if she knew the defendant.

'I met him fifteen years ago when I was still in high
school,' she said in a sweet, soft voice. 'He was a student at
the University of Minnesota.'

Another series of questions elicited the story of the
beginnings of her relationship with Phelps. Finally Strom
asked, 'Did the defendant ever put you in a position where
you feared bodily harm?'

'Yes,' she said. Her face tightened up. Fear replaced her
gracious expression and a vertical line appeared between
her eyebrows.

'Where were you at the time?'

'It was right after I graduated from high school. Tom had taken me to a party and we had quite a lot to drink, at least for me. I hadn't done that much drinking up to that time,' she said. 'Or since, for that matter,' and she looked at Rebecca as if she didn't want her to think she was a big drinker. 'Anyway,' she blew air through her lips like a smoker exhaling, 'he took me to his house after. He lived with his mother. I guess she was supposed to be away for the weekend or something.'

'Object, not responsive. I ask that counsel be directed to proceed with questions and answers,' said Harry Scott in his dark blue suit. Phelps sat next to him, his lips a straight line, but Rebecca thought she detected amusement in his eyes.

'Sustained,' she said. 'Please use the usual method of direct examination, Counsel.' Letting the witness tell her story was a clever way to get inadmissable material before a jury but Scott wouldn't let it happen without protest.

'What happened next?' Strom asked.

'He took me in to show me his mother's neat bedroom. She had a four-poster with a canopy. Well, we ended up wrestling around on her bed and I was getting scared a little, but he was laughing and acting playful, like there was nothing to be afraid of. And eventually he got both of my feet and both of my wrists tied to the posts on the corners of the bed with . . . I think they were the sashes from bath-robes or something like that. Anyway, I was helpless. I've never felt so helpless.'

'Then what?' said Strom, looking at the jury with a we've heard this someplace before expression on his face, his incipient beard clearly visible even at this early hour.

'He took his pants off.'

'Then what?'

'He took off everything.' A flush showed through her make-up.

'Then what?'

'I started to cry.'

'Then what?'

'He said, "You'll like this," and started to, you know, go down on me.'

'Did you like it?'

'No. I pleaded with him to untie me. I told him I didn't like it. I was very scared. I was a virgin.'

'Then what?'

'We heard this noise, like a motor running. He listened for a minute. Then he leaped up and pulled his pants on and his shirt. I was so relieved. I remember he put his underwear in his pocket. Then he started to untie the knots and he had trouble with one of them. He untied three of them, but he was still fumbling with the one when his mother walked in the room.'

'Then what?'

'She said, "What the hell are you doing in my room?" By this time I was crying pretty hard and she saw my leg was still tied to one of the posts. She took a pair of scissors out of the drawer and cut me loose. Then she told me to get the hell off her bed like I was the one at fault. I ran out of her room and out the front door and down one street after another until I found an all-night gas station. I called my dad to come and get me.'

When she was finished, Strom took her back through each of Phelps's actions, and asked if she had consented. Each time she answered with an emphatic, "No, I did not."

Strom glanced toward Harry Scott. 'Your witness,' he said.

Scott began speaking to the witness in the same intimate tone he would have used if the two of them had been out to dinner alone. 'Miss Daugherty, you testified that the defendant tied each of your limbs to one of the posts of the four-poster, is that correct?'

'Yes,' she said in her soft voice.

'Did you remove any of your clothes before he tied you down?'

'No,' she said more loudly.

'Did the defendant remove any of your clothes before he tied you down?'

'No.'

'Were you wearing panties or pantyhose?'

How about nothing as an option? Rebecca thought.

'Panties,' she said.

'Was it your impression that the defendant intended to have sexual intercourse with you?' Scott asked, now a little louder.

'Yes.'

'With your panties on?' Scott's voice had become incredulous, with a hint of sarcasm.

'Well, I—'

'Have you ever tried taking a pair of panties off with both ankles tied to posts?'

'No, but—'

'It's a fact, is it not, that the defendant made no attempt to take your panties off?'

'I guess not.'

'Even when, as you put it, he went down on you?'

'It's been so long,' she said, her voice anxious, full of doubt.

'What you're saying is that you don't remember what happened all that clearly, correct?'

'Well, some of it—'

'No further questions,' said Scott.

After the morning recess, Whit Strom called Marlene Mays, the strawberry-blonde Candice Bergen lookalike, as his next witness. Her connection with Phelps had been political, and within the last five years. Her experience was amazingly close to Dinah White's, including being tied down. The most important difference was that Marlene claimed to have been in a drunken stupor. It was the middle of the night in a hotel where a party function had taken place. Phelps had penetrated her, she said, without a condom, and she herself was without any birth control protection. She was terribly relieved that she hadn't become pregnant, but she had caught some kind of non-specific infection that had been promptly and successfully treated. She hadn't come forward when it happened because she thought the scandal would ruin her politically. Now, she thought she had a greater duty to women in general to tell her story.

Two or three of the women jurors appeared sympathetic

and moved by Marlene Mays's testimony.

Harry Scott opened his cross-examination. 'Was it your idea to come here and testify?'

'Yes.'

'When did you get the idea?'

'When I read about the rape in the paper. I remembered what had happened—'

'No one else encouraged you to testify?'

'Dinah White encouraged me, after she met me.'

'No one else?'

'Not really, I'm here on my own. Of course people who heard I was going to testify supported my decision to do so.'

'And who were these people?'

'Friends and . . .'

'And who?' said Scott.

'Barbara Bird,' she nodded her head slightly toward the prosecutor's table and again when she said, 'and Mr Strom.'

'What friends?'

'All of my friends.'

'Anyone else who's involved in this trial?'

'I think Sue Klein is going to testify. I guess you can say she encouraged me.'

'What did she say?'

'I really don't recall exactly.'

'Generally then,' said Scott.

'I don't recall really.'

'You don't recall any of the substance—'

'Objection,' said Strom. 'Asked and answered.'

'Sustained,' said Rebecca.

'Where was she when she encouraged you?'

'I guess it was on the telephone.'

'You don't remember whether or not you were face to face or on the telephone?'

'I guess it was both, actually.'

'When on the telephone?'

'At least a couple of months ago.'

'When in person?'

'Sue and I socialize,' said Marlene.

'On how many separate occasions in the past twelve

months have you and Sue Klein socialized?'

There was blood in the water and Rebecca knew Harry Scott had scented it.

'I don't recall.'

'Less than ten?'

'Yes, I would say less than ten.'

'More than twice?'

'Maybe.'

'Maybe three times?' Scott asked.

'Maybe.'

'Of those three times—'

'Objection,' said Strom. 'He's assuming facts not in evidence. The witness has testified she doesn't recall how many times.'

'Sustained,' said Rebecca.

'Would you agree that in the past twelve months, Ms Mays, you and Sue Klein have not socialized on more than four occasions?'

'Yes, I would agree with that.'

Now, Scott had what he wanted.

'If you socialized four or less times in the past twelve months, you must be able to remember where you were when you were socializing, correct?'

'I suppose, at least some of the places.'

'Would you please state for the jury just what places.'

Rebecca knew how quickly the reluctance of witnesses to give honest answers could lose a jury.

'Well, after a Central Committee meeting we went to the Palomino Club.'

'Is that one of the times Sue Klein encouraged you to testify?'

'I don't recall.'

'At what other place can you recall socializing?'

Marlene Mays's face took on a desperate look. Rebecca was sure that at this moment she was wishing she had stayed out of the Phelps case. Scott leaned back and waited.

'Her house.'

'When?'

'A couple of weeks ago.'

Scott went on to worm a detailed account of the agreement among Sue Klein, Jean Daugherty, and Marlene Mays to come into court and do their best to convict Tom Phelps, including an account of their apparently failed efforts to enlist Melody Sanford in the same enterprise. One thing Rebecca knew for sure was that Whit Strom and Barbara Bird had no knowledge of the meeting. Neither one of them was that stupid. Maybe it was her imagination, but she thought she felt a sickening pall settle over the courtroom, like a film of disagreeable dust. She could hear Harry Scott's final argument now, challenging the credibility of these women. It wouldn't be pretty.

Scott's last question was a duzy. 'Ms Mays, who was the instigator of this conspiracy to convict Tom Phelps of rape?'

'Objection,' said Strom. 'Assumes facts not in evidence, calls for a legal conclusion.'

'Overruled,' said Rebecca.

'I wouldn't call it a conspiracy,' said Marlene Mays.

'Call it what you want,' said Scott. 'Whose idea was it?'

'I guess it was Sue's,' she said glumly.

'No further questions,' said Scott.

Phelps's straight-lipped expression was turning slightly upward at the corners. Rebecca caught Graydon Williams's intense blue eyes for a second, and felt almost nothing. From a strictly analytical viewpoint, feeling nothing was real progress since yesterday. Could she ever be lucky enough to have him try to rape her again while she was still carrying that little five-shot revolver in her purse? From that day forward he'd be speaking in a higher register. God, girl, what the hell is to become of you? she said to herself.

To the assembled throng she said, 'This is a good time for the lunch break. The court is recessed until half past one.'

Six foot two and blonde, Sue Klein stood up straight in heels, right hand raised, swearing to tell the truth. In response to Whitlow Strom's questions she told a story similar to those the jury had heard from the other women. Heavy drinking, tying the limbs in what could have been playful foolishness, ending up with full penetration sex as

341

had happened to Dinah White and Marlene Mays. Sue said she didn't think anyone would believe her. She had gone to Phelps's apartment late at night of her own volition. It was only a year and a half ago.

Not wanting this witness to be ambushed by Harry Scott's cross-examination like Marlene Mays had been, Whit Strom made Sue Klein tell the story in detail, including the meeting at her place less than two weeks before the trial. Sure, they had agreed among themselves to testify, she said. Sure, they wanted Phelps convicted. But they weren't willing to go beyond the truth to see it happen. As a trial judge, Rebecca was aware how loosely that word was thrown around courtrooms. Truth to one was not always truth to another. Perceptions varied from person to person. *Rashomon* was not a far-fetched tale.

Harry Scott treated Sue Klein gently on cross-examination as he explored the meeting at her house in great detail. Her version varied little from Marlene's. Rebecca thought they had compared notes more than Sue Klein admitted.

'If I were to tell you that someone had come forward with a tape recording of the meeting at your home attended by Ms Daugherty, Ms Mays, Ms Sandford and you, Ms Klein, would you want to change your testimony or add anything to it?'

Strom broke in. 'Is counsel stating for the record that he has such a tape recording?'

'I'm not testifying here, Mr Strom,' said Scott. 'Your witness, Ms Klein, is testifying.'

'I object, your honor, to the form of the question,' said Strom.

'Overruled,' said Rebecca.

'You may answer,' said Scott.

'Could you repeat the question?'

Harry Scott asked the reporter to read it back.

'I've done my best to recall everything that happened and answer the best I can,' said Sue Klein, her voice much weaker and more uncertain than it had been. 'I suppose I could have forgotten something or made some mistakes.'

'But as far as any major or significant discussion of this trial or the testimony you were all going to give, you can remember nothing.'

'No, I don't think there's anything significant,' said Sue Klein.

I'll bet there is, thought Rebecca.

A nurse, a doctor and a technical expert consumed the balance of the afternoon's testimony. At the end of his cross-examination of each of them, Scott asked the same question: is there anything about your observations that is inconsistent with the assumption that Dinah White had engaged in spirited consensual sexual intercourse? They all agreed there were no such inconsistencies.

Extensive news coverage on four metropolitan channels that evening inferred that the prosecution's case against Tom Phelps was less than solid. Harry Scott's cross-examination had at times made the witnesses look foolish, one commentator said. A late evening call-in poll revealed that fifty-seven per cent of those calling thought Phelps had raped Dinah White; forty-three per cent thought he had not.

With Julie staying out at the lake, Rebecca had decided that Kevin was right. For now, the place for her was with him. Her bailiff Henry Pettiford had carried a gun ever since the botched attempt on her life, so staying with Kevin when she was away from the Government Center meant that she was protected at all times by an armed bodyguard. She had tried to talk Julie into going to Milwaukee and living with Papa Nathan, but she wouldn't hear of it. She had a major role in the freshman class play, for starters. That old woman is dead, Julie had exclaimed, and if Wilma Schmid was going to hurt us, she's had months to do it. It's you they want to hurt, Mom, she had said. *You* should go to Milwaukee.

On the way home, over dinner at Sidney's, Kevin told Rebecca they had nothing new on William Schmid. The Mankato police had carried his picture around to all inn-keepers and left copies for their employees to see. The same picture was run in the Mankato newspaper, and of course it had run in last Sunday's statewide edition of the *Tribune*. The pay phone that the calls were made from in Mankato was an outdoor telephone in a Mobil gas station where hundreds of calls were made every week, both local and long distance. The FBI had checked the South Dakota truck stop where the two telephone calls to the railroad law library had come from. They found nothing. Truck drivers made more than three hundred long-distance calls a week from that phone, but mostly on credit cards. These calls were made with coins, but the agent said that was not that unusual either.

A complete canvas of the lawyers and support employees who rented space from the railroad and were therefore eligible to use the library uncovered no one who had received such calls. Finally, the more than three hundred employees working at the headquarters of the railroad were contacted. None admitted to having received any of the calls in question. What all the interviews of people in the building meant, Kevin said, was that there was a good chance that Wilma had received those calls, and if she had, there was a very good chance they had been made by her brother.

As soon as they arrived at Kevin's apartment, Rebecca was on the phone to Julie. 'How's it going, honey?'

'Awesome,' said Julie, 'but Mom, I miss you.'

'I miss you too, sweetheart. You're being careful now, aren't you?'

'Sure, Mom. You're the one that needs to be careful.'

'I am. How's the play going?'

'Super. Except I gotta kiss this freak. Like no way, I said. But Miss Perkins said, this is a drama, we have to act like professionals. But I told the freak to keep his tongue to himself.'

'Is he—?'

'Yes, Mom, he's white.'

Heat spread through Rebecca's face. Why did she always ask those stupid questions that she had spent a lifetime contending were irrelevant? She changed the subject. 'What're you girls doing with all your time in that big house?'

'Monica's got a stereo in her room that's totally rocked. I mean totally. She's got hundreds of discs, at least twenty Duran Duran.'

'Sounds nice.'

'Sounds slammin',' said Julie. 'So far tonight I've been listening alone. This freak called Monica, and she can't get rid of him. She hates him, but he keeps calling. She's so super sweet she won't hang up on him. He was Cindy Brooks's boyfriend up to a month ago. He was just usin' her.'

'Does Denise know about this guy?' Rebecca asked.

'I don't think so, but don't you say anything. Monica'll freak out if her mother says something. You won't say anything, promise?'

'I promise,' said Rebecca with a sigh, 'but don't you think you should at least talk to Monica if he's that kind of a boy?'

'I do. I will again later on. I gotta help her with her algebra. But what can I say? She knows he's an asshole. I gotta go, Mom. I love you. Oh, you know what, Monica's folks are taking us snowmobiling tomorrow night. You wanta come? It'll be awesome. Her dad's so cool.'

'I can't with this trial going on,' said Rebecca. 'I'm ready to collapse right now and it's only ten after eight.'

'Gotta go, Mom. Love you.'

'I love you too, baby.'

Out on the ice William had already spotted the black face on three levels tonight. The weather had warmed a little and it was pleasant on the lake. He could do anything, expend any effort when he knew that eventually he would be going home to his lovely Mary.

49

Mary had driven into Long Lake, the closest town, and bought a week's supply of groceries including the makings of one of her favorite breakfasts. Toasting bread and frying sausage filled the kitchen with fragrances reminding William of pleasant mornings at the farm. These last few days had been the best of his entire life.

Two distinct persons had emerged from the one that had been William Schmid. One lived day by day for new-found pleasures of the senses: Mary's gentle touch and the warmth of her body under a pile of quilts in a winter-chilled room; watching the squirrels and blue jays in the snowy back yard fending off winter and eating the scraps Mary had thrown them; little sips of wine from crystal glasses and dining on wonderful meals she had prepared with loving hands; deep breaths of the natural perfume of her red hair and inhaling the civet aroma of their repeating rut; Mary playing a polonaise on the old upright and her soprano renditions of hymns he had heard but never before listened to.

The second person knew the first and liked him, and wanted to get to know him better, but that would have to await the denouement of his dreadful resolve. Like a planet in orbit, the second person was following a track through space preordained and immutable until some interstellar collision created chaos. The first understood the destiny of the second and could only imagine how life might be had fate decreed differently.

At this breakfast he chose to finalize his instructions. 'Mary, you remember when we talked at the farm, I told you I had an important task to accomplish?'

'I remember,' she said. Her wide-set eyes said show me what you want me to do.

'I need to use the basement for what I am doing. I want you to promise me that from this day forward you will not enter the basement for any reason.' He dipped his toast in the soft egg yolk and ate with relish.

'I promise, Frankie. Whatever you say,' she said. 'But it all sounds kind of scary to me.'

'I do not want you to become involved. There could be serious trouble. You must be able to honestly say that you had no idea what I was doing.'

'Why don't we just enjoy ourselves for a while longer?'

'I must complete what I have set out to do.'

'You know I would never tell anyone. I have never said anything about Kenny Speer.'

'You must defer to me in this.' He used the harshest tone he ever had with her, then got up and kissed the top of her head and went downstairs to the basement to make his preparations.

Because of a judges' meeting in the morning, Rebecca was unable to get day five of *State of Minnesota v. Phelps* going until two in the afternoon. All the seats were filled and the jury was already seated when Whitlow Strom said, 'The state calls Karen Crane.'

After the preliminaries, the smooth-domed prosecutor asked the witness if she knew Tom Phelps.

'When he was in the investment business I was his personal secretary for three years,' she said. Probably thirty or so, she had short brown hair and a pretty oval face, her cheek bones highlighted with blush.

'When was that?'

'I started with him about ten years ago.'

'I take it that means you worked closely with Mr Phelps.'

'That's true,' she said.

'Did you have any relationship with him other than business?'

'Not really. We had dinner a few times, but I had a steady boyfriend at the time.'

'Did Mr Phelps ever suggest anything more than a business relationship?'

'Many times. He was very aggressive about that.'

'How did you handle it?'

'Mostly with humor. I told him my boyfriend was very jealous.'

Rebecca saw Harry Scott listening very carefully, getting ready to jump in with an objection.

'Did Mr Phelps speak with you about his personal life?'

'Yes, quite frequently.'

'What did he say about his personal life?'

'Objection, no foundation,' said Scott.

'Sustained,' said Rebecca.

Unflappable, Strom started again. 'Can you recall a specific conversation he had with you about his personal life?'

'Yes,' said the witness, tossing a lock of hair out of her eyes with a shake of her head.

'And when did you have that conversation?' Strom asked. At his side, Barbara Bird in a navy blazer stared at the witness intently, as if she was about to reveal something terribly significant.

'It was just before Christmas about eight years ago, say about the fifteenth of December.' She sounded confident, her voice strong and smooth. In the preliminary questions she said she had become a stockbroker over the ensuing years.

'How can you be so sure of the date?'

'That was the year he met Wilma Schmid at a Christmas party. I got to know her pretty well after that. She came into the office often.'

'And who was present when you had this conversation?'

'Just Tom and me,' she said.

'And where were you at the time?'

'In his private office. He often called me in to dictate letters, or just to talk.'

As Strom started his next question he looked at Rebecca as trial lawyers do, his face saying, there you have your foundation, Judge. Who, when and where. 'What did he tell you about his personal life?'

'He told me he had met this sexy woman named Wilma Schmid at the Christmas party and he had taken her home and raped her.'

'Did you respond in any way?'

'I said something flip like, Tom, don't you know that's against the law?'

'What did he say then?'

'He said, "Nothing ventured, nothing gained." Then he told me he had tied her up on his mother's four-poster bed and had sex with her while she was crying for help. Then he said, "Karen, you won't believe this, but when it was over, she asked if I would do it again." '

'Did he say anything else?'

'He said, "See what you're missing." '

Beside Harry Scott, behind the counsel table, a deadly serious expression formed on Phelps's face.

'Did he ever say anything about it again?'

'When he got her brother a job at the university, he said it's the least I can do for somebody I raped, but that was a long time after and he had been sexually involved with her for months. He claimed she was insatiable.'

'Did she ever comment to you on the rape?'

'Objection,' said Scott. 'Hearsay.'

'Sustained,' said Rebecca.

'Are you involved in politics in any way?' Strom asked.

'I vote,' she said. 'Nothing more.'

'Do you have any reason to wish Mr Phelps ill?'

'Not at all. I got along fine with Tom.'

'How is it you happen to be here today to testify?' said Strom looking directly at the jury.

'I was served a subpoena.'

'Has anyone encouraged you to come here and testify?'

'No.'

'Did you attend any meetings wherein this trial was discussed?'

'No.'

'Do you have any idea why you were subpoenaed?'

'An investigator from your office interviewed me a couple of months ago. She asked me whether or not I had any

349

information about Tom's . . . Mr Phelps's relationships with women, with particular reference to forced sex or, she used the word, rape. I thought it was my duty to be honest so I told her the story I just told here.'

Harry Scott's cross-examination established that Karen Crane thought Phelps was a 'nice guy', that he had never tried to force sex on her, that he was a hard worker, and a compassionate and generous man. To wind up, Harry Scott surprised Rebecca by breaking one of the cardinal rules of cross-examination. He asked a question, not knowing the answer in advance. Or, did he? Rebecca wondered.

'Ms Crane, I understand that you worked very closely with Mr Phelps over a period of three years. During that time did you ever know Tom Phelps to lie?'

'Never,' she said emphatically.

Why in the world did that woman say that? Rebecca thought. Phelps, like all politicians, was an accomplished liar. Harry Scott knows it goes with the territory. He must have known in advance she was going to say never. Then it dawned on her. Karen Crane had been honest with the investigator and had had second thoughts when she knew she would be subpoenaed. She went to Phelps with her dilemma, and Harry Scott had told her how she could help them. With that one answer, Rebecca thought Karen Crane's testimony had helped Phelps more than it had hurt him. She wondered what Scott would use for the *coup de grâce* on Monday.

With Rebecca beside him, Kevin pulled his car into the warehouse in St Paul where the state cops had stored the station wagon William Schmid had driven into the Wolf River. The tripods with the floodlights were still there. With just the area around the station wagon lit, the enveloping darkness of the huge warehouse gave Rebecca the creeps. Kevin pulled some rented scuba diving equipment from the trunk of his car. When he got the oxygen tank attached to the harness, Rebecca helped him wriggle into it. He opened the door to the station wagon and crawled in across the front seat on his knees. When he was all the way in, he slipped his legs under the steering wheel and sat upright. He closed the door. The tank took up the area where the seat back had been. He had been ninety-nine per cent sure before, but now he was certain. It was no longer an assumption. William Schmid could have fitted into this car with enough equipment to stay underwater until he had traveled many miles downstream.

He opened the door and scrambled out. 'It's awkward,' he said, 'but no big deal.'

'But you can't be sure he made it. He had to survive the plunge and the weather.'

'That's true, but my guess is that they had a car stashed for him downstream,' said Kevin. As he spoke, Rebecca helped him out of the scuba gear. 'If they did and he didn't find it, the cops would have. Course if somebody had been waiting for him in a car, Cloris Schmid, for instance, and he didn't show up, they would've just left.'

'And his body would still be in the river under the ice,' said Rebecca, still hoping but not believing.

'True, but I wouldn't bet my life on it,' said Kevin, 'or, more importantly, yours.' He pursed his lips and shook his head. 'You know I been chasin' the bad guys for about twenty years now. Most of 'em are stupid. I mean more stupid than your run-of-the-mill stiff. They don't see ahead very far. Sure, there's a few smart ones, but just a few. We gotta remember that the guy we're dealin' with here is a frigging theoretical physicist. He's not gonna make a lot of mistakes.' He picked up the oxygen tank standing on the concrete floor and put it back in the trunk of his car.

William sat on the Wayzata Bay ice for the fifth consecutive night watching and waiting, thoughtful and patient. Sitting in the dark observing people who were unaware of his presence gave him a feeling of omnipotence. Their lives were in his hands as much as God's. More, really, he thought. He remembered a quote from Maimonides: 'God is not a meddler.' The means of their destruction was at William's fingertips. Intermittently, he lifted his right shoulder to feel the weight of the .38 in the button-down pocket of the snowmobile suit.

The wind was light but out of the north and biting. It wasn't as cold as it seemed, because the ice formed only very slowly on the hole he had opened for his fish line. There was more traffic than usual on the causeway. Probably because it was a Friday night. There were more snowmobilers too, darting around the lake randomly in the dark.

Sometimes William dared to believe his headaches had subsided for good. It had been two months since the last one. Without the medication, he had feared their return daily. Mary must be the reason. She had become his medication. Since the night the train had hit the truck, she had steadied him, warmed him, loved him. Too late, she had given him a reason to live. With him gone, she would go back to Mike and more beatings. Once Konrad Schmid had started beating Cloris, he had never stopped. That was the way with men who beat women. Their appetite whetted, they didn't stop. Add alcohol and only the worst could result. Mike Bohas, like everybody else, didn't know a good thing when he saw it.

The light went on in a big recreation room on the lower level of the Clark house. William refocused the binoculars. The same four people came into view, the Clark family and the judge's daughter. They were getting into snowmobile suits.

About fifteen minutes later, the headlights of two snowmobiles crossed the wide expanse of snow-covered lawn sloping down to the lake. They sped across the ice directly at William. He slipped the binoculars back inside his suit and sat with his head down, staring into his fishing hole. The powerful engines drew closer and the beams of their headlights swept across his legs, lighting up the snow around him. The noise receded as they headed up the lake toward the colored lights of Excelsior in the distance. Any expectation of the girls being left alone had vanished for tonight. William picked up his gear and headed for his car.

50

The landlady had kept a clean and cheery kitchen. Not yet daylight outside, fluorescent lighting recessed in a false ceiling behind large squares of frosted plastic illuminated every corner. The end wall forming the corner where William sat at the table reading the Saturday morning *Tribune* was papered in a delicate green print over which were hung three realistic slices of watermelon made of plastic.

The idea that there were seven deadly sins had always fascinated William. In a world where lust, greed, sloth, gluttony, jealousy and pride infected the character of society, he believed he had lived relatively free of those sins. The seed of the seventh, anger, had taken root in the fecund garden of his youth. Fertilized by parental abuse and unfairness, the poisonous vine crept through his essence, insinuating itself into the whole organism like Spanish moss drooping from a live oak tree. Mary's gentle influence had retarded its progress and it had wilted some, even withdrawn from sight. Saturday morning it sprang forth from every crevice of his character.

William had followed the Phelps trial in the *Tribune*. It kept him apprised of the whereabouts of Judge Rebecca Goldman and fed his contempt for Tom Phelps. He had hoped that Wilma had taken his advice and stayed away from the man. Karen Crane's testimony of yesterday as reported under Annette Rollins's by-line took William completely by surprise. WITNESS LINKS PHELPS TO KILLER'S SISTER, the headline blurted. He read the story of Phelps's light-hearted account to his secretary of never-ending sexual escapades with Wilma – 'sexcapades' Annette Rollins called them in her column on the editorial page. For the first time, William learned that his teaching job had been a by-product of his sister's rutting with this contemptible creature, even as he himself, from time to time, had shared her bed. Insatiable, the article said. Wilma was insatiable. What a fool he had been. What a fool he was.

'How about waffles,' Mary said, 'with walnuts and blueberries? I used to make that for Mike when we first got married. I've even got some maple syrup.'

William barely noticed how nice she looked, her face already made up with soft lipstick and light blush. The newspaper article stuck low in his throat like a chicken bone. The squeezing pressure in his temples had returned. The inevitable pain would soon follow. Something distorted Mary's kind face like an image in a flawed mirror. He rushed out of the kitchen and down the short hall to the bathroom. Twisting the faucet handle, he let cool water run over his wrists and splashed some on to his face.

'Frankie, what on earth is the matter?' Mary was outside the door.

He was unable to answer. The steady pressure became a throb. *Hoomb. Hoomb. Hoomb. Hoomb. Hoomb. Hoomb.*

'Frankie, I'm coming in,' Mary said through the door.

When she entered, William was seated on the closed cover of the commode, his chin resting on his chest as though his neck was constructed of soft rubber. Mary's feet shuffled into his line of vision. Her fingertips began a circular massage on his temples. *Hoomb. Hoomb. Hoomb. Hoomb. Hoomb.*

'That awful thing has come back,' she said, 'but Frankie, I know it will go away just like last time. You'll see.'

William didn't move.

Mary lifted his right hand from his lap and tugged gently. Like a retarded child he rose and followed her down the hall into their room. She nudged him toward the unmade bed and he sat on the edge, his head still hanging forward, his chin on his chest. It was a gray dawn. By adjusting the blinds, Mary effectively darkened the room.

She turned the switch on a halogen reading lamp on the bed table. Blinding incandescence flooded the area of the bed and splashed across the left side of William's head, drawing a faint auburn cast from his beard. Mary retrieved her pendant from the top drawer of the dressing table. She walked slowly back, stepping softly, the shiny pendant dangling on the end of its chain. A spot of lamp light glancing off the silver played across the rumpled bed-clothes. She held her hand steady until the dancing spot settled down. Gradually, she moved the chain toward William. The spot of light followed across the top of the bed and jumped on to his lap. It stopped on his right hand, lying palm down on his thigh. She held it still, her arm extended, trembling only slightly. One minute passed. Then another and another. Her arm grew weary. She backed up a little, the spot moving from the back of his hand to the blue denim covering his knee. William's head rose a few degrees. She stepped forward, drawing her hand back toward her bosom, maintaining the spot of light on William's knee. Her black woolen skirt pressed against his leg. She maneuvered the scintillant spot up the skirt on to the surface of her dark green sweater. As his head came up, she let the flash of light swing back across his lap, up over his shirt on to his face. She played the light on his left eye. He stared intently for a minute or two. She reached out with her left hand and pushed on his right shoulder, carefully holding the pendant's beam in his eye. Torpidly, he descended to the pillow.

'Close your eyes,' she said. 'It's time to go to sleep.'

At her command, the lids dropped shut. She bent over and lifted his feet on to the bed. She lay down beside him and pulled the quilt over them both. William dropped into a sleep as though he had been drugged.

Saturday morning was Miles Dickstein's turn to put his feet on Kevin's desk. Stacks of papers covered every flat surface in the drab office, on the wall was the picture of George Washington that had hung in schoolrooms earlier in the century.

'Shit,' Miles said, smoothing back his dark wavy hair, a cigarette flopping on his lip, 'we got nothin' new. The Eau Claire police are tearing their hair. Guy down there, O'Neal, he's sure Wilma Schmid smothered that old guy.'

'Me too,' said Kevin.

'Considering when she checked in at Madison, they can put her drivin' down 94 in the area of Eau Claire within the ME's estimated time of death,' said Miles. 'And we got Cloris pegged at a dump in Bloomington, so it wasn't her. But they got nothing else on Wilma, and they got no motive. Shit, they know they got no chance to extradite her on that. They're gonna try and come over here and talk to her. I gave 'em all I had.'

'She got a lawyer yet?' Kevin asked.

'Beats me. She's talked to me twice without one.' Miles lit another cigarette. 'Why the fuck you think she killed that old guy?'

'It was probably the easiest thing to do at the time. My guess is she promised Cloris she'd take care of him for the weekend and Wilma didn't want anyone spotting her car there or anything like that to connect her with Cloris.'

'Makes sense,' said Miles, 'if you're into killin' people.'

'That Eau Claire killing's got me thinkin' about something else,' Kevin said. 'We've been assuming that her brother's the nut. Maybe she's just as nuts as he is.'

'Don't forget one thing,' said Miles. 'There's a chance she didn't do that old guy in Eau Claire. The ME could be wrong on that time of death. Wouldn't be the first time.'

'Slim to none,' said Kevin.

'The tails have been with her most of the time, but they haven't given us anything to work with. When she wants to, she shakes 'em. But how do you figure? She's got a top job with the railroad.'

'When her boss reads the morning paper, she might get canned,' said Kevin.

'No law against fucking nowadays,' said Miles. 'Any more on the Mankato connection with her dear brother?'

'We got all the motel and hotel registrations for the night before the call. Like I figured, it's so full of phonies we gave up on that. I can't stand the thought of that sonofabitch runnin' loose around here.'

'That's only a theory, Kevin. One friend to another, the boys upstairs think you're over-reacting 'cause you're tight with the lady judge.'

Kevin grinned. 'Wasn't it Einstein or somebody said there is no reality, there are only theories.'

'Shit, Knuckles, you been hangin' out with the wrong crowd.'

As he slept beside the wide-awake Mary, colorful images flew in to haunt his semi-conscious mind. Phelps's face was green, Wilma's body yellow and his own head seemed to pass through her thatch of curly pubic hair and on through her pelvis. Phelps laughed hysterically. Wilma joined in. Alice Wahl, clothed in a white nurse's uniform, faded into view, her hair vivid red like his stepmother's, blood dripping to the floor from beneath her skirt. William opened his mouth to yell at them to stop laughing, but no sound came out. Alice Wahl began to cry and she held her hand out to him and said, William, I really liked you. I liked you too, he said. The images dimmed to blank space that began filling up with numbers, just ones and zeros. Like a voice-over, the laughter continued, and then only sobs, Alice Wahl's sobs. Her sobs became his and his body shook with sobbing. Fingers rubbed his temples as he awakened. Mary hovered over him in the shadowy room.

'Everything is fine now, Frankie,' she said.

His head felt cool and refreshed, with a faint memory of fleeting pain. Some of the images lingered, but he had seen them all before. He smiled at her. 'Are the waffles ready?' he asked.

'In just a few minutes,' she replied.

The sky had been scraped clean of the early morning cloud cover and the sun turned the kitchen table top into a glaring disk of gold. William was tempted to close the blinds, but Mary was enjoying the light. Awaiting his waffle, he went back to the morning paper. An article early in the

357

week on the trial had mentioned that Phelps lived downtown in the Dorchester, a thirty-story tower. William scanned the ads in the *Tribune*. Two apartments in the Dorchester were offered for rent. Today's article kept running through his mind. He remembered that Phelps had been interested in Alice Wahl. He had often suspected he had helped her get her job as a teaching assistant in the physics department. Now he was sure. Alice was the only woman William had seriously approached, the only woman in his life, other than Wilma. Alice and Wilma. Ironically, they had both deviated to Phelps.

The images of the photographs admitted into evidence at his trial came back: Alice's half-naked corpse, the close-up of her abdomen, the bloody scalpel. The scalpel itself, gleamingly clean, lying on the table in the courtroom glare. The most significant event of his life was lost totally to his memory. None of the other memory blackouts had resulted in harm to anyone, other than perhaps himself. Psychogenic amnesia, the psychiatrists called it, at least those who had believed him. It usually occurred after a profoundly disturbing event. It was unrelated to his schizophrenia, they all said. William often relived the psychiatrists arguing at his trial, the prosecution insisting he had a personality disorder that didn't excuse his horrible act. All so much water over the dam.

The preparations in the basement were complete. He decided to move the dynamite he had taken from Kenny Speer's farm from the garage into the basement. He stored the caps and fuses under the stairs and stacked the five cases of dynamite sticks against the wall. There was nothing more to do at the house. Perhaps tonight he would get the opportunity he had so patiently awaited, perhaps not. He would be in position shortly after dark.

51

High above the shaded canyon of Marquette Avenue, the early morning sun gilded the IDS Tower. Harry Scott would begin his case for the defense of Tom Phelps later today.

Vivian's voice on the intercom: 'Mr Phelps is here, and Chet Ronning is on the telephone.'

'Put Chet Ronning's call through, dear. Have Phelps sit down and read the paper.' With that nasty feeling you get when your mouth twists into a sick frown, he pushed the button. 'Hello, Chet.'

Chet Ronning had one of those telephone voices that hurt the ears. 'Harry, they'll go for the extra hundred thou cash if you can wind everything up including payment in full by the end of the month. Otherwise I think the ratfucker will go all the way with it. Your old lady hates you and her lawyer's hungry. The ready money tempts him. He's worried about when he's gonna get paid, I can tell. It's a hell of a deal; your practice remains unmolested and unappraised and so does your pension plan.'

'I haven't got that kinda cash right now,' Harry shouted into the telephone.

'Borrow it,' said Ronning.

'I'm borrowed out. There's a little thing I haven't told you about.'

'Jesus Christ, Harry, are you crazy? We've been representing that we made a full disclosure.'

'It's a wash, Chet,' said Harry. 'I co-signed a note for a pal of mine. He'll make it good. I'm not worried. An old client trying to stay out of trouble. It's a weakness. I'm a sucker for a hard-luck story. He covered it with a safe deposit box full of diamonds, strictly legit, not stolen. But I don't get my money for six more months. I get to keep six gorgeous solitaires for interest. No big deal, shouldn't affect anything in the divorce.'

'I hope you know what you're doing,' said Chet.

'I told you. Strictly legit. This guy's a straight arrow. I represented him in an arson beef years ago. I think by co-signing that note I might have kept him out of some trouble. Plus, I make some easy money for a change. You know how it is. You work your ass for what you get in this business. Besides, I'm running out of juice. I need a partner.'

'Is that an offer?' Chet asked.

'I love you like a brother, but I need somebody with a solid criminal law background, and somebody under fifty.'

'Hey, that's age discrimination.'

'Very funny. Besides, I've got somebody in mind.'

'Who?'

'I haven't even told her yet.'

'Her?'

'Yeah, that proves I don't discriminate. Chet, hold the old lady off for a little longer. Maybe I can think of something. At least till I finish this Phelps thing. Lover boy's waiting out in the lobby. I gotta go to court.'

Vivian brought Phelps in. He looked tired and unhappy, but he had on a freshly laundered pale blue shirt and blue striped tie with his expensive navy suit. They both mumbled good mornings.

'We better get going. We can talk on the way over,' said Harry.

They were alone in the mahogany paneled elevator. 'Tom, I've been thinking about something all day yesterday. Ever since that old secretary of yours testified on Friday, you've been down in the mouth. And Saturday when we were working on your testimony. You haven't said anything, but it's obvious. She helped us a lot. Damn seldom the prosecution calls a witness that is so obviously favorable to the defense.'

'You managed that,' said Phelps.

'No, she did. I just told her what she could do. She did it perfectly. She didn't have to. Everybody knows you never lie, right?' Harry led the way out on to the sidewalk along Seventh Street. It was cold, but they saved two blocks walking outside rather than in the skyway.

'I know. She's a good girl,' said Phelps.

'Then what gives?' Harry asked.

'Nothing,' said Phelps. 'Nothing.'

'This case is going well. Things have been breaking our way. I would think you'd be feeling pretty good, at least as good as a defendant in a rape trial can feel.' Some jerk behind the backed-up traffic was leaning on his horn. 'Guy must be from New York,' Harry said. 'Listen, Tom, you were way up all last week; then you dropped into a ten-foot hole. The jury's gonna know it too. You think I'm doing OK in this case?'

'Christ, you're great, Harry,' said Phelps. 'The best. Chairman of the fucking board.'

'Well then, let's do it my way. I gotta know what's bugging you.'

'I can't tell you.'

They waited for the light before crossing Seventh Street to the Government Center plaza, still heaped with dirty snow. 'Bullshit,' said Harry. 'You can tell me anything. I'm the one who can't tell anybody. That's the law. I could lose my license. This is what you call a—'

'I know,' said Phelps, 'a privileged communication.'

Harry turned and stepped in front of Phelps, barring his path right in the middle of Seventh Street, four lanes of morning rush hour traffic waiting to roar through the intersection when the light turned, like the starting line at the speedway. 'If I'm going to represent you I gotta know everything. Period. Everything.'

Phelps looked nervously at the cars.

'Or,' said Harry, 'I'm going up there right now and request the court's permission to withdraw.' He was running a calculated bluff. The light changed. Clamoring horns protested the two blue suits blocking the street.

'OK. Come on.' Phelps ran to the curb. Harry walked behind, to a chorus of honking. Phelps hurried ahead on the long sidewalk across the plaza leading to the first-floor entry of the Government Center. The twenty-story building sat astride Sixth Street like a giant toaster, the traffic bisecting the first level, presently bumper to bumper. When Phelps got into the lobby, nothing but an oversized collecting point for the escalators, he walked across into a corner well out of the pedestrian traffic pattern, Harry at his heels.

'I'm just gonna tell you what's worrying me. It's got nothing to do with this case, and I'm telling you only on the condition you promise not to repeat it.'

'I told you, it's privileged.'

'Promise,' said Phelps.

Harry had got into the habit years ago. He did not divulge clients' confidences. How often he had sat around bars and locker rooms hearing lawyers giving away their clients' secrets. 'I promise,' he said.

Phelps shuffled his feet around, backing Harry into the corner formed by two granite walls. Phelps moved up so close his lips were almost touching Harry's nose. 'William Schmid *is* alive,' he said. 'And he's not going to like what Karen Crane said about Wilma and me on Friday. It was all over Saturday's papers.'

'Do you know where he is?' Harry put his hand on Phelps's chest and eased him back just a bit.

'No,' said Phelps.

'Is he in this area?'

'I hope not.'

'Does Wilma know where he is?'

'No,' said Phelps. 'At least not the last time I talked to her.'

'When was that?'

'That's enough,' said Phelps. 'You wanted to know what was eating on me. Now you know. None of the rest has got anything to do with this case.'

Harry searched his mind for a way to keep Phelps going. 'She could come in and testify that Karen Crane was exaggerating.'

'She wasn't exaggerating,' said Phelps.

Harry glanced at his watch. 'We gotta get upstairs.'

Day six of *State v. Phelps* opened to another buzzing courtroom with the spectators cooling their heels. In Rebecca's chambers, Harry Scott moved for a dismissal. This morning when she had asked Whitlow Strom to commence, he had announced that the state rested. At the close of the prosecution's case, the lawyer for the defendant almost always argued that, considering the evidence that had been offered, the jury could not conclude that the defendant was guilty beyond a reasonable doubt; stated legalistically, the state hadn't made out a *prima facie* case. As much as she wanted to spend Sunday with Julie, Rebecca had painstakingly studied the brief Harry Scott had delivered to her office late on Saturday afternoon. Now Whitlow Strom, African princess Barbara Bird and Harry Scott, frequent visitor in Rebecca's dreams, took seats around her desk. Off to the side, the blonde curly-haired court reporter was ready to go. Her machine, set up by her knee, looked like a skinny dog who wanted his ears scratched. Rebecca's clerk Tess sat behind the court reporter, her eyes on a document. Rebecca said good morning and eschewed the small talk lawyers and judges often engage in when proceedings go down in chambers. 'You may proceed, Mr Scott.'

Harry scratched his nose and began, his eyes on a long yellow legal pad he held in his hand. All the testimony offered by the prosecutor that had any bearing on the issue of consent was tainted, he reasoned. Soon he ignored the legal pad and held Rebecca's gaze, urging her to try to understand the rightfulness of his position. Of course, the only witnesses to the alleged rape were Dinah White and his client, the defendant Phelps. The testimony of the women regarding Phelps's prior acts was so tainted by their conspiracy to convict over cocktails that it should be given no weight whatsoever. He pointed out the inconsistencies in Dinah White's own testimony. In conclusion, he said it was ludicrous to think that the prosecution had proved their case beyond a reasonable doubt. His built-in little half-moon of a smile assumed its regular place and the flying fingers of the court reporter abruptly stopped.

Whitlow Strom started to speak, but Rebecca interrupted him. 'I think Mr Scott makes a powerful argument, but I'm going to deny his motion without hearing anything further. The issue of whether or not Dinah White is telling the truth is for the jury. They will be amply instructed that they must believe that the elements of the crime have been proven beyond a reasonable doubt.'

The three lawyers and the court reporter got up and filed back into the courtroom. The trial judge had the power to stop everything right where it was and set Phelps free to prey on more women. Rebecca had considered it. Strom's office had done a reasonably good job of building a case against Phelps, but it had fallen apart. It might not have if they had checked the extent to which that hotel room was soundproof, and if they had taken greater care to keep their witnesses from having tea parties to discuss the case. Nevertheless, the possibility existed that enough jurors would believe Dinah White to convince those who weren't so sure that a rape had been committed. Rebecca would still have the opportunity to direct a verdict for acquittal after the defense had made their case. She might as well face it, she thought. If she didn't let this case go to the jury, her name would be shit in the feminist community. Worse yet, that felonious sonofabitch Graydon Williams might think his presence had influenced her. Did people really think that judges could keep these kinds of thoughts out of their minds? Rebecca believed she was better than most. She refused to be influenced by anything but the evidence, she told herself and others when appropriate. But it was a lie. She was human. Some of her sisters on the bench were much worse than she was, refusing to consider the possibility that an illiberal cause could have legal merit. She knew she didn't fall into that category. She did her best to do it right. In her opinion that elevated her to the upper ten per cent or less among her colleagues.

'Remain seated,' said Rebecca to the murmuring throng.

Quiet anticipation settled over the courtroom. 'You may call your first witness, Mr Scott.'

Travis Seymour, tall, graying, hair combed straight back, took the stand, flashing a quick, deferential smile at Rebecca. One of the sleeves of his upscale gray suit was empty. Everyone in Minnesota knew he had lost an arm in Vietnam. Apparently he was here to testify as to Tom Phelps's good character. If it was anybody but Harry Scott, Rebecca thought, she would question the strategy. Calling character witnesses opened a can of worms, inviting the prosecutor to present testimony from people who believed the defendant was a scoundrel or worse. In Phelps's case, Rebecca suspected there were legions of those. Harry Scott skimmed through the preliminaries effortlessly. Seymour was a banker, a member of Westminster Presbyterian Church, divorced, and the father of three girls whom he had raised alone, navy pilot, Vietnam veteran, and a community activist. Rebecca had met him on several occasions.

Harry cut to the chase. 'Mr Seymour, how is it you happen to be in court this morning?'

'I was served a subpoena commanding me to appear here this morning.' He pulled a document out of his inside pocket as if to offer further evidence.

'Are you aware of the name of the case?' Harry leaned back easily in his chair as if he was conversing with the distinguished Travis Seymour in his living room.

Seymour unfolded the document and read aloud, 'State of Minnesota v. Thomas Phelps.'

'Are you aware of the allegations the government has made against Mr Phelps?' After each question, Harry's smile returned. It wasn't the expression Rebecca remembered from her dreams.

'Mr Phelps is alleged to have raped Ms Dinah White.' Seymour's voice had the tone of somebody used to giving orders and having them followed.

'Do you know Ms Dinah White?'

'Yes, I do,' said Seymour in a matter-of-fact tone.

'How long have you known her?' Harry was still leaning back, acting as though he was about to notarize a deed.

Uh-oh, Rebecca thought, trying to glance at Whitlow Strom without seeming obvious. Harry appeared to be heading for the areas protected by the rape shield law. Strom was leaning over the table waiting tensely for the next question like a wolf ready to grab a stray lamb.

'I've known her approximately five years.' Travis Seymour gave each answer directly to the jury as if he, Harry Scott and those fourteen were the only people in the room.

'How did you make her acquaintance?'

'We were introduced by mutual friends at a political fundraiser.'

'What was your relationship exactly?'

'I guess you could say we were romantically . . .'

Barbara Bird poked Strom in the ribs. He leaped to his feet. 'Objection.'

'Involved,' Seymour finished his answer.

'May we approach?' said Strom. After the lawyers had formed a tight little knot in front of Rebecca, Strom whispered, 'Minnesota statutes protect the victim in a rape case. It is improper to offer testimony as to the sexual history of the victim,' said Strom.

Somebody who had been trying rape cases for the past five years rather than running the DA's office might have phrased that a little differently, Rebecca thought. Her eyes turned to Harry, implying, if you have something to say, now is the time.

'Your honor, I'm well aware of the statute,' said Harry. 'I can assure the court I have no intention of delving into the sexual proclivities of Ms White, however interesting they might be.'

'The objection is overruled,' said Rebecca, after the lawyers had returned to their seats.

Harry looked directly at the jury. 'During the five years you have known Ms White, have you had the opportunity to converse with her on a variety of subjects?'

'I have,' said Seymour to the jury.

'On how many occasions?'

'A great many.' A serious look spread over Seymour's face.

'Have you formed an opinion as to Ms White's reputation for truthfulness?'

'I have.' His face became even more serious. The furrow in his forehead deepened.

'Are you aware of the substance of Ms White's testimony in this case?'

'Yes, I am.' Two intense grooves formed at the bridge of Seymour's nose.

'If you were asked to believe it, would you?'

'Objection,' said Strom, on his feet. 'This line of questioning is prohibited by statute.'

Seymour twisted round to look at Rebecca. His blue eyes met hers. 'Overruled,' she said.

Seymour turned back to the jury. 'No, I would not believe her,' he said.

So much for the rape shield law, Rebecca thought. The legislature better go back to work.

Strom's cross-examination was perfunctory. Yes, Seymour knew Phelps. No, they were not friends. No, he had no reason to be angry at Dinah White. No, he was not a Democrat. Yes, he had made contributions to Democratic candidates. Like any competent trial lawyer, Strom knew that cementing in every answer the defense had elicited was stupid and unforgivable cross-examination. He let the witness go. Rebecca called a short recess.

Harry Scott made a quick trip to the men's room, then walked alone along the railing of the twenty-story atrium. He stopped and leaned over. People scurried in beelines across the granite floor far below. He remembered the day some despondent soul had leaped from up here somewhere, barely missing a judge on his way to the escalator. Of course, he had speculated along with the police that William Schmid might be alive. But speculation was one thing; terrible knowledge was another. Phelps was more than worried. He was terrified. Harry knew Schmid had no love for him either. Supposedly he had humiliated him, and then was unsupportive of his efforts to get a new trial. It wasn't true. He had had no choice but to testify honestly. But

Schmid hadn't believed him, and the state public defender, who hated Harry's guts anyway, had made a big scene. Rebecca Goldman had made a fair holding at the trial, and at the hearing where Schmid's lawyer claimed his choices had not been explained to him. The Court of Appeals had agreed with Rebecca Goldman. None of that meant anything to William Schmid. He was not a lawyer; he was a physicist – a discipline where if you processed the exact same data you got the exact same answer. That wasn't the way the law worked. No one really knew how the law worked, and with the courts at all levels loaded with mediocre minds, the law became even more unpredictable.

For the short time remaining before the lunch break, Harry called another witness. If Travis Seymour was distinguished-looking, this one was spectacular. Light shone off the broad brown planes of his face. His head was set on a neck like a tree stump, and his shoulders must have driven tailors mad. Well over six feet tall, Ernest Blankenship was known to sports fans everywhere. On the middle finger of his right hand he sported a Super Bowl ring. He had only known Dinah White for three years. He too had been very close to her. He too would refuse to believe her testimony. Whitlow Strom got no further with him on cross-examination than he had with Travis Seymour.

After lunch, the defense called its next witness. So far Harry was batting a thousand. His clean-up hitter was slim, bespectacled Neil Kemp, a certified public accountant. He had made trips with Dinah White to Barbados, New York City, and Steamboat Springs. He wouldn't believe her either, he said. Again Strom made no inroads on cross-examination.

Scott's last witness was Tom Phelps. The few empty seats had filled. Some of the faces in the jury box showed a flicker of renewed interest. Rebecca thought their minds were made up. But Harry must have decided he had to put Phelps on to deny the charges, make the rout complete. Phelps looked contrite and humble. After establishing who Phelps was, Harry asked, 'On the night in question, did you have sexual intercourse with Dinah White?'

'Yes,' said Phelps.

'Did Dinah White consent to your having intercourse with her?'

'Yes,' said Phelps.

'Your witness,' said Harry, looking at Strom.

Two hours later at five-thirty Strom, his eyes on Rebecca, said he had no more questions.

It had been a very short cross-examination of a defendant in a criminal case. Phelps had been extremely well-drilled. He agreed with Dinah White's description of the alleged rape in every detail except on the question of consent. She wanted to be tied up, he said. That was not unusual. Some women liked it that way. Rebecca wondered if she would. She doubted it. But how many women liked to be spanked? She loved it. Phelps managed to slide in with an answer that perhaps he had been set up for some political reason. Near the end, Strom said, it's a fact, isn't it, that your whole future in the Democratic Party depends on your answering in a certain way? Yes, Phelps said, I suppose that's why these women from the far left wing want to get me. Point, set and match, thought Rebecca.

52

Possessed by a manic obsessive patience, William had returned to the ice on Monday for the eighth consecutive night. The temperature was in the twenties. A sliver of moon hung in the blue-black night. Beneath it, a string of lights crossed the causeway like a moving necklace of diamonds and rubies. Judge Goldman's daughter might be leaving the Clarks at any time. The paper said there could be a verdict in the Phelps trial by Wednesday, maybe sooner. If he were delayed much longer, he would need a whole new plan. No matter what, he would take no unnecessary risks. He meant to succeed however long it took.

In a bedroom on the top floor of the Clark house, an etched glass light fixture cast shadows on dingy pea-green walls like a giant spiderweb. The door to the closet where boxes of Denise's old clothes were stored stood open.

'Awesome. Hold your chin up a little more,' said Julie.

Delicate Monica, dark blonde hair piled up on her head, a lit cigarette in a holder at least six inches long protruding from her mouth, stretched to her full height of four foot eleven. A low-cut lavender evening dress with a jeweled bodice hung from her tiny frame. With the hem pinned up, Julie thought it looked totally rocked.

'Take it, take the picture,' Monica said through clenched teeth.

The camera flashed. 'Cool,' said Julie.

'You want to try this one?' said Monica.

'I'm too tall for it. Let me try that red one with the short skirt,' said Julie. 'That should just come to my knees.'

'Geez, you'll look awesome in red,' said Monica.

'Wait'll I get this sweater off. Hey, let's get a couple of Cokes first.'

'You get the dress on,' said Monica. 'I'll run down and get the Cokes.'

Like a flimsy negligee, a thin layer of cloud had slipped across the crescent moon. Snowmobiles were tearing around the lake. The mother was clearing the dining room table. For only the second time in eight nights there was a light on in one of the dormer windows on the top floor. There was no sign of the girls. William assumed it was they who had turned on the light on the top floor. From the left, in shirt and tie, the father came into view. The mother and father embraced. He walked from the dining room into the foyer, then turned back, apparently talking to the mother. He opened the closet and withdrew his overcoat and a hat, then disappeared from view to the right. Seconds later he passed the kitchen window. In a couple of minutes a pair of tail lights moved up the drive.

Back in sweater and jeans, Monica ran down four flights of stairs from the attic to the main floor. 'Where's Daddy?' she said to her mother.

'He has a committee meeting. He hadn't planned on going, but Alex just called and said they needed his vote. He said he'd be right back, before nine for sure.'

'Mother, you should have seen me in your old lavender gown. I looked so cool. Julie said awesome. We're going to make up the coolest album, like a fashion magazine, you know.'

'Sounds great, honey.' Denise was in slacks, her dark hair pulled back with a rubber band round it, leaving a short pony tail.

The phone began to ring. Denise went to answer it. Monica followed her into the giant pure-white kitchen to get the Cokes.

'Yes, this is Dr Clark . . . ICU . . . She's dehydrated again . . . No, be careful. I better come down there . . . Yes,

I've been through it with her before. Give me a half-hour.'

'What's the matter, Mother?' Monica asked.

'One of my patients. I've got to go to the hospital. It'll be a couple of hours. I think you two girls should come with me.'

'No way, Mother, we're having a blast.'

'Get your coats on.'

'Mother, we don't want to sit around that hospital. Besides, it's a school night. Daddy'll be back soon.'

'Yes, he will be back way before I will.' She looked at her watch. 'Actually in fifteen or twenty minutes, no more than half an hour. Oh, OK. Keep the doors locked.'

'I always do. Mother, is there something going on I don't know about? You haven't asked me to go along to the hospital since I was nine or ten.'

'No,' said Denise. 'But you can't be too careful these days.' She picked up her car keys off the white Corian counter.

The mother walked briskly through the dining room into the foyer, opened the closet and pulled out a fur coat. William's body stiffened like a cat watching a bird fall out of its cage. Even before the car's tail lights disappeared in the dark, the snowmobile engine roared to life. With no lights on, William sped across the five hundred feet of snow-covered ice toward the sprawling house on the side of the hill. Braced for the bump at the shore, he jumped up on the land at thirty miles per hour. In five more seconds, he had run up the slope and stopped behind the dark hulk of the garage.

In the silence, each step he took along the back wall of the garage crunched loudly in the crusty snow. He reached the corner, turned and followed the north wall, covered with indistinct shadows cast by the trees in the scant light of the stars and sickle moon. At the front corner of the garage, he found what he thought was the telephone wire. From just under the eave it ran down the rough-textured wall into the ground. With cutters from his pocket he deftly cut the wire. He retraced his steps back past the snowmobile and down the slope to the lower level entry.

Removing the .38 from his pocket, he shoved it through a pane of glass in the door, reached in, and turned the dead bolt. The door stopped against a chain. He broke a pane higher up and released the chain. The door opened into a vestibule off the well-lit recreation room, paneled in cypress or some other open-grained exotic wood.

Three floors up, the girls continued their photography session. The red dress with the flounced skirt fitted Julie perfectly. She had found a wide scarlet ribbon, a perfect match to the dress, and tied it round her jet-black hair like an Indian headband, with the loose ends hanging down at the back.

'Oh, Julie, you look slammin'. I'm going to throw my pictures away.'

'Monica, don't talk stupid. Yours will be just as good, maybe better.'

'You look good enough for *Vogue*, no lie,' said Monica.

Julie raised her chin and looked off to her right, at least supposing she looked sophisticated. The camera flashed.

'I think we should take a whole roll of you in that outfit. You look just like Whitney Houston,' said Monica. 'Can you imagine, my mother wanted us to go with her to the hospital.'

'Why on earth for?' Julie asked.

'She didn't want to leave us alone. We're almost fifteen and *she* didn't want to leave *us* alone.'

'Where's your dad?' Julie's throat constricted.

'He had to go someplace. He'll be back before my mother. Totally rocked. Julie, you look totally rocked. If you wore that outfit to a dance at school, you'd stop the music.'

The image of the woman lying on the sidewalk, shot down, twelve stories below, flashed into Julie's mind. Monica seemed so calm. Of course, all she knew of William Schmid was that he had drowned. Rebecca and Denise had decided that Monica shouldn't be alarmed by Julie coming to stay with her. In that dingy attic room with the odd shadows on the wall, and fragile little Monica, the only other person in this big house, Julie felt alone and apprehensive. The worry that had begun with the scene on the sidewalk at Lake Vista returned.

'I think I should call my mom,' said Julie.

'Go ahead if you want to,' said Monica. 'There's a phone by the top of the stairs.'

'I'll be right back.' Julie stepped out into the long hall, poorly lit by two dusty ceiling fixtures about thirty feet apart. The many doors along both sides of the hall were all closed. The phone was mounted on the wall beside the door at the top of the stairs coming up from the second floor. She hurried toward it, her footfalls silent on the worn carpet. An old-fashioned key protruded from a keyhole lock under the brass knob. Julie picked up the phone. There was no sound. No dial tone. No nothing. A noise from below. A door, she thought. Maybe it was Monica's dad. She opened the door at the top of the stairs and listened. The landing below was empty. A creaking sound, as if a person might be walking up the stairs on the flight she couldn't see. It just had to be Monica's dad. She would call out and see. A figure in a black snowmobile suit appeared on the landing, its face enshrouded in a black wool mask with openings for the eyes and mouth. The breath she had mustered to call out was sucked involuntarily back inside her. She slammed the door and turned the key in the lock and stood looking at the door for a second. The constriction in her throat had become a lump the size of a baked potato and it sank down to the pit of her stomach. She ran back down the hall toward the room where she had left Monica. The door was open.

'Monica. Monica, there's a man on the stairs with a hood over his head.' The letters published in the newspaper two months ago assembled in her mind and the recent speculation in the paper. 'It's William Schmid. He's going to kill us.'

Monica gasped. They both ran into the hall and looked back toward the door at the top of the stairway. The knob was jiggling and turning.

'Follow me,' said Monica. She turned and ran down the hall in the opposite direction.

Monica opened the third door on the left. They both rushed through and Julie pulled the door closed behind them. There was no lock. In the darkened room, illuminated by only the faintest light sifting through one window, the furniture, just big shadowy lumps, was hidden under dust covers. From back down the hall came the crackling breaking sound of the intruder smashing the stairway door. Julie heard the creak of a hinge and followed Monica into what must have been a closet. Julie closed the door behind them. Inky blackness. As they moved, they bumped into heavy garments suspended on hangers.

'There's a little door in here somewhere,' Monica whispered. 'I've found it.' Another hinge creaked and Monica's hand reached back and grabbed Julie's dress, pulling her along into the cool, musty air.

'Careful, we're on a landing at the top of a real steep stairway. Don't fall.' Monica's voice was barely audible. A sound came from nearby. It could have been the door to the room they had just left. 'Just hold on to my hand. Don't forget to close the door real quiet.'

The hinge creaked. Julie pulled it a little further, another creak. The door hit the jamb and stuck. 'It won't close,' Julie whispered.

'Leave it,' whispered Monica, her damp hand gripping Julie's tightly. 'Feel for the first step.'

Julie felt her hand pulled forward and down. In the pitch blackness Julie's stocking-clad toe curled over the edge of the wood at the top of the stairs. Monica's weight brought a squeak from one of the stair treads. Julie had read about fear in Stephen King's books, but now she knew its reality. Fingers of terror tickled her skin. Every hair moved. Her stomach was full of wild birds flapping to get out. Step by step they descended, hand in hand, into blackness.

William played his flashlight around the wall until he found the light switch. This was the fifth room he had entered. He had spent only seconds in the first four; they had been completely empty with no means of escape, except through tightly closed windows. This one was filled with furniture draped with dust covers. He dropped to his knees and looked under the bed. Nothing. He held very still and listened with his head cocked to one side like a robin waiting to pluck a worm from beneath the sod. Only his breathing, then a sound. He got up and opened the closet door. Suspended from two rods on both sides of the large walk-in closet were coats, jackets, heavy sweaters and the like, some the bright orange used for hunting. He pushed the coats aside to expose the wall behind to the right. Nothing. Stepping to the left, he repeated the procedure. Hidden by the hanging clothes, a small door was set into the wall. It was not tightly closed. He pulled the door open and thrust his flashlight into the opening. Sweating heavily inside the black snowmobile suit, he crouched down and squeezed through.

Julie whirled her head round to the sound from above. At the top of the long narrow stairway a flashlight beam poked through the darkness. She quickly closed the door at the bottom behind her. They stepped out into an empty clothes closet on the second floor.

'Hurry,' said Monica. They ran through a bedroom and out into the main second-floor hallway. Monica opened a door and they headed down two flights of well-lit stairs. Before they closed the door at the bottom, they heard the door at the top open. Lights behind cut-glass sconces illuminated the central hall of the main level. Monica ran along the Oriental runner between walls richly paneled in polished wood, then through the first door on the left into the library. Julie pushed the wide oak door shut behind them and turned the dead bolt. Monica cut diagonally across another Oriental rug to a wall of books. Somehow she got one whole section of shelves to recede into the wall, then pivot at its center, allowing passage on either side. She and Julie darted through the opening on one side. Monica turned on the light and pushed a button on the wall. As the bookcase slid back into place, they heard a heavy impact on the library door.

★ ★ ★

William's shoulder ached from banging into the solid oak door. He kneeled and examined the lock. It was an ordinary keyed dead bolt. He could go outside and try the window, but then they could escape through the door. He glanced at his watch. He had been in the house almost ten minutes. He had hoped to be out by now. One of the parents might return at any moment. He must take a calculated risk. The house was large and the grounds spread out in every direction. It was winter and people kept their windows shut. The sound wouldn't be heard. He withdrew the .38 from his pocket, cocked the hammer with his thumb, and took careful aim at the point on the door jamb behind which he presumed the bolt was engaged. The blast of the revolver seemed loud enough to be heard in downtown Minneapolis. William's ears rang. He examined the splintered wood. The steel bolt gleamed from the depth of the bullet hole. He backed away, extended his arm with the muzzle close to the original point of entry. Again the loud roar. He tried the knob, but the door held. He knelt and examined the damage. More steel visible. He fired again. This time the door opened. From a supply in his pocket he reloaded the revolver's three empty chambers.

William pushed the door wide open. Thousands of books lined the walls. An immense Oriental rug in magenta tones. Two massive wooden reading tables. Period furniture. Chairs, tables, and sofas. Sculptures on pedestals. The girls were nowhere in sight. He crossed quickly to a large double window, with blue stained-glass border. To William's left the center portion of the south wall separated cases of books. In this space, papered with gold leaf, hung a portrait of a man wearing a high stiff collar with a mane of silver hair and heavy sideburns. The eyes followed William around the room. The lips curled in a slight smile. William walked along the cases of books looking for a clue. If there was a door to another route of escape, he might never find the girls, but more likely there was a hidden room of some kind.

When Monica and Julie heard the shots, they wrapped their

arms round each other and began to cry softly.

'Why does he want to kill us?' Monica whimpered.

Julie backed away and put her finger to her lips. 'He doesn't want to kill you,' she whispered. 'Just me.' But she remembered the two he had killed at the state hospital. The phone on the desk was worth a try, but it was just as dead as the one upstairs. Her eyes fell on Dan Clark's glass-fronted case of pistols fixed to the wall above the desk.

'Do you know how to use any of those?' Julie whispered.

'No, he's never let me touch them. I don't think they're loaded.'

Schmid would hear the breaking glass. They couldn't chance it. Monica's hands were clasped tightly together. Tears stained her face. Julie stepped toward her, her lips close to her ear.

'Is there a key?'

Monica pointed at the desk. Julie opened the top drawer. A pocket knife, letter opener, magnifying glass, scissors and other clutter. At the very back she found a ring of keys. A small round-headed brass one labeled YALE was the best candidate. She opened the glass door on the first try.

William stood in the center of the room pondering. He eliminated the outside wall; a hidden room there would be detectable. The opposite wall had the main hall running its full length. That left the two ends. The south wall with the portrait in the middle allowed less space for the required mechanism. The north was a solid wall of books; he would examine it first. The wall was covered with five floor-to-ceiling bookcases about ten feet high and four feet wide. Starting with the middle one, he began to sweep the books from the shelves on to the floor. The dictionaries and encyclopedias fell with resounding thuds. In a couple of minutes he had cleared all the books from the shelves as high as he could reach.

Julie stretched over the desk and lifted the smallest gun from its holder. It was shiny blue-black and had flat sides. She had seen toys like it, but its heft told her this one was no toy. At that moment she heard the first thunk of books hitting the floor on the other side of the wall. Monica's brown eyes were wide with fear and glittered with moisture.

'I have no idea how to work this gun,' Julie whispered. 'I don't even know if it's loaded.' There was a little lever on the side, pointed to the tiny word 'safe'. When she moved it with her thumb, it pointed to the word 'off'. Julie moved it back to safe. She assumed that if it was loaded it would fire if you pulled the trigger when the lever was not on 'safe', but she wasn't sure. Now, the books fell to the floor from higher up, making a continuous loud tumbling sound. Monica reached for one of the larger guns. It was more like the ones she had seen in Western movies, heavy and much longer. She could barely hold it with her long tapered fingers. Silence suddenly replaced the sound of the tumbling books.

The three center cases were completely empty of books, except for the top three shelves. William examined all of the wood surfaces carefully, using the flashlight beam to supplement the lamp light. He found nothing. After pushing with great force against each of the cases, he stepped back a pace and studied the configuration of the entire wall. The cases were identical. If one of them acted as a secret door, it had been ingeniously designed. Just as he decided to remove the books from the other two cases, he noticed that one book was extended slightly from the front of the shelf. The words *Keys to the Kingdom* were embossed in gold on the brown leather binding. He pulled the book out. Behind it on the back of the bookcase was a button like an ordinary doorbell. William pushed the button.

Suddenly the silence was broken by the hum of an electric motor. The four-foot section of wall through which they had entered the small room began to move slowly toward Julie. Monica screamed, and kept screaming as the wall continued moving. Julie, clutching the big gun in both hands waist high, glanced at Monica standing helplessly beside her. Julie's head moved from side to side; the birds in

379

her stomach flapped their wings with new-found energy
Her breath was short and shallow, her speeding hear
thumped in her chest. The wall began to turn. Julie raised
the gun and held it out in front of her, the muzzle wavering
The man in the black suit and the black mask came into
view in the narrow opening, a gun in his hand. Julie closed
her eyes and pulled the trigger. The only sound was a
metallic click.

William stepped through the opening in the midst of
Monica's shrill screams. With the .38 he motioned toward a
chair and said sharply to Monica, 'Sit.'

Monica abruptly stopped screaming and sat down, as if
she knew she had been given a reprieve. William turned his
attention to the tall black girl in the scarlet dress. Her arms
hung down in front of her clutching the gun she had hoped
to kill him with. He reached out with his left hand and
pulled the gun from her hands. He put it in the cargo pocke
of his suit and glanced at his watch. He had been in the
house twenty-five minutes. Far too long. 'Get in tha
corner,' he said to Julie, motioning with the muzzle of the
gun to the corner behind Monica's chair. She obeyed, tears
flowing down her face. 'If you co-operate with me fully, you
will not be harmed. Either of you. Turn your face to the
corner.' From inside his suit he produced a small roll of
duct tape. He tore off a short piece and with his left hand
on the back of her dark blonde head he plastered it across
Monica's mouth. Her shoulders still shook, but the tape
stopped the mournful sobbing. With longer pieces he fastened her ankles and wrists to the chair. 'Your parents wil
release you soon,' he said in a gentle tone.

'You come with me,' he said, much less gently, to Julie
'Your name is Julie?' She nodded. 'I will call you that and
you obey. If you do not, I will shoot you on the spot. I do
not wish to, but I will. Do you understand?'

She nodded, snuffled her nose, and inhaled a short serie
of abrupt sobs, then cleared her throat as if to speak, bu
she didn't. William reached out and grabbed her wrist with
his left hand and pulled her along behind him back into the
library, stepping over the piles of books on the floor. He

held the .38 in front of him and led her through the house and out the lower level door in her stockinged feet. When they reached his snowmobile at the top of the slope, he pulled a suit out of his pack. 'Put this on,' he said. Then he gave her a pair of pack boots. Finally he zipped the hood tightly about her face and pointed to the saddle. 'I have seen you riding before,' he said. 'This will be no different. You hold on to my waist. When we get to the car, you are to get in the back seat and lie down. If you make any trouble for me, your life will be over right at that instant. If you obey, you will be released completely unharmed, and,' he added purposefully, 'unmolested.' He turned the key. In seconds they were racing across the ice.

53

Kevin's cleaning lady had been in earlier in the day. His blue and white kitchen looked freshly scrubbed and polished for the first time since Rebecca had decided that living with him, at least temporarily, was far safer than staying at Lake Vista. The two of them had just finished eating carry-out Chinese from the Nankin.

'Let me read your fortune cookie,' Kevin said, reaching across the table. He broke it and held the little slip of paper close up in front of his eyes. 'There is a policeman in your future,' he said with a grin.

'Oh, that isn't what it says,' Rebecca said, trying to grab it.

''Tis too,' he whined, childlike. He rolled it into a tiny ball and snapped it into the sink with his thumb.

'There you go messing up the kitchen already.' She was kidding, but her penchant for perfection in housekeeping and organization had become a trifle tested over the past week. She had come home exhausted and overwrought every night, not feeling up to cleaning. It didn't seem to make that much difference to Kevin.

'Trial movin' right along?' Kevin asked.

'Faster than anyone expected. Should be over tomorrow, except for maybe the charge.'

'How's it look for our boy Phelps?'

'Good. Damn good,' Rebecca said. As close as she had got to Kevin, she didn't want to talk about her trials. She changed the subject. 'I tried calling Julie about an hour ago. The line was out of order. I better give it another try.' The phone on the wall beside the kitchen table rang as she reached for it. Rebecca handed it to Kevin.

'Hello? Yes, she's right here.'

'Yes, this is Judge Goldman.' She listened to the most hideous words ever to fall on her ears. 'I'll be right there,' she said. She put the phone on the hook. Kevin's face blurred through the tears. Her throat tightened and she tensed against the pain.

'Somebody kidnapped Julie,' she whimpered. 'Sounds like William Schmid.'

Rebecca slept no more than an hour on Monday night, and that not in a bed but fully clothed on the sofa in the Clarks' living room. Confusion was the order of the night. She and Kevin had dashed into the Clark home to find the family as distraught as Rebecca was. Denise, almost out of control, said Monica had been hysterical when Dan found her. Denise had given her a sedative and Monica had fallen asleep immediately. There were several Wayzata police officers wandering around the large house, plus two FBI agents, two state agents, three guys from the county sheriff's office, who had learned somehow that Judge Goldman's daughter had been snatched, and of course Kevin.

The Wayzata police had got only a little out of Monica before she passed out. One of the FBI agents seemed upset because Denise had sedated Monica before he'd had a chance to talk to her. Dan Clark told him to go fuck himself. He added that the guy had had a mask over his head, a gun in his hand like Dan's own .357 magnum. 'You know it's William Schmid,' he said. 'So find him, don't bitch about my little girl getting proper medical attention.' The agent left the room with his tail between his legs. By midnight Dan had apologized. That was about the time Denise completely lost it, and pleaded with Rebecca to forgive her. 'It was only for fifteen or twenty minutes, but I should have taken them with me,' she said. 'There's no excuse. I knew you were worried. I just failed you. I'm so, so sorry.' Rebecca wrapped her arms round Denise. Julie couldn't have been watched every minute, she said, with all the sincerity she could muster. If not tonight, it would have been another time.

Rebecca held tightly to what Dan Clark described as Schmid's assurance. He said Julie would not be harmed. Monica believed he meant it – for what that's worth, Dan said. Schmid or whoever it was had left with Julie only two or three minutes before he got home.

The various cops had set up floodlights all around the house. They found boot prints in the snow, and they were able to follow the snowmobile track up the lake for about three miles until they lost it among the myriad others of its kind. They were going to try again in daylight. But by 6 a.m. enough new snow had fallen to cover the pertinent details of any of the tracks on the lake. For various reasons the consensus was to withhold any information from the press until they heard from the kidnapper. Rebecca knew this would be impossible considering the number of people involved.

Kevin dropped Rebecca off at the Sixth Street entrance of the Government Center and vowed to work until he either found Julie or he keeled over. Looking at his face, Rebecca thought that might be any minute. At one point in the night when she was walking down the hall to the bathroom she had found him sitting by himself in a little room near the library with a Kleenex in his hand, tears running down his face. She had sat down beside him and kissed him on the cheek. She reminded him that there was a policeman in her future. 'You sure that cookie didn't say "men" instead of "man"?' she asked. He didn't smile. Inside, she felt they would never smile again. Not ever.

Now she had to go into the courtroom in a few minutes and act as if her child had not been kidnapped. Acting as if she had had more than an hour's sleep would be hard enough. In these slept-in clothes, she thought, I'm going to really appreciate my robe today. The tears came again as though they would never stop. Tess came through the door, then turned to leave. Rebecca called her back. She told her the story as briefly as she could and explained how they would have to behave today. Then she picked up the phone and called Annette Rollins.

'And is there anything at all I can do to help convict that sonofabitch? Lawdy, lawdy, lawdy.'

'I have something serious to tell you, Annette. Off the record. Completely.'

'You got it, Becka.'

'Julie's been kidnapped. It was almost certainly William Schmid.'

'Oh my God, honey. I'm so sorry. But he won't hurt her. I know he won't.'

'I thought maybe you could come over here today. At least at the lunch break.'

'Hey, I'll be there whenever you say. I'll take the day off.'

'You don't have to take the day off. There's going to be a big story in this, eventually.'

'I don't care about that. I'm comin' right over.'

Through her tears Rebecca said, 'I'll have Henry Pettiford put a special chair out for you by the door. There's some room for one back there. But we're trying to keep this quiet.'

'Don't worry about me, hon. I don't see how you can sit up there.'

'I don't think Harry Scott's going to call any more witnesses. They'll probably do the arguments this morning and after the break I'll do the charge. I've got that ready. I'll just read it.'

'I'll see you in a little while,' said Annette.

At the morning break Rebecca called Kevin. He was out, but the dispatcher had him call her back. 'I wish I had something to tell you, sweetheart,' he said. 'We can't even find where he left the lake. I take it you haven't heard anything.'

'Nothing here,' said Rebecca. 'Did you check the answering machines?'

'We've got your line and my line and the Clarks' line all fed into your phone in chambers. We have a policewoman answering it down here. If there's anything on Julie we'll get you out of court in a minute or two. I checked to see if anything had come in on yours or my answering machines during the night. There was nothing. We just left the railroad building. Both Miles and I thought Wilma was really surprised. But that's just a guess. You know we've had tails on her. It would be hard for her to do anything.'

'Doesn't she ever shake them?'

'A few times, but she's shown up at home, or that one time at Phelps's place not long after,' Kevin said. 'What's happening in the trial?'

He hadn't said a word about Julie's chances. Rebecca was hoping for a quick miracle, but she was running out of steam. She felt her shoulders shaking and her heart beating up high in her throat. 'Scott's finished his argument already. That's when I called a recess. I've got to get back in there now.'

'Keep your chin up,' Kevin said.

'Find Julie, please find Julie,' she said.

'We're working on it, sweetheart.'

She sat absolutely still for a minute. Tess stuck her head round the door. 'Are you ready, Judge?'

Rebecca nodded. Tess looked skeptical, but she let the door close, heading for the courtroom to tell the bailiff the judge was on her way.

'All rise,' said Henry Pettiford when Rebecca opened the door. Her feet felt heavy and she stumbled and grabbed the arm of her chair for support. 'Be seated,' she said weakly. She looked at Strom, his eyes narrowed behind his thick-rimmed glasses, his pate pinker than usual. 'Mr Strom, you may proceed with your summation.' When Strom stood up, Rebecca fell out of her chair. She could hear the sudden clamor of voices but she didn't feel capable of movement. In a moment, Tess, Henry Pettiford, Harry Scott and Whitlow Strom were all looking down at her, their faces strangely distorted. She wanted to scream out, 'That crazy psycho William Schmid has my daughter,' but her lips wouldn't move. Harry Scott, his neat face even more benign than when he had faced the jury, got down on one knee and raised her head up with his hand. 'Your honor, do you have any idea what happened?' he said. She barely shook her head.

Whitlow Strom began to speak loudly. 'Everybody back in

their seats. *Now!* If you want to spend the rest of the day in a cell, just hesitate a little bit.'

That brought even Rebecca slightly back to life. Strom and Harry took hold of her under the arms and lifted. She helped by straightening out her shaky legs. They led, carried, and dragged her back to chambers.

'The medics will be here in a minute,' said good old Henry Pettiford.

Rebecca mustered her strength. 'Henry,' she said, 'get my reporter. Bring her into chambers.' Barbara Bird, who had been hovering around in the hall, closed the door behind the five of them – herself, Strom, Harry, Tess, and Rebecca. The curly-haired blonde court reporter came in a second later. Harry and Strom laid Rebecca out on the leather sofa. The door opened again. It was Annette Rollins, all two hundred pounds of her done up in grey wool.

'For Christ's sake, no reporters in here,' said Strom.

'No. Let her come in,' Rebecca commanded in a raspy voice.

Annette gave Strom a fuck you sneer and knelt down beside Rebecca. 'What's the matter, honey?' She caressed her forehead.

The three lawyers backed away a step.

'Tell them what happened,' Rebecca said.

Annette summarized the kidnapping story. When she had finished, Strom and Harry fired questions simultaneously. Rebecca pulled on Annette's hand.

'You guys shut up a minute,' said Annette. 'The judge wants to be heard.'

'Charlene, set up over here,' Rebecca said to her court reporter. Charlene's face, as pretty as her hair, smiled an admiring smile at her boss. She had that kind of lovely expressiveness that made you think her face muscles were somehow connected to her heart.

'It would be a waste to declare a mistrial in this case because the judge got sick,' Rebecca said feebly. 'Therefore, counsel for the defendant and counsel for the state have stipulated that the state can complete its argument to the jury and the jury charge may be given by a substitute judge to be chosen at the discretion of the trial judge.' She would call Corny if he was available. 'Would you gentlemen please assent to this stipulation on the record?'

Harry's little smile was firmly in place, but Strom began to argue. 'I think this might be a little high-handed. I think—'

Rebecca took a deep breath and cut him off. 'Off the record,' she said to Charlene with a weak wave of her hand. 'Listen, Mr Strom—'

'I want everything *on* the record,' said Strom, directing his statement to Charlene.

The wide-set brown eyes in Charlene's perfect face said who am I supposed to listen to?

'OK,' said Rebecca, 'on the record if you wish, Mr Strom. I am ready to entertain a motion from the defense. A jury has sat here for five days, during four of which you put in a case that is at best doubtful. Would you like the jury to decide the case, or would you rather have me decide it right now?'

Strom seemed to hesitate. Rebecca knew he was thinking of the politics. Which way would he come off best? With a directed verdict by the court, or an acquittal from the jury?

Barbara Bird, pragmatist rather than politician, stepped forward. 'Your honor, we would rather have the case go to the jury.'

Rebecca looked at Strom. She felt ready to pass out.

'OK,' he said, 'the state so stipulates.'

'The defense joins in the stipulation,' said Harry.

Charlene's fingers, rapidly tickling the Stenotype, stopped.

After all but Annette and Tess had filed out of the room, Rebecca called Corny. He was in the middle of a long accident case. While Rebecca was riding to Abbott-Northwestern Hospital in a paramedics' ambulance, he gave his jury a half day off and reconvened the Phelps trial within three-quarters of an hour. Later that day, after just taking time enough to elect a foreman, the jury acquitted Tom Phelps.

★ ★ ★

William had made Julie quite comfortable in the special room he had prepared in the basement. She lay back in a half-tilted recliner watching TV. In spite of the handcuffs, she was able to use the remote control and surf through the channels at will. Chains led from her handcuffs to two large concrete blocks, one on either side of the chair. Her feet were manacled in the same way. Whenever she indicated the desire, William loosened her hands and feet and allowed her to use the bathroom. He had all kinds of snacks that he had asked Mary to pick up at the supermarket – he had told her he wanted them for himself. That's not like you, Frankie, she had said.

When he had first trussed Julie up the night before, William had told her that no matter what happened, she would not be harmed. He meant it, but he was not sure she believed him. He said he was very sorry that he had to put her in this position, especially the taping of her mouth, but he had no choice. She had cried off and on during the night, but today she had cried very little.

He spent the day working on a video tape of Julie juxtaposed with several sticks of dynamite, apparently attached to a clock radio. It was a ruse in all respects, but he was finally satisfied that the video looked real enough for his purposes. Mary still had no idea Julie was in the basement.

Just before five o'clock, the game show Julie was watching was interrupted for a news bulletin: 'Moments ago, special assistant to the Governor Tom Phelps was acquitted of raping Democratic political activist Dinah White.' After brief interviews with Phelps and White, they cut to the Governor's office. His face radiated satisfaction. 'This is a day for celebrating,' he said. 'Justice has been served.'

Rebecca saw the announcement of Phelps's acquittal on TV in a private room on the fourth floor of Abbott-Northwestern Hospital. They had hooked an IV to a vein in her left forearm. She had slept for at least four hours, waking refreshed, only to be devastated all over again when she remembered what had happened to Julie. While she was watching the Governor make a damn fool of himself with glowing statements about his predatory aide Phelps, Rebecca tried to get Kevin on the telephone. A dispatcher downtown assured her that Kevin would call her in a few minutes. Her head dropped back down and soon a steady stream of tears spilled on to the pillow.

The malefactor Phelps had been acquitted. William could not believe what he had heard. What kind of system could turn such a villain loose to find more innocent victims? He had felt certain that Phelps was on his way to jail, where he belonged, where Wilma would be safe from him. A wave of resentment swept over him not unlike his feelings toward Judge Rebecca Goldman and Harry Scott. Phelps was worse. Wilma had been the victim of his debauchery. Although the newspaper story had clearly stated that Phelps had had a long-time relationship with Wilma, William was sure he had worked some evil power over her like he had with the other woman. With his own life hanging by a thread, William suddenly decided that there was a reckoning due to Tom Phelps at least as important as the one he had planned for Rebecca Goldman.

A couple of minutes before five o'clock, William rang the Dorchester rental agent. 'I need to look at an apartment right away,' he said in the most ordinary tone he could muster.

'One or two bedrooms?' asked the agent cheerfully. 'I have two of each right now.'

'One will be fine. I may decide to look at a two-bedroom later,' William said.

They made an appointment to meet in an hour.

William returned to the basement. 'I must leave now for several hours,' he said to Julie. 'Your hands must be more restricted. I am sorry. Perhaps you should go to the bathroom.'

When she had finished with the bathroom, he removed the tape, gave her half a glass of water, and replaced the tape. After double-checking everything, he was satisfied that she was completely secure. He looked at her pleading eyes. 'Do not worry,' he said, 'this will soon be finished and you will be able to go home.'

Julie's eyes pleaded with him. Please don't hurt my mother, they said.

As William drove downtown, he listened to a WCCO radio reporter interviewing Tom Phelps.

'What is your reaction to the verdict?'

'I am elated,' said the voice that apparently belonged to Phelps.

'Was it a surprise?'

'No. Harry Scott is the best lawyer in the state and I expected to win because I am innocent.'

William remembered the glib tone, the condescending attitude. Intense dislike had turned to hate. The interview went on.

'How many members of the jury are here to celebrate your acquittal, Tom?'

'I think they all are.'

'Somebody said it was the quickest verdict on record.'

'They were back in less than an hour.' Phelps sounded smug.

'By the way, shake the hand of Graydon Williams, Deputy Assistant Secretary of Agriculture. He answered my call to come down and lend a little moral support during the trial.'

'Mr Secretary, what's your reaction to all this merriment?'

'Wonderful, wonderful. I'm so happy I had the opportunity to come back to Minneapolis to stand behind my old friend, Tom Phelps, a truly great public servant.'

'Thank you, Mr Secretary. Here comes the Governor. Governor, could we have a word with you?'

'This is my buddy, my right hand.' William recognized the familiar voice of the Governor. 'Nice going, big guy. I knew all along you'd be OK. I guess when the jury comes to the party, they must be pretty convinced that the guy's not a criminal.'

'Thank you, Governor. Back to the studio.'

William parked in a lot two blocks north of the Dorchester. When he was a boy, the Foshay Tower, an obelisk modeled on the Washington Monument, was the tallest building in downtown Minneapolis. Now, it was barely noticeable. And the Dorchester, a mere apartment building three blocks away, was just as tall.

The agent, a buxom brunette called Queeny Parks, awaited William in the sumptuous lobby. 'Mr Kroll?' she said. William nodded and walked past a liveried doorman who gave him a blank stare. 'Good evening, Mr Kroll.' She had a low-pitched mannish voice and a face like a bulldog. She threw her hand at him for shaking. He grasped a few fingers limply and mumbled a greeting. 'It's really warming up out there, isn't it?' she said. 'If it keeps this up, spring'll be along in no time.'

William looked around. Unfamiliar faces filed in and out of the lobby without giving him a glance. He followed Queeny to the elevators, the .38 heavy in the gray tweed overcoat he had found hanging in the house.

'Do you know anyone who lives in the building?' Queeny asked on the way up.

'No,' said William, 'but the newspaper mentioned that man Phelps lived here.'

'It was such good news to hear the jury found him innocent,' said Queeny. 'Tom's been here since the building was built. He's up on thirty.'

Thirty twelve, to be exact, William thought. He had got Phelps's apartment number by calling the building office and telling whoever had answered that he was mailing a package. The elevator stopped at eighteen.

William watched Queeny pick out the key when she opened the door to 1811. It had a red dot on it as if it had been marked with nail polish. After they had walked through the apartment, William suggested to Queeny that they look at a two-bedroom. When she opened the door to 2013, she used the same key. It was obviously a master key.

Ten minutes later, with Queeny's master key in his hand, William headed for the elevators. In the darkness of a bedroom closet in room 2013, Queeny Parks lay on the carpet securely bound and gagged with duct tape.

54

Kevin stopped at Rebecca's hospital room early in the evening. Every time she thought she was cried out, the tears returned, but she had been dry-eyed for almost half an hour. 'You look too tired to be standing upright,' she said.

Kevin sat down on the edge of the bed opposite the IV and took her hand. 'I know it's not logical, but I feel like I'm failing you. We have no idea where he is holding Julie.'

'Psychotics have their own logic,' Rebecca said.

'Maybe,' Kevin said, 'but I can't help remembering his brilliant ten-year career as a physicist. An absolutely clean record, not so much as a speeding ticket. No juvenile file. No nothing. By the way, did you know Wilma has a juvenile jacket? Miles Dickstein has talked to several people who knew her. She was a holy terror as a teenager. Promiscuous. Booze. Bad checks. Even one assault. All hearsay, but consistent. Then the twin brother commits one of the most ghastly crimes in city history and she becomes a model employee at the railroad.'

'As I said, he's a psychotic. He's no ordinary criminal.' Rebecca didn't want to clutter her head with scenes from that awful trial but the images of William Schmid as described by Dr Phillips jumped into full view as though they had been hiding under the bed.

'I sat through that trial too,' said Kevin, 'but I must admit I spent much of the time admiring the judge.'

That was a long time ago, Rebecca thought. Her new beau was hardly a fast worker. She let his remark lie, and hoped he would, too. 'Kevin, I want you to do something for me.'

'Anything,' he said, his bloodshot eyes wide open.

'Promise?'

'Sure. I promise.'

'Good,' she said. 'You go straight back to the apartment and get a good night's sleep. I don't want you to do a Goldman and end up getting a ride in an ambulance.'

'But—'

'You promised,' she said. 'I hold you to it.'

He looked exasperated. 'OK, you win, but if you think of anything I should know, or want anything, just tell Tony to call me.'

'Who the heck is Tony?' she asked.

Kevin's broad ruddy face looked as though he had given away a surprise party. His mouth opened and closed, like a goldfish in a bowl. Then he apparently decided to tell the truth. 'He's the uniformed officer outside your door. His shift goes till midnight. The nurse will call him in if you want him.'

The point came back to her as clear and irrevocable as the sentences she pronounced in her court. It was her that Schmid had sworn to hurt, not Julie. In a way it was a tiny relief, the first toehold in the climb up Everest.

Getting off the elevator on the thirtieth floor of the Dorchester, William tried to look as inconspicuous as possible. The gray tweed overcoat he had appropriated looked rather smart, he thought. It was like one he had had when he was teaching at the university.

He hoped no one would find Queeny Parks in time to thwart his objectives. He had checked the duct tape carefully. She wasn't going anyplace on her own. Her little pig eyes had searched his for some sign of mercy. He had ruled out hurting her. If someone found her, she would remember Phelps's name had come up. That was a mistake. Mistakes were much more frequent when one was not working from a carefully reasoned plan.

The master key worked perfectly in the door to suite 3012. William stepped inside. Phelps had a fine apartment. Not large, but luxurious by William's standards. Beautiful

394

paintings adorned the walls, and a bronze of an Indian brave stood on a pedestal where the sliding glass doors opened to the balcony. One would think a man of quality lived here. But William knew better. In this elegant place wrongs would be righted. He decided to wait in the bedroom.

Loretta, the nurse Rebecca liked, a young Native American woman with two-foot-long jet-black hair, pranced into the room showing a row of straight teeth and glittering dark eyes. 'There's a very good-looking man here to see you.'

'Oh God, I look like cat food. Who is it?'

'He says his name is Harry Scott.'

Instead of his face, Rebecca imagined the hard flat look of his belly. That feeling that only Harry Scott produced radiated out from the deep in the center of her. It wasn't a feeling she wanted to allow herself, with Julie in mortal danger. 'Tell him to wait a few minutes. Tell him I'm on the phone. Then check back with me before you bring him in,' Rebecca said.

After Loretta closed the door Rebecca pulled her purse, still heavy with the little revolver, out of the bed-table drawer. By the time Loretta came back, Rebecca had done a reasonable overhaul on her stressed-out face, especially around the eyes. 'Bring Mr Scott in,' she said.

'Hey, you look great,' said Loretta.

A minute later Harry Scott said, 'You look great, Judge.'

'The case is over. Call me Rebecca. It's thoughtful of you to drop by.'

'Everybody is worried about your daughter. I just wanted to tell you that. I know you've got more important things to think about than listening to another lawyer.'

'No, I'm glad you came. Gives me a chance to congratulate you on your victory. You did your usual fine job.' She looked straight into his blue eyes, just to see if she could.

'I've been trying to think of something to do to help,' he said. 'Especially since the consensus is that my old client Schmid has got your daughter.'

'I guess we can hope he might call you.'

'Doubtful, but if he does, it may be attorney-client. That would raise some weird issues.'

'Indeed,' said Rebecca, feeling a little pissed, but quickly understanding. When she was practicing, she had found herself in a position where she would have liked to reveal a client's secrets but couldn't. Sometimes it meant people might get hurt in some way when it could have been avoided.

They talked about Schmid and what he might have in mind but only in generalities. Harry seemed to steer the conversation away from the unpleasant possibilities. Finally, he changed the subject. 'Rebecca, there's something else I want to talk to you about,' he said.

Uh-oh, she thought. He was about to step from her dreams into reality again, and she wasn't ready for it. But it wasn't a date Harry Scott had in mind. He didn't leave for almost an hour.

What a grand party it had been. Tom Phelps had lost track of the number of times really important people had toasted his health. At the Dorchester, a woman in the elevator got off at nineteen. She reminded him of Wilma. It would really cap off the evening with a bang if Wilma were waiting for him on the top floor. But there was a good chance he would never see her again. He hoped he wouldn't. Maybe she had already left town. If she put that fifty grand to good use, she could put a lot of miles between Minneapolis and herself and brother William – the Minnesota twins, Phelps had called them when he wanted to get a rise out of Wilma.

He let himself in to his apartment, snapped on the lights, hung his coat in the closet and pondered mixing a Scotch and soda to sleep on, then decided against it. In the clear night, city lights stretched out before him for miles. The track lighting on the living room ceiling illuminated the balcony just beyond the sliding glass doors. What the hell was that out there by the railing? It looked like somebody's gray tweed coat.

Phelps slid the door open. He approached the coat and bent down to pick it up. It was tied to the top rail somehow.

What in hell, he thought, his brain clouded by alcohol. And then his mind cleared for that one paralyzing moment, perhaps less than a second, when you suddenly understand but you can't quite act simultaneously with the illumination in your brain. The interval varies with the talent, but the lag is inevitable. In that short space of time a pair of hands on muscled arms, conditioned to lifting heavy pails of hog feed, clamped on to Phelps's legs in front, just below the knees, and lifted in one motion. Phelps watched his large hands, as if of their own volition, grab at the top rail and miss. His body balanced level for a nanosecond. A last push to further an inflexible purpose tilted it downward toward the city lights below. He slid off the rail like a dead sailor committed to the deep. Phelps's grotesque scream indicated that he had joined the select few who knew those three seconds of indescribable terror, as the sidewalk thirty stories below rushed up to meet him.

Wilma Schmid was up before six and picked the morning *Tribune* off the stoop. Unseasonably warm misty air made rings round the street lamp on the corner. She unfolded the paper as she settled down on her cushioned toilet seat. Any hope that her bowels would move was immediately lost when she saw the headline: ACQUITTED PHELPS LEAPS FROM 30TH STORY. Wilma knew better. Tom Phelps didn't leap. He was pushed or thrown, and she knew who had done it.

The second paragraph of the article dictated Wilma's next move. There were no alternatives left. There was speculation that several computer disks police found among Phelps's personal effects contained a journal that he had kept over the past dozen or more years. A source that didn't wish to be named said Phelps eventually planned to write a book. Wilma knew about the journal. He had reminded her the night he gave her the money that he wrote things down. He had done it in a kidding way, but she had no doubt that he had wanted her to remember.

Wilma pulled on her clothes in the dark and, without turning another light on, descended the worn wooden stairs into the dank basement under her bungalow. She shoved a stool up beneath a window in the foundation wall facing the alley. Her skirt tore as she squeezed through, pulling her attaché case behind her. The police usually watched the front of the house. They would be knocking on her door again soon. If not, they would be back at the railroad. Wherever they came, this time it would be with handcuffs. She cut across the alley in the dark, then tramped through the dingy drifts between the little houses crowded into the old Richfield neighborhood. She barely noticed the icy snow crystals filtering into her shoes. At a gas station on Lyndale she called a cab.

Mary was sleeping when William came home on Tuesday night. The first thing she said when he opened his eyes in the morning was to tell him that she had called her mother in Mitchell the day before. Mike was in the hospital with a stroke. One side was paralyzed and he was unable to speak. The neighbors were taking care of the farm. You must go to him, William said. I think I must, Frankie, but I will come back. You can be sure of that. I love you. Two hours later Mary got into her car with all her belongings and headed down the road out of William's life.

Harry Scott got to his office early. Late yesterday afternoon Chet Ronning had left a message: 'We're running out of time.' Harry was about to pick up the phone to call him when the door to his office swung open. Jesus Christ. He had forgotten to lock the waiting room door. The face he saw didn't belong to the Schmid twin he had been thinking about. It was Wilma with a briefcase in her hand. He got up and shook her hand and invited her to sit down.

'Mr Scott, I need to talk to you.'

'About what, Wilma?'

'I need a lawyer.'

He didn't want to get involved with another Schmid. One was enough. Even criminal lawyers didn't like being scared of their clients. He pressed his knee hard against a button mounted out of sight under his desk. 'I'm afraid my representation of William will prevent me from representing you, Wilma.'

She said nothing. The brass catches on the attaché case in her lap snapped open with distinct little clicks. She stood up and turned it upside down over the desk. An impressive pile of packets of one hundred dollar bills dropped out on the blotter. She sat back down. From a zipper pocket in the cover of the case she withdrew a legal document and handed it across the desk to Harry. 'This is a deed to my house made out to you. It is free and clear. According to an appraiser I hired, it is worth between seventy-five and eighty thousand. As you can see, the date is open. There is fifty thousand in cash lying on your desk. That makes a total of at least one hundred twenty-five thousand. All I have that I can get my hands on. I do have a vested pension plan at the railroad, but I may need that to live on.'

Harry was astonished. Right now this money could end his troubles with his wife. Protect his practice from the divorce. Of course, he'd have to have the deed from the house dated after they executed the divorce stipulation. Very workable. 'Why do you need a lawyer?' he asked.

'I am in very serious trouble.'

'I take it the speculation I've read in the paper has some truth to it.'

'Will you take me on as your client? If not, I intend to hire another lawyer before I leave this building.'

Harry saw the money being quickly withdrawn and leaving with Wilma. She had only to walk down one floor and there were at least two lawyers ready to pounce on it – even if she planned to assassinate the President. There really was no conflict of interest. William hadn't been his client for six or seven years, maybe more. Even so, there wouldn't necessarily be a conflict. He knew where he was leading himself. Why wait? 'Just one more thing,' he said. 'If you are in any way involved in the kidnapping of Rebecca Goldman's child I will not represent you. Is that clear?'

'Yes,' she said, 'perfectly clear. I am not involved in any kidnapping.'

'Then I'm willing to take you on as my client.'

'That means this minute. I am now your client?'

'When Vivian comes in, I'll have her give you a form to sign, but yes, you are now my client.'

'Good. I want to tell the whole story from the beginning. Then I want your advice on what I should do next. You have all my money, so I cannot flee. I thought about that, but with all these television programs, it seems like there's very little hope of disappearing anymore.'

Harry hadn't expected the Phelps trial to be over yet, so he had plenty of time for Wilma. After he had visited Rebecca in the hospital, he had made a brief appearance at Phelps's party, then gone home and got seven hours' sleep for the first time in a long time. He hadn't listened to the radio or read a paper since yesterday. 'Go ahead,' he said to Wilma, 'tell me your story.' He stopped her only twice on pretexts, giving him a chance to change the hidden tape.

55

Sealed in the cocoon of Kevin's Ford, they headed from the hospital under a low gray sky. When they stopped for the light on Chicago and Franklin, Rebecca heard the movement of the automatic locks in the door beside her as Kevin touched a button on his door. Even cops were leery of decaying urban neighborhoods. 'Still nothing?' she said.

'Still nothing; no leads of any kind. We're hoping for a call. Somebody who's seen somebody like Schmid with a snowmobile. Chances are he's trailering it. He's too smart to operate right on the shores of the lake.' Kevin's normally ruddy face, now splotchy with red, sagged grimly.

Rebecca considered telling him about Harry Scott's offer, then thought better of it. Nothing seemed relevant, except Julie. Still, she had listened intently to Harry last night, glad to occupy her mind with something else for a little while. In spite of everything that was happening around her, she had been physically drawn to him. With Julie in deadly jeopardy, she felt ashamed of the feeling.

Kevin changed the subject to Phelps. The spectacle of his thirty-story dive after his victorious criminal trial would have been her only focus at any other time. Now, it didn't seem to matter. It only pricked her curiosity.

When they walked into the kitchen, the red light was blinking on Kevin's answering machine. He called his office.

Miles Dickstein answered. 'Some guy told the Wayzata cops that he remembered seeing a snowmobile parked out in front of the Clark place almost every night for a week or so. Said it looked like the guy was fishing. Best he could remember, the guy was alone but he wasn't sure. Couldn't even say for sure whether it was a guy; coulda been a woman.'

'Were there any other fishermen around?' Kevin asked.

'The guy said definitely not. It's not a place people normally fish. Anyway, they went out and cleared away the snow. They found a frozen-over fishing hole in the ice about five hundred feet offshore.'

'He must have been watching the place,' said Kevin.

'Wait a minute, Knuckles, it gets better.'

Kevin's skin tingled in anticipation.

'When they were clearing away the snow, they found a motel receipt for a place in Mankato. Turns out a guy fits Schmid's general description, except with a beard, was staying there for a couple of days with a woman, a redhead with lots of hair. She was the one that registered. The address she gave was a phony – nonexistent in Des Moines. Also listed an Iowa plate that doesn't exist. Clerk says they never look at the cars and check. She paid cash. No phone calls.'

'He's got a beard and he's with a redhead. We'll find him now,' said Kevin.

'If he's in the area.'

'He's in the area, all right.'

Harry Scott headed west on I-494 toward his townhouse in Chanhassen, a suburb to the southwest of the city. With the candor required to make the admissions she had made, he believed that Wilma had nothing to do with Tom Phelps's death. Nevertheless, because of what he had learned from her, he refused to talk to the police about Phelps, other than to tell them he hadn't seen or spoken with him after the party. Wilma's voice droned on in his mind, still telling her incredible story. Better he listen to it exactly as she said it. He reached into his inside suit pocket and retrieved one of the tapes. He shoved it into the slot in the dash. Not sure of where he wanted to stash them, he had taken the tapes with him when he left the office. The case full of cash was in the trunk. He hit the fast forward to get to the part that had taken his breath away.

A few minutes later he drove down a snow-packed drive between a long line of garage doors on both sides. He hit the rewind button. When he turned his headlights off inside his garage, he ejected the cassette and dropped it back into his suit pocket.

As much as he had grown to despise his wife Hillary, he hated even more coming home at night to an empty house. He opened the door from the garage into the small laundry room off the kitchen, snapped the lights on and moved quickly past the gleaming white washer and dryer into the kitchen. Bright light flooded a mostly white room with whitewashed oak cabinets lining the walls. From the kitchen he crossed the darkened living room and hung his coat in a closet beside the front door. A jet in its landing pattern droned above the silence of the house.

After he urinated in the bathroom off the hall, he headed for the kitchen to pick out a Lean Cuisine for dinner. A cold beer would rinse the dryness out of his mouth that had begun with Wilma Schmid's story. One step out of the bathroom, he felt a sharp jab in his back.

'Be very careful, Harry, or I will kill you on the spot.' The voice was unmistakably William Schmid's.

William ran his hands over Harry's body, feeling for a weapon.

'Whatever you say, William. Just take it easy. You have no reason to hurt me.'

'I disagree. But for now we have other things to discuss. Walk straight ahead and sit on that chair.'

William nudged Harry toward a leather wing-back chair near the picture window in the living room. The drape was drawn. He had left it open that morning.

Harry sat down in the chair. William walked round behind it and pressed the muzzle of the gun against the back of Harry's head. Behind his ear Harry heard a sharp click followed immediately by a louder, duller noise, the sound of a revolver being drawn back to the full cock position. The odds were even or better that Schmid meant to kill him, eventually. It was a hundred to one that he would if his instructions were not followed forthwith.

'How did you find this place?' Harry tried to keep the quaver out of his voice.

'Your wife was kind enough to give me the address. I told her I was a new client.'

'What do you want?' Harry's voice had regained its usual steady confidence.

'First, clearly understand me, Mr Scott. I no longer consider you an ally. You are my enemy.' William's tone left no doubt about his determination. 'Despite any reservations you may have about my sanity, I know precisely what I am doing. I will not allow you or anyone to stand in my way. Do you understand me?'

'I understand,' said Harry.

'Good. Then understand this. If I perceive the slightest effort on your part to escape, or in any way undermine my purpose, I will shoot you where you sit.'

The living room was still partially darkened, lit only by the ceiling fixture in the kitchen. Against the wall at the end of the room to Harry's left a portable television set had been placed on a low table, with what looked like a VCR beside it. With the cocked .38 aimed at Harry, William side-stepped across the living room and pushed the TV power button. Before a picture had formed, he pushed another button on the VCR. A grainy image appeared on the screen: a black girl in a scarlet dress with a red ribbon round her head, sitting in a recliner, her hands and feet manacled. She was bound to the chair with black bands, like those that might be used to hold a boat to a trailer. Bundles of what appeared to be dynamite sticks were fastened to the recliner at various points. On a table beside the chair was a telephone, a clock radio, a profusion of wires, and other mechanical paraphernalia. Even with the imperfect focus, the girl's face was obviously tear-streaked. Her full-lipped mouth hung partially open, and the tops of her lower teeth were just visible. A newspaper lay across her lap. The picture shook as the camera moved in close to the headline: ACQUITTED PHELPS LEAPS FROM 30TH STORY. Obviously, this morning's edition.

The camera withdrew and again framed the girl in the recliner. She spoke. 'Mom, I'm OK and I believe I will be released if you follow Mr Schmid's instructions.'

Harry studied the background for a clue. An out-of-focus concrete wall. Nothing else.

With the gun still pointed at Harry, William turned off the TV and the VCR. He returned to his position behind the chair and pressed the gun's muzzle into the hair on the back of his captive's head.

'Now, Mr Scott, if you are not already aware, the young woman you have just seen is the daughter of Rebecca Goldman, the woman who sent me to Wolf River – with your help, of course.'

Harry decided silence was best. It almost always was when you were unsure of the effect your words might have.

William's voice remained matter-of-fact, self-assured. 'The touch-tone telephone you saw on the table beside her is equipped to detonate the dynamite with one call followed by the appropriate code. There will be nothing left of her. If I do not return within twelve hours, the timer will detonate the explosives in any event.'

It could be a bluff, Harry thought, but Schmid's intellect could design and build such a device with little effort.

'Now, Mr Scott, the logic is as follows. I obviously have plans for the Goldman woman. My letters were not idle threats.'

That morning Wilma had told Harry that she had written them all, except the first one. Throughout her life, she had always done what her twin brother had asked, she said.

'I want you to ask Ms Goldman to meet us on an urgent matter. It is either that or her daughter dies. I do not want you to tell her that. I reserve that for myself. But I'm sure you must agree she would prefer to meet us, regardless of the circumstances, rather than have her daughter die. Ipso facto, as you lawyers say. Correct?'

Harry agreed, but remained silent.

Kevin had made tuna sandwiches and he and Rebecca were sitting at his kitchen table washing them down with Diet

Coke. He grabbed the phone on the first ring, then handed it to Rebecca.

'Rebecca, this is Harry Scott. I take it that was Detective Bannon who answered?'

'Yes,' she said.

'No one must know about this phone call. No one.' His voice was filled with the urgency she had heard in his summations.

'OK,' she said.

'What is the closest bar to where you are right now?'

She thought for a moment. Kevin, standing over her, leaned his ear toward the telephone receiver. She pushed him away. 'The Happy Hour,' she said into the phone.

'How far is it?'

'A block or so.'

'Hold on.'

She felt her pulse in her throat. This had to be about Julie. William Schmid was using Harry Scott as a go-between.

His voice came back on the line. 'Go there right now. Alone. You will receive a call precisely five minutes after I hang up.'

'OK,' she said.

'Now, I am going to read you something. Listen carefully.' He cleared his throat. 'If any attempt is made to interfere in any way, or if any contact is made with Mr Scott by law enforcement people or anyone else, you may be assured that you will regret it for the rest of your life. Do you understand?'

'I understand,' said Rebecca. The dial tone came on the line. She jumped up from the table, grabbed her coat and purse, and headed for the door. 'Don't follow me, Kevin. I believe Julie's life is on the line. And you know for sure Schmid's no ordinary kidnapper. He kills as a matter of course.'

'But—'

'No buts,' she said as she rushed through the door.

Two minutes after Rebecca left the apartment, Kevin

headed out after her. On his car phone he called Miles Dickstein. 'We've got to move. Tell the Feds and the Crime Bureau I've got good information. We're running out of time. Get the artist's drawings they made up with those motel clerks on the ten o'clock news. Stay mum on the kidnapping. We've got to find Schmid. Also, see if you can find out if Harry Scott is in his office. If he isn't, find out where he is. But you can't let anyone know you are looking for him.'

'Knuckles, how'n the fuck can I do that?'

'I don't know,' Kevin said. 'Figure it out.'

Kevin's mind was in a turmoil. He told himself he couldn't try to save Rebecca's life at the risk of Julie's. But she might be dead already. He pulled up to the curb and sat with his engine running across the street and half a block from the Happy Hour.

In the dim light of the Happy Hour, Rebecca picked the bar stool nearest the door. The over-heated air reeked of stale beer, cigarette smoke and fresh popcorn. There were four or five people at the bar and maybe a dozen in the booths along the wall, guzzling beer. She felt scared and weak, but she knew she would do whatever she was asked.

In a couple of minutes the phone rang and the bartender asked loudly if there was a Mrs Goldman present. Rebecca raised her hand and moved down the bar to where he held the receiver out. She pushed in between two solitary drinkers and grabbed the phone. She listened to Harry's instructions, repeated them back to him, and rushed out the door. Before she jumped into her car, she looked up and down the wintry street, seeing nothing unusual but not really knowing what she was looking for.

'Put your coat on and get your car started,' William said to Harry Scott. 'If Bannon knows it was you on the phone, he will show up here, probably sooner rather than later. I trust Judge Goldman will make sure she is not followed. Her child's life depends on it.'

Minutes later, with William in the back seat, Harry

guided his car between the long rows of garages and eventually on to the Interstate. They headed north in heavy traffic. At 169 they turned to the west. In fifteen minutes they were parked across from the drugstore in Chaska where William and Mary had picked up a newspaper when they first arrived in the metropolitan area.

Rebecca drove west on Lake Street toward the intersection with I-35W. A set of headlights two cars back had made the turn on to Lake from Cedar just after she did. She couldn't take the risk that Kevin, with all good intentions, was following her. Abruptly, she pulled over to the curb in front of a Subway sandwich shop. The car in question stopped a hundred yards behind. Rebecca ran back down the slippery street, oncoming cars brushing past, inches away. Behind his windshield, Kevin's face, well illuminated by a street-light, bore a sheepish expression of resignation. He got out and grabbed her upper arm and led her up on to the sidewalk. She twisted out of his grasp.

'Listen to me, Becka—'

'No, you listen to me, Sergeant. *I will not be followed!*'

A passerby in a down jacket and watch cap stood gawking, ebony face partially covered by a graying beard.

'Buzz off,' said Kevin.

'You need help with this guy, sister?' said the grizzled face.

'No, thank you,' said Rebecca. 'Please leave us alone.' He turned and left. 'Kevin, I have no time. I must do this my way. Don't make me drive through alleys to lose you.' She felt tears close to the surface. 'Please, if our friendship means anything, promise me you won't follow.'

His sad, sagging face nodded and he said, 'OK, I promise, but—'

'No buts. I'll call you as soon as I can.' She pecked him lightly on the lips and headed back to her car.

Sitting dejectedly in his car with the motor and heater running against the cold, Kevin contemplated his next move. For the first time since Schmid had made his fantastic escape in the icy waters of the Wolf River, they had a real lead. He picked up his car phone.

'Homicide. Dickstein.'

'Get anything on Scott?'

'His new address and phone number from his estranged wife. Strange, is what I should say. She wanted to talk about the divorce. Says he's a workaholic. Shit. He oughta try my hours these days.'

'What's the address and number?'

'I called. There's no answer. Not even a machine. Think a lawyer'd have a machine.'

'What's the address, Miles?'

'One six eight one six Grasslands Way. Unit three seven four. It's out in Chanhassen.'

'I can be there in ten, fifteen minutes.'

'Want me to send a car, Knuckles?'

'No. This is touchy. Don't monkey with it. I'll call you when I get there. Are those pictures going on the news?'

'Four channels. Be on *Nine At Nine*, the rest at ten.'

Kevin was already weaving through traffic on I-35W with his red flasher blinking.

56

Harry Scott and William sat in Harry's Cadillac across the street from Snyder's drugstore in Chaska. William had moved into the front seat. Harry's upper arms shivered under his overcoat, even though the air inside the car was warm. Customers in ones and twos entered and exited the busy store, inaudible words evidenced by puffs of vapor in the night. The temperature hovered in the twenties, balmy for Minnesota winter.

'Turn on the radio,' said William.

'You are listening to eight three oh, W-C-C-O,' said a mellow voice. 'It is eight o'clock; the temperature at the airport is twenty-seven. Now back to Williams Arena and Gopher basketball.'

William reached out and turned the radio down to a low murmur. It had been almost half an hour since Scott had talked to Judge Goldman. If she was coming, she should be here momentarily. He wasn't sure what he would do if she didn't show. Shoot Scott? He was an afterthought. Goldman was the culmination of years of planning. It was her he had to kill to make good on his promises to himself and to the judge in writing. His name came through the murmuring radio. He adjusted the sound.

'We repeat. Schmid, who escaped from Wolf River State Hospital more than two months ago and was then presumed drowned, has been sighted in the Mankato area. He is said to be traveling with a woman with abundant long red hair. When last seen, Schmid was wearing a short dark brown beard and glasses. Local TV news shows will be carrying pictures of Schmid and artist's renditions of the woman

Schmid is presumed armed and extremely dangerous. He should not be approached by anyone except law enforcement officials. If you have information regarding the whereabouts of William Schmid or the unidentified woman, please call your local police or one eight—'

William turned the radio off. Rebecca Goldman was getting out of a car across the street. 'There she is,' he said. 'Wave her over.'

It wasn't necessary. She had spotted them. She was wearing a dark knee-length down coat. She waited for a car to pass, then walked directly toward them. William got out and held the door open. Without a word from anyone, she got in the front, William in the back. He reached over her shoulder and grabbed her purse.

'A gun,' he said. 'You will need more than a gun. Drive north on Forty-one.'

Harry pulled the car away from the curb and headed out of town as instructed. He looked at Rebecca. 'I'm sorry. I wasn't sure—'

'Shut up,' said William. 'Neither of you is to speak unless I say so. I am going to state three basic facts, Mrs Goldman. One, your daughter is alive. Two, she will only remain that way if the two of you do exactly as I say when I say it. Three, if I do not return to where she is within eleven hours, a timer will detonate enough explosives to make her and the building she is in disappear. Mr Scott has seen a video tape that verifies what I am saying is true. Correct, Mr Scott?'

'Yes,' said Scott. 'That appears to be what I saw on the tape.'

Rebecca began to turn in her seat to look at William.

'Look straight ahead,' William said. He poked the muzzle of the .38 hard into the back of her seat.

Her head snapped to the front. The car moved slowly on a two-lane highway with cars immediately in front and immediately behind. Headlights passed in the opposite direction every few seconds.

He would tell Scott to turn off on a dark country road, William thought. Stop somewhere. Shoot them both in the back of the head. It would be finished; promises kept. He thought of Mary and the farm. Nauseous doubt shivered through his gut and upper body.

His obsession, they called it. Call it fate. Call it destiny. Whatever. He had seen his own death as if it had already occurred. One step remained in his commitment to balance the scales. These lives had been delivered to him. His work had been rewarded. Then why the disquiet? He must get out of the traffic. They would be looking for Harry Scott's car. Afterward, he would have to drive back to get his own car before somebody spotted him. By then, what would be the difference? Death today was as good as death tomorrow. The difference was, with Mary on her way back to the farm, someone had to release the girl. He would telephone the police when the time came.

Harry caught a glimpse of Rebecca's profile in the dim light of his peripheral vision. This might be getting out of hand. Somehow, he believed Schmid would release Julie. Crazy or not, he had always thought there was a certain honor about the man. Wilma's rambling tale had confirmed the thought. In twenty years of criminal law, he had never heard such a story. Of course, it was protected by the privilege. No one else would ever hear it. It would likely die with him. No. The tapes were still in his suit pocket. The police would listen to them when they found his body.

'Turn left there, where that car is waiting to get on the highway,' said William.

Harry flicked on his left indicator. He turned after the waiting car had pulled out. They were headed west on a gravel road covered with patches of packed snow. A few flakes spun in the headlights. The cops would listen to Wilma's story, but what could they do with it? Having found it on her attorney's body, it would be suppressed. No jury would ever hear it.

'Slow down,' said William.

He must be looking for a place to turn off. Was he bringing them to the place where he was hiding Julie? No. He seemed too unsure of himself. This was new territory. He was looking for a quiet place to shoot them.

412

'Here. Turn here.'

Harry slowed the car almost to a stop. There was no sign of cars either ahead or behind. He swung into a narrow lane; tall trees extended up into the dark on either side. There were no tire tracks in the snow. Fear radiated out from the top of his gut, through his arms and down his legs. He was going to die. Criminal lawyers often wondered if they would die at the hands of a deranged or vengeful client. Schmid was both. After hearing Wilma's story, he had felt William had a right to be nuts. Her story. Maybe that was a hope. 'William—'

'Shut up,' said William. 'Stop up ahead, there in that wide spot.'

There was nothing to lose. 'William, Wilma came to see me this morning. I want you to hear what she said.'

'What difference could it possibly make? They would only be your words. I've heard you lie when it was important to me that you tell the truth.'

Harry stopped the car in the center of the lane, a couple of hundred feet short of the spot William had indicated. 'It will make all the difference,' Harry said.

'You are just buying time,' said William.

'My God. You intend to kill us here and now,' blurted Rebecca. 'Where is Julie? Is she all right?'

'She is all right. She will be released as I have promised.' To Harry he said, 'And you could say Wilma said anything.'

'No.' Harry reached inside his suit. Inside the car the expanding sound from the roar of William's gun assailed Harry's eardrums. He felt as though he had been hit in the shoulder with a hammer. Still, he jammed the tape into the slot in the dashboard and turned up the volume. Wilma's slightly nasal tone was unmistakable.

'You see I loved Tom Phelps. I wanted him for myself.'

He had grabbed the right tape. It was playing on side two of the first cassette, the part he had replayed earlier, on the way home from the office.

'Tom and I had an intense relationship. I devoted most of my time to him. Politics and sex. That was what it was. Of course my twin brother took plenty of my time before they locked him up.'

Harry Scott's voice: 'Why would you help him escape?'

'I was all he had. He was dependent on me, like mother and child, even for sex. For his very life. I thought he might kill himself. You knew all about his spells. But beyond that, William was my twin, my family, the only family I have. Even if it had been his own fault that he was locked up, I had to try to get him out. If there was any possibility at all.'

Harry Scott's voice again: 'What do you mean by "even if it had been his own fault"?'

Earlier she had admitted her involvement in the killing of the old man in Eau Claire, and in putting her stepmother up to trying to assassinate Rebecca. It would all be in Phelps's diaries, she had said.

The tape went on: 'I guess I don't need to hide anything from you. You can never tell anyone. Right?'

Harry's assent was barely audible over the hiss of the tape.

'Even my brother. You can't tell him anything I tell you either. Right? That's right for sure, isn't it?'

Again, Harry's voice assured her of the inviolability of the attorney-client privilege.

'It wasn't his fault he was locked up – because he didn't kill that girl.'

Exquisite pain spread out from Harry's shoulder. In the light from the dashboard Rebecca's expression was fixed in horror.

'You know, Tom Phelps had an in at the physics department. That's how William got his job. Well, Tom got Alice Wahl her job, too. She told Tom that my twin brother was the smartest one in the department. William was infatuated with her, but it was Tom she cared for.'

Harry felt the blood soaking through his shirt under his shoulder blade. Some trickled down his side like sweat.

'When her belly started swelling, brilliant William didn't even know she was pregnant. He didn't even know she ever saw Tom. Tom told me the baby was his. He wanted it, he said. He intended to marry her. Marry Alice Wahl? It was unthinkable! I would become just another party worker and an occasional fuck when Alice had a headache. I have never known such rage. Sure, my temper had caused trouble before but I prided myself on my control. When Tom told me he was going to marry Alice, I lost control. For several hours nothing else mattered to me but that Alice Wahl be dead.'

William Schmid made no sound in the back seat. Rebecca was softly crying, her head bent forward, her chin on her chest.

'Tom had told me of his intentions in the afternoon. William was working in the lab that night. He stayed late about half the time. He and Alice would eat at that hamburger shop by Oak and Washington. Then they'd go back to work. It was routine. That night he had a project of some kind set up in the lab with some prisms. There was no one else around. Alice walked through the lab and into the small office they both used. I was waiting. Furious. I cut her throat with a scalpel. She made a little whimper, but I had cut through her trachea. She couldn't make a sound loud enough for William to hear. Then I pulled up her skirt and cut her belly. I put the tiny fetus in a petri dish that was sitting on the desk.'

Rebecca remembered the glossy photos of Alice Wahl's abdomen. They argued for weeks over whether or not William Schmid was a sociopath. No one questioned who did the crime. He had no record. He had never done anything criminal. That trial had created a criminal. What new hate he must be feeling at this moment.

'Of course when William discovered the gruesome scene a few minutes later, he blanked out. Went into one of those headache spells of his. He even picked up the scalpel. That was all I needed. He was arrested.

'At first, he swore to me that he hadn't done it. He was sure he could not have done it, he said. He had never hurt anyone, he said. It wasn't in him to hurt. I knew that. I had been with him his whole life. He was a gentle creature. My fury had subsided. I wished desperately that I hadn't done it. With William in jail and facing a life sentence according to the newspapers, I made my choice. It was either him or me. I decided to let him go to prison rather than me. I worked on him. I told him that he must have had one of his spells and he must have been outraged when Alice told him she was going to marry Phelps, have his baby. But, he said, she had never told him. How would he know? I kept reminding him that he didn't remember anything when he had one of his spells. Eventually, he came to believe he had killed her. You, Mr Scott, and that woman judge, and that high and mighty prosecutor, and all the psychiatrists did the rest, not to mention the jury. But of course no one ever considered for a moment that maybe he hadn't done it at all. That maybe someone else had done it. Not even you, Mr Scott. Now you and I are the only ones who know I did it and you can't tell anybody.

'When he escaped I urged him to run. Everyone thought that he was dead. But he was obsessed with getting his revenge on that judge and, other than me, Alice Wahl was the only woman he ever cared about. He saw himself as her killer, not deserving to be free.

'I'm sure you already guessed that I gave him the cyanide. Tom Phelps got it for me. I don't know if that will turn up in the—'

The tape made the clicking noise of autoreverse.

'You can turn it off,' said William. 'Now get out of the car.'

Rebecca was sure the end was near. Maybe she should make a run for it. That would be better than being shot in the back of the head. But what about Julie? She believed him when he said no harm would come to Julie. Only losing her mother, she thought. She opened the door and stepped out. William was right behind her.

'I'm pretty stiff,' said Harry.

'Get out if you want to live.'

Want to live. Was he going to let them live? Frail hope returned to Rebecca. 'May I help him?' she asked.

'Go ahead,' said William.

He followed her round the front of the car. She opened the driver's side door and grabbed Harry's arm. He groaned, but he got his left foot out on the ground. Soon, he was standing up, supported by Rebecca.

'Now, go round to the back of the car,' said William.

Rebecca worked her way to the back with Harry leaning heavily on her. The engine stopped. William must have turned it off. He walked past her and in the dim light he opened the trunk lid with the keys he had apparently pulled out of the ignition lock.

'Get in,' he said.

Kevin's headlights led the way between the rows of garages until he saw the numerals: 16816. He pulled up close to the garage door. The townhouse looked dark. He rang the bell. And again. He turned the knob, and when he pushed, the door swung open.

'Anybody home?' he yelled. Nothing. He stepped in. Ahead, the kitchen light was on. He quickly walked through into the dark living room and saw the VCR and TV. He pushed the eject button on the VCR. There was no tape. He moved on into a hall. No one replied to his shouts. He flicked the light on in a bedroom, then relieved himself in the bathroom. A white telephone hung on the wall in the kitchen. He picked it up and looked at it, then pushed the redial button. After two rings a voice answered: 'Happy Hour, Bernie speakin'.' Kevin put the phone back on the hook, then picked it up again.

'Homicide, Dickstein here.'

'Miles, I'm at Harry Scott's. Nobody here now, but they were here less than half an hour ago. I haven't looked in the garage. Hold on.'

The garage was empty.

'Miles, they musta gone together. To meet Rebecca Goldman, no doubt. He'll kill them both. We gotta find him.'

'I'll get Scott's car out on the wire right now. Knuckles, hang in there. Anything can happen. They had the—'

'Yeah, tell that to Slim Olson's widow. What's the latest on Wilma?' The line was silent for a minute and Kevin visualized Miles Dickstein taking a deep drag on a Camel.

'Stakeout says she's in her house. Listen a minute, Knuckles. They had the pictures on *Nine At Nine*. Just before I answered your call a clerk from Kenny's grocery store in Long Lake called. Says he thinks he mighta seen the woman a couple a times. New in his place. Last time the day before yesterday. I got his address.'

Minutes later Kevin, with his red flasher blinking on the roof, wove in and out of traffic heading north on I-494 at eighty miles an hour.

Rebecca had crawled into the Cadillac's trunk first, then reached out to help Harry get in. When William slammed the lid above them, she pulled Harry up against her body.

'Even getting shot has its compensations,' he murmured. 'I'm getting kinda cold.'

Unlike the interior of the car, the ambient temperature in the trunk felt only slightly above freezing. Rebecca remembered how important it was to keep an injured person warm. Wriggling and struggling, she managed to get her down coat open and drew Harry's body tightly against the front of hers. She pulled his head to her shoulder and rested her cheek on top of his ear, much as she would hold a pillow when she slept. A tuft of his hair brushed against her eyelid. In the absolute blackness of the trunk she thought of how blind people spent their lives. She thought of Julie and she clung tensely to the hope that they would both live. At least Julie. Please God, at least Julie. But what would Julie's life be like without a mother? Maybe she would go live with the Clarks in the big house on Wayzata Bay.

The road was a little bumpy at first, but then she was sure they were back on the highway. Perhaps Wilma's voice on the tape had saved their lives. Perhaps not. What strange impulses were controlling the man at the wheel? Had he been culpable in any of the tragic circumstances that had brought him to this point in time, racing down the highway with two people in the trunk? Was he just another one of the victims of his twin sister's treachery?

'Harry, can you hear me?' Rebecca's lips brushed his ear lightly. 'Are you OK?' His head moved in assent; she heard nothing but the wheels whirring on the highway.

★ ★ ★

Long Lake was a village on US Highway 12 in the outer ring of suburbs. Jimmy Wunderlich lived in a narrow old house with a porch across the front. It was he who had called Miles Dickstein less than an hour ago to report that he thought he might have seen the red-headed traveling companion of William Schmid. Now, he opened the door and invited Kevin into his home.

After the usual small talk about the weather, Kevin withdrew from his inside coat pocket a copy of the artist's drawing that had been made based on the advice of the motel desk clerks from Mankato. Unfolded, he held it out to Jimmy, still standing just inside the door.

'Yeah, that's the same picture they showed on the news, ain't it?' Out of a round, fat face, Jimmy's blue eyes fixed on Kevin, his head nodding as he looked up from the drawing.

'Same one?'

'It's that spot up on her cheek. I noticed it when she came in the store first time. Wife's a redhead too. She's at PTA. Got that real light skin. Burns easy. Spot's kinda reddish. Doesn't spoil her looks at all. She was a nice lookin' lady.' Jimmy stopped for a moment and glanced back down at the picture. 'Yeah, 'bout the size of one of them little shirt buttons. Y'know, like the ones on a dress shirt.'

'Any similarity besides the spot?' Kevin was in a hurry. He worked at being polite. Anxiety tightened his upper body, his gut felt vaguely sick.

'Oh yeah,' said Jimmy. 'S'good likeness. Great head a red hair, long and thick. Y'know what I mean? About forty. Body, too.'

'When did you see her?' Kevin prayed for the right details, but he stuck to the routine.

'She was in the store – y'know I work up at Kenny's, right on the main drag in Long Lake – day 'fore yesterday. An' at least once before that. I think maybe twice. I remember she wanted some real maple syrup. We only carry the other kind.'

'You catch her name?'

'Don't think she used it. Paid cash.'

'Can you think of anything unusual? Anything that might

help me find her. Like the kind of car she was driving.'

Jimmy's serious scrunched-up expression indicated great effort to remember something. Lives depended on his memory if there *was* anything to remember. Maybe he hadn't seen the woman at all. But Kevin had interviewed hundreds of people trying to ID someone. Jimmy produced that feeling of veracity within him that he had come to trust. The woman had been in the store twice for groceries. It was likely that she and William Schmid were based close to Long Lake.

'Oh, I remember.' Jimmy looked excited. Kevin's heart seemed to stop and he held his breath. 'She bought some bird seed. Said she had a feeder outside her window. Said there were blue jays hangin' around. Imagine anyone likin' those damn jays.'

Kevin thanked him and left his card.

57

William eyed the speedometer of Harry Scott's Cadillac. It wouldn't do to be stopped for speeding. Cars and trucks passed him by as he proceeded east on 169. The object of six years of planning lay a few feet behind him in the trunk. For William, not killing Rebecca Goldman now was like a climber stopping ten yards short of the summit of Everest. But even if he hadn't heard Wilma on the tape, he wasn't sure he could have killed the judge. He had known from the time he grabbed her daughter that he couldn't kill the lovely young girl. He liked the kid, just as he liked Mike Bohas and Mary. He loved Mary. You don't kill people you like. But he had killed Slim Olson and Thurgood. He had liked both of them. And Kenny Speer and now Phelps. Of course Kenny Speer was despicable. And Phelps. He was worse.

He remembered Wilma's words on the tape. 'It wasn't in him to hurt anyone.' In fact, he had never as much as slapped another person. What a thin line existed between kindness and malice, between sanity and insanity, between good and evil. And now to know he had not harmed his beloved Alice. It had been Wilma all the time. Oh, how he had trusted her, loved her, depended on her. The wreckage of his rationality blurred his vision. A twinge of pain trembled behind his eyes. It was time to get together with his sister, time to recognize her for what she was. They had agreed that two rings and a hang-up followed by one ring and a hang-up would bring her to the Camden post office. Of course, if the police had read Phelps's diaries, they might have already arrested her. In his troubled mind, the tape played over and over and over again.

In the blackness of the Cadillac's trunk, Rebecca held on to Harry Scott. She hoped the bleeding had stopped. He continued to acknowledge her whispers in his ear with a slight movement of his head, but he said nothing. Was he going to die in her arms? Once again the car rolled to a stop. This time the hum of the engine ceased. A door opened. The whole car moved slightly. A door slammed. Footsteps squeaked by outside. The door of another car opened and closed. An engine started. The sound moved away. A cold quiet descended upon the two bodies huddled together in the dark.

In a Holiday gas station, William waited for the two rings, then hung up. Dialed again. One ring, then hung up. He hoped Wilma had heard them. After another brief call, he checked a Minneapolis map, then headed north on I-94 for the Camden area.

Kevin drove toward downtown on US 12, pondering his next move. All he could do was wait. Hope for another call from the public. Hope that Schmid made a mistake – the non-fatal kind. Maybe it would be worth a visit to Wilma. He called Miles Dickstein on the car telephone and headed toward Wilma's. A female voice answered.

'Miles is on the other line,' she told him.

'Have him call me in my car.' Kevin said. He was no more than fifteen minutes from Wilma's on the freeway.

As he approached Wilma's exit on the Crosstown, Miles called.

'More news, Knuckles. They found a woman tied up in a closet at the Dorchester. Apparently Schmid used her key to get in Phelps's apartment. She's OK. They've got her at HCMC for observation. Might wanta talk to her. She was showing Schmid apartments for rent. Name is Mildred Parks. They call her Queeny. We got a uniform down there. Never know what that bastard might do next. Never know. Still no sign of Scott's Cadillac.'

'I talked to the guy in Long Lake,' said Kevin. 'I think he actually saw our redhead. But he's no help. She didn't tell him anything. Didn't notice her car. But he's sure she's the woman in the drawing because of a small mark on her face. She was in his store two or three times. Schmid must be holed up somewhere out there.'

Kevin passed Wilma's exit and swung off the Crosstown on to I-35W and headed downtown to talk to Queeny Parks. Just one little lead. He needed one little lead.

Rebecca let out another yell. 'Get us out of here!'

Harry mumbled something about 'stiff'. She patted his face and told him it would be just a little while and they would be in warm beds.

Rebecca had waited five minutes after she heard the other car drive away before she had begun to yell. Her throat was already hoarse and sore. She counted to one hundred between each set of yells. Two or three cars had driven by. She no longer worried for herself. Lying there, she reasoned that if Schmid wasn't going to kill her, he wouldn't kill Julie unless something went wrong. But for Harry, time might be running out. She tried rubbing his wrists. The cramping cold continued to close in around their bodies.

Rebecca heard the engine of a car pull up close. She waited until she heard a door open and then started to yell.

'OK, OK. We know you're in there. Just a second.'

Tears and more tears. She was safe. She would be reunited with Julie. 'Harry. There's somebody out there. They're going to get us out. Out, Harry! We're getting out!'

Harry moaned. Somebody was making a scratching noise with a tool.

'Harry, do you hear me?'

His head nodded against her cheek. The trunk lid popped open. Two figures in the dark. One blinded her with a flashlight. 'Chanhassen police,' the voice said.

'Thank you. Thank you,' she said. 'I'm Rebecca Goldman, this man has been shot.'

'There's an ambulance on the way. We got a call.'

Around midnight, a yellow cab stopped in the well-lit area

at the curb in front of the post office. Wilma, in a fur-trimmed coat with the collar turned up round her face, got out and stood on the sidewalk. The cab moved on. The cab had come up Lyndale Avenue from the south. A pick-up truck and an old clunker passed. For the moment no other headlights. Parked a hundred feet north on the opposite side of the street, William blinked his lights. Wilma crossed the street. He sat still and waited. She opened the door on the passenger side and slid across the seat. She wrapped her arms round his neck and kissed him full on the lips.

'Oh, William, my sweet, it's so good to see you.'

He started the engine and pulled away from the curb. In minutes they were on I-94 heading north.

'How did you shake them?' he asked, glancing at his mirror.

'Easily. I went down to the office. They followed me right into the garage. Inside the building there is a stairway between floors from the president's office down to engineering. I'm sure they're still standing outside the door I locked behind me on seventeen. Then I went down to the basement and took the tunnel under the street and waltzed out the back door of the Crossman building. I caught the cab on Hennepin.'

'Good,' he said. Nothing more. He swung west on I-694, heading for Long Lake.

'Where are we going?'

'Where we can talk.'

'You're so quiet. Tell me what's been happening.'

'I am very tired; we'll talk when we get there.'

The awful revelations on the tape had pushed Mary out of his mind. Now he thought of her. Was she back on the farm? Was Mike recovering? Perhaps he had died. Mary would be alone. If only things had been different. Going way back, if only things had been different. He had tried hard, but Wilma's jealous rage had deprived him of a life. And he had paid for her crime.

Fifteen minutes later, William triggered the automatic garage door. He had been gone more than six hours. Wilma followed him into the room where Julie was manacled in the chair. A late-night talk show was on the TV. Julie was sleeping. He touched her shoulder. Her dark brown eyes opened and she looked up at him and then at Wilma.

'I wet my pants,' she said.

'I am very sorry,' William said. 'It will not be much longer.'

'Who is she?'

'This is my sister, Wilma.' He wanted Julie to see Wilma, to remember her.

'Did you kill my mom?'

'No, I did not,' William said.

'Are you going to?'

'No, she will be fine.' He wasn't so sure about Scott. Perhaps he was already dead.

Julie looked skeptical. 'Where is she?'

'I assure you she is unharmed.'

'Did you see her?'

'Yes.'

'Where?'

'I have no time to discuss this further. You will soon be free. You will soon be with your mother.' William loosened her restraints and led Julie to the bathroom.

Wilma stared at the scene. When the bathroom door was closed, she asked, 'What are you going to do with her?'

'Nothing,' he said.

'Was what you said to her true?'

'About what?'

'Did you really let that judge go?'

'Yes, I let her go.'

'I am glad you did. There are too many other problems, but I still don't understand. You were so determined.'

The bathroom door opened. In a couple of minutes he had secured Julie in her chair again, turned the TV off and covered her with a couple of blankets. He pointed to a door and followed Wilma up the stairs. In the darkened kitchen she turned toward him and reached out to embrace him. He switched on the light. Wilma glanced around the empty room and beyond.

'Where is the woman you had with you?'

'Gone,' he said. 'Come with me.'

She followed him through the dark living room, then down the hall to the bedroom. In the bedroom he snapped the light on and turned toward her. Her arms were once again spread out and her eyes said, come to me, I'll hold you. When she saw the .38 in his hand, a deep frown replaced the smile; her lower lip protruded stiffly.

'Why are you pointing that at me?' Her tone conveyed total disbelief.

'Lie down on the bed,' he said.

'Oh, dear William, you know you don't have to force me. I can take care of you.' She managed a smile and moved toward him.

William stepped back. With his arm outstretched, he aimed the gun directly in her face. Her mouth dropped open, eyes wide. He moved the gun slightly to the left and fired past her right ear into the wall behind her. The roar of the shot filled the small room. She leaped back.

'Lie on the bed,' he said.

She stretched out supine on the colorful quilt. 'What are you going to do?'

Her voice sounded unfamiliar. He had never heard Wilma sound frightened. 'Just lie still,' he said.

With four leather belts he tied her spread-eagled and then stuck a swatch of silver-gray duct tape across her mouth.

Kevin had to get cop-tough to get by the nurses' station on the way to Rebecca's room. He flashed his badge and told them that Judge Goldman was in grave danger.

Rebecca heard the commotion through the door. When he stepped into her room, she said, 'Kevin, it's OK. He had me and let me go.'

He grasped her right hand and squeezed. There was an IV in her left arm again. When he tried to kiss her, she turned her head. 'Julie's still out there somewhere. I can't let myself relax until I've got her back.'

Kevin pulled back and sat on the edge of the bed. 'Of course not,' he said. 'We haven't let up for a minute. At least we think we know the general area now.'

He told her about the Long Lake sightings and she told him what had happened in Harry Scott's car. She told him the details of Wilma's brutal attack on Alice Wahl. Kevin's eyes widened in horror; his lips spread in an anguished grimace.

'I know what you're feeling right now,' Rebecca said. 'I had the same feeling when I heard her say so matter-of-factly that she had put the tiny fetus in a petri dish.' She looked into Kevin's face, her eyes overflowing. 'We turned William Schmid into a murderer. Our system took a benign brilliant college professor and turned him into a killer. We just assumed too much. All of us.'

Kevin felt his teeth clenching together in frustrated regret. He deserved the gutload of guilt that filled his insides. He just sat there staring at the IV bottle on the other side of the bed. Then, the rote of longtime duty regained control for the moment. He had to find Schmid before he killed again. Part of Kevin's penance would be to lock up William Schmid again.

There was no time for sleep. In the basement area between the garage and the room in which Julie was sleeping, William leaned over a small electric grinder mounted on a work bench. The whirling wheel screamed against the edge of a hatchet he held tightly in his hands. A partially opened stick of dynamite lay off to the side. Beside it was a small blue tank of propane with a torch attachment. He expected the task laid out in front of him would take the rest of the night.

58

Kevin got the call early the next morning about an hou
before daybreak.

'Sergeant Bannon?'

'Speaking.' Kevin knew the voice.

'This is William Schmid.'

'I am very glad to hear from you.'

'I am ready to give you the girl.'

'Is she OK?'

'She is fine. I have taken good care of her.'

'Where do I pick her up?'

'You must follow my instructions carefully. Write then
down. Do you have a pen?'

'Yes. I'm ready to write.'

'You must follow these instructions to the letter or the gir
will die. Please believe that. The girl will die. It will be
beyond my control. Do you understand?'

'I understand fully.'

'I am located on a dead-end street in the suburbs. The
house I am in – by the way, if this call is being traced, if you
approach me in any way other than the way I am instructing
you, the girl will die.'

'The call is not being traced.'

'The house I am in is at the end of a dead-end street
There are no other houses and the street is close to five
hundred feet long. The house is set back in some trees. Are
you writing this down carefully, every word?'

'Yes, I am.' Kevin's hand trembled as he waited for more

'The house is set back from the street about a hundred
feet on the north side.'

'I got it.'

'You will bring one car to the head of the street where it intersects with the main road called Haggerty Lane.'

Kevin remembered Haggerty Lane. It ran into US 12 a couple of miles west of Long Lake.

'You will stop at the head of the road. You will approach no closer than the intersection with Haggerty Lane. Do you understand?'

'I understand.'

'Anyone or anything any closer from any direction will be in great danger. Please believe me. If you or anyone attempts any other approach, you or they and Judge Goldman's daughter will die.'

'We'll do it your way, William.' Kevin was wide awake; he had been half-asleep when he answered, his mind fogged with fatigue.

'Sergeant Bannon, please remember, this plan has no margin for error. I want to release the girl unharmed, but I will not jeopardize the balance of my plan to save her life.'

'I hear you, loud and clear.'

'Stop your car across the head of the road so no other traffic may pass. When I see your car there, I will walk from the house with the girl and one other hostage. We will walk down the drive to where the road dead ends and where I will have a car parked. I will enter that car with the other hostage.'

'Can you identify the other hostage?'

'The girl will tell you. When I have closed the door of the car behind me and the other hostage, the girl will be allowed to proceed to your car. But you must wait for her. If you don't, she will die. After she reaches your car, you may do anything you like. I expect you will be here in less than an hour. If you take more than an hour I cannot guarantee the girl's safety. Do you have any questions?'

'What's the address?'

'The intersection is Haggerty and Gailey Way.' He spelled Gailey.

'I'm on my way.'

The dial tone came on the line. Kevin hung up and the telephone rang again.

'Kevin, is there anything new?' It was Rebecca.

'Schmid just called. I'm going to pick up Julie.'

'Oh my God. My God. When?'

'Now.'

'Where?'

'Out by Long Lake.'

'Pick me up. I'm almost on your way.'

'No way.'

'Did he insist you come alone?'

'No, but—'

'How much time did he give you?'

'An hour.'

'I'll be at the front door of the hospital in five minutes. You pick me up. That's an order from a district court judge. And I'm not fooling.'

Kevin grabbed his binoculars from a drawer in the kitchen cabinet before he rushed out the door.

William sat in the living room peering out the window and up the road in the morning light. Wilma and Julie, wearing coats, sat side by side on the sofa. In a storage closet, William had found an old pair of shoes that fitted Julie reasonably well. Wilma's hair was in disarray and her mouth was covered with duct tape. Her hands were tied behind her back and her feet were tied at the ankles so she could walk with little short steps like a hobbled horse. William had the .38 in his hand. He had been up all night. In the corner, the TV screen flickered. News of Rebecca's rescue had been repeated several times. William thought he detected signs of appreciation in the girl's face, but she remained silent. Harry Scott was expected to live.

Kevin made the turn north off US 12 on to Haggerty Lane. Other than tense words of hope and anticipation, there had been little conversation since he had picked Rebecca up in front of the hospital. He had handed her his notes and recounted the telephone conversation with Schmid. Trees, fences, houses and cars flew by in a blur.

Kevin swerved to miss an old dog ambling down the road

and then on the right they both saw the sign at the same time: GAILEY WAY. Kevin slowed abruptly and parked across the opening to the street. Under a paste of gray clouds, the road sloped down through thinly wooded rolling land on both sides. At the very end on the left, just visible through the barren trees, was the outline of a house set far back from the street. A dark-colored car was parked across the road where it ended. Behind it was a lowland marsh, thickly tangled with brush and a scattering of blue-green cedar trees. The roof of a house a couple of hundred yards beyond the car was partially hidden by the tops of the trees. In every direction the earth was encased in an even blanket of white.

From the living room, William saw the car stop. The time had come. From her seat on the sofa, Wilma's stare burned like a cornered ferret's. At her side, Julie's dry-eyed face was relaxed in quiet anticipation. She still had the red ribbon round her hair. William stood up.

'It is time to leave,' he said. He pointed the .38 at Wilma's face.

Both of his captives rose from the sofa. He motioned with the muzzle of the gun. When they stopped in front of the door, William grabbed hold of the two-foot long loose end of rope dangling from Wilma's wrists.

He looked at Julie. 'You lead the way to the car down by the swamp. My sister and I will be right behind you. If you attempt to escape, I will shoot you in the back. If you do as I tell you, you will soon be in your mother's arms.' He reached in front of her to open the door.

There was movement in the trees near the house. Kevin pulled his binoculars out of the glove compartment. Behind the distant filigree of tree trunks, three figures walked very slowly toward the road in a single file. Glimpses of scarlet flickered through the forest.

'I see her,' said Kevin. 'She still has the red ribbon in her hair.' He handed the binoculars to Rebecca.

'Oh my God. My baby.'

'She's going to be fine. Just sit tight.'

Without a word, she handed the binoculars back to Kevin.

'They're almost to the road,' he said.

When the three figures reached the end of the driveway, they turned left on to the road and headed for the car less than a hundred feet from where they were.

'The middle one, that must be the other hostage.' Kevin noticed the long hair. 'It's a woman. She's hobbled. That's why they've moving so slowly.'

'Very good,' said William, 'Now open the car door,' he said to Julie.

She reached out and opened the front door on the passenger side. The odor of gasoline was strong. William walked past her with Wilma's tether in his hand and stepped into the car. He crawled across the front seat. The driver's side door was open. Kneeling on the seat in front of the steering wheel he jerked on the rope. 'Get in, Wilma,' he said.

Hobbled as she was, she could barely raise her foot high enough to struggle into the passenger side. He reached behind her seat and grabbed a loop of rope lying on top of one of the cases of dynamite. The other end was tied under the seat. With a tug the loop just reached over Wilma's head. When she moved, it cut into her throat. William reached in the back seat and lifted a case of dynamite from the cushion where it sat among four other cases and some red gas cans. He hefted it into the front and on to Wilma's lap. She began to struggle despite the rope on her throat.

William looked past her at Julie. 'Just as soon as you close that door, you may go to that car at the end of the road. Sergeant Bannon is waiting there for you.'

'Knuckles!' Julie's voice was elated.

'Close it and run as fast as you can.'

She did, and turned heel, heading up the sloping road at a dead run.

Rebecca watched her beribboned daughter running up the road toward her. She wanted to get out and meet her, but she remembered the instructions. Nothing must go wrong now.

Kevin had the binoculars up to his eyes. 'Two hundred yards to Mama's arms. She looks great, like a track star. Jesus, look at her come. Look at that kid run.'

Like light electric shocks, Rebecca's nerves prickled the skin all over her body. Every hair moved. Her heart rate must have doubled, and then there she was twenty feet away. Rebecca opened the door and Julie jumped in on top of her. As Rebecca pulled the door shut, the car at the end of the road disappeared in an enormous flash. A second later the sound wave blasted into Kevin's car and the windshield popped out in one piece. The accompanying roar rendered Rebecca completely deaf for several seconds. Everything near the far end of the street was on fire.

'Shhhhit,' said Kevin, blowing a stream of air through his lips.

'Shit,' echoed Rebecca.

For several shattered seconds the three of them stared down the street, Rebecca's mouth and throat as dry as sand. After the blast, the quiet that descended upon them seemed even more silent than before. From that distance they could only imagine the crackling of the flames.

'Mom, he blew her up, and him too.'

Kevin started dialing his car phone. 'Who did he blow up?' he asked in a high-pitched voice Rebecca had never heard before.

'His sister,' said Julia.

Rebecca agreed to stay with Julie, and Kevin trotted down the road toward the destruction. There were bits of metal lying just a few feet from his car. The sound of a siren came from the direction of Highway 12. Further down the road was a piece of metal that looked like part of a door. The light west wind on Kevin's back blew the smoke away. The fire spread through the trees and totally engulfed the swamp. The snow had disappeared from a large area surrounding the spot where the car had been. Now, from where he stood, he could see most of the house on the far side of the marsh, not just the roof as before. It appeared unharmed, but the brush fire might reach it soon. He turned back toward his car when he heard the siren winding down. A state trooper was getting out of a maroon and white patrol car. Kevin waved at him, then turned and kept on walking.

Pieces of blackened metal were scattered all along the way. The house where Schmid had been hiding was blown flat and burning. Most of the trees for more than a hundred feet around the crater were broken off from five to ten feet above the ground. A burnt powder smell hovered over the whole area. The entire end of the road for fifty or sixty feet looked as though it had been scooped out with a giant shovel. He looked back toward Julie. The patrol car was trying to get around Kevin's car by driving up the bank beside the road. Kevin broke into a run to meet them, his hands held high, palms out. 'Stop!' he yelled. 'This is a crime scene.' The highway cop got the idea.

Kevin's eyes focused on the ground. There, next to the toe of his shoe, was something like a little piece of burnt meat. He hesitated to touch it. Then did. He poked at it, then picked it up between his thumb and forefinger. He held it out in the best light. It was a piece of a finger, nail and all. He carved a big X in the dirt where he had found it, then wrapped it in a piece of Kleenex and dropped it in his shirt pocket.

The highway cop was walking toward him. Now a fire truck was trying to get by Kevin's car. Apparently, someone was moving it. He ran toward the assembling crowd of emergency personnel, hoping to explain things as best he could.

59

Rebecca brought Julie home to Lake Vista. They both dropped into the big soft pink cushions of the living-room sofa. Julie rested her head on her mother's shoulder and Rebecca undid the ribbon in her hair.

'How are you doin' now, sweetie?' she asked.

'I'm just fine, Mom. I want to call Monica as soon as I change my underwear.'

'That'll all wait. Besides, Monica's in school. We're going to sit right here for a while and you're going to tell me the whole story.'

When Julie was through almost an hour later, Rebecca had absorbed all of the shocks one by one and marveled again and again at the resilience and courage of her child. She leaned back and let the relaxed feeling of the end of something big spread through her entire being. She knew the answer she was going to give Harry Scott. On Kevin's car phone she had learned that they were getting him ready to remove the bullet this afternoon. The surgeon had said he was in no danger. She imagined her business card: SCOTT AND GOLDMAN – TRIALS IN ALL COURTS. Except for maybe Harry, she hadn't seen any trial lawyers that she couldn't equal or better. And who knew where it would lead. It was nice having two good men interested in her. She was ready to put any serious choices on indefinite hold. That would be a whole new story.

The telephone was ringing. 'Honeybunch, I'll get that. You can change your underwear.'

'OK, Mom. Bet it's Knuckles.'

Julie was right. 'Is her honor enjoying the homecoming?'

'You bet,' said Rebecca.

'Guess what?' said Kevin. 'You know the finger I found?'

'What about it?'

'The lab checked the print. It's William Schmid's left pinky.'

'Oh my God!' said Rebecca.

'It's finally all over, your honor.'

'So it is,' she said. 'So it is.'

60

A hot wind buffeted the South Dakota landscape, driving fine particles of the rich soil ahead of it, along with the stink of the liquid pig manure the Mennonites had spread on their fields a mile to the west. Mary Bohas was used to it. She had lived on the plains with the suddenly changing weather moods all her life. The planting was done and there had been just enough rain. That easy contentment only farmers know filled her breast.

The past half year had been the best of her life. Last winter when she had got back to Mitchell, Mike had been near death, but from the day she had walked through the door of his room, he had begun to rally. The doctor said it was remarkable. By late March he was on the mend. But he would never be able really to take care of himself. His right side was paralyzed and he was unable to speak. With the left side of his old smile on his face, he pushed himself with a cane in the platform swing Mary had bought at an auction last week. Round Mike's neck, on a long cord, hung a slate in a wooden frame about eight inches square. A piece of chalk dangled beside it on another string.

As Mary poured him a glass of lemonade from the pitcher, the big green tractor motored to a stop behind her. Mike's smile stretched far off to the left, accentuating the lifeless droop of the right side of his face. He put the glass down and printed on the slate: 'NINE IS AS GOOD AS TEN.' With a glottal grunt he held it up with the thick stubby fingers of his good hand. As Mary handed him his glass of lemonade, Frankie Kroll said, 'I guess you are right, Mike. I do not even miss that one little finger any more.'